Family
TIES

M...my lemon pie.

FAMILY TIES

STEPHIE WALLS

Edited by THE WORD LYRICIST
Proofread by JUDY'S PROOFREADING
Cover Design by WICKED BY DESIGN

PROLOGUE

JUDE—EIGHT YEARS OLD

IT HAD ONLY BEEN A COUPLE OF HOURS SINCE THE CASEWORKER dropped me off at the Shaws'. Ernie and Hensley seemed nice enough, but I hadn't spent much time talking to the adults. Or Portia —a strange name that somehow suited her, even with the little bit I knew. The three of them showed me my room and the mounds of books they'd stocked on the shelves, and I stayed holed up alone until dinner, lost in the pages of a made-up world.

It was weird to eat with anyone other than my mom, or anywhere other than at our table for two. Ours was nestled into a corner of our living room to create a makeshift dining space. Even at eight years old, I knew it wasn't much, but it was ours, and my mom worked hard to make sure we had a nice place. It wasn't as big as the Shaws' house. Our carpet was flat from walking on it all the time, and my twin bed didn't have a matching dresser, much less a nightstand and a lamp. The walls were white and our dishes mismatched, but at home, my mom tucked me in every night. When I was there, she brought me novels from the used bookstore every couple of days. And I knew I'd miss hanging out after school at the diner where she worked—they had the best lemon pie.

There was no lemon pie here. And even though there were tons of new stories to read, they weren't stamped with the logo of my mom's favorite shop. And they didn't smell like they'd been loved. But I had to make do. This wasn't permanent—my mom *would* get better. And I *would* go home.

"Jude's a weird name."

I cocked my head to the side and considered what Portia said. I didn't think she meant it to be cruel; it sounded more like curiosity.

"My mom loves the Beatles." The first smile I'd worn all day tugged at my lips. I thought of my mother dancing around our apartment, listening to songs I'd memorized in the womb.

We moved to the couch after dinner. I read a book on one end of the long, leather sofa, and Portia watched a kids' program on TV that I'd never seen since we didn't have cable. She'd sat silent for so long, the sudden conversation surprised me. I'd seen her eye me, and I waited for her to pounce the way other kids did. I wondered whether she would pick at my red hair or the abundance of freckles, or maybe how tall and skinny I was in comparison to other boys our age.

"My biological mom was into Janis Joplin. I hate hearing her songs." She shrugged, and her face contorted into a funny expression, like she'd sucked a lime and didn't care for the taste.

"Does it make you miss her?"

"Hardly," she scoffed. "She did me a favor."

I set my book down, curious to hear what she wanted to share. "I don't understand."

"It makes me think back to the day I found her." She rolled her eyes and let out an exaggerated huff. "And all the days before that, when I'd come home from school and find her tanked."

There was something she wasn't telling me. She glanced over her shoulder into the kitchen, I guessed to see where Ernie and Hensley were. When she gave me her attention again, her words didn't match her tone. "She did drugs. A lot of them. And those stupid songs were always playing in the background. The day I found her dead, one was stuck on repeat. It played over and over. Even after the cops got there, no one turned it off."

"How long have you been here?" I murmured, as though someone slept nearby and I might wake them. Ernie and Hensley had to be as aware of Portia's background as they were mine, so I wondered what the secret was and why we were whispering.

She wiggled a bit and snuggled deeper into the corner of the couch. Her rosy grin quirked to the side, and she stared up as though the answer might be on the ceiling. "Since right after Christmas." Her finger bounced on her chin three times. "So, six months, maybe. Yeah, that's about right." Then her gaze returned to me.

I wanted to keep her talking, but I was more of a listener. And I wasn't big on sharing things about my life. The kids at school made fun of me any time I did, so I had learned a long time ago not to tell my stories. Portia seemed different. Genuine maybe.

"You'll love it here. It's so much better than anything we know." Portia absentmindedly twirled a chunk of her dark hair, and her eyes glazed with contentment, assuming the two of us came from the same mold. "I hope if I'm good, the Shaws will adopt me. That's what they want, too." Her voice was sweet like cotton candy, light and fluffy. I imagined if it were a color, it would be pink —pale pink.

Listening to her ramble on made the day a little more bearable. I should've corrected her and told her that my mom didn't do drugs. I wouldn't be here forever. Yet I was afraid if I did, she'd think I thought I was better than her. And I was certain, even in the short time I'd spent with her, I wanted Portia to be my friend.

"Can you imagine? We could be brother and sister. I've never had a brother." She paused, and that dreamy expression floated across her eyes again. "Or a sister." When she giggled, the room got brighter, my heart grew larger, and I was warm all over.

"I don't have any, either." Sadly, Portia wouldn't become one.

I would go home when my mom finished treatment...even if I didn't know how long that might be.

1

JUDE

NINE YEARS LATER

MOTHER NATURE SHADED THE SKY IN HUES OF GRAPHITE, VIOLET, and a morose blue in a sullen farewell. The threat of rain was appropriate as I stood next to my mother's casket. Everyone had said their goodbyes and told me what a lovely service it was—I didn't think a funeral could be anything other than gruesome and depressing. I'd learned over the past nine years, and the last few days, when people don't know what to say, they repeat cliché phrases when silence would do better. Today was no different.

I understood my mother's friends' desire to pay their respects, to show her their love one final time. I just wished they realized that I didn't want to share those moments with them. I wanted to have my own, one that no one else would be privy to. My feelings volleyed between sadness, grief, anger, and rage, and the emotional shifts had only become more swift and unexpected after my mom took her final breath. Today, I hung between overwhelming sorrow and blinding fury. It took everything in me to bite my tongue, shake her guests' hands, and watch the parade of people until it ended.

Not even Portia's presence eased my suffering, and she knew it the moment she saw me. Unlike everyone else, she respected sorrow and kept her distance. I was aware of her without being suffocated. Ever since the two of us were kids—me eight and her nine—I'd welcomed the comfort she offered, and I'd leaned on her. Now, I wanted nothing more than time alone to tell my mother how much I loved her and how I'd miss her.

When I left here, I would be an orphan. I had been for several days, but I'd been able to avoid that reality by staying busy. Hensley and I had spent the majority of that time packing the old apartment and making funeral preparations. No seventeen-year-old should have to bury their parent; nevertheless, I was lucky to have the Shaws to fall back on. I didn't know where they were at the moment, though. Alone, I sat in one of the empty chairs and scooted it closer to my mom.

"I know you're not in pain anymore, and I'm grateful for that. But selfishly, I wasn't ready to let you go." I spoke as though she could hear me and might respond. "I can't imagine a world without your dancing and renditions of endless Beatles songs, or eating lemon pie from the diner while we talk about books."

The knot in my throat grew unbearable—large and painful. I couldn't swallow around it, and I choked on the words I needed to make sure she heard. "There won't be anyone around to remind me that copper is a beautiful color and every one of my freckles is a mark where you kissed me as a baby." My safety net from the world had been stolen. The woman who believed I was perfect—even in all my awkwardness—ripped away unjustly.

I eased off the chair, not caring if I ruined my slacks, and kneeled on the ground. Words were too messy, and tears streaked my face shamelessly. The casket still sat on the lowering device above the hole, so I pressed my cheek to the shiny, chestnut wood and sobbed. I longed for her to tell me one more time how much she loved me. I wished I could hug her and protect her. Through the tears, I croaked the lyrics to "Hey Jude," and when I finished, I wiped my eyes, kissed her goodbye, and stood to find Portia waiting for me on a bench not far off.

Over the years, Portia and the Shaws had become as big a part of my family as I had theirs. I'd never known my dad, or even his name, and Ernie stepped in to fill that role from the day I met him. Every time my mom had to go through chemo, I'd gone back into foster care, and I had gotten a family that defied all odds. They weren't the couple that people read about who appeared to be wonderful on the outside, only to find out they abused the system for money and neglected the kids in their custody. Ernie and Hensley Shaw just wanted children and hadn't been able to have any. I became an extension of the family they'd tried to have, and none of the three of them ever missed out on anything I did—even if I wasn't living with them at the time.

Regardless of how tough the last few weeks had been, Ernie, Hensley, and Portia hadn't left my side. It was an unconventional arrangement to most—thankfully, it worked for us. I'd been back and forth to their house for weeks or months at a time for the better part of a decade, and they'd welcomed me just as they always had.

When I got within a few feet, Portia stood, and I drowned in the sight of her.

"Hey, Jude." Her voice was still as sweet as spun sugar, and her smile was the stuff lipstick commercials were made of.

She slipped her arms around my waist and laid her head on my chest—even in heels, she didn't clear my shoulder. Reciprocating her embrace, I held her to me and placed my cheek on the top of her head. I welcomed the familiar smell of mint and rosemary and found comfort in the way her long hair tickled the tops of my hands on her lower back. Portia didn't try to make a hasty exit or encourage me to put on a brave face. Just as she'd done since the day we met, she accepted me exactly as I came to her—broken.

I didn't know how long we lingered in the cemetery. The quiet of the world hugged us, not allowing the wind to rustle leaves or give the birds their cue to chirp. And when it started to drizzle, I held steadfast in the same spot until water dripped from my hair and onto my face. Drenched, Portia pulled away enough to peer up so I could see her eyes and lifted onto her tiptoes to kiss my cheek.

"You ready?" I asked her, knowing she would stand here all day.

She nodded and took my hand. The warmth of her skin on mine was in sharp contrast to the chill of my emotions and the rain. The heat soothed a piece of me that wanted to run wild. Together, we walked away from my past and into my future. I didn't look back; my mom was gone, so there wasn't any point. I'd have to carry her in my heart from now on.

When we got into Portia's car, she shivered, undoubtedly cold from the rain. Even with her long hair plastered to her cheeks, spilling down her back, and spread across her arms and her makeup ruined by the weather, she was still the most stunning girl I'd ever known. Her beauty went beyond her slender physique and her exquisite facial features. Just past her eyes—irises the color of a green parakeet—her soul shined. As a kid, I thought the glitter was a dreamy expression. Now I knew it was a glimpse at her greatest treasure, and I prayed no one other than me ever saw it.

I cranked up the heat and then strapped on my seatbelt. Her house wasn't far, but the silence between us grew painful. "When are you leaving for school?"

She glanced at me before giving the road her attention. "Two weeks."

When the school year had ended, I thought we would have the summer to hang out—it didn't turn out that way. Since my mom had worked a lot in the past, Ernie always made sure to take me camping; we all went to the lake, and otherwise spent the majority of our time at the pool, wasting the hours away. But when my mom got sick right after summer break started, it was far worse than it had ever been. At seventeen, I didn't have to go to the Shaws', and when Mom decided not to undergo another round of chemo, I had opted to stay home. Unfortunately, that ate away the time in the sun and the annual vacation I took with Portia and her family.

Portia patted my hand. "Don't worry. I've saved all the fun stuff for us to do together."

I snickered half-heartedly. "Yeah? What's that?"

"Dorm shopping, packing, cleaning out my room." She tapped her finger on her chin the way I'd seen her do so many times before while she thought of anything she might have left out. "And if that's not enough to make you giddy, then you can help me load up all my crap and take me to school."

My groan reverberated throughout the car.

She swatted at my arm. "Oh hush. You don't have anything better to do. Your books will still be there after I'm gone."

Those last two words hit me harder than I expected—a sucker punch to the gut. My sharp inhalation clued her in.

"I didn't mean *gone* gone. I'm sorry, Jude."

I shook my head. "It's okay. I don't know why I'm being overly sensitive." I knew why, but I didn't want her to feel bad. "It's just going to be weird being at the Shaws' house without you there."

"I'll only be an hour away." She stopped at a red light and glanced toward me. "You can come visit. I can introduce you to college chicks, and you can drool over the campus library."

"The library alone would be worth the drive." Not that I had a car.

"What about *me*?" she shrieked, as though she wouldn't be the reason for any trip I made.

"Yeah, you'll be there, too."

"Consolation prize?"

"Something like that."

She tilted her nose up with a smug look on her face. Even with the smudged mascara under her lashes, she was still cute. "I'm the best consolation prize you ever won."

"Your humility is something I've longed to mirror."

Portia glared at me without any real punch in her stare. My

laughing at her only caused her lips to tilt in a smirk of her own. Even on my darkest day, that smile lit up the sky.

She pulled into the driveway of the house I'd now call home. It was all familiar, from the white siding to the black shutters and the red, front door. Even the flowers and bushes could have names, they'd been around so long. Only, in the past, I'd known I would go back to our little apartment a few miles away. This was now permanent.

The alarm chimed as I opened it, and Ernie and Hensley met us in the foyer. Hensley had been a wreck for days. She'd tried to hold it together for me, but she and my mom had become close over the years. Her death hit Hensley almost as hard as it did me. Portia shut the door behind us just as Hensley swarmed me in emotion. It didn't take long for Ernie to wrap the two of us in his own awkward hug. I was seconds from losing my cool when Portia wiggled her way between Hensley and me, pressing her front to mine. My heart swelled when I peered down my nose to find her staring up at me with a wicked grin.

"Enough of all these tears. Carrie would want us to celebrate her life, not wallow in her death." Portia was right, and my mom would have high-fived her for breaking up the sobfest.

"Did you have something in mind?" I wasn't sure what Portia was up to, but I prayed she didn't lead me into a pit of darkness or allow me to get sucked into a black hole.

The four of us broke apart as she pushed her way out as though she were in the midst of an enormous crowd and suffered from claustrophobia. "Indeed, I do."

"Oh lord, Ernie. What's that child up to?" Hensley swiped at the tears on her face through a smile. She adored Portia—and me, too.

Here were two people perfectly suited to be incredible parents who were never able to have children of their own. I'd asked once why they hadn't adopted babies—they could have gotten them— and Ernie just shrugged and said, "Babies are like kittens and puppies; they're easy to find homes. But kids of all ages need love and family."

I'd thought at the time his comparison of children to animals was odd until they took Portia and me to the humane society to adopt a pet. Of course, we were both drawn to the adorable little baby animals. But the moment Portia found out that a dog—with a neon-green sign reading "Dog of the Day" on its cage—would be put to sleep if it wasn't adopted, it clicked for both of us. There was no doubt the cute, fuzzy critters would find homes, but Baker—the mutt who came home with us that day—only had hours for someone to pick him, or he would be euthanized.

We—Portia and me—were very similar to Baker. But just like that lazy, old dog, the Shaws gave us a home and more love and attention than either of us dreamed possible, although our stay outlasted the dog's. Ernie went out of his way to be a positive, male influence in every aspect of my life, and Hensley was kind and patient. They never replaced my mom, but they enriched my life. And without them, I couldn't bear to think where Portia might have landed.

The familiar riffs of the guitar and beats of the drums came from the speakers in the living room where Portia had disappeared. My eyes burned, and the knot reappeared in my throat until she came slinking into view, exaggerating each movement of her arms and legs in time with the music. The moment she started to sing the lyrics to "Come Together," my heart melted. I let the tears flow as I took her extended hand, and as I'd done with my mom so many times in the past, I danced.

Ernie and Hensley joined in, moving awkwardly on the hard-wood floors. It didn't matter that we were all sad, or that Portia and I still wore wet clothes. The only thing I cared about was that people I loved surrounded me. Portia had obviously *planned* her "impromptu" dance session. The playlist consisted of nothing but the Beatles and only upbeat songs that kept us moving. From "Here

Comes the Sun" to "Help" and every song she'd chosen in between, she never let go of my hand. The girl couldn't carry a tune in a bucket, but her voice lulled my heart to peace. Cotton candy.

SWEAT COVERED MY SKIN, AND A CLAMMY CHILL CLUNG TO ME through the thin fabric of my pajamas. They were the only thing I recognized in the dark. It took me a minute to remember where I was, and it wasn't home. My mom wasn't down the hall, my stuff wasn't strewn about the floor, and I wouldn't be eating at the diner tomorrow morning when daylight took over the night, illuminating the room.

"Are you all right?" A voice startled me.

Jerking my line of sight toward the sound, I waited. I prayed my eyes would adjust and the shadows would stop tricking me into thinking things moved around the room. I'd woken up in here hundreds of times and never felt the panic I did now.

Portia didn't wait for me to respond. My heart hammered in my chest, although I didn't know if it was the nightmare that woke me, the unfamiliar fear clawing at me, or the girl crawling into bed next to me. Portia slinked between the sheet and the comforter. When the blankets moved, the swirling air from the fan hit my skin, causing me to shiver, which likely had to do with my damp clothes. I didn't want her to think I'd peed in the bed, but I wasn't quite ready to put my foot on the floor, brave the empty space between the mattress and the dresser, and change my pajamas.

"Do you feel bad?" She pressed her hand to my forehead. "You don't have a fever."

She laid her head on the pillow next to mine and shifted onto her side to face me. The moon gave off enough light to make out her features. Her smile was soft and gentle even though I couldn't see the crooked, front tooth that made her grin unique. Portia's eyes

12

were wide and bright, even covered by a shadowed veil. There was nothing sleepy in her expression, contrary to my own, which was foggy and unclear. She pressed her hands together and laid her cheek on top of them like an angel. It wasn't the first time Portia had come to comfort me in the midst of a nightmare, yet every time, I wondered briefly if God had sent her to me because he knew I was afraid.

"I just had a bad dream." I finally answered one of her two questions, although those few words answered them both.

She nodded and ran her tongue over her lips. I watched with rapt attention, mesmerized by the sheen that remained. She wiggled a bit and snuggled farther into the pillow and comfort of the blankets. "I had a lot of those after my mom died, too."

I knew that. Even though it had happened months before I met Portia, when I came to stay here the first time, she still had them. Only, she didn't wake me up screaming; she woke herself and often found her way to my room and into the same spot she was in now. We'd hide together for a few hours and then she would retreat to her room before the sun came up.

"Does it get easier?" It was a dumb question; nevertheless, I needed something to cling to—hope that I'd recover and life wouldn't be so painful.

Her shoulder escaped from beneath the blanket when she shrugged. She was thin, and a bone jutted out on top of her shoulder, now exposed by her tank top. I'd admired that little knot for as long as I could remember. I'd never seen another girl that had it—it was all Portia, just like her crooked tooth.

"I don't think my situation was anything like yours. So, it might be easier for me. Or maybe harder. I don't know. My mom wasn't like Carrie. We didn't have lemon pie." It was a euphemism for the good things I had that Portia didn't. She had gained a ton with the Shaws, although I doubted, in her mind, they were the same as having them with her real mom. One day she'd realize Hensley *was* her real mom. But that was a conclusion she'd have to come to on her own; I certainly wouldn't push it or even point it out.

"Do you still miss her?" I whispered into the darkness the same way I had when we were little, never wanting to wake Ernie or Hensley for fear they would get mad or stop these moments from happening. I often wondered if they realized all the secrets Portia and I shared, or if they grasped the gravity of the bond foster children clung to.

"I think I miss the idea of who I wanted her to be." She sighed. "Then I think how disrespectful that is to Hensley and Ernie, who were more than I ever dreamed."

"I don't believe they expected to replace her. They just love you." I huffed out a little laugh. "Warts and all."

"I couldn't ask for better. But you asked if it gets easier, and I can't say yes or no. There are days where you will forget, and other days it will consume you. It's been ten years, and I still struggle." Portia brought the blanket up close to her chin. "Just don't think you have to do it on your own. You've always got me."

"Except you're leaving. I'll be lost in this house without you."

"Meh. You'll still have Ernie and Hensley. They'll even listen to you talk about your boring books."

I yanked the pillow out from under her head and swatted her with it just before I pretended to smother her. While Portia was shorter than me—and didn't weigh a buck and a quarter soaking wet —she was strong. Her thighs grasped my waist, and her arms wound around my ribs. In the blink of an eye, she threw her weight into a barrel roll, and I landed on my back with Portia straddling my stomach.

She ripped the pillow from my hands, laughing loud enough to wake Ernie and Hensley. I cupped my hand over her mouth to quiet her victory. My gaze strolled from her glittering irises past her perfect nose and down her long neck. Stopping at her chest, her nipples were taut under her thin tank top, and even in the darkness, I could make out their dusky outline beneath the fabric. The top had ridden up her belly in the struggle and now exposed a sliver of her flat stomach and milky skin. Her long hair fell over her shoulder and onto her arm, and when she stopped squirming long enough to tuck it behind her ear, I quickly moved my hand from her mouth to join my other on her hips. I feigned a struggle and lifted her off my stomach to prevent her from noticing my arousal.

"Jesus, do you have rocks in your pockets?" I joked.

She rolled over and back into the spot she'd inhabited moments before…on her side of my bed. Far enough away that she couldn't feel the heat that flushed my skin or witness my growing erection under the blanket.

"Is that a crack at my weight?" She laughed as she spoke.

Before I could respond, she crossed her hands on her stomach and turned her face toward me. "Just a piece of advice there, sunshine"—I secretly loved when she got perturbed enough to make fun of my hair—"you're never going to win over the ladies with those kinds of jokes in your arsenal. Lucky for you, I'm here to school you in the ways of wooing." Her satisfied smirk made me chuckle.

To my knowledge, Portia had only shared one kiss with Bryson Kilpatrick, and that had been forced while playing spin the bottle. For all her rousing of me, she was just as inexperienced. "What do *you* know about being wooed?"

She stammered before acknowledging she knew nothing in absolute truth. "I've read a lot about it." Her brow pinched with indignation.

"Smut doesn't count. And when did you start reading?" As long as we'd known each other, my affinity for literature had been a source of amusement for Portia. It was all in good fun, but she let me know in her own way that it might be the reason I wasn't all that popular at school. I was never sure if she hadn't figured out that other kids believed I was awkwardly tall, overly skinny, had Irish-red hair, and was covered in freckles, or if she thought that my love of reading was one characteristic I had the power to alter. Either way, I was who I was, and that wasn't going to change.

"Around age five, I believe."

I moved onto my side, intrigued by this revelation. "Smart ass. You know what I mean."

She moved around in an attempt to get under the covers, clearly insecure. When she settled, I assumed she'd answer. She did not.

"Well?"

"What's with the interrogation?"

I hadn't meant to embarrass her, and I wasn't sure how to fix it. Social awkwardness was my forte; charming ladies was not. "I- I didn't mean…"

"I had a hard time when you'd leave. I'd get used to having you around and then you'd be gone again." This was unbeknownst to me. "I started coming into your room because I missed you." Her vibrant, pear-colored eyes glistened with unshed tears. "But there was nothing to do in here other than smell your stinky boy scent. You don't even have a TV." She giggled self-consciously and ran her fingers under her eyes to remove the evidence of her emotion. "Anyway, I was sitting in here after your mom had gotten better, but you'd stayed over one weekend, and I picked one up."

"What was it?" I didn't know why it mattered.

"*Huckleberry Finn.*"

A classic, although not something I thought Portia would enjoy. "Did you like it?"

She shrugged one shoulder. "I liked feeling close to you."

She could have slapped me across the face and I wouldn't have been more shocked than I was right that second.

"I know, it's dumb." It wasn't dumb at all. In fact, it made me love her even more. "So, I read them all."

There were hundreds of books on the shelves in this room and had been even then. I'd added to the collection tenfold over the years, but it was the single greatest kindness the Shaws gave me upon my arrival, because it allowed me to live in a place where my troubles didn't exist. "You mean the ones that were here then?"

She shook her head. "No. I mean every book you've ever brought into this house. And those you didn't leave, I bought and added to your shelves after I read them. And when we came to pick you up at your apartment, I'd look in your room to see if there were any new ones and ask Hensley to buy them."

Portia left me speechless. All these years, I believed she hated reading. "Why didn't you tell me?"

The emotional mess that threatened to spill over was replaced by the snarky banter I loved to share with her.

"And risk you thinking I was as big a dork as you are? Pfft. As if." She ruffled my hair playfully and awarded me with a cheesy smile, crooked tooth and all.

I found it hard to believe she'd held onto that secret all these years. If she'd done that, I could only imagine what she was capable of. "What else have you been keeping from me?"

"Nothing." Portia took my hand under the covers and closed her eyes. "Shh. It's late. Go to sleep." Without another thought, she shut down. Once she was done, there was nothing I could do to lure her back.

I couldn't stop myself from adoring her in the darkness. The moonlight cast an ethereal glow to her porcelain skin, and I had to will myself not to lean over and kiss the lips I'd admired since I was eight. I drifted off to sleep, wondering how it could have been the worst day of my life, burying my mother, and the best day, finding out Portia was a closet literature lover.

And when we woke in the morning, she had retreated back to her own room to keep our secrets safe.

2

JUDE

PORTIA'S ROOM LOOKED LIKE A BOMB HAD DETONATED. I DIDN'T
know how she planned to find anything, and I wasn't sure I could
locate her amidst the toys, clothes, and general crap piled on every
available surface.

I peered around the mounds to locate her. "Are you in there?"

Her head popped up on the opposite side of the bed, and a huge
smile broke out on her face. "Yep. I'm glad you're here."

"Do you need my help escaping? This place is like a landmine."
I took a couple of steps in, trying to find a safe place to put my foot
without fear of breaking something.

"No, silly." She glanced around with a confused look. "It's all
organized."

"Yeah? Into what, chaos?"

Portia squinted and turned her head a bit, giving me an eat-shit
look. "Can you go get some of those big, black trash bags from the
garage? The ones Ernie uses in the yard."

"Are you giving up? Just going to throw it all away? Burning it
in the firepit in the backyard might be easier." I raised my brow in
question, to which she launched a stuffed bear in my direction. I
caught it before it hit me in the face. The matted fur had a hard

texture like it had been singed at some point, although it might have been syrup or jelly that had petrified. "Gross. What's on this thing?" I held it out to my side, pinching it by the ear.

"Aww. That's Woobie. Don't you remember him?"

I hadn't ever seen the thing in my life. "Nope."

She huffed. "You got him for me at Chuck E Cheese's." It didn't ring a bell. "At my tenth birthday party." Still nothing. "Right before Sherlynn Gossman pulled your pants down in front of everyone there." Ah, it was all coming back to me and not in a pretty light.

"You always did have poor taste in friends." I tossed the grungy stuffed animal back at her. "You should get rid of it. That bear should have a biohazard warning on it."

Portia clutched the dingy thing to her chest. "No way. It was the first thing you ever gave me. And that was the first real birthday party I'd ever had. I felt like a princess."

I blew it off and went to get the bags she requested. Girls were weird about that kind of crap. I couldn't remember the first thing Portia had ever given me. In fact, I couldn't remember the last thing she gave me. And it wasn't because her gifts were thoughtless or meager; I had just never cared...as long as she'd been at whatever event warranted a present.

When I returned, Portia hadn't moved, even though it seemed everything else had. There were now defined piles with pathways between them.

She stood and grunted. "What took you so long?"

"I was gone for maybe two minutes." And in that amount of time, she'd put on music and done whatever it was to distinguish the mounds from one another.

Portia was an odd bird. Not on the outside so much as the little nuances that made her who she was. She was the girl next door. I thought she was stunning even if other guys weren't standing in line to date her. Truth be told, maybe I thought she was so beautiful because she was so exceptionally ordinary—like a dandelion growing between cracks in cement. Her music tastes were eclectic, to say the least, and she never listened to the radio. I never quite grasped how she found these indie bands. I just sat back and enjoyed what she uncovered. Today was different, though. Still a playlist, only instead of it being indie-grunge, the room filled with sounds of the Grateful Dead.

"What's up with the music?"

"Just feeling nostalgic." It didn't escape my attention that she refused to make eye contact. "It's a cool mix. You'll like it." When I didn't respond, she peeked up from the pile she was stuffing into the bag. "What?"

"Nothing."

"Grab a bag. All those clothes are going to Goodwill."

"You know you don't have to get rid of your stuff just because you're going to college, right?"

She moved over to the closet and opened it for me to see she wasn't. "I'm not. Just the stuff I don't wear." For a girl who lived in jeans and T-shirts, she had more clothes on the floor to give away than I did in my entire wardrobe.

I sat down between two large piles and began shoveling things into the bag. It took all of two handfuls for me to come across some-thing I didn't want her to let go. "Why are you getting rid of this?"

"Pink Floyd was so ten years ago," she mocked.

"We loved this album." I'd never been a fan until Portia was. I swear, I was so lost—she could have told me she was Dorothy, and I would have followed her down the Yellow Brick Road. Even then, I'd wanted to fit in, if with no one other than her.

"You can have it if you want it."

I just gaped at her, waiting for it to dawn on her. When she stared back, blinking slowly, I stripped off the shirt I wore and put on the one in question.

She giggled. "So maybe it doesn't fit. Fine, give it here. I'll keep it."

Satisfied that I had persuaded her to keep a memento from our past, I continued with my assigned task. Not two minutes later, it was a Disneyland shirt. "So you're keeping some stinky bear but not things that are useful?"

"Seriously? You want me to wear a shirt with Minnie Mouse written in glitter on the front?"

It took everything I had not to tell her to shrink it in the dryer, cut it off, and wear it without a bra. That and a pair of white, cut-off jean shorts would have me salivating from here back to California. "That was an awesome vacation." And it was. The Shaws had even taken my mom with us on that one.

I finally conceded. "Fine. It might be a tad immature." As I continued through the stack, I realized how many of her clothes held memories. And what a girl I was being. In that moment, it dawned on me, I hadn't seen most of these on her in years.

My eyes flicked up, and I realized, staring at her, that the girl I'd grown up with had become a young adult. I'd seen glimpses of it here and there, but today it smacked me upside the head. The youthful, ordinary chick who'd worn jeans and T-shirts now had a very distinct style of her own. If she were in a band, she'd be a natural for the cover of *Rolling Stone*. The innocent appearance she'd had for years still lingered behind the perfect makeup—not overdone— and the skinny jeans with holes in the knees. Even her hair had an edge to it that I hadn't noticed at the funeral because she'd curled it.

"What are you staring at?"

I hadn't noticed I was staring...well, that I'd been doing so without reservation.

"You look different. When did"—I waved my hand around in her general direction—"*that* happen?" My dick stirred at the shock of seeing the woman before me. She was undeniably hot.

"That's mean." The pout on her pink lips did nothing other than encourage my body's poor behavior.

"I didn't mean it in a bad way. I just—you grew up."

Her face beamed with pride, and her eyes sparkled. "Thank you."

In that moment, it occurred to me that I would face something I'd never experienced with Portia—competition. She was going to college, and I wouldn't be around. Even when I hadn't been living here, the two of us had gone to the same high school. We didn't hang out with the same crowds, but it was no secret we were very close, and rumors roamed the halls that more existed between us than ever had. Although, that wasn't due to a lack of desire on my part. I'd just never had the balls to tell her. I was always afraid of how it would look.

The student body thought we were siblings—even though there was zero blood relation between us—because I stayed at the Shaws' as often as I did my mom's. The handful of friends I had referred to her as my sister, and likewise with hers. But part of me believed—or maybe just hoped—that guys left her alone because they thought she was taken. That was an unspoken proclamation on my part...her being mine, that is.

I wouldn't have any claim to her when she wasn't in town. No one at the university would know our history or our tie. And looking the way she did, there was no doubt in my mind, guys would go after her. My heart nearly split in half at the mere thought of anyone touching her, and it about shattered when I entertained her growing close to another male, sharing her secrets and feelings.

When I filled the second bag, I stood to move it out into the hall and caught sight of myself in the mirror. Six foot three and a hundred and ninety pounds. Scalding-red hair, freckles on every bare inch of skin, and sad, brown eyes. There was nothing in that image that could appeal to her—not that any freshman in college would want to be with a senior in high school.

Just when my self-esteem was about to tumble over the edge of a cliff, that damn stuffed bear hit me upside the head. "Come on, Fabio. We'll be here all day if you don't stop gawking at yourself in the mirror."

With wounded pride, I gave my attention to Portia, and her crooked tooth and gorgeous smile knocked me back on my feet and solidified my desire.

———

"COME ON. GET UP. GET UP. GET UP." PORTIA WOKE ME BY bouncing on my bed in animation. Her dark hair flew around her, blocking her face from view, but her voice gave away her excitement.

"God. What time is it?" I pressed the heel of my hands into my eyes and tried to rub the sleep away. "If it's before noon, come back at twelve." Yanking on the covers, I rolled onto my side to block her out.

She tugged on my arm and used her weight to pull me into a sitting position. "It's already ten. By the time you shower and eat, it will be noon before we get on the road. And then it's an hour drive. Come on."

I hated it when she pouted and even worse when she whined. Portia was the only female in the world who could spin me upside down by puffing out her bottom lip and lowering her voice half an octave. I was a goner the instant she did it.

"Fine. I'll get up when you get out." There was no way in hell I was tossing back the blankets to give her a visual of all the things I'd dreamed about. It was difficult enough to hide morning wood with something covering me; in nothing other than boxers, she'd see all I had to offer.

There was no denying how nice her ass looked as she crawled off the side of the mattress. It was perfectly round, and the bottom peeked out beneath her shorts. "Promise you won't go back to sleep?"

I grunted, crossed my heart, fell back onto the pillows, and waited for her to go. The groan that escaped my mouth could only be satisfied under the veil of running water and a locked door. Like most guys my age, I did my best thinking in the shower—and Portia monopolized my thoughts. I'd never seen her naked; however, I'd had the pleasure of sunbathing on the beach next to her. Portia had sported some pretty skimpy bikinis that I couldn't believe Ernie had let her out of the house in. My imagination was vivid enough to fill in the blanks.

It hadn't taken me anywhere near as long as Portia believed it would, but I kept dragging my feet. The two weeks I'd had with her before she left for college flew by faster than I could blink. I dreaded leaving today to drive her to school. I knew just how hard the solitude would hit me. My entire life, I'd had my mom or Portia at my side, and in a matter of hours, I'd have neither.

Ernie and Hensley had hovered since the funeral, even though they hadn't pushed. It was as if they were waiting for me to fall apart, which hadn't happened since I'd left Mom's grave. Ernie wanted to have one of his father-son talks, but wisely, he hadn't pushed the subject. I could only hope that starting back to school in two days would keep all that at bay. I didn't believe in the whole grief process thing; I'd experienced all those stages before my mom died because I knew it was coming, and then again in the few days after. Since then, I'd been kind of numb.

The only good part about Portia going to college was that I got her car. As a freshman, she wasn't allowed to have a vehicle space, which meant she either had to find a place to park off campus or leave it at home. Ernie and Hensley thought the second option was best. Selfishly, I appreciated it—until I realized she wouldn't be able to come home whenever she wanted. One of us would have to go get her—not that I'd complain—or she'd have to find a ride. And so far, Portia didn't know anyone attending the same university.

Hensley straightened my shirt and smoothed it down my chest. "Jude, make sure you call us when you get there. And again as you're leaving so we know when to expect you back." She didn't make eye contact with me until after she'd finished her sentence.

I nodded and stepped back so she and Ernie could give Portia money, an emergency credit card, the same list of rules she got every time she left the house, hugs, and then poorly hidden tears. It was hard to imagine what this would be like for a parent, and even more so for one who hadn't had the full eighteen years with their child. But as the kid who sought independence, I wasn't sure how Portia hadn't pushed them off and darted to the car to speed off into the sunset. My heart swelled watching her play the part of a doting daughter. She loved them both beyond measure and was well aware of how different her existence would be had they not found each other.

I had taken their role in my life for granted until recent weeks. I never saw them as my parents, more like those of my best friend. Even though they'd been there for me at every turn—good or bad—it never occurred to me that they were an extension of my mom. It wasn't until the day she told me the cancer returned and she had opted not to do another round of chemo, that it dawned on me where I fell in the pecking order of their lives. They hadn't prayed for my mom's demise, but they had, however, made her a promise to fill in wherever she left off.

I stared at the three of them in a communal embrace and listened to them cry tears of happiness that their little girl was growing up. Portia rolled her eyes even though she'd bend over backward to please them.

Ernie clapped me on the shoulder when the blubbering ended, startling me from my thoughts. "Drive safe. Make sure you call us."

"Got it." I tried to soften my tone when I realized how sharp my words were. "Promise."

Portia blew Ernie and Hensley kisses—she was such a girl—and settled herself into the passenger seat. While I buckled up, she entered the address into the GPS, and I stole a glimpse of her, capturing a screenshot in my memory. She caught me staring at her while she fumbled with the radio. We maneuvered out of the neighborhood, and she slowly tilted her eyes up to meet my stare. I glanced away, as though the road garnered my attention, yet from the corner of my eye, I watched her watching me. I wondered if she were making memories of her own to recall later when she was alone at school or if she just thought I was an odd duck. Either could be true.

Once she settled on a playlist, she sat back with the volume cranked up and proceeded to sing every lyric to each song that barreled through the speakers. Some she sang to me as though I were her ravenous audience of one. Others she belted out like she was alone in the world, staring out the window. And then there were a handful she knew I recognized and forced me to join in as though it were a hallelujah chorus. This was the Portia I'd loved as a kid, through the various awkward stages of puberty, and now into adulthood—although each with a different passion.

I could see the pieces of her that had grown and matured along the way in everything she did; even the way she laughed hadn't changed, just aged.

"Stop staring at me, Jude. You're making me all self-conscious."

"How can I be staring at you when my eyes are on the road?" Regardless of whether I admitted it, I'd been caught, and I smirked.

"I bet you still believe that if you can't see me, then I can't see you, huh?"

"You'll never let that go, will you?"

"It's funny." She chuckled and then broke out into laughter, almost choking on the words as she forced me to relive a memory she loved and I hated. "How could you think I wouldn't see your body hanging out from under the couch just because you had covered your head?"

I turned onto the campus, and I hoped when I pointed at the sign that she'd drop the topic. "It wasn't one of my finer moments. Gimme a break. I was eight."

"And oddly enough, the smartest guy I've ever known...you just needed a little schooling in the ways of the streets...some world knowledge."

"Oh yeah, you brought that to the table in spades with your vast history on the streets of Carondale when you were nine."

"There!" Portia smacked my arm and pointed to an enormous building with the words Sander Hall etched above the brick facing. "That's it. Find a place to park."

That was easier said than done. We weren't the only people who had shown up to move in on "Moving Day." The roads were congested with families trying to find the closest spot to the building.

I stopped to wait for three guys to cross the street and hoped they were going to a car where we might snag their parking place. As they hung out, talking between two vehicles, I got frustrated, not wanting to give up the possibility of a spot, and not wanting to wait all day for something that didn't exist. I huffed, and she shoved open the passenger door.

"Portia, what are you doing?"

She didn't wait to answer. Instead, her lean legs carried her thin, smoking-hot body straight up to the three strangers. Her hair blew behind her in the breeze, and her oversized shirt slid off her shoulder to expose the black strap of her bra and that knot of a bone I loved so much. It was a strategic move on her part; I just wasn't aware it was one that was in her arsenal. I couldn't see her face, yet I had no doubt she was talking because her hands were moving. Each of the guys had turned toward her, forming a little circle with the girl they'd never met and obviously wanted to get to know by the grins plastered to their faces. Portia pointed to the car, and I hoped I was far enough away that they hadn't seen me glaring. She smiled and returned her attention to the tallest of the three. He leaned in and said something only she was privy to.

I saw red. The guy had about fifty pounds of solid muscle on me, even though I had three inches on him. I wasn't a fighter— never had been. Still, had Portia not come back to the car sooner rather than later, I would have gotten out and removed her. She strutted toward me with confidence I didn't know she possessed and glanced over her shoulder, waving to the same guy who'd whispered sweet nothings in her ear.

She got back in the vehicle. "Bartholomew is going to move his car so you can park there and—"

"Who?" My tone was snotty and unwarranted. Thankfully, Portia missed it.

"Bartholomew. He's the RA for Sander Hall."

My anger morphed to sullen disbelief. "Your dorm is co-ed?"

"Oh. Go. The spot's empty." She patted me on the arm to grab my attention. "Hurry before someone else gets it."

Parking squelched the discussion. Portia was out and lifting the hatch. All around us, vehicles were open, people carried boxes and bags—some lamps and odd-looking chairs—and Portia was in the zone.

I tried to remember why I was here. This wasn't about me. She'd chosen to have me bring her, not Ernie and Hensley. The two of us had a bond that I believed only twins and other fosters understood. Nothing—not distance, not another guy, not school—could change that. Even if it didn't stifle my jealousy.

For the next hour, I acted as Portia's pack mule, toting her stuff up to the third floor of her dorm. Waiting for elevators was pointless; everyone and their mama—literally—had them in use. I opted for the stairs, making trip after trip while she found places to put things in the tiny space she now shared with Jet Ashmore. I couldn't say with any certainty that Jet wasn't her real name, but I was confident in going out on a limb to say that it wasn't. At first glance, she seemed a perfect fit for Portia. Then, as I caught pieces of their conversations while I came in and out of the door, I realized her look didn't match her personality, and Portia would call her a poser. I just hoped Portia managed to make friends with her; otherwise, Portia would have a long year in this crackerjack box of a room with a girl she couldn't stand.

On my final trip to the third floor, I dumped the last of Portia's stuff on her bed and realized she'd be just fine. She already had her indie-grunge music pumping, and even though Jet didn't seem to know the words, it appeared she liked the beat. The two of them were dancing, and Portia had started singing—God, help us all.

"Jude, you forgot to call Mom and Dad to let them know we were here."

I'd gotten distracted by Bart and company in the parking lot. "Did *you* call?" I hadn't gotten used to her referring to Ernie and Hensley as Mom and Dad. She didn't do it often, so when she did, it threw me for a second.

"They called me. I think they were afraid of you talking on the phone and driving at the same time." Pleased with herself, her eyes narrowed playfully, and her smile widened.

Jet beamed at me and continued to put stuff away as she danced around. "I think it's cute your little brother brought you to school."

Portia didn't correct her. And by the time I realized she wasn't going to, I'd waited too long—it would now seem odd for me to announce that we weren't really related. I cocked my head in question, but Portia either didn't get that it bothered me that she let this girl think I was her sibling, or she completely missed me staring at her.

She came over and ruffled my hair like I was five instead of seventeen. "He's awesome to have around." And then she snaked her arm around my waist and gave me a quick squeeze.

"Too bad you're younger. You're super cute." Jet wasn't the least bit shy, even if she was full of shit.

"He is, isn't he?" The proud look Portia gave me made my heart swell, and I forgave her for rubbing my head. "Can you imagine how hot he'll be when he fills out in a year or so?"

It was like I wasn't even standing there.

"Damn." Jet jutted her hip out and ran her gaze from my head to my toes and back. "That red hair, and as tall as he is…if he puts on some weight, you won't be able to beat the girls off him with a stick." She shook her head as though she were fantasizing about a more mature version of me standing before her.

Invisible.

"Aren't his freckles perfect?" Portia cooed at her new friend.

"It's those big, brown, puppy-dog eyes that are going to steal the hearts of ladies." Jet wagged her brow at me and winked.

She was a pretty girl: long, blond hair, bright-blue eyes, and a body guys would drool over. If Mattel ever created an Indie-Rock Barbie, they could use Jet—name and all—as inspiration. Yet she paled in comparison to Portia's unique vibe.

Without warning, Jet popped me on the ass and giggled. That's where I drew the line.

"Before this gets out of hand, Portia, is there anything you need to do around campus?" I already knew there was.

"Oh, yeah. I'm glad you mentioned that. I don't know how late any of these places are open." She turned to Jet. "Do you want to go with us to get a student ID and meal card? I need to get my books, too."

I hoped she would let me go around campus with her to find her classes, as well. I wanted to be a part of this. And I hoped that if I knew where she was during the day, I'd feel closer to her. Being able to visualize where she was when I talked to her somehow set my mind at ease. I'd done the same thing when I'd been with my mom instead of at the Shaws' house.

"Nah, I'm going to stay here and finish unpacking. You two go. I'll see you later."

I let out a breath that I hadn't realized I held. Jet seemed to be a nice enough girl; I just wanted what little time I had to be spent with Portia and not competing for her attention. We'd almost made it out the front of Sander Hall when Portia's new BFF stopped her to ask where she was headed, as though I weren't standing next to her.

And after telling him, she drove a knife straight into my heart when she asked, "Wanna come?" I couldn't have snapped my fingers as fast as Bartholomew took her side.

"Oh, I forgot. Bartholomew, this is my little brother, Jude."

I tried—unsuccessfully—to hide my disappointment in her introduction as I shook the guy's hand.

"Please, call me Bart." He glanced at her and then back to me. Bart had to shift his eyes upward. He wasn't short by any means, a solid six feet. I was just three inches taller. I took pleasure in that tiny nuance. "Not very *little*. You play basketball?"

I hated that question almost as much as I detested sports. "Do you play miniature golf?" It wasn't nice even if I said it with a smile. Nevertheless, he chuckled.

"Jude! Don't be like that." Portia came to Bart's defense.

And then she touched him.

It was a casual exchange—her hand on his forearm. All the same, it fueled the green monster growing inside me. "He's more of an intellectual than an athlete." Her eyes shifted to mine.

"No shame in that, man. It's good to meet you."

Bart made it awfully difficult to dislike him. He was respectful, courteous, and seemed laid-back… I could acknowledge that women would find him easy on the eyes. And I had to admit, he made every effort to keep me engaged with the two of them.

Although, I still seemed to be the third wheel in this trio, which was odd since I'd known Portia for years to his handful of hours.

As we proceeded around campus, Bart showed Portia where all her classes were, bought us both coffee, introduced her to what seemed to be every soul we encountered, and gave her an inside tour of the campus. When we circled back to their dorm, I offered to excuse myself.

I thought for sure Portia would tell Bart she'd see him later and beg me to stay…that's what I got for trying to manipulate the situation to get what I wanted. Bart was new and exciting. I was reliable and always around.

"Don't forget to call Mom and Dad when you get in the car." And in that handful of words, Portia managed to make me feel like a child.

She wrapped her arms around my waist and pressed her head against my chest. I reciprocated and took the opportunity to inhale the scent of rosemary in her hair and try to memorize the way she felt next to me. I didn't have a commitment for when she'd be home, and I knew the second I got in the car, loneliness waited to hold me hostage.

"I won't."

Bart smiled at me and then looked down at Portia. He clapped me on the shoulder which prompted her to release me. "It was good to meet you, man. Don't be a stranger. I promise I'll take good care of your sister."

I wanted to correct him. Tell him we weren't *really* related. Threaten him about touching her. Pee on her leg and stake my claim. Instead, I pussed out. "You too."

3

PORTIA

BART KNOCKED, AND JET OPENED THE DOOR TO OUR ROOM. THE two of us had spent the last hour getting ready for our first frat party, and Bart, Chet, and Todd were here to escort us. Bart whistled through his teeth when I spun around, but it was Chet who scanned my body from head to toe. There was no way he missed the blush that warmed my cheeks with his attention.

Bart took Jet's hand and lifted it above her head so she could twirl for him, and then he repeated the same with me. "You guys look fantastic."

"Thank you, thank you." My roommate beamed with his praise.

Bart wasn't at all shabby himself. There wasn't a flaw that I could find anywhere on his body, and he was a nice guy to top it off. Ever since I'd met these three the day I'd arrived, they'd all spent time getting to know me, and by default, Jet. Bart and Todd were older than I was and both juniors. Chet, however, was the little brother of a guy Bart went to high school with, and he was a sopho-more. One year didn't seem that monumental until I realized just how much I didn't know.

Jude was the only guy, other than Ernie—who didn't count—

that I'd ever been close to. The attention these three lavished on me sent me soaring.

Jet bounced in her heels, and her hair moved with it. She was gorgeous, every guy's fantasy come to life, which was probably why Bart, Todd, and Chet welcomed her with open arms. The first few times we'd all hung out, I'd believed I was the go-between for one of them to get to her. Oddly enough, if they had wet dreams about her, none of them made a move toward changing any of them into a reality. Chet, on the other hand, made a noticeable effort to grab my attention.

We had Chemistry 101 together, and since I wasn't friends with anyone in the class, he picked me as his partner. It didn't escape my attention the way the other girls in the lab glared at me. Chet was on the lacrosse team, chiseled, and had piercing, blue eyes. His dark-brown hair was long on top and shaved on the sides, which I thought went out in the nineties, yet it worked on him. And while his confidence could be suffocating, once I'd spent a little time with him doing labs and homework, I enjoyed his company.

"Portia, you ready?" Chet leaned against the wall with his ankles crossed.

Just hearing my name roll off his lips brought unfamiliar sensations to strange places. It wasn't that I didn't like it; I did. I just didn't know how to extinguish the fire or fan it. Chet was the first guy who'd ever shown any real interest in me. I couldn't stop staring at his mouth, and when he chuckled, I snapped my attention to his eyes. Bright blue. They reminded me of the ocean, pretty to look at but danger lurked inside.

I dismissed my trepidation for inexperience and smiled.

"I'll take that as a yes. Come on." He jerked his head toward the hall as he pushed off the doorframe, and when I met up with him, he extended his hand.

I took it with hesitation. I didn't want to stare at his fingers, and I was afraid to let him see the insecurity I tried to disguise. The warmth of his palm pressed to mine, and the gentle, yet confident way he held on to me as we walked the halls of Sander set me at ease by the time we hit the quad. Heads turned with each step we took. I wasn't sure if it was the guys or Jet who people took notice of, but for the first time in my life, I ran with the big dogs.

Bart, Todd, and Jet were close behind us, even though Chet and I were in our own bubble. I had no idea what to expect when we got to this party, and my heart raced with anticipation—not just the magnitude of what we were about to walk into, but whose arm I would do it on. Chet's thumb stroked the top of my hand. Obviously, I wasn't doing as well as I'd thought at hiding my emotions.

Frat row consisted of eleven houses that each flew a flag—with letters I didn't know—indicating which fraternity lived there. And there wasn't just one porch covered in people; they all were. People lined the streets and the sidewalks and shadowed every window. It was after ten, yet it was easy to spot those who had started to party earlier than the rest. I didn't drink, and I didn't do drugs, nor had I ever hung out with anyone who did. I didn't have a problem with alcohol when consumed responsibly. I was not a fan of knee-walking drunks, who slobbered on my ear or pulled at my clothes when they staggered.

We hadn't been there fifteen minutes, and I'd already been felt up by a chick trying to get to the guy who held my hand. She spilled beer down my arm, and all I could do was smile. I recognized her as one of the other students in our chemistry class, but I didn't know her name and had never spoken to her. I didn't want to be *that* girl...the one who thought she was better than everyone else and acted like a snob, but I had a hard time not pushing her off me with a grunt of irritation.

Chet dropped my hand and pried the girl off my leg. "Let me find some paper towels or something to clean off your arm. I'll be right back."

I twisted around in the mass of people, expecting to find Jet and the other two guys behind me, yet none of them were there. In a continued search, I located Jet and Todd dancing in the living room, although there was no sign of Bart. In the other direction, I came face to face with the girl Chet had just removed from my thighs. She now stood—wavering—with a stare so hateful that if it had a fist it would have packed a mighty punch.

"He's just using you." Her words were slurred, yet the sentiment was loud and clear. The girl's neck twisted, and her eyes bulged. Cleary, she believed she illustrated a bold point, regardless of how foolish she appeared doing it. "Upperclassmen only have interest in fresh meat for one thing. As soon as he gets it, he'll drop your naïve ass faster than he can chug a beer."

Before I could respond—not that I had a clue what to say—Chet returned with a handful of napkins.

"Here you go, Portia. I couldn't find anything else." He ignored the blonde to my left, who still hovered inches from my face and reeked of vomit and beer.

She stumbled, but remained upright. "Portia? Like the car? That's rich. Or maybe just trashy." The beer in her red Solo cup sloshed over the side and onto the floor.

"Carolyn, why don't you back off?" Chet's jaw was set, and the muscles ticced with each passing second.

My eyes flitted between them both, wondering what kind of history they had to make her so aggressive. I kept my mouth shut, and when he wadded up the napkins, he took my hand and led me away from the monster who'd dumped beer on me.

"Sorry about that," he apologized as we walked into the kitchen to a large trash can.

"Why?" I wasn't sure I wanted the answer.

Chet had been nothing other than kind to me. He was attentive in class, and we often ate lunch together with Bart or Jet, and sometimes Todd. I'd get random text messages from him, and he always stopped to talk when he saw me around campus. At first, I hadn't seen tonight as a date so much as friends hanging out—special friends, maybe. The guys were aware Jet and I didn't know very many people, and they had kind of taken us under their wings to show us the ropes.

"That was uncalled for." He took a cup of beer from the guy manning the keg and then lifted our twined hands to point toward the spot we'd last seen Carolyn. "I don't understand why girls think that kind of behavior attracts guys."

When he met my eyes, I relaxed. It was easy to see how he could get a reputation from women who felt slighted after he'd rejected them. I wouldn't say Chet and I were close; we hadn't known each other long. Although, his reputation and perception were important to him. He took pride in his position on the lacrosse team, he made sure to talk to anyone who said hello, and he was part of a handful of clubs and organizations. Chet played an active role on campus. He was a popular guy. It would be easy to mistake his confidence for cockiness if I hadn't spoken to him.

"Do you want something to drink?" he asked, as though he'd just realized he had a beverage and had been rude not to offer me one.

"I'm not a fan of beer. Thank you, though."

"I'm pretty sure there's a stash of wine coolers in the back." Charisma oozed from his smile, and I was putty in his hand. "Come on, you can pick whatever flavor you want."

I debated refusing. It wasn't that I wasn't interested in having one. I'd just never done it before, and I wasn't certain this was the best place to let loose. Chet had proven he'd take care of me and would be attentive, but he wasn't Jude. This wasn't a boy I'd known most of my life. He wasn't someone I wouldn't question…yet, here I stood, not opening my mouth to refuse him. Like a sheep to the slaughterhouse, I held his hand, ate up the envious glances in my direction, and took the peach cooler he offered me. Then in an even dumber move, I put it to my lips, and we moved back to the front of the house.

The concoction was as sweet as Kool-Aid without a hint of alcohol. I hadn't realized how hot it was inside with all the people crammed into a space meant for a twentieth of the number it now held. The liquid went down with ease, and before I could blink, Chet held out another bottle with the cap already removed. I wasn't sure where it had come from, but I took it regardless. I liked the peach better, but strawberry wasn't half bad.

"You want to dance?"

I couldn't hear him over the music and people talking. "What?"

Chet snaked his arm around my waist—the one holding his beer —and kept my hand in his. In a move Rico Suave couldn't repeat, he'd brought me flush against his hard chest. Every ripple of well-defined muscle pressed against my breasts and stomach. Heat flooded my core, and I had to fight not to rub against him to alleviate some of the sexual tension rolling through me. Chet's masculine scent overtook my nostrils, and I couldn't inhale him fast enough. But I came close to losing control of my legs and my ability to stand when he spoke close enough to my ear that his breath tickled my skin and sent chills down my spine. My body warred with the hot and cold, back and forth, tension and ease. I hadn't heard a word he had said, even when spoken close enough to my head that I could have licked his cheek if I were so brazen.

I refused to ask him to repeat himself again. Instead, I just nodded while I floated on a cloud of lust...or maybe the early stages of love. I didn't know which, nor did I care. Any hesitation I had when Carolyn snarled at me left at the end of the first bottle. By the time I'd finished the second, he could have taken me just about anywhere, and I wouldn't have refused to go. A warm hum buzzed through my body as he led me to the makeshift dance floor.

It was far too loud to talk, so instead, I found the beat in the music and let go. I didn't have a clue if I could dance, all I could say with any certainty was Chet seemed as into what we were doing as I was. He didn't let me get far, whether the song that played was upbeat or slow. If his front was to my back, his arm held me close. If we stood face to face, he still had an arm securing me to his body, and I rode his thigh like it was a champion bull at the rodeo. If people stared, I missed it. I was too lost in my own pleasure to notice anyone else.

Until Jet tried to politely intervene.

And then not so politely jerked me away.

I felt Chet's loss, although it was quickly replaced by the heat of Jet's wrath.

"What are you doing?" she growled through clenched teeth, and for some reason, I had no problem deciphering her words over the music.

"Dancing."

She grabbed my wrist and headed toward the front porch. Just before we disappeared outside, I turned back and met Chet's eyes. The confusion cleared when I mouthed, "I'll be right back."

If Jet didn't slow down, I was on the verge of stumbling much the way Carolyn had—not that I was drunk, just warm and sated. She finally stopped in the grass on the opposite side of a large tree. It provided a little seclusion, although not much. People were everywhere—as if the entire campus came to frat row to drink tonight.

"Portia, seriously, *what* are you doing in there?"

I wasn't sure what she misunderstood. Jet wasn't a dumb girl. She'd seen me with Chet...*dancing*. "Dancing." My brow furrowed with confusion.

"Girl, you're using his leg as a pole. Guys were starting to pull dollar bills from their wallets to stuff into your shirt." She folded her thin arms across her chest and waited.

"Pfft." A raspberry blew past my lips. "I wasn't doing anything every other girl in there with a hot guy wasn't doing." I heard myself dismiss her warning and wondered how I could be so passive about what she'd said. I'd only had two wine coolers, yet still, I couldn't bring myself to be mortified or believe it was as big a deal as Jet made it out to be.

"My guess is they didn't arrive with three guys, either, Portia." She let out a heavy sigh as though it saddened her to have to be the one to inform me.

"You act as if my reputation is at stake." She was making a big deal out of nothing. No one cared that I'd come in with three guys. I'd also come in with another girl. I only held the hand of one of those four people. I'd only touched one of them.

"It is. Do you realize how many people are here? And it's not the nobodies from class. Every major player on campus is roaming this block right now. You're setting the stage for the next four years." She put her hand on my arm, and her posture softened when my eyes filled with tears. "Just be careful. That's all I'm saying."

I swiped at the tears now rolling down my cheeks and nodded. Jet took my hand and squeezed my fingers. Together, we maneuvered our way back through the crowd, and I noticed my roommate was right. It wasn't the same people on the porch that were here a few minutes ago when we walked out. And while I didn't know any of them personally, I recognized most of them. This was the "in" group at the university, and getting a reputation that was less than pristine wasn't what I wanted.

Bart waited for the two of us just inside. He glanced at me, and then his attention darted to Jet. There was no doubt he could see that I was upset, and I giggled when he didn't know what to say. It was the wine coolers relaxing me, but I didn't want him to worry, either. Just as I leaned in to hug his waist and tell him I was all right, Chet met us at the door.

With one look at my puffy eyes, his features hardened. He didn't have a clue what took place outside or why Jet had ripped me from his arms in the middle of a song. And now he stared at me, clearly wondering why I'd been crying. I backed away from Bart, who kissed my cheek and patted my arm, although he didn't ask any questions. The pity on his face made me think he might have been the one to send Jet after me so he didn't have to be the bearer of bad news.

Chet held out his hand. I glanced between Bart and Jet even though I didn't know why. Confirmation, acceptance maybe. Neither gave me much to go on. Bart remained stoic while Jet just shrugged. A shrug could mean anything. It could be acknowledgment that it was okay to let Chet take me away, or it could have been her way of saying, "I warned you, and now you're on your own." I should have read it as the last. Instead, I chose the first.

My fingers intertwined with Chet's, which hadn't relaxed in the slightest. He ensured no one would come between us...wherever we were going. Once I made the decision, I didn't hesitate. And when he couldn't create a path for the two of us to go safely through without worry over separation, Chet used his grasp to pull me so I could walk in front of him. He put his hands on my hips to direct me to the stairs. The man was the size of a Brahma bull—when people saw him coming, they stepped aside, essentially staying out of my way.

It didn't occur to me that every one of those students we passed saw the two of us on the dance floor and now heading up the stairs together. Alone. I ignored those who showed us any interest and kept the path he pushed. And when we reached the second floor, it was quieter than downstairs where the music blared.

Chet braided his fingers through mine again when we reached the dark hall. He seemed to be intent on a particular destination. I heard a noise behind me, and a giggly girl—and a guy I assumed to be her boyfriend—knocked at one of the other rooms while making out in front of it. A guy appeared, invited them in, and the two disappeared at the same time Chet tugged me out of the hall.

He flipped on the light and then closed the door behind me. He moved around the space as though it wasn't the first time he'd been in it, turning on the lamp and straightening the comforter on the bed. I had been in several of the dorms, but this was the first frat house I'd been to. The room didn't appear much different than mine in Sander Hall, except there was a queen-sized bed here, versus the two twins in the meager dorm room Jet and I shared; however, these accommodations were much more masculine than ours.

Sirens should be going off in my mind, warning bells blaring in my ears, lights flashing—something. Instead, a dopey smile formed on my mouth, and my cheeks heated when Chet drew nearer. I watched him lean past my shoulder with one hand, while the other settled on my hip. And in one smooth motion, he'd extinguished the overhead light, leaving us standing in the dim bedroom that belonged to some random guy. Chet was close enough that the warmth of his breath tickled my nose, and his fingers dug gently into my side when his eyes met mine. I swam in the blue. Lost myself in the atmosphere. And drowned in his presence.

His lids fell slowly, and mine followed. Our lips met, and his tongue slid across the slit, begging me to open. As if he could smell the desire that radiated off me, his hand slipped from my hip and around my lower back, drawing me impossibly close. The fire I'd felt before was merely kindling compared to the raging inferno that now consumed me. Our mouths moved together, and every swipe of his tongue sent an electric current straight to my pussy. I wound my arms around his neck and dove in for the most intense experience of my life. Nothing compared to the fireworks that exploded behind my eyelids, and I willingly moved with him to the bed, hoping to keep the colors bursting.

With ease, he held me to him as he lowered us both to the mattress and then shifted to his side. Our mouths never parted, our tongues didn't stop dancing, and his fingers began to roam. His calloused hand dipped beneath the hem of my shirt and tickled my skin with eagerness. The fabric rose as he explored further, and with the flick of his wrist, the clasp on my bra released. I didn't even have time to process what he'd done before those rough nubs tweaked my nipple and cupped my breast, kneading it with his palm. I moaned against his mouth, and he eased his thigh between mine. The pressure he applied between my legs brought a wave of satisfaction until he started to use it to excite me.

Every move he made was precise and calculated. I wasn't insecure about my body; I was, however, worried about my inexperience where men were concerned. This was the first real kiss I'd ever had, and I'd definitely never made it to second base. Yet, here I was sliding through them one by one on my way to home plate so I didn't lose the game. Chet slid my shirt over my head and then freed me from my loose bra straps. With my breasts completely exposed, he leaned back to take in the view. I watched his head dip, and my eyes rolled back in my head when he secured his mouth around my peak. Unable to keep my head up, it fell, and my back arched when the sensations took over. He shifted sides, lavishing attention on the other nipple. The sublime aura that engulfed me caused my brain to cease functioning. The synapses no longer fired, connections weren't made. I didn't think to put the brakes on until the sudden knock brought me out of my lust-induced haze. Before I could grasp what was happening, the hall light flooded the room, and two couples stared at us as if we were a porn show set up for their viewing pleasure.

I tried to find something to cover my exposed chest, and when that failed, I flipped over while Chet enjoyed a casual conversation with our audience. It wouldn't have surprised me for Chet to have them sit down for coffee. He wasn't the least bit put off that I'd been caught in a compromised position or even concerned that half of my body lay exposed to strangers. This wasn't the way to introduce myself: Hi, I'm Portia Shaw. C cup. Never been felt up before. Nice to meet you.

For some reason, my mouth and my brain refused to work together. I thought to politely ask them to close the door with them on the other side. It occurred to me to nudge Chet to remind him I remained facedown on the mattress. It even dawned on me to flip the edge of the comforter—the side he wasn't lying on—over me to conceal my goods, at the very least. Instead, I lifted my head enough to cover my eyes and dropped my shoulders, mortified.

Minutes ticked by like hours, and by the time our guests—and I use that term loosely—left, the moment had passed. Chet tried to pick up where he'd left off as though there had been no interruption, and I had just become the whore of Alpha Sigma Phi.

Every muscle from my jaw to my toes tensed when he nuzzled into my neck.

"Mmm. You smell so good." He had to be kidding—the guy just gave me my first voyeur session, and now he wanted to compliment my body wash.

I turned, pushed him away, and sat up. Chet took that as an invitation to use my tit as a pacifier, and I jerked back. "Do you know where my shirt is?"

He huffed and then laughed. "Don't be like that."

"Chet, four strangers just stared at my breasts."

Nothing I said clicked for him. It appeared he thought that with a little cajoling, I'd settle back in and let him have his way. My buzz was gone, and so was my patience. When he tried again, this time with his hand and his salivating mouth, I slapped his fingers away and spun around to get off the opposite side of the mattress. In a search for my top and lingerie, I moved around the room, hunched over to see if they'd managed to get lost under the bed. There was nothing on the damn floor—including my bra and shirt. I couldn't leave here without them. Panic coursed through my veins, and my mind reverted to the worst possible scenario—having to walk out of here and across campus half-naked.

"It's not a big deal, Portia. Do you think this was the first time any of them have seen tits? I can assure you, it's not. Come here." The smile that had bartered with my defenses all night—the one which stole my ability to make rational decisions—once again lured me in.

I took his outstretched hand and allowed him to tug me back to his side. "It's a big deal to me."

"Sweetheart, you're in college. This kind of thing happens all the time. No one cares."

Maybe that was the problem—this was so common that women no longer respected themselves. I didn't want to be one of them.

"What do you think is going on behind every one of those closed doors in the hall? I can assure you, they aren't just making out. And most of them probably have more than one couple fucking inside."

My face quirked into an uneasy expression. I couldn't believe what I'd heard. He didn't even apologize or pretend that my discomfort mattered. This was someone I thought—at the very least —was my friend. I didn't know boys who acted this way. Jude sure as hell wouldn't have been this disrespectful to a girl. Jude would have remembered to engage the lock. Jude would have shielded me with his body. Jude would have pushed those gawking, uninvited strangers into the hall. Jude would have found a way to conceal my nudity and ease my embarrassment. Because that's what a *man* should do. It shouldn't matter if they had a spoken commitment between them; a guy with any integrity would protect any girl from that level of shame.

Yet here I sat with a great-looking guy every girl on this campus would give her right arm to have, and he couldn't care less about how I currently felt. He just wanted to convince me that my reaction was over the top and unwarranted. Maybe it was. Maybe it wasn't.

It didn't matter. The only thing that mattered was that was how I felt, and a friend should care about that more than their desire to get their rocks off.

He waved his hand in my face to get my attention. "Earth to Portia."

"Honestly, I didn't think about what was going on in any other room, because that's not who I am, or how I am."

"Exactly, no one's thinking about what anyone else is doing. Stop worrying about it and let me make you feel good."

All I could do was glare at him, dumbfounded that he'd not only dismissed my concern, but all he cared about was getting into my pants. I couldn't stand to look him in the eyes and see the irritation he tried to hide. As my gaze dropped down his chest to avoid the unspoken confrontation, I noticed the strap of an aqua-colored bra peeking out from under him. The second I reached for it, Chet appeared to believe I'd consented to resume whatever he had in mind. His solid arms lifted me in one swift motion and returned me to the place I'd just vacated at his side.

His mouth met mine in an unwelcomed exchange, and when I pushed against his chest to break free, he held on tighter, refusing to let me go. I didn't know if he thought this was some coy game girls played to get his attention, but it wasn't a joke. My anxiety ratcheted exponentially. Sweat broke out on my skin, my heart raced, and fear oozed from every pore. Chet was twice my size, and it was abundantly clear, I couldn't stop him if he chose to ignore my refusal.

As I continued to squirm, his lips left my mouth. He nipped at my ear and then my neck. Suddenly, he bit down in what might have been an erotic gesture had I not feared I was about to lose my virginity to a guy I didn't love in a stinky frat house covered in drunk co-eds.

I jerked back with all my might and forced my elbow to lock between us. "That fucking hurt!"

Chet wagged his brow. "Most girls like it rough. They want to know who's in charge." The chuckle that rolled from the mouth I'd thought was so sexy when he stood in my dorm and said my name, now made me want to slap the taste off his tongue.

He had one thing right. I wanted to know who was in charge—and it damn sure wasn't him. Chet propped himself on his elbow, and I used that opportunity to snag not only my bra, but my shirt. I jumped up as quickly as my arms and legs allowed. Dressing at the speed of a Tasmanian devil, I had my bra on in the blink of an eye and tugged my shirt over my head, while simultaneously rounding the end of the bed.

Chet grabbed my hand as I stormed past him and prevented me from leaving. Screaming was useless; nothing could be heard downstairs over the music. And if what Chet had said was true about girls liking it rough, the other people on this floor who *might* hear my cry for help would probably assume it was nothing more than a guy and a girl having a good time.

"You're making a mistake, Portia." The confidence in his statement had saliva pooling on my tongue ready to launch it at him if he didn't release me. He'd managed to move his clutch from my fingers to my wrist, and his nails pinched at the skin the tighter he held on.

My chest heaved with the tension that hung in the air. I couldn't fill my lungs fast enough, and staring him down only served to further steal my breath and my words.

"Do you know how many girls at this school would kill to be where you are right now? To have a place at my side? My social status around campus would skyrocket yours—completely changing your entire college experience." He couldn't be serious, yet every indication he gave told me he was.

"In exchange for my virginity?" I gawked at him with my mouth partially open.

"That explains a lot."

Those four words were a slap to the face. "My inexperience, or your inability to capitalize on it?"

He leaned back on his hands, taking a casual stance and ignored my question. "The two of us could be good together, but I don't beg."

I wondered if he believed that would entice me to reconsider, although I didn't bother to ask. The longer I stood there with my lips parted in disbelief, the dryer my tongue got. Either I needed to say something, or I needed to leave. I took a deep breath and dared to voice my thoughts.

"I'd rather be a nobody for the next four years than sell my soul or my body." I grabbed the knob and twisted. As I moved, I heard him rise from the bed behind me, and even with the music floating down the hall, there was no denying the steps he took in my direction.

I'd made it two feet out the door when he called my name. Foolishly, I stopped and faced him. I could never prove it, but he seemed to sense people were coming up the stairs, and he waited for an audience.

"You're a fucking tease and a damn prude. There's not a guy on this campus who's going to come within spitting distance of you after tonight."

The danger I'd seen in the ocean of his eyes was a shark that lurked just beneath the surface. It had come to shore in search of blood. A tear seeped down my cheek and clung to my jaw. I nodded slowly, and without another word, I grabbed the rail and took each step with purpose. I held my head high and swiped at the emotion on my face. Clearing any sign of distress from my posture and my expression, I smiled when I made eye contact with Jet, and then Bart and Todd.

"Where have you been? I was looking all over for you. Bart and Todd created their own little search party of two." She giggled, oblivious to anything I'd just gone through—and that was exactly how I wanted to keep it.

I held out hope that if I kept my mouth shut, rumors wouldn't fly. There was the possibility that Chet would let it drop and not mention my name to anyone. It might be wishful thinking, but for tonight, I pretended nothing had changed...when in fact, everything had.

4

JUDE

As adamant as I was that the stages of grief were nothing other than crap some shrink created to sell books and services, the truth remained. I had hit stage two with guns blazing shortly after I dropped Portia off at school. Anyone in my path could testify to that fact, and most made excuses for my poor behavior.

Hensley tried harder than anyone to get me to talk. "Jude, I don't understand what happened."

If I weren't careful, I'd find myself in a counselor's office exploring my feelings—as if I needed to explore how fucking bad it hurt for my mom to die. I experienced that shit every day—talking about it wouldn't bring her back or take the pain away.

"I got into a fight." And suspended for three days.

Ernie and Hensley sat with me at the kitchen table. I'd done my best to ignore them, and Ernie had done a lot of yelling.

"Over what?" She pleaded with me to let her in—she'd be happy with a few crumbs.

It didn't matter over what. They wouldn't understand, and I sure as hell wasn't going to explain it in any detail. "A guy said some things about Portia."

Ernie's shoulders finally relaxed, and Hensley leaned over to cup my cheek in her hand.

"Sweetheart, I love that you want to defend your sister, but fighting is never the answer."

My sister. And that's why I'd never tell them the truth. "Okay."

She stroked her thumb over my swollen cheek. The guy had gotten in one solid shot. While I'd never thrown a punch, I hadn't realized what kind of advantage my height gave me when push came to shove.

"Are you sure you won't consider talking to Dr. Vanderhugh? He was such a help to me when we had family planning issues." *Yeah, because family planning and infertility were the equivalent to losing your mom.*

"I'm fine. I just refuse to let anyone say things about Portia that aren't true. Neither of you would have stood by while someone talked shit about her, either."

"Jude!" Ernie's defeated posture became determined. He and I had always had a bond that Hensley and I didn't share. I had a mom, but Ernie filled in the empty space left by an absent father. "Language."

Seventeen years old, yet they believed I never cussed. Or just that I shouldn't. "Sorry." I wasn't.

"I'm concerned that you've suddenly started defending with your fists instead of words. You're such an articulate boy. It just doesn't make any sense." Hensley said all the right things; I just had no interest in hearing any of them.

My own mother would have slapped me upside the head—not only for my behavior but my attitude in general. That thought only served to elicit internal shame. I sighed, desperate to end the discussion and wrap up the family powwow. "I won't do it again. I'm sorry. It got out of hand."

I didn't want to disappoint them, either of them. They'd been good to me for the better part of ten years. Not once had they missed anything going on in my life, skipped out on a holiday or birthday, or taken the easy path when my mom was sick—they deserved better than I currently gave. Even with that realization, I couldn't stop the anger that poured from every part of my soul.

"Can I go now?" This wasn't getting us anywhere. Either they needed to punish me or leave me alone. I deserved the first and needed the last.

Hensley made to say something, and Ernie put his hand up, halting her. "You can. But be prepared to spend the next three days working around the house. Your suspension will *not* be a vacation."

I pushed the chair back more forcefully than intended and knocked it over. "Understood." Instead of apologizing and picking it up, I left it lying there and walked out.

I hadn't even made it to the bottom of the stairs when the sting of a firm grasp jerked my bicep. The force at which the hand held me indicated it was Ernie; even so, I glanced at the offending hand and then at my captor.

"I know you're hurting right now. I get it. But you will be respectful in this house. And you will act like you have common sense outside of it. We are more than happy to get you someone to talk to if you don't think it can be either of us."

I glared at him through squinted eyes and jerked my arm from his grasp.

"Don't push Hensley and me out, Jude. We both love you." The pity that radiated from his expression and dripped from his words ate at me. This wasn't the relationship the two of us had always had, and it wasn't one I wanted now.

Ernie's prying wouldn't change anything, and it certainly wouldn't solve any of my problems. I wished he understood that I needed him to be normal, not protective. If he wanted to serve a purpose in helping me through this, then he needed to act as though nothing had changed. But he wasn't going to handle anything that way, and I wasn't going to direct his parenting path.

"I'm fine." And I stomped up the stairs. I didn't slam my door, even though I wanted to. Instead, I closed it, locked it, and put on headphones. There, I listened to the Beatles playlist Portia and I danced to the night of my mother's funeral.

I tried to think back to that night, dancing with her while she attempted to relieve me of some of my grief, but I couldn't let go of Chad Hartman taunting me in the halls about Portia.

"I heard she's become quite the free spirit since she's been gone."

"Rumor has it, if she was a virgin when she got to school, she sure isn't now."

"Frat parties just aren't the same without Portia Shaw. Seems everyone on frat row has taken their turn."

The guy had never cared for Portia, although I didn't have a clue why. He'd teased her mercilessly last year, and somehow, she had managed to ignore him. Not me. The first words out of his mouth, I'd shoved him against the lockers in the D hall. The second insult, and my fist met his face. That was the one time he got in a shot. I'd hit him again, which spun him back into the foot traffic away from the wall. He'd wiped at his bloody lip and then spewed the filth that brought the teachers running. It probably wasn't his words that grabbed their attention so much as me laying him out on the floor of the senior hall, straddling him, and punching him until someone pulled me off.

I wasn't sure if I struggled with the horrid things he said or that I couldn't be sure they weren't true. Portia had been gone a month and hadn't come home once. Her calls happened less frequently and were shorter when they came. I didn't want to believe anything Chad said, yet I couldn't deny it with any certainty. Something had captured her attention. It might just be growing up and independence. Or it could be all of Phi Beta Kappa.

Just as my top was about to pop, contemplating it, my phone lit up with a text message and the sounds of "Help" faded out and back in through the speakers that covered my ears. I pressed pause on the music to read it.

Portia: Hey, Fido. Got a minute to talk?

Great. Either Ernie or Hensley had told her what happened.

Me: What's up?
Portia: I hear you've got quite the shiner defending my honor.
Me: Something like that.
Portia: I'm going to come home this weekend.
Me: Why?

I shouldn't be a dick. I wanted to see her more than I wanted air or water or food. What I didn't want was sympathy, and that was the only reason for her visit.

Portia: Spend time with you.
Me: I have plans.

I didn't have anything to do.

Portia: Change them. I'll see you at dinner on Friday. And stop being an ass.
Portia: I love you.

Without responding, I pressed play. Not even the Beatles were salve to my wounds. I didn't know what I expected; I should have anticipated pain, agony. The pain of my mother's passing. The pain of Portia leaving. The pain of being alone. Yet even though I knew it would come, I hadn't foreseen the way it would wrap its arms around me, dig its talons into my flesh and soul, and tear at me like a starving animal devouring prey. I couldn't escape it, couldn't welcome it, and struggled to handle it. The only time I'd felt any control since my mother died was when I pounded my fists into Chad's face.

Nothing I did for the next three days gave me that same relief. No matter the level of exertion or the menial task at hand, I couldn't release the rage that brewed and bubbled inside.

Then she walked in the door. I hadn't heard the car in the driveway, and her presence in the foyer surprised me, along with the large duffle bag she'd dropped at her feet.

I came the rest of the way down to stand in front of Portia. "What are you doing here so early?"

"I left after my last class. I'm done at two on Fridays."

There was something wrong. Something was off. Portia's focus flitted from mine to the floor and back. For whatever reason, she refused to maintain eye contact and seemed as surprised by me as I was by her. Except, I lived here, and she knew I'd been suspended.

"Look at me," I commanded, as though she were destined to do my bidding. The bite in my words erupted out of fear, though I doubt she recognized that.

Her eyes widened in surprise. She swallowed hard and squared her shoulders. My tone scared her, and it was written all over her face.

"What's wrong?"

"Nothing," she lied. Her normally pink lips were crimson, almost purple, and her voice didn't come off as cotton candy. There was nothing fantastical in her tone or her features, and for Portia, that was a telltale sign of unhappiness—the glitter was missing in her eyes, and she'd closed the windows to her soul.

I nodded slowly, unsure of why she wouldn't be honest. Portia was rattled, and I was higher strung than normal. Her refusal to confess what was going on only served to skyrocket my unease. Then I heard noise in the kitchen, and it dawned on me that Hensley was within spitting distance…even if she hadn't heard the two of us yet. Portia's eyes darted between me and the rustling of pots and pans, and then she shut down. I'd seen her do it time and again.

"Portia, sweetheart, is that you?" Hensley called out from the kitchen. Her voice stole Portia's attention along with the strain between us. "Oh, it's so good to see you." She appeared, honing in on her daughter. "Oh, Jude. I didn't know you were down here, too. Come in the kitchen. I made cookies."

Hensley's inability to notice something was off with Portia surprised me. She normally picked up on even the slightest change, especially when she hadn't seen one of us in several weeks. It was one of my favorite things about her when I was growing up. I'd go home for a couple of weeks or months, then when Hensley saw me again, she'd notice my haircut or that I'd grown, or that five more freckles had sprouted on my nose where none had been previously. Every minute detail caught her attention—maybe she already knew what was going on with her daughter and didn't want to cause me to worry.

I sat there silently, mesmerized by Portia's transformation—she was a damn chameleon. When she'd walked in, I would have bet money that she carried the weight of the world or an enormous secret. Yet now, listening to her talk to Hensley, it was as if she just needed to share how different her new life was than the one she'd had here. And the chasm between us—a valley prior to this moment —became the Grand Canyon.

"Jet has to be one of the funniest people I've ever met." She carried on about things going on in her dorm and people I'd never heard her mention.

I only half listened, lost in thoughts of how each passing day she got further away.

"Have you met anyone special?" Hensley wiggled her brow suggestively, and I furrowed mine at her unsubtle insinuation.

"Guys don't see me that way." It wasn't disappointment I heard so much as pragmatic resolve. Even if she were dead wrong, Hensley wouldn't be able to convince her otherwise, and I wouldn't try.

Maybe that made me a schmuck, but no guy tries to convince the girl he loves that guys would flock to her if she opened her eyes. Jet was a good person for her to be friends with...any *female* on campus worked for me.

"I don't believe that's true. Do you, Jude? Your sister's a beautiful girl."

There was that word again, but I forced my mouth shut. It took monumental effort not to remind Hensley there was no relation—by blood or legally—to Portia, or her for that matter. Instead, I just grimaced. "How would I know?"

Portia's face fell right before she cocked her head and stuck out her tongue. It was a dick comment, but they shouldn't put me in the position to have to make such proclamations. That was Hensley's job, maybe even Ernie's—certainly not the kid they had temporary custody over who was in love with their adopted daughter.

I stood, pushed in my stool, and excused myself. "There's far too much estrogen in this conversation for me. I'm going to my room."

"Have you finished the list of things Ernie left for you to do today?" Hensley played the role of a dictator. Unfortunately for her, I was acutely aware that if I had put up any resistance toward their punishment, they both would have caved. But the alternative was counseling, so I chose manual labor—gladly.

"Yes. My sentence is complete." I held my wrists out to her as if she might unshackle me by releasing the lock on my handcuffs.

Hensley swatted playfully at my shoulder, and Portia just shook her head. I held Portia's gaze a beat longer, inhaling her. Maybe I'd mistaken change and maturity for unhappiness. It was possible I'd completely missed the mark when she walked into the house. Her playful, youthful coloring returned, sitting at the counter in the kitchen, and so did the sugar in her voice.

I DIDN'T HAVE A LOT OF FRIENDS, AND THOSE I DID WERE homebodies. I should be embarrassed that as a senior in high school, my weekends consisted of music and books; although I wasn't. It might not be the "in" thing now, but it would serve me well later in life. I'd gotten a text from Ethan that he and Carson were playing video games tonight if I wanted to join them. I wasn't sure if my sentence had been commuted, or if it extended through the weekend. Instead of asking, I opted to stay in.

The light knock stirred me from the pages of the book in my hand, and I glanced up to see Portia entering without an invitation. "What's up?"

She came in and closed the door behind her. "Just wanted to see what you were up to."

I held up the novel. "Reading."

"Do you want to watch a movie or something? Talk? Tell me why you've been on an angry rampage?"

"Subtle."

She chuckled. "Hensley and Ernie are worried. They thought I'd have more luck than they have. You know I don't beat around the bush, so I might as well just ask, right?"

I sat up, and Portia took that as a green light to join me on the mattress. The thin fabric of her shirt and her tiny sleep shorts made it difficult to focus on anything other than her teasing nipples and taunting long legs. When she tied her hair in a knot, I almost came undone and groaned at the hint of her exposed skin. Thankfully, she believed my reaction was in response to her question and not to the sight of her in my bed.

"What do you want to know?"

She propped pillows on the headboard and situated herself against them. "If there's anything I can do to help…"

I bit my tongue to keep from telling her to come home. "I'm fine."

"Jude, you got into a fistfight. You're the most passive person I know. Clearly, you aren't fine."

I refused to debate the legitimacy of my interaction with Chad to the girl I had defended. She never needed to know what had been said. Based on her comment in the kitchen, there'd been no truth in any of it, anyhow. If she didn't believe guys saw her that way, then she certainly hadn't become the campus slut.

"He's a dick." That was profound. Spoken like the average, teenage guy.

"He's been a dick since the day I met him. You didn't kick the crap out of him then or any time since. Why now?"

I took a deep breath and then released the air. "Is this really what you want to talk about? Chad Hartman?" I prayed it served as a distraction from this topic, and mentally groaned at the prospect of the other one she'd put on the table—grief.

Her tongue swept across her lips just before her teeth snagged the bottom one. She chewed on it in contemplation and finally lifted her eyes to mine. "I'm worried about you, Jude. We talked all the time when I lived here. Even when you were with your mom, there wasn't a day that went by that the two of us didn't communicate, either at school or by phone. Now I never hear from you."

I hadn't made much effort, and neither had she. "The phone rings both ways, Portia."

"Jude, I send you text messages all the time. You never respond."

"Once a week is hardly all the time, and you send them during the day when I'm at school." We were on the verge of an argument, and it was one I didn't care to have. "It's not a big deal. What difference does it make?"

Her eyes flooded. "It hurt to tell you that I loved you and you not respond."

"I was pissed that Ernie and Hensley told you I'd been suspended." And those three words meant something different to me than they did to Portia—vastly different.

"You don't have to keep it all bottled up inside, you know?" A chunk of hair fell from her knot, and she tucked the strands behind her ear. The innocence in her eyes was just another reason why I loved her the way I did.

I wanted nothing more than to move that piece of hair, to cradle her jaw in my hands and kiss her in a way that would make her blush, and hold her close to me as though nothing else in the world existed.

Instead, I lashed out. "There's nothing to bottle up, Portia. My mom died. It sucks. It's only been six weeks, yet everyone seems to think I should be happy-go-lucky and dance around because I'm still breathing. I'm pissed. Why her? There are so many people in the world who should have gone before her—murderers, criminals, drug addicts—"

As if I'd slapped her across the face, she blanched and her entire body stiffened.

"I'm sorry. I didn't mean that about your mom. Of all people, I figured you'd understand. You lost your mom. Did you sit around and tell the world how sad and angry you were?"

She hadn't. She also hadn't gone to counseling or any other grief-processing bullshit.

"I wasn't angry, Jude. And I was nine."

"How could you not have been angry that your mom was taken from you?" We'd never talked much about her situation. By the time I'd gotten to the Shaws' house, she'd been there for months and the subject—although unspoken—was off-limits.

"She wasn't a mother to me. I don't remember a time when she wasn't high. Do you realize that when I was five years old, I could have taught an adult how to mainline heroin? Five. Probably earlier but with confidence in kindergarten. I'm thankful now—I didn't realize it then—that she managed to stay sober when she was pregnant so I wasn't born a cracked-out drug baby."

I rolled my neck to stare at her, but she'd turned away and stared straight ahead while she spoke.

"There were hundreds of situations she put me in or left me in that could have resulted in a horrible sexual encounter, or worse—my death. If it hadn't been for the next-door neighbor, most days I wouldn't have eaten. So no, I wasn't angry so much as relieved."

"I guess I'm a selfish bastard then."

Her attention reverted to me. "How can you say that?" Her eyes reminded me of a shamrock. They were so green, I wondered how anyone missed the glow against her ivory skin, surrounded by her inky hair.

"Because even though she was in pain, I didn't want to let her go. And if I had the choice today to bring her back riddled with cancer, or let her exist in a realm where she doesn't hurt, I'd want her here. I'd sell my soul for one more piece of lemon pie. And I'd dance with the devil to hear her sing another song."

Portia snuggled down in the pillows as she rolled onto her side. She folded her hands under her peachy, flushed cheek, and her eyes shimmered. "It's okay to feel that way. And it's okay to be angry tomorrow. Sad the next day. Or even confused and torn in between. You lost your mom. You're allowed to be selfish and have warring emotions. Give yourself permission to experience them, acknowledge them, express them—whatever you need to do to find peace so you can welcome her memory and spirit back here." She placed her palm flat on my chest over my heart.

I prayed she didn't detect the pace of my heart accelerating in my chest the longer the heat of her hand radiated against my bare skin. And that she didn't notice the change in my breathing.

"She's with you, Jude. But you won't be able to sense her or find comfort in that until you process the range of emotions you're fighting. Until you can silence those, you're missing out on having her and her presence."

I placed my hand on top of Portia's, in hopes she wouldn't move it. Her skin on mine lit an impatient fire—one I struggled not to fuel. I desperately wanted to lean over and place my lips against hers. Drowning in dreams of how her mouth would taste, I didn't realize I'd lifted my free hand to stroke her cheek. She leaned into my touch, and her fingers dug into my chest. My eyes flitted from hers to her lips and back. Slowly, I moved forward, waiting for a sign of hesitation or her to push me away. Portia appeared as hungry for me as I was for her. Time stood still, the world stopped, her eyes closed, and I went for it.

It was everything I dreamed it would be—heaven's gates opened and angels sang. Her mouth was soft and supple yet electric and mesmerizing. Her nails clawed into me as she relaxed into my hands when my fingers tangled in her hair.

"Portia? Sweetheart, can you come downstairs?" Hensley's voice snapped me out of the daze Portia's kiss had buried me in.

Portia jerked back breathlessly…and mortified. She snatched her hand from my sternum and wiped her palm over her mouth to remove any evidence that I'd touched her. Fear replaced the luster I longed to see, and she raced out of my room.

Her footsteps shuffled down the stairs, and I threw myself against the pillows, wondering what the hell I'd just done.

I didn't see anyone else the rest of the night. I'd hoped Portia would come talk to me, and I kept my light on so she'd know I was awake. Staying up did nothing other than make a long night into a lonely one and cause me to toss and turn when I finally tried to sleep.

When I dragged myself out of bed the next morning, I needed a shower to even think about facing another human being. My mind was cloudy, my heart ached, and I desperately wanted to make things right with Portia. If nothing else, I had an hour-long car ride to take her back to school tomorrow. I just didn't want to wait that long or feel like a prisoner in the house if any awkwardness lingered between us.

I stopped by her room after I shaved and got dressed. Her door was open, the bed made, but none of the typical signs of Portia's life marked the space. Clothes didn't litter the hardwoods, the contents of her purse weren't on the bed, and the duffle bag of clothes Hensley washed last night was nowhere to be found.

It was only ten o'clock. I couldn't imagine she was up and braving the day already. Normally, she spent half of Saturday slumming around the house before she even got in the shower. I trotted downstairs and found Hensley in the kitchen cleaning up breakfast dishes. Somehow, I had missed an entire morning of activity.

I opened the fridge to find something to eat and acted as casual as possible without sounding aloof. "Where's Portia?" The cold air chilled my heated and guilty skin. Hensley didn't have a clue I'd kissed her daughter last night, but my conscience had something to hide.

"Her friend Bart came to pick her up." There was no accusation in her tone, no confusion—just matter of fact.

With the milk in my hand, I reached for a bowl in the cabinet. It was safer to continue moving about the kitchen to make cereal than stop and face Hensley for fear she'd see shame written all over my features. "I thought I was taking her back tomorrow?" The bite in my tone apparently didn't reach Hensley's ears; either that, or she ignored it. The thought of Portia running off with Bart had me grinding my teeth and ready to put my fist through a wall.

From the corner of my eye, I watched Hensley wave her hand in the air and twist her face. "You know how girls are. She probably had a party or something she wanted to go to. That's what happens when kids go off to college—they forget about their parents at home…and their brothers." She winked at me.

It was safe to say Hensley wasn't aware of last night's blunder. What I didn't know was how to approach any of it with Portia. I had little doubt she'd left this morning because of what happened in my room. But I didn't know if it was because she enjoyed it and didn't think she should, or if I freaked her out and repulsed her with my incestuous behavior.

Things were black and white for me, although I could see from an outsider's perspective how the morality of my feelings for Portia might blend into unidentifiable shades of grey. No court in the land would find a relationship between foster kids scandalous or unlawful—I couldn't say the same for those who knew us personally.

And it was painfully obvious, Portia had never considered anything deeper with me.

5

PORTIA

ALL I HAD THOUGHT ABOUT WAS GETTING OUT OF THE HOUSE, escaping the crash before it happened. I couldn't deal with what had gone on with Chet, then Jude, and following that, Hensley and Ernie. I'd sent Jet a text last night to ask her to pick me up this morning, but she'd gone home at the last minute and wasn't around. Bart was the only other person I considered, and he'd surprised me when he didn't hesitate. It was a little over an hour's drive each way, and gas was a precious commodity to college students.

Bart showed up this morning at nine sharp. It was a safe bet Jude wouldn't be awake, but Ernie and Hensley would. That enabled me to tell them goodbye *and* pretend there was something fantastic going on at school that I didn't want to miss. I'd played the dutiful daughter. I came home, I talked to Jude and tried to reason with him—I'd even reported back on how that had gone…sort of— and I'd listened to my parents give me the most crushing news I ever could have received. Through it all, I never dropped the smile or hinted at my devastation. I hadn't let on that anything bothered me. And it had nearly broken me on more than one occasion in the eighteen or so hours I was there.

"You're awfully quiet." Bart never pried. He was one of those guys who got that sometimes a person sought company without conversation.

As much as I wanted to keep it all inside, I became a bomb ready to detonate, and I needed to get it out. I couldn't talk to the one person I discussed everything with. The fight with Chad Hartman only proved Jude wouldn't hesitate to come to my defense; the kiss with Jude confirmed I couldn't confide in him about Chet. And then there was the topic around the dinner table last night that had eliminated my parents as viable options, as well. I loved Jet, but she had a tendency to gossip, and none of this was crap that needed to get around.

I rolled my head on the back of the seat, exchanging the view through the window for one of Bart. "I just have a lot on my mind."

"We've got at least an hour on the road if you want to talk." Bart's understanding smile told me that if I turned him down, he wouldn't be offended.

"I'm not sure I should." It wasn't Bart that worried me, it was what I would be admitting out loud. In my mind, the moment I uttered the words, each of the three things that weighed me down would cease to be ideas, and they'd become reality.

He took his hand off the gear shift and laid it on top of mine. With a gentle squeeze, he said, "Anything you say stays between us, Portia."

"I'm not worried about you telling anyone. I don't want you to think differently of me." Regarding any of it…but I didn't add that last part.

"Not possible." The traffic came to a halt on the interstate, and he released my hand to shift gears.

I groaned. There was nothing I wanted more than to get this off my chest, yet the repercussions could be irreversible. "Honestly, I'm not sure why I'm upset about any of it."

Bart lifted the emergency brake and let the car idle. We weren't moving, and the longer we sat there, the heavier my heart got.

"Any of it? More than one thing is bothering you?"

I took a deep breath, ready to start with something I didn't think anyone could hold against me. "Yeah, several."

He leaned back in the bucket seat of his BMW Roadster and met my gaze with acceptance and understanding. "Let's start with one." There was no telling how he did it, but he'd released the pressure from the balloon without it popping.

I chewed on my lip and tried to figure out how to start this conversation. Bart was friends with Chet, and I had to be careful not to badmouth him. "Last weekend, when we went to the frat party…" As I tried to formulate the words, it all sounded juvenile in my head.

"What about it?"

"Ugh, I don't know. Now that I'm actually trying to say it, it seems stupid."

Bart shifted in the seat to face me with his shoulder against the back, although his head still rested on the leather. "If anything bothered you, it doesn't matter how it sounds. Your feelings are valid, Portia, even if no one else understands them."

That was something Jude would say, and what I'd expected from Chet that night.

"Okay. But promise you'll let me know if I'm being immature and tell me to suck it up?" I watched his head bob when he nodded. "I need you to be honest. I was kind of sheltered growing up"—at least past the age of nine. I just didn't mention that part —"so it's totally plausible that I'm blowing this out of proportion."

He stuck his pinky out and waited for me to hook mine and seal the promise. "Pinky swear."

"Remember, you guys couldn't find me when you were ready to leave?"

"Yeah, you were upstairs." There was no judgment behind his words, just confirmation that we referenced the same thing.

Before I said another word, my eyes pooled with tears, and when I blinked, they fell.

"Hey, hey." His voice was soft and soothing. "Talk to me." Bart leaned toward me, extended his hand, and wiped away the moisture with his thumb.

"I'm sorry." My voice cracked.

Concern lined his forehead in the form of three stark creases. "Don't be."

"I made a lot of mistakes that night. Things I shouldn't have done. And it started with drinking wine coolers to impress a guy who didn't give a crap about me."

When he dropped back against the seat, I saw the disappointment in his eyes as his face fell. "Chet?"

I nodded, and more tears appeared. Bart didn't wipe these away; instead, he waited. "I don't know what I thought would happen upstairs, or why I went. He'd just been so nice to me since the first day of class. We'd spent time hanging out, and I believed he had a genuine interest in me."

The muscles in his jaw ticced, and his chest heaved, but he didn't say a word.

Twisting my hands in my lap, I kept talking. "I only had two wine coolers, but it was enough to give me a little buzz, and I just wanted to enjoy his attention."

"If he hurt you, I won't be able to stand by and not do anything, Portia."

"Huh? God, no. I mean he did, but not what you think."

His shoulders drooped, and he stopped grinding his teeth.

Embarrassment took over. My cheeks flushed with heat, and I struggled to admit the truth. "I've never dated before." It didn't surprise me when his brows raised in shock—even dorks dated. "And other than a game of spin the bottle, I'd never been kissed." I rolled my eyes when he cocked his head, intrigued. "So, as shallow as it sounds, Chet's attention was similar to winning the lottery. He's gorgeous, an athlete, built—"

"I got it." He stopped my description of his friend. "He's a catch. Noted." The wink he sent my direction eased my worry slightly.

"I didn't know what to do or what he expected. I had no idea that going upstairs with him would mean anything more than some heavy…" I tapped my finger on my chin and searched my mind for a word that wasn't detailed, yet descriptive. "Petting."

I needed to stop pussyfooting around and just spit it out. Drawing this out implied more than it was, and even though Chet was an ass, he hadn't forced me into anything. Not really.

"We were kissing, and four people barged into the room. The lamp was on, and I couldn't hide."

His eyes went wide. "You were *naked*?"

I couldn't help but laugh at the animated way he asked the question. "Not from the waist down." I tilted my head while he pondered that scenario. "Granted, he didn't know they were going to come in, so I can't fault him for that."

"He could have locked the door to prevent it." Well, there was that.

"Bart, he didn't try to shield me or cover me. He rolled over and had a conversation with them."

"While you lay there…topless?"

I nodded.

"What the hell did you do?"

"Acted like an idiot. There was nothing to hide behind, so I flipped over onto my stomach and buried my face in my hands until they finished talking."

"Did you slap the shit out of him when they left? Please tell me he didn't offer to share the room." Bart ran his hand through his hair. I wasn't sure which one of us was more upset by Chet's behavior, but at least it was obvious that Bart didn't think I'd exaggerated.

"No." I hated that I didn't have more of a reaction—one that carried a punch. "All I could think about was how inconsiderate he'd been. And even after they left, he never apologized. When I told him it bothered me, he told me I was blowing it out of proportion."

"What?" If a guy could screech, Bart just had.

"Yep. Since everyone else upstairs was having orgies, I shouldn't care that strangers had seen me topless. But Bart, *no one* had ever seen me topless. I'd never even really kissed a guy until that night. Maybe I should have told him that earlier—although, I'm not sure when I would have worked that into a conversation. He didn't care that I was worried about it or upset. The only concern he had was getting back to where we left off."

"Portia, so help me God, if you tell me you let him touch you after that, I might have to hurt you myself."

"No. I mean, I sat down in front of him to talk since I couldn't find my bra or my shirt." My face burned with that admission, but it had escaped before I could censor it. "I thought maybe he had realized how much it upset me. But he just tried to get things going again."

"How'd you get out?"

"He was lying on top of my clothes, so I grabbed them, yanked them out from under him, and put them on. But before I got out the door, he stopped me and told me how good he would be for my social status and what a catch he was for a girl in my position."

Bart's jaw dropped.

I felt like a fool and glanced at my fingers in my lap when I said, "I told him I'd rather be a nobody for four years than sell my soul or my virginity."

He hadn't spoken when his hand came into view. His fingers slipped underneath mine, and then they intertwined. I downcast my eyes and watched his thumb trail circles on the top of my hand.

"I thought he was done. He told me he wouldn't beg and that I was making a mistake, but I walked out anyhow. Then he stepped into the hall and loudly announced to the people witnessing my *Carrie* moment"—I glanced at him to make sure he got the reference to the seventies film—"that I was a tease and a prude, and no guy on campus would have anything to do with me after that night."

"Is that why you haven't left your room all week other than to go to class?"

I shrugged. He didn't need me to confirm his assumption.

"Portia, the guy's a tool."

I perked up, surprised by his proclamation. "He's your friend." I laughed nervously, not knowing what to expect.

"No. He's my best friend's little brother. We hang out, but we certainly aren't close."

"What's the difference?"

"He doesn't know anything about me other than what he's witnessed firsthand. We don't have history. And honestly, I've never been a fan of how he treats girls."

"Then why did you let me spend time with him?"

He laughed. "I didn't *let* you do anything. Plus, he seemed different with you. I hadn't ever seen him hang out with anyone, much less do homework. And when he took your hand to walk across campus, it was a statement."

"Yeah, well, I believed he liked me, too. Now, I just feel like an idiot."

"You shouldn't. It takes a lot of courage for a shy girl—who by her own admission doesn't have a lot of experience—to turn down Chet. I'm not into guys or anything, but I'd have to be blind not to see the way women respond to him. I'm proud of you for holding your ground and not caving."

I picked at my cuticles and tore at my lip with my teeth. "Why would a guy like him have any interest in a girl like me? I should have known what he was after, but I was too naïve to see it."

He took a deep breath and slowly released it. "That's not a bad thing."

"I'm just not used to guys who treat girls that way. Jude..." I stopped before I launched into another topic entirely.

"Your brother is an anomaly, Portia. Granted, I didn't spend a ton of time with him while he was here, but certain people just give off a vibe. He's a good kid. But I'm sure you guys have great parents. Unfortunately, not everyone does."

I wanted to set the record straight, and now was the time to do it. It was easy to explain why I hadn't the day we'd met at Sander Hall, but that wouldn't be the case a year from now. And if I wanted to tell him about my conversation with Ernie and Hensley, I couldn't keep any of it a secret.

"He's not my brother." I tossed the truth out there and let it hang in the air.

"What do you mean?" A horn honked behind us when the traffic started to creep at a snail's pace.

It didn't occur to me that we hadn't moved the entire time we talked. This would end up being a five-hour trip at this rate.

"Just what I said. He's not my brother." I saw the confusion, but Bart wouldn't ask. I shook my head and gave in. I'd hopped down this bunny trail. "We were both foster kids. My parents adopted me when I was ten."

His focus remained on the stop-and-go traffic in front of him. "What about Jude? They didn't adopt him?"

"No, but they want to." I just couldn't keep my mouth shut. Here I hadn't even wanted to admit we weren't related, and now I was diving right into the third problem on my list.

"Isn't he a little old for that? You said he's seventeen, right?"

Maybe I could explain Jude's history away without confessing any of my own. "Yeah, but it's more symbolic than necessary. Jude's mom entered him into the foster care system voluntarily."

"Why?" His eyes and nose scrunched in what appeared disgust.

"She was diagnosed with cervical cancer when he was eight. They didn't have any family for him to stay with. It wasn't supposed to be permanent, even then. He was going to stay with us while she went through chemo, and then when she got on her feet and could take care of him, he would transition back."

Disgust transformed into shock. "Did she die?"

"No, not then. He stayed with us for several months, but Carrie —that was his mom—had a hard time after the chemo. She was terribly weak and got tired fast. My parents helped her out, and we ended up spending a lot of time at their apartment until she'd regained her strength. I'm not sure what the legal arrangement with the state was, but we all fell in love with Jude."

Bart smiled as I reminisced. It wasn't a happy time for Carrie, and often not Jude, but we had a lot of great memories that never would have happened had the situation been any different.

"So even after he went back to his mom's house permanently, since he didn't have a dad, Ernie—my adoptive father—made sure to keep up the relationship. Our families sort of became one that lived in two separate houses. We attended his school activities, he went on vacation with us, he'd spend a few days a month at our house. I don't know, it probably doesn't make sense to anyone who didn't live through it."

"I think it's cool your parents were so open to that kind of arrangement." The car jerked when Bart slammed on the brakes to avoid the vehicle in front of us. "Sorry, I wasn't paying attention. So, what happened after his mom got better?"

"She got sick again. And again. And again. It was awful, Bart. I swear, every time the doctors got her into remission, a year later, the cancer metastasized. She had countless surgeries to remove the growths, but it was destined to take her."

"That's horrible."

"Last spring, maybe early summer, she was just a shell of her former self. Skin hung on her bones, she had almost no muscle tone, and she hadn't been able to work much, anyhow. When the cancer returned, she told Jude she couldn't fight it anymore. She passed away two weeks before classes started."

His head jerked toward mine, back to the road, and then back to me as he came to another stop on the interstate. "As in six or seven weeks ago? The guy buried his mom right before he brought you to school?"

"Yeah."

"Holy shit. How's he handling it?"

"Not well. He got into a fight last week at school. That's the whole reason I went home. He got suspended, and my parents wanted me to talk to him. They're worried."

"Is that why they want to adopt him?"

"No. They don't want him to feel alone. They want him to know he's part of a family that loves him. And since he's almost eighteen anyhow, or will be in the spring, it doesn't really mean anything legally. If Carrie had passed away when he was eleven or fifteen, it wouldn't have mattered. They still would have wanted to do it."

"Do you think he's going to appreciate the gesture for what it is?" Skepticism lined his voice. I had to keep in mind, he only had what little information I had given him in the last ten minutes, not years of life in our family dynamic.

"I think it will mean the world to him. Ernie has always been Jude's dad. I mean, he doesn't call him Dad, but they have that bond." I giggled, thinking about the two of them working in the backyard when we were kids and just how awkward Jude was. I'd never seen a child so uncoordinated in my life, yet Ernie was patient until they had flowerbeds that Hensley fawned over. "And Hensley has never acted as a replacement, just a supplement."

"Then why do I get the impression you're not excited about it?"

Jesus. I'd managed to conceal my disappointment from two people who knew me better than anyone in the world—besides Jude

—yet Obi-Wan Kenobi here picked up on my unhappiness in a handful of words in a few measly minutes.

I shrugged. It was noncommittal, and I hoped he would let it go.

"Are you afraid it will change your relationship with them?"

"God, no."

"Then if you think it's important to Jude, why do you care? I'd think you'd be happy for him."

I stared at the taillights in front of us, praying they'd start moving and Bart's attention would return to the road. The car didn't move, and it started to drizzle. Knowing the way people drove in this state, whatever currently had us backed up would double in size with accidents once the roads were wet...even with us sitting still.

There was no real way to explain this to him without sharing information I'd never told another soul. I offered him a shrug, but my new bestie didn't take that as an answer.

"That's not much of an explanation, Portia. You should think about why you wouldn't want him to have the same security you do." There wasn't a hint of judgment or condescension in his voice. The way he said what he had, indicated that Bart believed it was something I needed to resolve, so I didn't hurt Jude.

"I know why." Shame laced my tone, and I hung my head at the weight of my guilty conscience.

"You just don't want to tell me?"

I hesitated. Fear clung to my thoughts like a bat to an eave.

"It's okay. You don't have to explain."

The silence between us was deafening. I'd kill to crank up the stereo and drown it out with an angry playlist that would change my mood and help me work through the nagging in my mind. But this wasn't my car, and Jude wasn't the one driving. I wasn't sure Bart would appreciate me synching my phone to his stereo so I didn't have to talk to him.

When he'd said it was okay, he'd meant it. Now, he didn't say anything further. But I just couldn't leave it alone. Maybe I wanted to tell someone so I could let my feelings go. This could be my opportunity to do just that—all I had to do was open my mouth and speak.

"Judgment-free?"

Bart came to another stop—approximately seven feet from the last one we'd made—and turned in my direction. With a look I'd only seen from one other person, his eyes spoke to me in quiet contemplation. "Always. You never have to ask."

I pulled my hair down and combed through it with my fingers before I wound it back into a knot on top of my head. It was a nervous habit that I hoped Bart didn't call me out on while he waited for my confession.

"Jude and I have a very different relationship than any other guy and girl I know."

"That makes sense. I don't know anyone else who shared a childhood the way you guys did."

I prayed he still felt that way five minutes from now. This had the potential to destroy my friendship with Bart, and I'd already alienated Chet, which would only leave me with Jet—not that she was a bad person to have around, I just didn't want to be isolated and away from home.

"We didn't go to elementary or middle school together, but even when we were younger, both of our friends—his and mine—lumped us together like brother and sister. He spent the night at my house. We vacationed together. Holidays always included the other." I paused, trying to determine the best way to explain this. "Foster children in the same home have a different bond than true-blooded siblings. Jude says it's similar to the one twins share. I'm not a twin, so I don't know. I also don't have any biological brothers or sisters, so I can't attest to that, either. All I know for certain, is that when two kids land in a house, scared and alone, they cling to each other because it's safer than the adults."

I'd kill for one Violent Femmes song right now. Anything to break up the monotony of my own voice.

"By the time I reached high school, Jude was the guy I compared all others to. I didn't date, but looking back, I wonder now if boys weren't interested in me because—"

He snickered and then muttered, "I seriously doubt that."

I eyed him but didn't question his comment. "Or if I was never interested because they didn't measure up...to Jude. I wasn't attracted to him"—then—"and nothing ever happened between us"—until last night—"and I didn't even think about any of that before the frat party."

"Did you guys go to parties together back home?"

"Ha!" It was laughable. "Jude Thomas go to a social gathering? Never."

"Then what made you think about it?"

"The way Chet acted. I was repulsed by his behavior because I'd never witnessed anything that resembled it. And when I thought about what Jude would have done had he been there, I realized how difficult it would ever be to find someone who loves me the way Jude does."

"Is that what you want? Jude?"

"No," I answered too quickly. It came off defensively, when I'd wanted it to sound confident. Scrambling to clarify, I started word vomiting. "I want a nice guy. Someone who treats me the way he does, that would defend a girl's honor even if he didn't know her, but someone I can just as easily joke around with and be playful." I thought about the fight Jude had gotten into at school, and his image filled my head. I stared at him through my mind's eyes while I described every-thing I loved about him. "Smart, funny. Definitely an avid reader—"

"I didn't know you loved to read." Bart had mistaken a quality I described in Jude as one of my own. It was, I just hadn't been refer-ring to myself.

"It's not something I broadcast. I have enough going against me without having my nose in a book publicly." I laughed as though it were a joke, but I'd hidden it from everyone I knew because of the stigma attached to bookworms in high school.

"You know, it wouldn't be unusual for you to have developed an emotional attachment toward him." Bart made the statement as if it didn't hold huge implications.

"What?"

He let off the brake as traffic started to move again. I watched him work his way through the gears, and I waited for him to respond as cars took off in front of us.

"I think maybe it's natural for you to struggle with your feelings for him. You're not related—not really. And you'll never be as close to any man who comes into your life as you are to him. Like you said, there's the foster-kid bond."

"Isn't that considered Stockholm syndrome?"

"No, that's people who fall in love with their captors or abusers and their mind idealizes the offender until the victim believes they saved them instead of hurt them."

"He's *like* my brother."

"Yet, you don't want him to actually have that title."

I shifted in the seat to face the windshield and watched the rain pelt the window. It didn't matter what I wanted. I'd told Jude it hurt when he didn't tell me he loved me back, and he'd made an excuse for why he hadn't returned the sentiment. But minutes later, one of the two of us—I wasn't entirely sure which—initiated a kiss. My toes had curled when I finally had his lips on mine, and I'd left claw marks on his skin with my nails. I couldn't speculate what would have happened had Hensley not called me downstairs, but after hearing what she and Ernie had to say, I'd gone to bed. There, I'd replayed every minute I'd spent with Chet, wrongly believing his interest was genuine. Then Jude hadn't responded to my text, making me believe—possibly because I was already wounded from the incident the previous weekend—that I wasn't significant to him, either. And by the time I fell asleep, I'd convinced myself that Jude had been no different than Chet. He'd just wanted a field to play in, and mine was available.

In the last week, my emotions had bounced around more than a ping-pong ball, and just as I'd started to acknowledge a deeper connection to Jude than I understood or admitted, my parents sprung adoption on me—eliminating him and those emotions as possibilities.

It didn't matter what I might or might not want from him. He deserved the same happiness I got from the Shaws adopting me, and if I loved him in any capacity, I needed to encourage Ernie and Hensley.

I'd been quiet for the remainder of the ride. At some point, Bart had switched on the radio, but I'd tuned it out. Commercialized music wasn't my thing. And as he drove into the parking lot, I meant to thank him for the ride, but something entirely different came out.

"You're right."

He parked and lifted the emergency brake. "Oh, yeah? About what?" His whiskey-brown eyes weren't quite as rich as Jude's and definitely not as sad, but he had a beautiful smile that he wore more often than not.

"I should be happy for him. Excited, even." My unidentified relationship intentions toward Jude couldn't prevent my parents from adoption. I wouldn't let it.

Bart leaned over the seat and kissed my cheek. "Just think, this way you'll be legally tied to him. You *can* claim him as your brother, and the two of you will always have each other."

"Lemon pie." I hadn't meant to actually say it and hadn't realized I had.

"What?"

"Nothing, just something Jude says when good things happen to him."

"I think this is definitely lemon pie then."

I unbuckled my seatbelt and hid my face so Bart couldn't see just how tart that pastry was. Ernie and Hensley had enough to deal with surrounding Jude and how he handled his grief. I couldn't take this from them, or him. Nor could I even imagine how I'd approach requesting them not to ask Jude. They'd flip out, thinking they'd failed us both, or at the very least, me. They'd blame themselves if I were possibly—though not certainly—in love with a boy who'd lived with us off and on for the better part of a decade. Hensley would go into meltdown mode convinced Jude was the reason I'd never dated.

Nothing good could ever come out of me exploring anything with Jude or acknowledging just what that single kiss had done to me emotionally and physically.

Mentally, I slammed the door shut and refused to keep the key.

6

JUDE

A WEEK LATER, PORTIA STILL AVOIDED ME AND KEPT HER TEXT messages short. I tried to act as though nothing had happened, yet it seemed that tiny kiss sent her far away. The closeness we'd always shared now strained under the weight of my actions, and I didn't know how to fix it. Other than Portia, I had a total of two friends. Ethan and Carson. The three of us had grown up together. We'd gone to the same elementary school and middle school, and with only one high school in our small town, we landed there as class-mates, as well. They hadn't met Portia until the start of our freshman year. Even though they knew of her, and heard me talk about her, their paths didn't cross since I didn't see them when I was at the Shaws' house.

Ethan was insanely intelligent even though common sense wasn't his strong suit. Carson was bright and street smart. Though we looked nothing alike, we were all similar in that we'd been outcasts early on and remained that way. Our friendships were forged by that alliance alone. It wasn't until we grouped together that the bullying stopped, and we recognized that we actually liked each other.

None of us dated, we didn't do high school events, and for the most part, we were rather anti-social. In the last year, Carson had branched out a little, not much—just enough to figure out that he enjoyed smoking pot and found being buzzed made life much more bearable. It hadn't taken Ethan long to give green a chance, and he, too, enjoyed the serenity they both swore accompanied marijuana. I'd stayed strong, resisted peer pressure—until today.

I nearly choked when I took a deep breath of the stinky substance. I didn't have any idea how they stood the smell, and the taste was rancid. If cigarettes were the equivalent to licking an ashtray, then pot was like sucking Pine-Sol through a straw. Carson swore that woodsy flavor spoke to the quality of the buds; personally, I thought it just tasted bad and medicinal. When I finally managed to stop coughing and wiped the tears from my face, I felt nothing.

"It's good, huh?" His slowed speech and squinted eyes reminded me of Hyde on *That '70s Show*. If he'd had a beard and glasses, they could have passed for twins.

"No. It's awful. And I don't feel any different than I did before willfully exposing myself to lung cancer."

"No carcinogens, man." Carson believed in the healing powers of the herb, or at least that was how he justified his use of it. "There is no medical proof that smoking pot causes cancer the way cigarettes do. Don't lump the two together."

I didn't have a clue if that was true or not. Surely, he didn't need the surgeon general to tell him that inhaling smoke of any kind into one's lungs wasn't healthy.

Ethan handed me the joint. "Try again."

I held it between my thumb and pointer ready to inhale when a car door slammed across the street, and I jerked toward the noise. The two of them laughed hysterically at my paranoia. Carson's garage wasn't airtight—I knew from experience the smell traveled beyond the space we were in and into the driveway. His parents were hippies who didn't care, although that didn't mean the neighbors shared their blasé attitude toward the illegal activity.

There was no reason for me to take another draw off the joint. The first one had been awful, and it had taken me five minutes to recover from the experience. Yet there I sat, pulling in air with my mouth pinched around the paper—slower this time so I didn't cough—and I held it in the way Carson showed me. My lungs burned until I allowed it to seep out slowly in an exhale. Still, nothing.

"Give it a few minutes. It's your first time." Ethan encouraged me as if I were trying out a new language or learning to ride a bike, not doing drugs.

I leaned back in the canvas folding chair and watched the sky through the windows at the top of the garage. The clouds moved by the glass panes, unaware of what we did. I realized when I'd been lost in thought for an exorbitant amount of time that my arms and legs had grown heavy, my eyelids drooped, and my mouth was drier than the Sahara desert. Lazily, I gave my attention to Carson and Ethan who were high as kites and pondered them through the haze that the lingering dust in the air created.

I didn't notice when I slid down in the chair and my back ended up almost parallel with the floor. Or that I had a permanent grin on my face.

"You're so blitzed, dude." In a few short minutes, Carson had gone from well-spoken to a surfer who'd spent too much time in the sun.

The moment I tried to deny his accusation, I sat up, smiled like a jackass, and started laughing uncontrollably at my friends. It was an obnoxious, girly giggle I couldn't contain or control. And just as quickly as it occurred to me I was high, it dawned on me how much better this felt than anything else I'd dealt with in the last few months. Ethan and Carson talked around me, and mentally, I ran through the checklist of crap that had gone on in my life, while simultaneously ignoring them. Cancer. Hospice. Death. Funeral. The Shaws. Portia.

"Why the long face, Droopy?" Ethan stared at me, waiting for an answer.

"This whole Eeyore thing you have going on isn't really all that welcoming, you know?" Carson peered at me over the edge of the paper he licked to finish rolling another joint. "I mean, I get that your life has sucked this summer, but moping around isn't gonna make it any better. You gotta let that shit go. Don't allow all that negative energy to drain you."

If the same thing had come from anyone else, I probably would have laid them out the same way I had Chad Hartman. Carson grew up with parents who believed you got out of the earth what you put in; they believed in chakra and karma and the effect of the stars on the moon— the things most people found hokey. He wasn't being cruel, he was essentially telling me to lean on nature the way a Christian would advise prayer and faith. His logic might be less conventional, but it was heartfelt, just the same.

"You ever going to tell us what happened with Portia? Why didn't you take her back to school last weekend?" Ethan had as much finesse as an elephant in a china shop.

Carson shook his head but never lifted his sight from the joint he still rolled. "How can someone be as smart as you are yet totally lacking in basic social skills, like the art of conversation?"

"She went back early."

"Can't blame her for that. Not that Ernie and Hensley are bad people or anything." Carson was a live-and-let-live kind of guy.

"But *why*? You've been acting funny ever since that whole thing with Chad in the hall. I thought for sure you'd come back to school with confidence. Instead you're just...I don't know...pissed at the world." When Ethan was high, he reverted to the vocabulary of a ten-year-old. "Who cares what he thinks about Portia, anyhow?"

In my already fractious state of mind, I was convinced guilt was written all over my face. That if I made eye contact, they'd know I'd done something that sent her careening from the house as if her ass were on fire. "Can we talk about something else?"

"Let's talk about getting your sister to hook us up with college babes." Ethan lifted his brow twice in an awkward attempt at luring me into agreeing with him.

"She's not my sister."

"Whatever, dude. You're connected to her. She's in college. The end result can still be the same." Carson finally plucked the twisted end from the joint he'd worked on for the last five minutes and sparked a flame to enjoy it.

The high I was on brought clarity I hadn't experienced before, or so I believed. These two were idiots. I stared at them both in disbelief and wondered how we'd been friends as long as we had. And the uncontrollable laughter began again.

"What's wrong with you?" I didn't know which one asked; I couldn't decipher the voice over my hysteria.

Nothing was as funny as I made it out to be, but I didn't care. Clutching my stomach that hurt from the muscles tensing for so long, I finally barked out, "High school girls aren't interested in the three of us. What would make you think college girls would be any different?" If either of them understood a word I said, I'd be shocked.

"Dude. That's not cool." Carson took another drag and passed it my direction. "Lots of girls dig intellectuals. They're called sapiosexuals. Your sister needs to find three of those for us."

"She's not my sister," I repeated adamantly. "And I don't see her setting us up with anyone." I didn't mention that I had no interest in her friends, just her.

"Did you piss her off when she was home? Because she likes me. I'm sure she'd set me up." Ethan lived in a world the rest of us only visited. Portia liked Ethan simply because he was my friend, not because she had any particular interest in him.

Carson chimed in. "I'm better looking than both of you; maybe she should start with me."

I'd stepped into another realm. "She's not setting either of you up with anyone." I'd lost my cool listening to them ramble. "She's not even talking to me."

"Did you steal her makeup or try to wear her shoes?" Ethan was a lost cause.

"I kissed her!"

The garage got eerily quiet, and the outside world came back into focus when I heard a car drive by and a kid scream in the street.

Ethan and Carson looked at each other, then at me. Carson finally spoke. "Isn't that illegal?"

"We aren't related. We share foster parents, not blood."

"But doesn't that make you first cousins?"

"No, Ethan. It makes us of *no* relation. Nada. Zilch. None."

"But you basically grew up together."

I pulled my hair at the roots, kicking myself for letting that secret slip. "So, by that rationale, if Grace Dawson decided tomorrow she wanted to give you her virginity, you'd say no because you two grew up together? You know, since your parents are best friends?"

Grace was the head cheerleader and queen shit on turd hill in our high school. She was also gorgeous and had done some print modeling last year. In other words, so far out of our league we weren't even playing the same game.

"Totally different." Ethan shook his head and turned his mouth down. "We lived in separate houses."

"Newsflash, genius. So did we. Remember when I was home with my mom and Portia wasn't there—for months at a time?" I wasn't going to debate this. I never should have said anything even if I'd wrongly assumed they had some inkling I'd loved Portia for years. There was no way they'd been blind to the way I talked about her or how I acted around her or the fact I protected her.

"Dude, don't get mad. You don't have to leave. We won't talk about you loving your sister anymore. Or how fucked up it is that you tongued her." Ethan was about to meet the same fate Chad had in D hall.

"Fuck off, Ethan. Carson, I'll talk to you later." I folded my chair, put it back on the shelf, and grabbed my backpack.

When I stormed out, I realized I was high and going home in this condition wasn't a well-thought-out plan. Even so, I didn't have anywhere else to go. I'd just have to hope Hensley wasn't around when I got to the house.

SINCE I'D NEVER BEEN DRUNK, AND THIS WAS MY FIRST experience being high, I didn't quite grasp that reaching out to Portia in my current state wasn't the best idea. She'd kept me at arm's length, responding to texts with short answers, but I hadn't been brave enough to call. I had a hard time hearing her voice—it made me miss her—so I'd avoided phone calls since she left. When I got home from Carson's, I snuck into my room and locked the door. Any witness to my behavior might believe I was part of a covert operation...or possibly breaking and entering. I hated to think just how sketchy I appeared from an outsider's perspective.

I grabbed my cell from my backpack and searched for a place to hide. Ernie was at work, and Hensley's car wasn't here when I'd shown up, so I wasn't sure who I was hiding from; it just made sense. The closet proved to be my best choice for full coverage. I didn't bother with the light and closed myself in. The glow of the screen illuminated the small space enough for me to safely have a seat without the risk of sitting on a shoe or a hanger.

There was no hesitation on my part, although there probably should have been. I hadn't thought any of this through, because it never occurred to me that Portia would be able to tell I'd been up to something.

She answered on the second ring. "Hello?"

"Hey, Portia."

"Jude? Are you okay?" The panic in her tone rang through the line, and even though I heard it, I didn't understand it.

"I'm fine." I drew out each word, confused by her alarmed voice. "How are you?"

"Why do you sound funny?" Concern morphed into irritation.

I looked around, unsure of what I'd said that was off…as if the clothes on the rod or the crap on the floor would give me insight. "Umm. I wasn't aware I did. Is it the acoustics?" Maybe the sound echoed in the small space.

"Jude Thomas, have you been drinking?" Her use of my full name made me think of my mother, briefly. But I wasn't able to hold on to the thought.

"Portia Shaw, have you?" She didn't think I was nearly as funny as I found myself.

"Does Hensley know you're intoxicated?" I didn't have a mother; Portia didn't need to try to fill in.

"I haven't had a drop of alcohol."

"Where have you been?"

"Can you stop with the interrogation? Damn. All I wanted to do was call and hear your voice." The line went silent on the other end. "I miss you and feel bad for what I did." And then, I started rambling. "Not bad like I didn't enjoy it. Bad like it scared you or pushed you away or grossed you out. I get it. What girl who looks like *you* wants to be seen with a guy like *me*, right? You don't have to say it." I let out a huff and kept going when she didn't stop me. "You probably think I'm as crazy as Ethan and Carson do. God knows you tell enough people I'm your little brother. Oh shit, wait, did you—did you think it was incest? Fuck. I'm sorry, Portia, I—"

"Jude. Stop."

I did as she instructed and waited. The silence lingered. The sound of a door closing in the background signaled her need to find privacy before she continued. Hope hung in the valance, until she smashed it with a curtain rod and then hung it out to dry.

"Did you say you were at Carson's?" she hissed under her breath.

"Well, yes." My confirmation sounded funny—the *Y* and the *S* bounced around in my head and vibrated my tongue. "That's typically where I go after school." I drew out the sentence as though I were muddled over her uncertainty. I never understood why people asked questions they already had the answer to. I'd just told her I was at Carson's. At least, I thought I'd told her I was there—maybe I implied it without actually speaking the words. Or possibly, I assumed she knew that was where I was because he was my best friend and—

"Are you *high*?"

This was a bad idea.

"Answer me, Jude."

"There's no need to yell."

"I'm not yelling, but if you don't start talking, I will be."

"I *was* talking, and you interrupted."

"You were babbling. What the hell are you on?"

I raked my palm down my face and wondered why I'd bothered to pick up the phone. "It's not a big deal, Portia. Calm down." Not even the sound of her voice was worth listening to this.

My mouth was so dry, my tongue clung to the roof, and my lips stuck together. The saliva was thick—cottonmouth, my ass. It tasted the way kitty litter smelled. I flung the closet open and practically threw myself into my room.

Portia talked on the other end of the call. I, however, was laser-focused on the water in the bathroom faucet rather than on anything she said. Once I'd downed a cold cup, I was able to revert my attention back to the girl on the other end.

"Are you even listening?" Ranting.

I'd discovered why Portia didn't have any dates. If she treated all guys this way, mothered them, acted self-righteous, hell, I wouldn't want to have anything to do with her either. Then I thought of her pouty, pink lips and remembered how they felt against mine—even for the briefest of seconds—and I knew I'd listen to this shit until the cows came home for one more kiss.

"Why are you screaming?"

"Just tell me if this is something you do all the time."

"No, Portia. It's not. This was a one-time thing. Believe it or not, I've had a few shit months and just wanted to unwind a little. It's just pot."

I heard something about a gateway drug and a vague promise not to do it anymore. And while I couldn't recall the exact words—I'd only been half-listening while I studied the freckles on my face in the bathroom mirror—I was fairly certain I'd agreed to her terms to keep her from telling Ernie and Hensley.

"I love you, Jude. I don't want to see you go down the wrong path." Cotton candy.

IT HAD TAKEN ME ALL OF THREE WEEKS TO BREAK WHATEVER agreement I'd made with Portia not to smoke pot again. The truth was, I thought all her vibrato was overkill. It came from a place of concern, but if marijuana was legal in a handful of states and decriminalized in several more, it couldn't be the death sentence Portia made it out to be. Cancer patients had used it for years to fight nausea and pain. And I was proof it warded off mental anguish, as well.

My grades hadn't suffered, Ernie and Hensley were none the wiser, and it hadn't affected my ability to take care of my responsibilities. In fact, the more I smoked, the happier my foster parents believed me to be. I'd simply made a mental note not to call Portia after school, and since we texted most of the time, it didn't matter, anyhow.

Portia: I'm coming home this weekend.
Me: Are you actually staying the whole weekend or is it a quick trip?
Portia: Depends. Can you keep your hands to yourself?
Me: Do I have to?

This was where I walked the line. I was never this brazen sober. But over the last few weeks, it helped ease the tension between the two of us to remain playful. We hadn't talked about that kiss. While I wanted to make it out to be something monumental in my mind— it was my first kiss—there was no tongue, no embrace, no heartfelt sentiment. It was a rash decision that had backfired. I had played my hand before it was time, and it cost me the game.

Portia: Mom and Dad have a surprise for you.

She ignored my question, the one about keeping my hands to myself.

Me: What?
Portia: If I told you, then it wouldn't be a surprise.
Me: Yet you suck at keeping secrets.
Portia: Mum's the word.

If she were home, I'd simply tickle her into submission. My normal interrogation methods were useless with her an hour away.

Me: Are you ever going to invite me to spend time with you at school?

Portia: That would depend on your ability to behave.

Me: Yes, that's me...social deviant.

Me: Of course, I'd behave. Why would you think I wouldn't?

There was a long period without a reply. Either she'd gotten busy or she needed time to organize her thoughts. I held the phone in my hand, willing it to ding with another message. Instead, those emerald-green eyes and pink lips showed up on my screen when her picture indicated she had decided to call. Portia knew I was around; we'd just been chatting. I almost didn't answer the phone, not wanting to be lectured again; nevertheless, at the last second, I swiped right and connected the call.

"Hello?"

"Hey, Jude." Her voice was laden with anxiety, which didn't bode well for me.

"To what do I owe the honor of an actual phone call?" I needed to keep my answers shorter if I hoped to hide the fact that I'd smoked with Carson and Ethan before I came home.

"This just wasn't something I wanted to text you."

Shit. That couldn't be good.

"I'd love for you to come see me and hang out for the day."

"But?"

She sighed into the speaker. "I'm kind of seeing someone."

Silence was no longer a problem. I didn't have a clue what to say. Portia had never even been on a date that I was aware of. Now she was "seeing" someone—not that I knew what *that* implied, either.

"Do you remember Bart?"

It wouldn't be possible for me to forget—I'd tried, unsuccessfully. "Yes."

"He's a great guy. Super funny and smart. At first, we were just kind of friends and hung out in groups, but things shifted after he picked me up from the house a few weeks ago. We started getting together one-on-one, and he's taken me out on a few dates."

There was more to this than her having a study buddy or someone to eat dinner with at the cafeteria. "Okay…"

"Ah—" The nervous sigh seconds earlier became something entirely different when she spoke of him. "He kissed me. It was magical. All the way to my toes." Portia said all the right words— and it was possible I hadn't heard them correctly in my altered state of mind—but I didn't sense the oomph that should have come with that description. Something lacked in her tone that I couldn't quite pinpoint.

Nevertheless, my imagination kicked into overdrive. Here's where I envisioned her with her arms out, spinning in a circle, with her head back in total abandon…like Julie Andrews in *The Sound of Music*. She hadn't convinced me that she was as over the moon for this guy as she wanted me to believe, but it didn't take a rocket scientist to figure out what she was doing. Whether *Bart* was the one or not, Portia just told me in a passive way, that I was not.

"Since then, we've spent just about every day after class together."

I didn't understand why she needed to heap on the details. Her declaration alone held the power to bring me to my knees. The weight on my chest was crushing enough already. My heart pounded painfully while my ribs constricted, closing it in a cage it desperately wanted to break free from.

"Are you still there?"

Physically, yes. Mentally, I'd drifted a thousand miles away. "Yeah."

"Say something, silly." If she wanted my acceptance, I wasn't ready to give it.

"Something silly." *Brilliant.*

"Come on. You have to have an opinion. You have an opinion on everything."

Oh, I had an opinion. It just wasn't one she wanted to hear. Portia had confided in me, practically begging for my approval. I couldn't stop the nagging realization that this was her way of telling me she didn't hold me in the same regard I did her—without actually saying the words. Whether it had been her intention or not, it was the only thing I focused on.

"Why don't you bring Bart home with you this weekend? We can hang out, and I can get to know him." *Utter horseshit.* The only desire I had in getting to know *Bart* was to find his weaknesses, determine his intentions, and reconcile the best way to get rid of him.

"I already told you, Mom and Dad have a surprise for you. Probably not the best time to bring a guy home. Plus, isn't that a huge step in the world of dating? Meeting the parents?"

"Well, if it's a surprise, those are typically good, right? Unless Bart doesn't like surprises."

"What about meeting the family?" She didn't have the first clue when it came to dating. She also happened to seem disappointed by my suggestion—further proving this conversation wasn't about Bart.

Sadly, I was as clueless as she was when it came to matters of the heart. So, asking my advice wasn't particularly bright on her part—I couldn't be held responsible for what happened if she took it. Although, secretly, I hoped it freaked him the hell out and caused him to run screaming into the night. "I don't see a problem with it." Most guys would. That step was the neon sign of commitment. It was doubtful Bart was ready to hop on the marital train those introductions implied was leaving the station.

"Okay. I'll ask him and see what he says."

Fantastic. I couldn't wait.

"You promise to be nice?"

Cordial, *maybe.* "Sure."

"Jude…"

"Portia…"

Several long seconds passed. I didn't know if she sensed the unease from my end, but it seemed palpable to me.

"Well, I'll let you know tomorrow if he's coming. Okay?"

"Yep."

If she wanted to say anything else, mention how few words I'd actually spoken in this conversation, or chastise me, she didn't. My thoughts and emotions were more random than stars in the sky. I wasn't at a point I could convey any of them in an articulate fashion, so I bit my tongue.

"Later."

"Bye, Jude."

7

PORTIA

JUDE'S EASY ACCEPTANCE OF MY RELATIONSHIP STATUS STUNG. I didn't know what I had expected, some sort of fight, hesitation, anything to indicate his kiss had meant something. Jude wasn't Chet, but I had a hard time differentiating between the two when it seemed a cheap feel was all either wanted. Unfortunately, I couldn't discuss Jude with anyone, and Chet was just an ass. I could talk until I was blue in the face about the lacrosse player the girls on campus lusted after, and it wouldn't change anything about him.

Sitting cross-legged on my bed, I held the phone in my hand and wondered when the shift had taken place with Jude. I'd always believed he cared about me, and I still wanted to. I just couldn't reconcile his ability to change gears and hand me off to another guy with so little fight—not that I'd given him an opening to do anything different. I flung myself back onto my pillows and let out a loud grunt. The door swung open during my anxious release, but I didn't bother to glance over to see who it was.

"What's wrong with you?" Jet was one of those perpetually happy girls. She always had sugar for the lemons life threw at her, and there were days I wanted to replace it with salt.

I stared at the ceiling as I spoke. "Do you ever annoy yourself?"

"Umm, have I done something to upset you? If so, you can just tell me."

I rolled my head toward her and saw the hurt in her eyes. "Oh, no, Jet. Not you. You haven't done anything. I'm actually asking about me. I'm aggravating myself. My thoughts are like a ping-pong ball, and I can't land on anything. The back and forth is driving me bonkers."

She lay down on her mattress so she could see me. Her sky-blue eyes sparkled, and her lips tilted into a soft smile. "Bart?"

Jet didn't always come across as the brightest bulb on the porch, but I had to give it to her. While she only had half of the answer, it was impressive she got that much. I'd done everything I could to outwardly express more devotion toward Bart than my heart actually held. "How do you do that?"

"It's not hard to see, Portia. He's a good-looking, charming, all-American guy."

"But?"

"But there aren't fireworks or sparks. He's just a close friend."

"I like him a lot. Maybe I just don't know what I'm supposed to feel. I've never had a boyfriend."

"Or maybe you know exactly what you're supposed to feel and don't want to admit you aren't feeling it for Bart. It's possible to want to like someone differently than you do, just like it's possible *to* like someone the way you do."

She'd just summed up my wishy-washy mentality in two sentences. "How do you figure out which is the real emotion?"

Her thin shoulder raised a couple of inches and then fell. "Give it time. You're young. You don't have to make any decisions today. Just make sure that when you figure it out, you're honest with yourself and him. Bart's a good guy."

"I wish I was better at this," I grumbled under my breath.

Jet chuckled. "This is what dating is about. It's how you get better at picking a partner, and I guess, hopefully a spouse."

"I do like him. And I'm definitely attracted to him. He gives me the warm fuzzies in all the right spots…"

"Then what's the hang-up?"

"I wish I knew." I did know; I just refused to share that information with anyone. I had a hard-enough time denying my emotions to myself. If I verbalized them, not only would I have to face whatever ridicule followed my declaration, but it would make it all real. I didn't have the energy to hash out my issues over Jude with anyone, and the last thing I needed was my roommate thinking I was into some kinky, brother-sister thing. And even if I could get past that, I couldn't ignore the doubt Chet had caused. Regardless of whether he was an ass, the entire experience left me gun-shy where men were concerned.

"You know it's okay to just enjoy dating someone. Have fun together. Just don't let him believe it's going somewhere that you know for sure it's not."

I stared at the dingy, popcorn ceiling. "Jude wants me to bring him home with me this weekend."

"Bart?"

"Yeah."

She rolled onto her side, set her elbow on the mattress, and propped her head in her hand. "Why?"

"To get to know him?" I shrugged. "I don't know."

"I wish I had a little brother who gave a crap about the boys I dated." She snickered, but she didn't know what she was saying. "Maybe that will help you figure things out. Anytime my family has met a guy I've dated, it either confirmed or denied the attraction. As much as I want to believe I don't care what my parents think, I totally do. If they don't care for someone I'm seeing, it's only a matter of time before the guy gets the ax."

I couldn't deny her point. There was no way I'd date anyone my family didn't love. Although, if they loved him, I wasn't sure how that would help my dilemma. Thinking about this made my head hurt. "How are things going with Todd?"

She hadn't admitted to dating Bart's friend, but I'd have to be blind not to see how much time the two spent together. "We're just friends." Disappointment lingered in her words, even though the glitter in her eyes and her smile didn't fade.

"Seriously?"

"I like him, but he hasn't asked me out."

"Maybe he's shy. Why don't you ask him?"

She flipped onto her back and draped her arms down her sides. Her chest rose when she took a deep breath, and then it lowered when she exhaled. "Don't laugh."

"I'm not going to laugh at you. I'm the last person to make fun of anyone else when it comes to guys." I sat straight up and tossed my legs over the side of the mattress. "Wait...you do prefer guys, right? I mean, I don't care if you don't. I just assumed you did. I'm cool with it either way, and—"

"Yes, I prefer guys." She chuckled, but she didn't look my direction. "I just believe guys should pursue girls. It's old-fashioned, but it's the way I was raised. I think it's romantic for a man to make his intentions clear."

I couldn't argue against that, and I had no experience either way, but I could attest to fear being a deterrent. "But what if he just needs that initial nudge to know you're interested?"

"You don't think I've given him that? Without me passing him notes or spray-painting my feelings on the quad lawn, there's not much else I can do, short of asking him out myself."

This seemed counterproductive. "Didn't you just tell me to be honest with myself and Bart?"

"Yeah?" She posed her response as a question.

"Then doesn't the same apply here? Shouldn't you flat-out tell him and then see what he does with the information?"

When Jet finally decided to make eye contact, she glared—the sparkle in her baby blues was gone. "*Now's* the time you choose to be logical?" She tried to hide the grin threatening to break loose, but she was unsuccessful.

"My bad. I'll try to keep my logic to moments where it doesn't make sense."

She sat up and tossed a pillow at me. "I'd appreciate that."

I shouldn't be happy that my friend was as lost in the dating world as I was, but I was glad to see I wasn't the only one who didn't have a clue. I'd blamed my inexperience, but Jet had dated a lot during high school, yet she wasn't in any better shape.

"I just stopped by to drop off my books. I'm done for the day and going to get some lunch. Wanna join me?" Jet stood and moved to the mirror to check her face while she waited for an answer.

"Nah, I have a bunch of homework to do. Save a place for me at dinner, though, okay? Unless you ask Todd out and have other plans." I winked, and Jet shook her head.

"Hey," I greeted Bart.

He popped a quick kiss on my lips that felt warm and good. Although I had to admit, it wasn't electric—but maybe rocking chairs and growing old wasn't about explosive moments, and instead, relied on deep-seated friendship and mutual attraction.

"Hey, yourself. You want to grab some dinner? I'm going to meet Jet and Todd in the cafeteria." He leaned against the doorframe.

My shoulders relaxed, and I fell under the charm that captivated me anytime we were together. When I was physically in his presence, I was content, happy. Unfortunately, when he wasn't within reach, my mind wandered endlessly. For the time being, I decided to focus on the here and now. At eighteen, I didn't have to make any life-altering decisions—he asked about dinner, not marriage.

"Actually, I'm starving." I grabbed my keys and then tugged a sweatshirt over my head. "I wanted to talk to you about something, anyhow." I moved past him and locked my room behind me.

Bart took my hand and laced his fingers through mine. "Yeah? What's up?" He had a habit of stroking the top of my hand with his thumb, and it was almost hypnotic—I loved it.

"Feel free to say no."

He didn't speak when we stopped in front of the elevators and he pressed the down button. When he stared at me, it was as though he waited on me to keep going.

"Do you want me to say no before you tell me what it is you want to discuss?" He laughed as he spoke. Bart let go of my hand and drew me into his chest in order to wrap his arms around my waist. He kissed the top of my head and then said, "You know, whatever it is, if I can make it happen, my answer will be yes."

This was one of the things I loved about Bart, yet it also caused me turmoil. Although, I couldn't be sure which bothered me more— the fact that he went out of his way to be good to me or that I was keeping a mental checklist of Bart's pros and cons.

The elevator dinged, and he let me go as it slid open. There were other people inside, so I held my question, and his hand, until we were out of the tin can. The group tailed us down the front steps and finally parted when we hit the sidewalk.

"You were saying?" he reminded me.

"Remember when I told you about Ernie and Hensley wanting to adopt Jude?" I kept my eyes trained on the cement, not caring to see his face if he refused the trip home with me.

"Yeah, the morning I picked you up."

I tucked my hair behind my ear with my free hand, and Bart stopped walking. I didn't get the message until my arm met the resistance of his standing still. Our sight met, and there was no denying he understood—before I even asked—that whatever was on my mind was important.

"They're surprising him with the paperwork at dinner on Friday night."

His eyes roamed my face, and I wondered what he expected to find hidden there. "That's great, right?"

"Oh yeah, it is. Well, Jude doesn't know—hence the surprise part. Anyway, when I told him I was coming home, he asked me to bring you. I didn't know if you'd want to go, and I'm not just asking because Jude suggested it. I really do want you—"

"Portia." My name on his lips stopped my rambling. He cupped my cheeks in his hands, and I waited for the rejection. "I would love to meet your family…"

"But?"

His arms dropped to his sides, and the loss of his warmth allowed the chill of the breeze to assault my cheeks. "Do you think this is the best time?"

"I'm sorry. I wasn't trying to pressure you. I knew it was too soon." I turned to walk toward the cafeteria, but he snagged my fingers, halting my steps.

"That's not what I mean. This is a family thing. I don't want to intrude."

"I told Jude my parents had a surprise for him, and he still insisted that you come. He said surprises are good things, so you wouldn't have any reason not to be there…if you wanted to, I mean." I dropped hold of his gaze in favor of staring at my feet.

Bart tilted my chin and forced me to look at him. "If Jude and your parents don't mind, I'd love to go."

"For real?" The surprise in my voice cracked the second word, and I rolled my eyes, once again irritated with myself.

"Of course. Why wouldn't I?"

I bit my cheek as I considered my answer. People milled about around us; there were guys playing soccer in the courtyard and girls chatting in front of the library. None of them paid us the slightest bit of attention, yet somehow, I was on display for the entire student body to witness my embarrassment.

"I haven't done this before, Bart. I just didn't want you to think it meant…I don't know…that I had expectations."

A laugh rolled through him, starting deep in his chest. "Portia, your family is important to you. I wouldn't feel any differently if you wanted to introduce me to your best friend. I'm honored you want us to meet." He hesitated, clearly not finished. "But again, it doesn't have to be this weekend. If this needs to be a family thing, we can go next weekend or any other time. What did your mom say?"

Hensley didn't care. I hadn't asked because I already knew the answer. She'd be so ecstatic that I had a date, it wouldn't surprise me if she rolled out a red carpet to welcome him to the house. "I haven't mentioned it to her."

"I tell you what. Why don't you call your mom, and if she's cool with it, then I'm all in. If she hesitates, then we can go next weekend. Deal?"

Bart was perfect in every way, and I wondered how I could possibly doubt what a great catch he was. He never pressured me the way Chet had, he treated me with respect, he was fun and funny, gorgeous—everything any girl would want.

I lifted onto my tiptoes and put my hands on his hips to steady myself. My eyes closed as our mouths met. His arm wrapped around my waist, bringing me close to his chest, and he took my affection a step further when he encouraged my lips to part to allow his tongue to tangle with mine. It wasn't crass or long-lived. It was perfect.

A bit winded, he broke away. "Come on. Jet's going to form a search party if we don't show up soon." He kissed my forehead, and then he led me across campus to meet our friends.

The four of us sat there for an hour, eating mediocre food and laughing about nothing. I noticed the little things Todd did to indicate his interest in Jet. I made a mental note to point them all out to her, and then slap her when she tried to argue them away as polite gestures. Guys didn't carry girls' trays or clean up after them. She might be able to convince me that they held doors open because they were polite, but I refused to believe they pulled out chairs for every female near them. Todd wasn't blazing a path for the world to see; he was trying to win her heart with action.

When we'd cleaned up our table, Bart and Todd planned to head back to their dorm, and Jet and I to ours. The two of them coupled off. If I questioned Jet, she'd swear it was to give Bart and me time to say goodbye. Personally, I thought she wanted time of her own with Todd.

"Why don't you call your mom before I go?" he suggested.

I wasn't certain this was the best time, but if I was going to bring him home, I guessed I needed to ask Hensley. Just as I suspected, the idea of meeting someone I was interested in thrilled my mom, and Bart heard every word she said.

"That's settled then?" he asked when I hung up.

"You're sure you don't mind?"

"Can't wait." He gave me a kiss on the cheek and then popped me on the butt as he turned toward his dorm. "I'll text you before I go to bed," he called as he grabbed Todd by the sleeve to drag him away.

Jet and I stood there, watching them disappear across campus.

"So, you want to tell me again how you think Todd isn't pursuing you?" I didn't try to stifle my giggle. Jet was so full of crap, she stunk.

"Hush." She rolled her eyes and hooked her arm through mine. "So, you're taking Bart home to meet the rents, huh?"

"Ugh. Yeah. Do or die, right?" I didn't have a clue what the hell I was doing. At this point, I was just going with the flow to avoid swimming upstream.

She winked at me. "That's one way to look at it." I knew that regardless of what happened this weekend, Jet had my back.

8

JUDE

THE FESTIVITIES WERE SET TO BEGIN PROMPTLY AT SEVEN. HENSLEY was giddy over Portia bringing home a boy, Ernie appeared defensive, and I just had to sit back to watch how it played out. Neither Hensley nor Ernie mentioned a surprise of any kind; however, Hensley had made a roast, which was my favorite. It also happened to be the best thing she cooked, so I couldn't be certain it was for me and not Portia's "guest."

"Do you know anything about this boy, Jude?" My foster mother had to be one of the kindest, most sincere, gentle women I'd ever known—the thought of a twenty-year-old guy being a "boy" might have made her a tad naïve, as well.

"I met him the day I dropped Portia off." Indifference dripped from my words and expression.

"And what's he like?" Her eyes were wide with anticipation. She mixed the ingredients for cookies together with her electric mixer, waiting for me to divulge the inside scoop.

I hadn't committed him to memory. "Nice, I guess." I'd tried to forget him. If I couldn't see him, he didn't exist—like when I had my head under the couch. It worked for me.

"You can't tell me any more about him?" She smiled and offered me a ball of uncooked dough.

I refused the raw cookie and her attempt at interrogation. "His name is Bartholomew."

She dried her hands on the towel and then threw it at me. "That's very helpful."

The front door opened, and Portia called out to find us.

"There you go, Hensley. Now you can get all the dirt on your own." I tilted my head toward the foyer.

Hensley grabbed my hand to pull me off the stool and then wrapped her arm around my waist with a squeeze. I escorted her to meet Portia's new beau sporting a fake smile. The moment Hensley got close enough, she let go of me to hug her daughter and then Bart. He quickly returned her embrace as though it were natural to linger in the arms of a woman he didn't know.

Bart.

He didn't look like a Bart.

As the introductions took place and Ernie quickly joined us, I wondered if Bart was a family name—maybe he was Bartholomew the Fourth. Not knowing his last name gave him far too much grandeur in my mind—he wasn't a king, but with Portia at his side, he resembled royalty. The only other Bart I knew was of the Simpson variety, and that didn't do, either—no sense in ruining a long-running, animated sitcom.

"Jude, it's good to see you, man." He stuck out his hand.

Being a dick, I just lifted my head in a quick nod of acknowledgment, until Hensley elbowed me and forced me to play nice. I shook his hand. "You too."

I chuckled when my gaze finally met Portia's. Terror. That was the only word to describe the fear in her eyes—the normally bright green was more of a dingy olive. The way she rubbed her thumb on her jeans over and over was another indication of her anxiety, but the rolling of her right ankle was most telling. Instead of helping her mitigate the discomfort, I shook my head and walked back to the kitchen, where I busied myself with cookies and dinner preparations.

Bart made it incredibly difficult to dislike him. His confidence made conversation around the dinner table easy. He flattered Hensley's cooking just enough without it being overkill or insincere. And I had to admit, he had a decent sense of humor. What he also had was Portia hanging on his every word and staring at him as though he'd hung the moon and each individual star, and then named the brightest one in her honor. But the light that normally made her eyes twinkle wasn't glowing, and instead of pink sugar, her voice was tough like taffy. Although, no one else seemed the slightest bit put off by those nuances, and clearly, I'd spent far too much time evaluating them.

After eating dinner, the five of us sat around the kitchen table while the four of them talked. My dead weight in the circle was awkward, so I opted to clean the dishes and put away the leftovers while they chatted.

"Bart, are you a coffee drinker?" Hensley had an array of flavors, brewing methods, and creamers that rivaled Starbucks.

"Yes, ma'am." He glanced at Portia, put his arm around the back of her seat, and crossed his ankle over his knee. Bart was perfectly at ease with our family, and I wanted to hate him for it.

Hensley got up to make drinks to serve with her freshly baked cookies; she also had quite an assortment.

There was no need for her to leave her guests in order to play hostess when I was desperate for excuses to keep me away. "I got it."

When the pot finished brewing, I gathered mugs and dessert plates to take to the table. Portia joined in helping me.

She stared over the island and into the dining room with a dopey grin. "Isn't he fantastic?" I wasn't certain if she was trying to convince herself or me.

"Sure, if you prefer the good-looking, outgoing, athletic type." I didn't. "Personally, I prefer brains to brawn. Testosterone just doesn't do it for me."

She hit me playfully on the arm. With her hip against the counter, she looked up and met my stare. "Are you excited?" The vivid green had returned, and her eyes sparkled.

"I mean, Bart seems like a nice guy, but I can't say that he revs my engine, Portia."

Her brows rose, and a smirk appeared. "Not about him. About your surprise."

"No one's mentioned anything other than you. Hard to get riled up."

She grabbed my hand and squeezed it. Then she lifted onto her toes and kissed my jaw. "You're gonna love it." Her hair grazed my forearm when she grabbed the tray of desserts, and her ass swayed like a pendulum as she returned to the table. When she glanced over her shoulder, an emotion I couldn't name flashed across her expression. It wasn't present long enough to identify, but it sat heavy on my chest, making it hard to breathe.

Once I joined them at the table, Ernie got up and came back with a manila envelope. He resumed his seat next to his wife. They exchanged a satisfied glance and left the rest of us to wonder what was going on. Or maybe just me—it appeared I was the only one not in on the secret.

"Jude." Ernie cleared his throat. "From the first day you came into our home, we thought of you as our own. Your situation was different from Portia's; even so, we hoped that, regardless of how many nights you actually spent under our roof, you would forever remain a part of our lives."

Whoa.

This is way too personal and far too sentimental for Bart to witness. My eyes darted from Ernie to Hensley, then to Portia with a glare of uncertainty. Her eyes brimmed with tears that contradicted her radiant smile. The emotion that had clung to my chest only moments earlier now pressed firmly on my shoulders.

"Our only goal throughout your childhood was to stay involved and help your mom in any way we could. We never wanted to replace Carrie; we only wanted to add to the love she gave you. If anything had happened earlier than it did, this would have come then, but we hope that you'll still want it as much as we do."

Lost.

Not a clue what was in the envelope he slid across the table.

I took it hesitantly, the paper rough on my fingertips, and flipped it over. After bending the brass clasp to allow me to pull out the contents, I chanced a final look at each person sitting near me. Every one of them—well, not Bart—fought tears. Portia's hand covered her lips, and she leaned closer, sitting on the edge of her seat in anticipation.

I lifted the flap and produced a stack of papers.

"Petition for adoption." I hadn't intentionally read it out loud. My mind just hadn't caught up with my mouth. I kept reading—this time to myself—not certain this was what I thought it was, and Hensley started talking.

"I know you're seventeen, and in a few months, you'll be leaving to go to college…"

There was a topic that hadn't come up—me and college.

"So, it's more symbolic than necessary. The court isn't going to move you or anything. We—the three of us—just want it to be legal. For you to know you aren't alone."

Not what I expected.

Not what I wanted.

A piece of paper wouldn't change that my mother had died, and

I certainly had no intention of changing my last name. In this great state, I could be tried as an adult, and the age of consent was sixteen —this was an unnecessary gesture. Even if those weren't reasons enough, there was one final nail in the coffin of legal adoption—one I didn't intend to share. *Portia.* And as ungrateful as it would make me, as much as it would hurt the three people I loved who sat around the table with me, my mind was made up.

"No." I slid the paperwork into the envelope and moved it back to Ernie. Clearly, that wasn't what any of them expected to hear... including Bart. "But thank you. It's a very kind gesture."

I couldn't bear witness to the disappointment I'd caused. So I excused myself without saying anything further and walked out the front door, quietly closing it behind me.

I hadn't made it to the end of the driveway before I heard the latch and footsteps down the sidewalk.

"Jude! Wait."

Portia.

My feet kept going. I'd heard her; I just didn't want to talk to her. And the idea that Bart had sat in our dining room during this fiasco made me want to slap Portia silly. She should have known better than to present this with someone at the house.

She'd run to catch up to me, and her fingers wrapped around my arm. "Jude. Stop. Would you?"

My hands were stuffed in my pockets to ward off the chill of the night air. I wished I had grabbed a jacket on my way out. "What?" Snapping at her wouldn't change anything.

"I thought you'd be thrilled."

"Really? What part of you thought this was a good idea?" I only referred to the adoption paperwork at this point, not the fact that she'd brought her boyfriend home to witness it.

"We're your family. I assumed it would make you happy to know you still had one after your mom…"

"My mom's been dead a handful of months. Her casket hasn't even had time to settle into the ground." I waved my arms at my side to accentuate each sentence. The only time I talked with my hands was when words nearly failed me, and right now, they flailed like wings I wished would carry me away. "Yet, somehow, the three of you believed I'd just write her off? Sign on the dotted line to become a Shaw and drop Thomas? Relinquish my lineage and forget about my past just because it hadn't lasted until I was sixty?"

"I just—" Tears flowed freely from her rimmed-red eyes, and the green was now a lackluster sage. The soft, pink-turned-crimson of her lips indicated her frustration, and her shaking shoulders told me just how sorry she was.

"What? You *just* what, Portia?" Screaming at her in the street wouldn't solve anything; it was simply the way my anger and grief manifested, and she was the victim taking the brunt.

She stared at me with her mouth ajar. Saliva clung like a web between her parted lips until she licked them.

"What? You assumed I'd take on another mother when mine gave out? Mine wasn't a heroin addict, Portia. I don't want to replace her or let her go. I don't want to share the Shaw name with you. All I want is to serve my time here and leave the day after I graduate."

Her neck jerked back in the same manner it would if I had slapped her. I could have easily smoothed part of that insult over by explaining that I wanted her to be a Thomas someday, have her take *my* last name. Instead, I let the verbal beating hang in the air for the neighbors to hear and the weight of it to defeat her.

Bart appeared on the front porch of the Shaws' house; I assumed he'd been drawn out by the screaming. I rolled my eyes, wondering what he believed his presence would do, other than serve to irritate me. This sure as hell wasn't something he needed to assert himself into. Had Portia thought about it, she would have realized he shouldn't have even known about it.

I jerked my head in his direction. "Your boyfriend wants you."

She looked over her shoulder, and I walked away.

WHEN I GOT BACK TO THE HOUSE, BART'S CAR WAS GONE, AND I assumed Portia had left with him. It was late, although I didn't know what time since I hadn't grabbed my cell phone when I'd stormed out after dinner. The house was dark, and a heavy silence hung in the air. Every step I took equated to walking in water, and the tension I'd left in the house still gripped every surface and available space.

The stairs might as well have been Everest, as hard as they were to climb. A chill ran down my spine that prickled my skin, taking a substantial burden with it and making every step laborious. I didn't find the atmosphere to be any different on the second floor than the first, except there was even less light to illuminate the hall without windows. It wasn't difficult to navigate the familiar path, just uncomfortable. I hadn't felt like a stranger in this house since the first day I'd arrived—now it was as though I was an intruder.

After entering the second room on the left, I closed the door and switched on the light.

"I wondered when you'd come home."

Portia scared the shit out of me. I clutched my chest and let out a long breath as my eyes adjusted to the changes. "What are you doing in here? I thought you'd gone home with lover boy." Sarcasm dripped from my words, and I wondered when I'd become the kid who hated everything anyone tried to do for me.

"Nope. I've been here. Waiting for you. Mom and Dad gave up and went to bed."

"What time is it?" Cell phones eliminated the need for traditional clocks in the world of teenagers, and I didn't have mine on me.

She glanced at her watch. "Eleven fifty-eight." Portia sat up from the supine position I'd found her in to address me. "Where the hell have you been for almost four hours?"

I took off my shirt and threw it in the laundry hamper. She averted her eyes when I removed my jeans, even though I'd left my boxers on. It didn't take me long to pull on a pair of basketball shorts, but I opted not to put on anything else. She was in *my* room—uninvited. If she didn't care for my attire or lack thereof, she could leave.

"Well?"

"I went for a walk."

Portia folded her legs in front of her, sitting Indian style. "To where? The state capital?"

"Down to the park. Around. What difference does it make?"

"Believe it or not, your safety is a priority."

I held my arms out and watched her gaze scan my face to my shorts and flick back up. "Here I am, safe and sound."

"Don't be an ass, Jude. Mom and Dad were worried, too."

I rolled my eyes and sat on the edge of the mattress. "Clearly. They sent out a search party and went to bed."

"I don't understand why you're so angry. Even if you don't want to be adopted, your response was totally over the top. You could have just said no."

With my head in my hands, I let out a long sigh. "That's what I said. I didn't explode or cause an argument. You created the scene when you chased me out the door."

Her face scrunched in dismay, as though she couldn't fathom she'd played a part in the evening's demise. "Your response was rude. We had company, and you just left after basically slapping Mom and Dad in the face."

"What was rude was presenting me with that in front of someone not involved in the picture. The three of you should have thought it through better."

"You said you didn't care if he was there for the surprise!"

"And you said it was something good. We disagree on that."

"I see that...*now*." The whites of her eyes appeared as she rolled them, shaking her head slightly. "Gah, Jude. They just want you to know how much they love you. That's it. They weren't trying to take anything away from you."

I yanked on my hair and wondered if I'd have any left by morning. "Portia, that was similar to proposing marriage on the Jumbo-Tron at the Super Bowl to someone you started dating a month ago. I was blindsided and exposed—the expectation for me to say yes to an audience was more than I could handle. I'm sorry if you weren't a fan of my reaction."

She didn't get it. And she probably never would.

I didn't want to hurt her. I didn't want to hurt them. Maybe if my feelings for Portia were different, then my reaction would have been, as well; I couldn't speculate on that. Either way, I thought it was too early—too soon after my mom's death. Although, I realized if they had waited what I considered an acceptable amount of time, I'd be eighteen, and once I was legally an adult, there would be no point.

Her stare caught my attention, and when I chanced taking in her features, the frustration eased, and the weight on my shoulders lessened. Portia's eyes were wide and innocent, the color soft and welcoming. And when her hand touched the bare skin on my shoulder, heat radiated through me—a comforting warmth. "I'm sorry." Her sentiment was sincere.

"I shouldn't have said what I did about your mom—or implied it."

She nodded and pursed her lips.

"My anger is never an excuse to hurt you, Portia. I'm truly sorry." I searched her face for acceptance, taking in her delicate features and the way the knot in her hair accentuated her high cheekbones. Everything about her was feminine in the most unique ways.

"They're just looking for a way to connect you to something. Even with the back and forth in your life, you always remained grounded and levelheaded. But recently, you've been all over the place, and they don't know how to help you, Jude."

"I'll talk to them in the morning."

She gave me a curt nod, and she swallowed hard past the lump in her throat. I waited for her to say more. When she didn't, I did what I've done since the night I met her, anything I could to keep her talking. I needed to hear the sugar of her voice. My ears were desperate to dine on the pink cotton candy.

"What happened with Bart?" I didn't want to know. It sucked that he bore witness to the shitshow that was his introduction to our family, but I refused to accept all the blame for the atrocity.

Portia made herself comfortable on my bed. "He went back to school. He thought it was best that we deal with this as a family."

"Sorry this was his first interaction with the Shaws." I lay back and leaned over to switch off the overhead light, bathing us in darkness.

"Bart's a nice guy. I don't think he'll hold any of it against me."

I folded my arms behind my head and listened to the quiet hum of the heater and the creaks of the house. As my eyes adjusted to the shadows, I stared at the ceiling fan spinning in circles and tried to lock my sights on one blade to follow it around. I never got more than three or four rotations before I lost hold. I snickered, wondering what Bart would think about his girlfriend in my bed.

WAKING THE NEXT MORNING, I'D HOPED TO FIND PORTIA HOGGING the bed and the blankets, but I found her space empty. I dreaded what I had to do and figured a shower would serve me well before facing the mess I'd created last night, although I wasn't the only one responsible for the turdshow at the manure corral. The shower ran cold while I played different scenarios in my head for how to word things with Ernie and Hensley, and I ended up deciding spontaneity would play in my favor. I never did well with anything rehearsed.

By the time I made it downstairs, it was nearly eleven, and the house was relatively quiet. Portia and Hensley were nowhere to be found, and I started to wonder if this was going to be a habit of Portia's every time she came home.

Ernie sat at the table with a cup of coffee and the newspaper in hand. "Hey, son." He set the paper down when I took a seat across from him.

"Is Hensley around?"

"She and Portia went shopping."

Good to know she hadn't escaped under the cloak of darkness again and run back to school with her tail tucked between her legs.

"Did you need something?" He was like a dog begging for scraps, and by the looks of it, he'd take anything.

I hadn't planned to do this separately, but it wouldn't hurt to talk to each of them one on one. Maybe it would make approaching Hensley easier if I'd had practice. "I was hoping I could talk to you both."

He finished his coffee and got up to refill the cup. "I'm all ears if one set will do instead of two."

He moved about the kitchen with an expectant look on his face. I didn't say a word while he poured his creamer, added sugar, and settled back into his chair.

I took a deep breath. "I wanted to apologize about last night."

Ernie leaned back and crossed his legs. "Jude, there's no reason to be sorry."

"I wish I'd handled it better. I just wasn't expecting it and felt blindsided. And having Bart there didn't make it any better."

"You can't help your gut reaction, and your home should always be a safe place to have those—"

"Even still, you guys have been good to me. The gesture was huge, and I appreciate it. I just...I don't want to dishonor my mom, and I don't want to give up my last name."

His forehead lined with creases. "Is that what you thought?" Ernie quickly uncrossed his legs, set his coffee cup down, and leaned forward on the table. "No wonder you were out of here like something bit you."

"It hasn't been that long, Ernie, and adoption would brush over her significance in my life."

He scrubbed his face with his hands before settling them on the tabletop. "Before Carrie died, Hensley and I spent a lot of time with her."

"I know." As soon as my mom had decided not to continue treatment, the three of them—Hensley, Ernie, and her—all spent the majority of their free time together. I never asked what they were doing. I assumed she was making final preparations for herself and me, and it was a fact I hadn't been ready to face.

"Did Carrie ever tell you what all we talked about?"

I shook my head. "Nah, I didn't ask." Other than the fact that the most important woman in my world was dying, it had been the most perfect time in my life. Both of my "families" were together constantly, and I never had to pick who I wanted to see, or sacrifice time with the other.

"Carrie asked us about our intentions regarding adoption."

My throat tightened even contemplating my mom having to consider giving me to someone else. Instead of speaking, I nodded as though Ernie had asked a question.

"The three of us thought it was the right thing for everyone. It was important to Carrie that she knew you were taken care of and that you'd always be a part of something."

"She *wanted* you to adopt me?" My voice cracked several times as I croaked that pitiful excuse for a sentence.

"If you were open to it, yes. But Jude, we never had any intention of you changing your last name. You're almost an adult. Heck, you might as well be one now. The paperwork was symbolic."

They'd spent a lot of money on an attorney to put in place something that would essentially be meaningless in six months. "I appreciate what you guys are trying to do. I know you mean well…" It just didn't change anything—not for me.

"We don't need a piece of paper to know we love you. If you don't need it, then there's no hard feelings. But if you want it, for any reason, the offer is there—and you wouldn't have to change your name." He patted my hand across the table and gave me the same smile I saw every time he was proud of me. "Either way, Hensley and I love you. We're grateful we've had so many years with you. The situation was tough, but Carrie made the most of it, and in the process, she gave us two huge blessings."

The fact that Ernie and Hensley considered my mom as great a blessing as they did me tugged on my heartstrings. I realized at that moment that I'd spent most of my time hiding my emotions completely—regardless of what they were or who they were about. My throat hurt from the length of time it had constricted, blocking that dam from breaking. But with Ernie's hand on mine, and my mom's wish hanging in the air, I lost control.

Tears came.

Quietly at first.

The sob that tore through my chest ripped the air apart around me, and I wept for the woman I ached for and loved. "I miss her." I lowered my forehead to the table and covered my head with my arms in a vain attempt to mask my pain.

Ernie didn't make a sound when he relocated to the chair next to mine. I hadn't realized he'd even moved until he put his arm around my back for comfort. Not once did he try to soothe me or convince me to stop crying. When I screamed and growled over the injustice of her death, he didn't try to calm me or hush my rage. What he did do was remain at my side until I was so spent he had to help me up the stairs to my room. There, he put me back in bed, pulled the blankets over me, and turned on my sound dock. As the sounds of the Beatles filled the room, he closed the door and let me spend some much-needed time with my thoughts.

9

PORTIA

BART AND I HAD EXCHANGED SEVERAL TEXT MESSAGES, BUT HE hadn't encourage me to come back to school early in any of them. In some weird, girly way, it hurt, and in another, it didn't bother me. I was grateful to have a couple days with my parents and Jude, even if he wasn't a barrel of laughs to be around. I hadn't gotten all the details, although I heard enough from the top of the stairs to understand that Jude had finally let go of the emotional wall he'd erected around his heart.

I shouldn't have eavesdropped when I heard Ernie retelling Jude's apology to Hensley. It was wrong. I was also a nosy girl who loved the boy my parents were talking about—every teenager in America would have done the same. So, I stood still and listened to their conversation downstairs. Oddly, Ernie wasn't concerned about Jude's breakdown or the fact that he'd stayed holed up in his room all day. In fact, he thought it was the healthiest thing he'd seen from Jude since Carrie died. At that point, I didn't need to hear any more. Regardless of what my tie was to Jude, and whether it would be as siblings or best friends or just fosters, the idea of him in pain hit me with the force of a tidal wave—it threatened to knock the wind out of me.

My hands were full, and I had to take the bags to my room. I didn't bother unloading any of them. Hensley and I had been at the mall the entire day, and we'd bought something from nearly every store we went into. I tossed the purchases on my bed, kicked off my shoes, and quickly changed clothes. If I was certain of anything, it was that it would be a long night.

When I got back to Jude's door, I debated knocking. If I did, then he'd have the option not to let me in. I chose not to ask for permission. I hadn't expected to find him curled into a ball in the center of his mattress in the dark with "Hey Jude" on repeat. The volume on the music was so low I wasn't sure how he even heard it, but once I settled on the bed, my body curled around his, it suddenly seemed to overtake the silence like a symphony.

Jude was under the comforter, which made it difficult to get close enough to him, although at some point, he moved his arm out to lace his fingers with mine and naturally brought us together. There wasn't a need for words, and it certainly wasn't a time for jokes. I couldn't comfort him or make things better—I just wanted him to know I was there. He fell asleep at some point, clutching my hand as though his life depended on his hold. I lay there and awkwardly ran my free hand through the top of his hair and even tried counting the freckles on the back of his neck, wondering how I could possibly help him through any of this. And just as I closed my eyes, but right before I drifted off, I resigned myself to finding something to lift his spirits.

THE NEXT MORNING, I POPPED UP BEFORE THE SUN. JUDE'S DEATH grip had relaxed enough during the night to allow me to find freedom. Quietly, I opened the door and peered into the hall. Once I was certain it was safe and I hadn't been seen sneaking out of Jude's room, I raced through a shower, dried my hair, and got dressed, and then flew downstairs.

One of the two had to be around somewhere. "Mom? Dad?" It was far too early for either of them to have gone anywhere on a Sunday. "Mom?" If I didn't want to wake the dead, I probably should keep my voice down, but I was a woman on a mission.

"Sweetheart, what are you hollering about?" Hensley wiped her hands on a dishtowel and turned to the fridge.

I didn't want to miss her omelets, but I wasn't sure how long Jude would hang around after everything that had happened yesterday. I needed the car, and more importantly, I needed him home when I got back.

"Where are my car keys?"

"Probably on the hook in the laundry room. Why? Where are you going? You haven't even had breakfast."

"I need to run an errand."

She pointed to the bar stool. "Sit. You can go after you eat."

I wasn't sure when she'd gotten all assertive, but today wasn't the day for her to display a new personality trait. "Mom, I need to go."

"It won't take you ten minutes to eat. Get yourself something to drink."

"Sit, fetch… If you tell me to heel or roll over, I'm out of here. I'm starting to feel like a dog."

"Where are you going?"

I quirked my brow, and she waved me off with a whisk. Seriously, I couldn't win. "To the fridge to get a drink."

She glanced at me while scrambling eggs in a bowl. "You know what I meant. Your errand. What's so important?"

I'd always loved watching her cook. Somehow, she made it look fun, although it never was when I tried it. Food seemed to dance for her, the eggs swam in the bowl, the cheese mingled with the green peppers and onions. When she poured the mixture into the hot skillet, the edges rounded perfectly like a ballet dancer curving her spine. Even the chunks of ham appeared to have assigned spots just before she flipped the side on top of itself, creating the fluffiest, tastiest omelet ever made—every single time.

"Portia?"

"Huh?" I'd gotten lost in the egg performance. "Oh, um, just across town."

"That doesn't tell me much."

It was a small town; across was only about four miles. There weren't many places *to* go. "A bookstore and a bakery."

Hensley's metal spatula clanged when it hit the counter. "Portia…do you think that's a good idea? Jude had a pretty rough day yesterday."

"That's exactly why it's a good idea, Mom. He finally acknowledged—with more than two words—that he misses Carrie. He needs to see that he can still have pieces of her and still enjoy her without her physically being here."

"I don't know, sweetheart. I think you're playing with fire."

"He might not realize it right away, but I think with a little time, he'll appreciate the gesture. And hopefully, he'll start doing it for himself."

She shook her head, still not convinced I was right. "If anyone can get away with it, that would be you. Just don't be surprised if it doesn't go as well as you'd hoped. Jude's in a vulnerable place right now—it could send him over the edge."

"Would that be so bad? If he doesn't hit the bottom of this pit, he can't start to come back up."

She scrunched her nose and made some funny duck face to illustrate her disapproval. "I get the sentiment. Nevertheless, it might be a little ill-timed."

"Or perfectly timed. We won't know until I try."

"Be careful, Portia. Remember, you're not cheering him up because he had a bad day at school. He's yet to deal with Carrie's passing. He's just started to process that grief. Take it from me, based on the whole adoption snafu, meddling might not be well received."

I swear. This woman was bound and determined to convince me not to get in the car. I'd think after ten years she'd know that once I made up my mind to do something, nothing short of being mowed over by a bus going eight-four miles per hour would stop me.

An hour later, I sat with Jude in the center of his bed with forks in our hands. And together, Jude and I consumed an entire lemon pie in one sitting, while he thumbed through the books I'd picked out at The Blistered Pear. Lemon pie and old novels—with Jude. I studied his face with each bite he took, watched with undivided attention when he'd sing the lyrics to one of his favorite Beatles songs, and stared in awe as he skimmed the used novels. I couldn't remember the last time I'd seen him so content...nor when he started to look more like an adult than the kid I grew up with.

His neck had thickened, and he'd put on some muscle since he'd started his senior year. His brown eyes were still just as sad, but his features had sharpened—not that he'd ever had any baby fat. Or maybe that was it—where he'd been skin and bones since the day we'd met, he now appeared bulkier, although still fairly lanky. But his freckles and hair were, by far, his most unique features—and definitely my favorite...

And both had gotten better with age.

———

I climbed into the passenger seat of Bart's Beamer as my family looked on from the front porch. Ernie and Hensley waved, but Jude stood silently with his arms crossed. His eyes never drifted from mine. I hated to leave him, knowing how much pain he was in. I worried that he'd shut back down instead of processing what had bubbled to the surface and boiled over.

As I buckled my seatbelt, I gave the three of them a forced smile and mouthed "goodbye" before I faced Bart. "You know, I could have gotten a ride to school. You didn't have to drive all the way back out here. Not that I mind, I just don't want to take advantage of you." I tried to take his hand to affectionately show my appreciation, but just when I reached out, he moved it to shift gears.

He focused on the road and the traffic in front of us. "That's what friends do, right?" There wasn't a hint of tension in his voice, but the use of the word "friend" sent me into high alert.

"Uhh, yeah. Friends." I tried to laugh it off, and instead, a bark came out that I was clearly uncomfortable with.

After he ran through the gears on the highway, he settled back into his seat and took my hand. "I wanted to pick you up so we could talk, Portia."

That couldn't be good. Even with my limited dating knowledge, I was well versed in the hidden meaning behind "talking." It might be easier for him to say what was on his mind while holding my hand, but it was easier for me to be defensive with my arms crossed and my body angled toward him. I withheld the glare that itched to take over my eyes while I waited.

"Please don't be like that. You haven't even heard what I have to say." His voice was gentle and his touch soft when he placed his hand on my knee. Clearly, whatever his message, he needed to maintain some form of contact to deliver it.

"I'm listening." Although I didn't uncross my arms.

"I've spent most of the weekend thinking about Friday night."

My shoulders fell, as did my arms. I took his hand in mine, ready to launch into an apology. "I had no idea things were going to go that way, Bart. I thought it was going to be a celebration."

"I know, Portia. I don't think you intentionally brought me to your parents' house to witness anything else. But that's not what I'm referring to."

I straightened my spine and squared my shoulders. "What are you talking about then?"

"The way you look at him."

"Look at *who*?" I blanched and nearly hit my head on the window behind me.

"Jude." Bart glanced my direction, knowing he'd struck a nerve. "Remember when we talked about your parents wanting to adopt him and I asked you why it bothered you?"

"Of course, I remember."

"I don't think you were very honest with yourself about why you didn't want him to be a part of your family."

I didn't bother hiding the offense I'd taken at his words. "What are you trying to say?"

"I'm saying that I can't imagine the emotional warpath the two of you have had to navigate since you were kids. It would be perfectly logical for you to have fallen for him along the way because the two of you share something no one else will ever understand."

I tried to dismiss his words, even though my heart ached to acknowledge every last one. "Most foster kids are that way, Bart."

"Maybe, but that doesn't make it any less true. I saw your face when he said no, and it wasn't disappointment—you were relieved. And when he left the house, you were on him like white on rice. Your body language in the driveway, the way your voice cracked, I don't know how else to make you see what I saw."

He didn't have to draw me a picture. I just hated that I'd been so obvious that he'd noticed it. And it sucked to know he'd witnessed it when I was in a relationship with him.

"I'm not trying to make you mad. I love being your friend, and I don't want that to change. I just can't be in a relationship with a girl who's in love with someone else…even if she desperately wants to love me."

I closed my eyes to absorb the weight of his words. "That's all kinds of messed up," I mumbled.

He squeezed my knee, but I didn't open my eyes to see him

when he spoke. "Maybe I'm way off base. Either way, I'm clouding a picture that needs to be clear. And until you can say with a hundred percent certainty that Jude isn't who you want to be with, it's not fair to either of us to pretend we're together."

My lids rose slowly as tears filled my eyes. "So, you're breaking up with me?"

"Come on, Portia. We spend all of our free time together, yet other than holding hands and kissing, nothing about our relationship is any different than it was prior to sticking a label on it."

"That's not fair. I told you I wanted to take things slow after everything that happened with Chet." It was true. I needed to believe Bart was with me because he cared about me and not because he thought I would be an easy lay.

"I'm not talking about the physical part of our relationship; I'm talking about our connection. I'd wait however long you needed to move forward with the affection. It's *us* that isn't getting any deeper. We're great friends, and I don't want that to stop."

"I guess I don't know the difference. I tell you everything. I'm just not that interesting." I chuckled under my breath as though it were funny—it wasn't, and I was well aware of what he meant. That connection I shared with Jude should be withheld for the guy I dated...not my pseudo-brother.

His thumb stroked my knee, and he offered me a sincere expression. "I think if you allow yourself to experience what you really feel for Jude, versus what you do for me, the difference will be evident."

I felt totally defeated. I wanted to unload and tell him the truth. I needed someone to confide in, yet I couldn't bear the thought of his being repulsed by my desire or the relationship I wish I had with a boy I'd grown up with.

"You can talk to me about this, too." It was as if he read my mind. "I imagine you'd be pretty freaked out, if you've actually acknowledged it...which I think you have."

I turned to face the road, effectively removing his hand from my leg, and closed my eyes again. This time, I prayed the miles would tick by faster and we'd be at the school before I had to answer any questions or admit to anything that might be held against me. Yet even with my eyes closed, a tear ran down my cheek. I didn't swipe at it to prevent drawing attention to it, although Bart saw it all the same.

"I'm right here. All you have to do is open up. I'm not going to judge you or repeat anything you say."

We'd only known each other for a handful of months, yet Bart was by far my best friend on campus, even more so than Jet. I believed him. I trusted him. I also needed him.

"It's not that easy."

"Sure it is. Even if you haven't sorted through it, I can help you if you'll just talk."

"Jude isn't an option. He never will be."

"Why not?"

I inhaled deeply and exhaled as I leaned back into the seat. We weren't even halfway back to the school. As much as I didn't want to get into this, another part of me was desperate to. "I think my relationship with Jude is different, even more than most foster kids."

"How so?"

"I could be wrong, but I don't believe there are a ton of moms out there who go to the state looking for help with their children. Carrie was alone when she got diagnosed with cancer, so she did some kind of voluntary program. It was never supposed to be permanent." I chastised myself thinking about what I'd just said. "No, fostering is never supposed to be permanent. The hope is that all kids will go back to rehabilitated parents—it just doesn't work out like that. Anyway, Jude was at our house for several months at a time, but then he'd be at his house for a couple of years when she was in remission. He'd spend the weekend with us or go on vacation with us, and we went to his birthday parties and attended recitals at school. But Jude was my best friend, not my brother. He just happened to be the only friend I got to spend the night with and have over on holidays."

"That makes sense. If he was always in your home, I can see how the lines wouldn't be so clearly defined."

"Exactly. In my parents' eyes, he was the son they always wanted, and they treated him that way. There is zero difference between me and Jude in that respect. They just saw us both as kids. Not to mention the age difference—I mean it's only a year, but he's in high school, and I'm in college. And his mom passed away—that adds a whole other dimension to this messed-up situation... I don't know when it happened, Bart."

"When what happened?"

"My feelings changed. Or I recognized them for what they are."

"So, you admit there's something there?"

I shrugged. "It doesn't matter whether there is or not. It would destroy my parents. They made a promise to Jude's mom to take care of him as if he were their child. I don't think that meant allowing him to have some twisted relationship with their adopted daughter."

"Maybe that's exactly what it meant. If I see it, surely your parents do too."

I shook my head. "Oh, no. They absolutely do not. If they did, they certainly wouldn't have us share a room on vacations—"

"You and Jude sleep together? Alone?" Shock was written all over his face and laced in his words. It was funny that nothing else he'd heard garnered a reaction, yet somehow, the thought of us sharing a hotel room riled him.

I couldn't help the giggle that escaped. "Not the way you're suggesting. What are they going to do, put us in sleeping bags on the floor? You have siblings. When your family goes on vacation, do you share a room with your brother and sister?"

"Yes, but I'm their brother."

"My point exactly. The Shaws see Jude and me the way your parents do you and your brother and sister. It may be naïve, but that's how it is. Your parents don't worry about any of you doing anything inappropriate, and neither do mine. They'd never suspect anything odd was going on, because it never has. We've never given them any reason to even consider it."

Bart seemed to ponder my point. I just wasn't sure he believed it.

I sighed. I wanted him to understand our childhoods weren't filled with perversion. My parents hadn't been blind because nothing existed. "Jude and I have shared a bed for years and nothing has ever happened. Ernie and Hensley never knew about it, but when we first went to the Shaws' house, both of us had nightmares. I think it's pretty common when you're shipped off to an unfamiliar place with unknown people who want to play house. Anyway, I got into the habit of sneaking into his room in the middle of the night when I had a bad dream or I heard him have one. We were eight and nine years old—it was innocent, I assure you. It was comforting to have someone's hand to hold, but I always snuck back out before the sun came up."

Bart's features had relaxed, and he didn't appear quite so tense thinking Jude and I had been sleeping together since we were children. "When did you stop?"

"Stop what?"

"Sneaking in and out of his room at night?"

Full disclosure was overrated, but I gave it a shot. I was already in this neck deep. I'd either figure out how to swim or start to drown. "I haven't."

His eyes went wide.

"Don't look at me like that." Shock, pity, possibly disgust—I didn't like the way any of those made me feel. "When it started, Jude was the only other person in the world who I thought knew what I was going through. Turned out, our situations were vastly different. His mother was nothing like mine, but by the time Jude let me in on that secret, the bond—and the habit—had already formed."

I waited for Bart to say something. Anything would have been nice. He'd gone from openminded to closemouthed in minutes.

"The point of this whole trip down memory lane was to show you that Ernie and Hensley absolutely see us as siblings—they call us brother and sister. They treat us that way. They definitely wouldn't understand. I can't imagine how mortified my mom would be if she even had an inkling."

"Maybe she'd be more understanding than you think." Bart must have the most amazing parents to ever walked the face of the earth. Either that, or he was terribly naïve...even more so than I was.

"I'd never risk it. They've done too much for me to chance hurting them that way. And then what if it didn't work out? Can you imagine what a nightmare holidays would be?"

"So, Jude could be your soulmate—"

"You're getting awfully deep here for a dude who just broke up with his girlfriend." It took a lot of effort to make this light.

"Hush," he said, playfully. "Hear me out. He could be *the one*, and you'd walk away from that to keep from upsetting your mom and dad?"

I shrugged. "Well, yeah." It wasn't what I wanted to do, and I'd hate myself for having to do it. But Ernie and Hensley had sacrificed more for me than I'd ever be able to repay. They'd always made sure I was their top priority. And I'd do the same.

"That's the dumbest thing I've ever heard."

I angled toward him to find him shaking his head while he watched the road. "Well, what would you do?"

"I'd figure out where my head was at first. Then I'd figure out where Jude's was. And if we were in the same place, I'd hope the two of us could sit down with our parents to discuss it."

I couldn't stop the laughter that poured from my mouth. "Did you hear what you just said?" It wasn't as funny as I made it out to be; nevertheless, releasing it lifted an enormous weight from my shoulders.

"What?"

"The two of us can sit down with our *parents* to discuss having sexual feelings toward each other."

He grimaced and then fell into fits of giggles with me—not that guys giggled. "Okay, maybe I see a little bit of your point. Either way, I think you have to be honest with yourself before you worry about anyone else."

Bart parked on campus, and I wondered where the second half of the trip had gone. It seemed as though we'd flown here in fifteen minutes instead of the hour it actually took to drive. He lifted the emergency brake, although neither of us made a move to get out. We both stared straight ahead. I didn't want to even twitch for fear that when I did, everything would change and I'd be lost and alone.

"So, this is it for us?" I asked hesitantly.

The right side of his mouth tipped up in a half grin when I faced him. "Hardly. We're just getting started. I don't want anything between us to be different. I just want you to be open to where you're meant to be."

"We'll still hang out?" I feared his answer, and worse, I worried that even if he said the words I wanted to hear, that tomorrow I'd realize they'd been just that—words.

"Jude isn't here. Regardless of how you feel about him or whether or not you're with him—you can still have friends. So, we just won't hold hands or kiss anymore." He shrugged as though it weren't a big deal. "I still need someone to do my homework with and a buddy in the cafeteria."

I hated the way that sounded. If I couldn't have Jude, Bart would have been the next best thing—he was nothing short of fantastic. It was selfish as hell even in my thoughts. He was an amazing guy and hot as sin. He just wasn't the guy for me, and pretending he was the right one wasn't fair to either of us. So, I had to hold fast to his words and pray that nothing between us changed.

I stuck my pinky out in some weird ritual of hope. "Promise?"

Bart hooked his with mine and then kissed them both to seal the deal. "Promise."

"BART'S GOING HOME FOR CHRISTMAS. IT WILL JUST BE ME THIS weekend. Sorry to disappoint you."

"I assure you, I'm not disappointed that your boytoy isn't joining us for the holiday." Jude huffed on the other end of the phone. "I assumed that's what couples did—spent time off together. It suits me just fine to have you home by yourself. Do you want me to pick you up from school?"

I hadn't been home since Thanksgiving, and I'd only stayed Thursday and Friday before racing back to campus. "Yeah. I hate that you'll have to drive all that way just to turn around and drive home, but everyone is leaving, and no one is going that direction."

"I don't mind. I'll just crank up the radio and sing at the top of my lungs for an hour. That way I won't feel cheated when you get in the car and put on your angry-girl crap."

"I don't listen to crap."

Jude laughed on the other end of the phone. "But you admit they're angry girls?"

"Maybe."

"I gotta go. Hensley's hollering for me to come to dinner. I'll text you when I leave on Tuesday and head in that direction."

"Sounds good."

I hung up and set my phone on the table, not realizing I had an audience. Bart sat next to me, and I wasn't sure how much of the conversation he'd heard...until he put his tray down and started talking.

"At what point are you going to tell him that we aren't dating?"

"At the same time you decide to stop being the voice of reason." I took a large bite of my turkey sub. It was dry without mayo and needed something to keep it from sticking to the roof of my mouth.

"Why don't you want him to know?"

I swallowed hard, forcing the clump of bread down my throat to answer. "I'm not lying to him and telling him we've gone out on dates or hooked up. He happens to call when we're together, and he makes assumptions."

"Yeah, because the last he knew, we were, in fact, dating. Come on, Portia. We talked about this, and you'd agreed to consider your feelings."

"I have considered them. And I'm still in the same place I was when we talked about this weeks ago. Nothing about the situation has changed. He's still in high school, he's still not dealing with his grief, and my parents are still his legal guardians." Stuffing my face gave me something to do besides address the heart of the matter.

Bart slammed his fist on the table, and I nearly choked on the food in my mouth. "I'm not going to let you use me as a scapegoat."

"Meaning what? You're not going to be my friend if I don't tell Jude that we aren't dating anymore?"

He ran his hand through his hair and then opened his little carton of milk. I thought it was cute that he always got the little boxes instead of the bottles, and it was always white, never chocolate—like his mom might find out and ground him. The smirk on my face didn't endear me to him.

"Stop that."

"What?" I shrugged.

"You know I can't be mad when you make that face." He pointed at my lips and swirled his finger in the air just in case I wasn't sure what he meant.

"I'll tell him. I just need to do this in my time."

"This weekend?"

"If it comes up."

"Portia…"

"Bart…" I swear, so much of our relationship was similar to mine and Jude's. I hoped that when he found a girlfriend that he didn't ditch me in favor of her. I'd miss hanging out with him.

"Fine. I'll tell him. I just didn't want to do it over the phone, and Thanksgiving wasn't the right time. As soon as I tell him, I'm going to have to deal with the ki—" I stopped, catching myself before I spilled my secret, although unfortunately, not fast enough.

"With what?" His eyes narrowed as his head tilted in consideration. "What will you have to deal with?"

I tried to wave the thought away, but Bart was a damn dog with a bone—he wasn't letting go.

"You're so nosy."

"And you've been keeping something from me. Spill it."

I set my sub on my tray, took a swig of my Diet Coke, and wished I could wash away the words before I had to share them. Technically, I could refuse, and Bart would let it go, but then I'd be hiding something, and he'd be hurt that I didn't trust him to share it. Boys sucked.

"Remember the day you picked me up from my parents' house?" I acted like it had been so long ago he might have forgotten, when in reality, it was only eight or nine weeks—ten at most.

"The day we talked about the adoption stuff?"

"Yeah"—my lids fluttered, and I took a deep breath —"that one."

"What about it?"

"I might have left out a detail about why I fled so early that morning."

He sucked his teeth before folding his hands in his lap, facing me to wait for more.

"Do you have to look at me that way?"

Bart didn't respond. He just raised his brows and waited. Asshat.

I could draw this out and make it into more than it had to be, or I could spit out the words and pretend it meant nothing. I opted for the latter. "Jude kissed me the night before."

In the most dramatic display of disbelief that Bart could possibly pull off, his chin dropped, mouth parted, and he let out an animated, "Huh." Then he waited to hear more, but I didn't have anything else to say. "And you're *just now* telling me this?"

"It wasn't a big deal."

"I'm going to pretend you didn't say that."

"It wasn't," I lied. "Okay, so maybe it was a little important."

"Portia, it's monumental. That only confirms that he holds you in the same regard you do him. Why have you kept that a secret in all the times we've discussed this?"

I stared at my partially eaten sandwich and wondered if I shoved the remaining half in my mouth and tried to talk around it if that would get me out of answering. Somehow, I didn't think so. Bart would politely wait for me to swallow before he continued his interrogation.

"Or that he's a horny guy who saw an opportunity and took it," I said around a glob of bread.

"You don't believe that."

My chest rose with the deep breath I took. "It was right after all that stuff happened with Chet. I didn't know what to believe. I'd never had anyone show any interest in me, and then all of a sudden, two people had. Chet's wasn't genuine, and I didn't know how to process Jude's."

"You *have* to know Jude and Chet are not the same person."

I did know that. And I was thankful that Chet had slithered away into the night and left me alone. He'd even managed to switch partners in chem lab without making a fuss over it. I wanted to believe he'd just had a lapse in judgment, but the fact that he had steered clear of Bart, Todd, and Jet told me that wasn't the case—he truly was a goon. Jude was nothing like him. I didn't want to believe it meant anything to Jude because that would force me to acknowledge that everything Bart had tried to cram into my head over the last few weeks might have some validity.

Deflecting occasionally worked. "Why is this so important to you, Bart?"

"Because you're one of my best friends, and I want you to be happy. You've tried to convince me that this was one-sided, or that your parents would have issues with it. And the truth is, it's not and you don't know that."

"Maybe it's not as one-sided as I make it out to be. I don't know. I haven't given Jude the opportunity to tell me any differently because I still don't believe it's a viable option, given our situation."

"I can't argue that. All I can tell you is that you need to come clean with him—at the very least, tell him we aren't together. See where that takes the conversation." Bart chugged his little carton of milk and then folded the cardboard opening together. He was such a tidy eater.

"He's picking me up for Christmas break. We'll have plenty of time to talk. Happy?"

Bart slid his arm around my back and pulled me in for a side hug. "Happy."

10

JUDE

"WHERE ARE YOU OFF TO?" PORTIA ACTED LIKE MY GOING OUT ON a Friday night was peculiar. A year ago, it would have been; this year, not so much.

"To Jamison Hart's house for a party." I stared in the bathroom mirror while Portia watched me from the doorway inside my bedroom.

"You should go with him, sweetheart. You don't want to sit here all night with your dad and me."

I hadn't realized Hensley had joined us. I poked my head past Portia to see what my foster mother was doing, only to find her putting away laundry and smoothing out the wrinkles on my bed.

"It's okay. I don't want to intrude."

"Nonsense. I'm sure Jude would love to have you go with him. Isn't that right, Jude?" Hensley hadn't bothered to pick up her head to look our direction. She just talked as she worked her way around my room.

I shrugged when I faced Portia. "Yeah, why not? You can go if you want."

"Wow, with that welcome invitation, how could I resist?" She folded her arms over her chest.

Playfully, I swatted at her elbow as I ran a brush through my hair. "I didn't mean it that way. I assumed you wouldn't want to hang out with a bunch of high schoolers. That's all. Carson and Ethan are going, and you know the rest of the student body." I tried to play it off, hoping she wouldn't tag along. It wasn't that I didn't want to hang out with her, I just knew this wasn't her cup of tea.

Portia should have been aware of that as well. She was never into parties around town, and she certainly didn't hang out with the likes of Jamison. The mere mention of his name should have sent up warning flags that would have her running in the opposite direction. Yet somehow, Portia missed the memo.

"Yeah, okay. If you don't care, I'll tag along."

I managed to keep the disappointment from my face and averted my gaze so she didn't see it in my eyes. I wanted to hang out with her—I just didn't want to do it with an audience. I wasn't sure Ethan and Carson could keep their mouths shut, much less behave.

"I'm leaving in about thirty minutes." That was my signal to her to go put on something she wanted to be seen in.

Forty-two minutes later, I got behind the wheel of Portia's car. It was odd to have her in it. I'd been using it since she had left for school, expecting to tote her back and forth between home and the campus, yet other than delivering her the first day and picking her up for Christmas break, I hadn't done anything other than play around in it. As soon as I cranked the ignition, she acted like her ears bled from the music coming through the speakers.

"Oh my God, Jude. What is this crap?" She wailed as though she were in pain...a rather melodramatic performance, I might add.

"The local radio station."

In seconds, she had her phone synced and one of her playlists filled the car. Portia moved in the passenger seat as I drove down the street to pick up my friends. Both of whom were shocked to see her when they piled in the back.

"Hiya, P." Ethan's eyes were glassy and his speech slow.

Either Portia didn't notice, or college had lessened her need to bitch about the effects of marijuana. "Hi, Ethan...Carson."

Carson didn't speak. Instead, he lifted his head to acknowledge her as he slid across the upholstery. I couldn't be certain, but something seemed off with him. Asking in front of our unexpected guest wouldn't prove fruitful, so I kept my mouth shut and waited to see how things played out.

"To what do we owe the pleasure of your company, Portia? I'm surprised you'd want to come to this kind of thing." Ethan didn't even try to hide his drug use as he rolled a joint in the back seat.

I didn't have a clue how he did it. It was dark outside—and in the car—yet when I looked over my shoulder to back out, there in his lap was a paper and broken buds. Tempted to tell him to put that shit up, I almost barked at him, but I bit my tongue at the last minute. Portia hadn't said anything, and I really didn't care except for her well-known opposition. It was no secret Ethan and Carson were potheads, so maybe it didn't bother her as long as she didn't think it was me.

"Nothing better to do. You know that crap fries your brain, right?" So, she hadn't missed it.

"I can do without a few brain cells." Ethan would still be insanely smart if he killed off half his brain. "Although, I could use some help in the social department."

"So, you think if you kill off working brain cells it will make fitting in easier because the masses are dumb?" Portia had turned around in her seat to watch him, and her shoulders shook as she laughed at his stupidity.

"Something like that."

I couldn't see him or Carson with them both behind me, and it being dark in the car made the rearview mirror useless for catching a glimpse. I'd heard Ethan's theory several times before, and thus far, it was working out for him. Actually, for all three of us. I didn't know if people thought we were cooler because we smoked pot—*I* didn't think it made us cooler. It was just easier to talk to people who otherwise seemed out of reach or off-limits when we were sober. Everyone in the school knew each other—we'd all grown up together—but somehow, we'd gone from social pariah to middle wrung on the high school ladder in just a few short months. I couldn't confirm that it was the pot or the fact that we now actually spoke to other students. All I could say with any certainty was that other kids talked to us in the halls, and we no longer seemed invisible.

"Carson, you're awfully quiet tonight. Are you okay?" Portia asked.

I wanted nothing more than to pull the car over and stare at her while she spoke. Her voice was filled with concern, and it was the same voice that came to me in the middle of the night—the one of comfort…it was the palest of all her pinks.

"Yeah, I'm fine." His answer was short and to the point, which for Carson meant something had ticked him off.

Portia faced forward with a plop. Thankfully, we didn't have far to go. I wasn't sure I could stand all the excitement oozing from the vehicle. When we arrived at Jamison's house, the place was busy, although not as bad as I had expected. Typically, his parties were pretty pumping, and everyone in school attended—this appeared to be all upperclassmen.

The four of us had no sooner walked in than Chad Hartman appeared with a condescending smirk on his face and a gleam in his eyes. If he thought he was going after Portia, he had another thing coming. He scanned her from nose to toes and back, tsked his tongue, shook his head, and wisely strolled off. It wasn't long after that a girl caught Portia's attention, and she left us in favor of friends.

"Thank God." Carson let out a sigh loud enough to be heard over the music. "I thought we were going to have a babysitter all night." He backhanded me across the chest. "I love your sister, but she can be a real buzzkill."

"She's not my sister."

"Whatever, same sentiment." Carson walked past Ethan and me to find a nook he'd camp out in for the evening. The only time he'd get up would be to get a drink and take a leak. The odd thing was, people would flock to his little corner. Somehow, in the last couple of months, he'd become cool amongst the outcasts.

I followed behind Ethan as he trailed Carson. There were a handful of people here I didn't recognize, which was always the case at Jamison's. Even though there was only one high school in the county, he had friends that lived a town over. I'd never bothered to learn any of their names since they'd never shown the slightest bit of interest in us. I was pretty good about keeping to myself. Even though Carson and Ethan had found their footing in the social world, I still preferred to keep my head down.

I'd never figured out how Jamison got away with having these gatherings. I'd asked him several times if his parents smoked, and he'd always told me no. They were social drinkers, but that was the extent of their deviance. Yet when I asked how they didn't know people spent the weekend smoking pot in their living room, he'd just shrug and flip his hair out of his face. Jamison was perpetually high. I couldn't remember the last time I'd seen him when his eyes weren't glassy and bloodshot —maybe his parents gave up and would rather know he's home safe than on the streets. They sure as hell left him home alone often enough.

Ethan lit the joint he'd rolled in the car, and as he passed it to Carson, I searched for any sign of Portia.

"She's out back." Carson pointed toward the door. "You're safe." And then he handed me the joint.

I wasn't anywhere near the avid smoker Ethan and Carson were. In fact, I typically only smoked on the weekends...well, Thursday through Sunday because Fridays at school didn't count. And I never smoked and then went home and called Portia. As far as she knew, I'd kept my promise not to dabble anymore. I still held firm to the notion that what she didn't know wouldn't hurt her.

Not long after we'd found our spot for the night, Jamison joined us, snatching the joint from Carson's hand. He took a long drag with the paper pinched between his fingers, and simultaneously stuck his fist into the middle of our little circle. I was the only one of the four of us still sober, although it wouldn't take long for the effects to kick in. My eyes were glued to his hand, and one by one his fingers uncurled until he exposed a handful of pills in his palm. They were neon pink and roughly the size of an aspirin, but that was about all I could make out from my vantage point.

Jamison jerked his bangs out of his eyes, and I wanted to scream at him to get a damn haircut, but I kept my mouth shut. He waved his hand around, enticing us to reach out and take whatever candy he offered. He passed the smoke to Ethan, who took it and one of the pills, then Carson reached out, Jamison grabbed one, and his hand swung toward me. All three sets of eyes watched and waited for me to pick up the pink tablet.

"Your sister won't know, man. Just pop it and have fun. She's occupied with the Spice Girls on the deck." Jamison nudged his head in the direction of the back porch as though I didn't know where the deck was.

"She's not my sister. And who the hell are the Spice Girls?" The band reference wasn't lost on me; I just didn't have a clue who in our school fit that bill.

Jamison coughed into his elbow and smiled as he said, "Ginger Peterson and her crew." He thought he was funny.

Ginger was the only one who had a "spice" name, so I guessed the rest of her friends got dubbed with the heinous nickname by association. Portia included. I stared at the door, wondering just how stupid I could be. It took little convincing by Ethan, Carson, and Jamison to get me to swallow whatever they'd just given me. It wasn't until after I washed it down with a bottle of water that I bothered to ask any questions.

"What was that?"

"*E*." Jamison was now upside down on the couch with his back on the seat, and his legs thrown over the top. His hair dangled to the floor, and his face was an odd shade of red—flushed from hanging in a precarious position.

I stopped myself from choking on the revelation, and I had to physically restrain myself from racing to the bathroom to induce vomiting. I had no idea what the hell I was thinking taking drugs from Jamison without question. "What's it do?"

"In about thirty minutes, you'll love the world and crave human contact." Jamison never picked his head up to face me when he talked, so it seemed like he spoke to the wall across the room.

"How the hell am I supposed to keep Portia from knowing I took this shit?" Probably a thought I should have considered three minutes earlier.

Ethan piped up and waved off my concern. "Dude, she won't know. She'll just think you're in a good mood."

Carson snorted with laughter. Snorted. Like a chick. "Except that Jude's about as anti-affectionate as Portia is anti-drug. Maybe she'll miss the fact that your pupils are the size of your iris, the cold sweats, and your desire to be petted like a dog. I mean, it's possible she left her brain at home."

I groaned, worried about just how bad this would get. But thirty minutes later, it wouldn't have mattered if Portia had shown up with Ernie, Hensley, and Jesus himself in tow. I was lighter than air, had a permanent grin on my face, and felt perfectly warm inside. I'd just thought pot gave the world a smile. It was nothing compared to the euphoria ecstasy left me with. A halo of light around everything I looked at, and when Carson brushed up against me, I almost let out a satisfied groan that might have sounded a bit orgasmic.

When I trusted myself enough to speak without my voice cracking, I asked, "How long does this last?" My words were slow, and the sentence seemed to stop time because it took so long to say.

Jamison didn't answer, and I wondered how long he could let blood flow to his head before he did permanent damage. Ethan stared at Carson as though he held all the answers. So, I too turned my attention toward Carson, raised my brows, and leaned forward to wait on his response. It took monumental effort as heavy as my body felt, but it was a good weight—solid. Grounded and stable.

Carson shrugged and took a sip of water. "I don't know...six or seven hours, maybe eight if it's good."

I pulled my phone from my pocket to check the time and nearly fell over when I realized I might still be rolling tomorrow morning when Ernie and Hensley got up. I didn't know where the time went or if he meant seven hours from now or seven hours from when we took it, and I didn't want to be the paranoid loser who asked a bunch of questions.

"Jude, man, your eyes look like pools."

Ethan was a moron. My eyes were brown, so I wasn't sure what he was used to swimming in.

"They're all glassy and watery." He narrowed his focus as he inched forward to get a closer look. "Are you about to cry?"

I pushed him back into his own space with my hand against his sternum. "No, but I am wondering how the hell any of us are going to get home in this condition."

"Easy, Portia can drive." Stupid hit Ethan at the speed of light anytime he got near pot, much less smoked it.

I smacked him hard against the chest, and he flinched at the blow. "What happened to her not knowing, dumbass? How the hell am I going to get this past her? She's going to blow a gasket."

About that time, Melanie Pratt dropped down onto the couch between Jamison and me. I'd known her most of my life. She was nice enough, kind of a drifter. Melanie had friends in every social circle, which meant she didn't belong to one and was accepted in them all. It was no secret she had an affinity for Jamison, although over the last few weeks I'd started to believe her interest was more in his stash of recreational substances than the man himself. Tonight seemed to be no different. But one look at her, and I knew there was no chance of my hiding from Portia. If I looked half as blitzed as Melanie did, I might as well have a sign with a flashing arrow pointing at me.

Just as I was about to comment, Melanie dropped one hand on my wrist and one on Jamison's. Each one of her nails lightly stroked the skin on my arm with waves of pleasure radiating from each. I was in heaven, and there was nothing that could drag me out of this nirvana. I closed my eyes as I moved my hand to her thigh and reciprocated. I lost myself in the motion—her hand, my hand—it didn't matter. It might have been thirty minutes or four hours. I didn't have a clue, nor did I care.

Until a familiar hand landed on my shoulder. My head rested on the back of the couch, and my eyes were still closed when she squeezed her fingers. "Do both sides." I moaned. A massage from Portia would be perfect right now.

She swatted at my arm. "You're out of your mind. Come on. It's late. We need to get home."

I still hadn't bothered to lift my eyelids and kept hoping she'd put her hands back on me—anywhere. My head rolled from side to side, and Melanie's fingers continued their magic. The last thing I wanted to do was get in a car and drive home.

Portia shook my shoulder as if she thought I might be asleep. "Come on, Jude. It's almost three. I don't want Mom and Dad to worry."

Lazily, I pried my lids apart to stare at the most beautiful girl I'd ever known. Only the instant she made eye contact, her gorgeous, green eyes disappeared behind narrow slits, and her expression morphed from angel to shrew.

"Jude Thomas! What the hell are you on?"

And that was my cue to get out of Dodge before Portia made a bigger scene. The atmosphere was rather calm, the music had been lowered, and people were relaxed. I didn't need her nagging, much less shrieking at me in front of the entire senior class.

I leaned forward and lost contact with Melanie's magic fingers. Ethan and Carson were kicked back with their feet propped up, and I couldn't tell if Jamison was even still breathing—I assumed he'd have gotten cold to the touch if he wasn't, and Melanie would have noticed.

"Seriously, Jude. Answer me."

I didn't have to look to know Portia had her hands on her hips and her expression hadn't changed. I chose to ignore her in favor of finding some place a little less public to be humiliated. I kicked Ethan and Carson—their feet, not them—to get their attention.

"Are you two coming?"

Portia continued to talk behind me, though I'd tuned her out. And both of my friends made eye contact with her and then quickly shook their heads.

"We'll find another way home." Carson's eyes went wide, and he stretched his lips across his teeth in some strange expression that told me he wished I could hide.

"Cowards," I muttered.

"I'd like to see graduation. I'm not sure how well you're going to fare when you leave." Ethan quirked his brow and then his head in Portia's direction. I still refused to turn around.

"Whatever. I'll see you guys later." I stepped over Melanie's legs without falling and made my way out. I could sense Portia on my heels, and I'd swear her breath hit my skin every time she exhaled, which seemed to be a lot. At least she'd quit bitching once I started moving out of the house.

Until the front door closed behind her and we were alone in the driveway.

"Seriously, Jude. I want an answer."

I needed to give her the keys so she could drive, yet in order to do that, I had to acknowledge that she had spoken to me, which would then require me to answer her, which I wasn't ready to do. Her fingers wrapped around my elbow, and she spun me toward her as I pulled the ring out of my pocket.

"Can you *not* make a big deal out of this? Please?"

She didn't let go of my arm, although she did take the keys, and her glare didn't soften when she made eye contact. "Are you kidding me with this shit? You promised me you weren't going to do any of this anymore."

I stared over the top of her head toward the house, wondering just how bad it would piss her off if I walked back inside. I could get a ride home and not have to listen to this.

"Jude."

I stuck my hands in my pockets and continued to ignore her. Her once pretty, pink voice became a harsh shade of red and hinted at purple—but not the girly kind, an ugly eggplant. The only sign that I was listening was the tic of my jaw in response to her grinding my name through her clenched teeth.

"Jude!"

With a deep breath in, I slowly closed my eyes and then reopened them with my gaze firmly on her face. "Yes, Portia."

"Are you listening?"

"How could I not? People in the next county can hear you complaining."

She eased her head back and shut her mouth. I hadn't raised my voice, but she acted as if I'd slapped her. Portia was the one who caused the scene and drew attention, not me. Luckily, no one was outside since it was cold as shit.

"Can we go? I'm freezing, and my coat is in the car," I sneered.

"I'm surprised you can feel anything, as high as you are."

"What is your problem, Portia? No one pressured you into doing anything. You didn't get caught with something you weren't supposed to have. Nothing I did tonight holds any consequence for you. So how about chill the hell out. Damn." I didn't wait for her to respond. Hearing what her problem was didn't interest me, and she'd still answer whether we stood in the icy, December air or sat in a car with the heat running. There was zero chance I'd escape her wrath—I might as well be warm listening to it.

Once I'd slammed the door, with me on the other side of it, she marched her happy ass to the driver's seat and slid in. She cranked the engine, but I wasn't fortunate enough to hope she'd concede and drive home in silence. Instead, she pulled out of Jamison's drive-way. The clock glowed three-three-three...so much for kissing that lucky number or wishing this away.

"You want to know what my problem is, *Jude*?"

I hated the way she emphasized my name, and I didn't care what her problem was. I just wanted her to shut up. It wasn't going to happen, so I reclined the seat and covered my eyes with my fore-arm, doing my best to tune her out. If I couldn't see her...

She rambled incessantly, from the time we left Jamison's until we parked in the Shaws' driveway, about her mother starting with easier drugs and moving into hardcore stuff when pot didn't do it for her. And how partying became a lifestyle that left her pregnant, single, and an addict. I just let her yammer, never bothering to respond or retort. Portia had convinced herself I was on a path straight to hell and the road had been paved with her mother's intentions.

I felt too good to fall into her pit of despair, and I refused to engage with her. She almost dragged me into the conversation when she tried to compare alcohol to drug use—both of which were illegal since we were under the age of twenty-one—and instead, I tickled my own arm to incite peace inside.

When she finally put the car in park, and I managed to remove my seatbelt, she caught me by the wrist before I got out.

"I love you, Jude. I thought you were better than this."

"You worry too much, Portia. Maybe *you* should swallow a pill and relax for a bit. You're too high strung. Do you bitch at Bart like this?"

Her eyes went wide, and her mouth parted. I threw open the passenger door, and a gust of wind raced through the car. I couldn't tell if that was what made her eyes water or the next thing she said. "We're not together anymore."

I'd waited for weeks to hear those four words, yet they lost their luster after twenty minutes of Portia weighing me down. Tomorrow I'd regret not capitalizing on this moment and using it to bring her back into my world, to comfort her, but tonight, I just wanted the solace of my bed and some peace and quiet. My feet hit the ground, and I stood without further thought, leaving Portia inside her car, alone.

When I got to the house, I realized I had to wait for Portia to get out and let me in, since my key was on the ring she currently possessed. I shivered on the front porch and bounced slightly on my toes to stay warm. She finally joined me, but I didn't bother to acknowledge her. I couldn't fix this tonight, and there was no point in trying. The key entered the lock, the deadbolt clicked when it disengaged, and I watched her delicate fingers press the button on the handle and push inside. I didn't wait for her to come in. I took the stairs two at a time in the dark and found my room without turning on a light.

I kicked off my shoes, shed my shirt and jeans, and lay down on the bed. In a matter of minutes, I found my headphones and a playlist, and there I lost myself in the sounds of the sixties and memories of lemon pie, old books, and my mom's smile.

"ARE YOU FUCKING KIDDING ME WITH THIS SHIT, PORTIA? WHAT the hell is your problem?"

I'd woken up filled with regret and the intention of making things right with Portia. The problem was, by the time I got out of bed, took a shower, and felt human enough to form sentences, I was dehydrated. I'd screwed up. It didn't matter if I'd thought it was all in good fun or believed she wouldn't find out, much less be hurt by my actions. I loved Portia, and that should have trumped anything else I thought was going on last night. I didn't have a reason for why it didn't, only that it wouldn't happen again.

I'd been ready to make that commitment and that apology until I had strolled into the kitchen—feeling like death—to find Ernie, Hensley, and Portia waiting to pounce.

"I did what I thought was in your best interest, Jude. And that was telling Mom and Dad." Portia tried to maintain her resolve, but she was seconds from breaking down.

"And you thought telling them I went to a party last night was the best way to handle that?" I needed to lower my voice, yet I couldn't stop from screaming every word inches from her face, which only served to make my head throb with each syllable.

"Jude, you need to watch your language and calm down." Ernie was about to find out just how foul my language could get.

"I'm not going to apologize for saving your life." Portia truly believed that shit.

"And you thought my getting blitzed at one party was a suicide mission? God, you're like a wet, fucking rag. No wonder Bart didn't stick around. He was probably afraid you'd call the cops to report underage drinking on campus..." I paced around the room, throwing my hands in the air and lobbing grenades. "Oh, wait...no, you think drinking is okay. Even though it's just as illegal as pot because you're not twenty-one. Explain that one to me. Can you spell the word hypocrite?"

"Portia, sweetheart, maybe it's better that you let us talk to Jude alone." Hensley patted her daughter on the thigh.

She wanted to argue, but at the very last second, she snapped her mouth shut, nodded her understanding, and excused herself from the table. When she moved by me, I hovered over her, hoping to make her feel small and insignificant. She had no clue what the hell she'd just unleashed and what I'd have to deal with after she went back to her ivory tower in Sander Hall. Never, in all the years I'd known Portia, had she thrown me to the wolves the way she had this morning.

"Jude, son—"

"I'm not your son, Ernie." Those five words cut through the air like the knife I'd just stuck into his back.

"Okay, Jude…how about you sit down and let's talk about this calmly."

I wanted to rage, throw things, tell him and his wife to go fly a kite. I didn't have a clue why I was so angry other than Portia had violated the only trust I had in this world. Neither of us had ever ratted out the other. She didn't have to do this. She could have come to me when I was sober. Instead, I threw myself in a chair and waited for them to punish me.

But it never came. I watched the minutes tick by on the clock— ten, fifteen, twenty—neither Ernie nor Hensley ever raised their voice. I heard bits and pieces of what they said, but the moment my mom's name came up, I shut them down. Being a senior and playing around with drugs didn't have anything to do with my mom's dying—it was just that, being a kid. I wasn't out vandalizing property or snorting coke. Prior to last night, I'd only smoked pot, and I could probably count the number of times I'd done that. They were making a mountain out of a fun little molehill. It wasn't anything more than that.

At the seventy-one-minute mark, Ernie asked if I had any questions.

"What's my punishment?" I'd probably be grounded until spring break. Maybe, if I was super lucky, Portia would come home for that, too, and ruin it, as well.

Ernie held my stare, but it was Hensley who answered. "The way you feel right now is punishment enough. You've alienated your sister and caused her to worry that she'll lose you the way she did her own mom and—"

I slapped my hands on the table and leaned forward to accentuate my point. "For the love of God, she's *not* my sister."

Hensley talked over me and missed my statement. "And we're going to insist you start counseling."

I let out an exaggerated sigh. It was worse than being grounded. There was no expiration date on therapy. It could go on for years, whereas being grounded had a time limit. It also didn't require me to interact with anyone; in fact, it did the opposite—it prevented me from having to deal with people or even speak.

"I'd rather be grounded," I huffed like a petulant child. "Can I go?"

Ernie and Hensley stood, and I pushed away from the table, my chair scraping across the floor. They were both going to hug me in some familial ceremony they believed fixed everything. That and chocolate chip cookies—both of which were horseshit and solved nothing. I didn't return their earnest embrace. In fact, I stood there with my arms at my sides and waited for them to let me go.

"We love you very much, Jude. I know you're upset with your sister, but she did the right thing by coming to us. Kids aren't equipped to handle these types of issues on their own."

"You're making something out of nothing, Hensley. I'm fine."

She patted me on the arm, and they both released me. I took the stairs two at a time and nearly knocked Portia over as we crossed paths. Never would I have believed she would have been capable of this level of betrayal.

And I wondered how our relationship would ever recover…or if I even wanted it to.

11

PORTIA

"IS JUDE PICKING YOU UP?" JET STOOD ACROSS FROM ME, PACKING her things for spring break.

"No, Ernie and Hensley are. He's still doing his best to avoid me."

"Have you two not talked since Christmas?" She spun around so quickly, her blond hair whipped around her body. Once her locks stopped, she plopped down on the bed, clearly stunned I hadn't talked to him in three months.

I shrugged, embarrassed. "I've sent him text messages, which I get one-word answers to if he bothers to respond. And I've tried to call a few times, but he doesn't answer." I took a seat next to my bag on my mattress and let out a heavy sigh. "I shouldn't have told my parents—or at the very least, I should have talked to him when he was sober before I did. I overreacted."

She reached across the small space between our bunks to touch my knee and bring my focus to her face. "You did what you thought was right."

My brow rose in hope that she'd confirm I hadn't screwed up. "So, you would have done the same thing?"

"No." Jet chuckled. "But, Portia, my mom didn't die from an

overdose. It's safe to say most people's reaction wouldn't be the same. Jude knew how you felt about it, and he didn't respect you enough to not do them around you."

"He shouldn't do it at all," I grumbled.

"Probably not, but most of the people we know do something illegal, and you don't condemn them."

Jet was right. I'd replayed that same sentiment over in my head since I got back to school after Christmas break. No matter how many times I repeated "everyone else does it," I couldn't convince myself that it mattered—they weren't Jude.

She leaned back and propped her hands behind her. "Do your parents know you guys aren't on speaking terms?"

"Yeah, why do you think they're forcing a family getaway over break?" I fell backward and stared at the ceiling. A week alone in a bungalow with Jude should be a dream come true, but I'd been dreading it since my parents announced our little vacation.

"The least they could do is take you somewhere fun. Who wants to go to Cape Cod in April? You guys are going to freeze your butts off."

"I think that's the idea. Not the freezing, but there won't be anything to do, which will force Jude and me to interact. Not a real well-thought-out plan if you ask me."

"Why is that?"

I continued to stare at the ceiling and wondered how I hadn't noticed just how dingy it was before now. I didn't have a clue how to clean a ceiling, but we definitely needed to look into that. "Because Jude will just stuff his nose in a book or put his head-phones on and tune everyone else out."

"Surely he can't live like that for a week." Clearly, she didn't know Jude.

I snickered. "He could live like that for eternity and be happy." My phone buzzed next to me, and when I picked it up, there was a text from Ernie informing me they'd be in front of the dorm in a few minutes.

"Is that your taxi?"

I forced myself up as though I were going off to war and this might be the last time I ever saw my roommate. "Yes," I groaned, making one syllable into four.

"Call me if you get bored. I'll tell you all about the beach and all the hot guys in Palm Springs. It's not too late if you want to back out of family fun time. I'll squeeze you into my bag and tell your parents I haven't seen you in days."

I stood and slid the strap to my bag over my shoulder. "I appreciate it, but at some point, I do have to face this. Might as well be now."

Jet gave me a hug and held onto my forearms when we separated. "I'm sure you two will work things out."

I patted her hand and gave her a reassuring smile, even though I felt none of it. "I'm sure you're right. I'll see you next week."

Walking through the dorm and down the stairs seemed like the green mile. It was melodramatic, but the truth remained. I couldn't remember the last time I dreaded something as much as I did this trip. I'd rather give a speech in public without clothes on than deal with Jude Thomas and his angry vendetta, which hadn't waned since Christmas.

I slung my bag across the back seat of Ernie's SUV and climbed in after it. "Hey." I'd become a master of disguised voices and hidden emotions where my parents were concerned. It wasn't them I was upset with, so I didn't want them to know just how much what had happened at Christmas affected me—although I was an idiot to believe they weren't aware.

"Hi, sweetheart," Hensley cooed over her shoulder as Ernie pulled away from the curb. "How's school been? We're so glad to see you."

"You know—it's school." I'd rather stay here and stare at the dirty ceiling than make this trip. "A bunch of my friends are going to Palm Springs tomorrow." A bunch, two, whatever—the point was, they were going and I wasn't.

"Portia, dear, you can do spring break with your friends next year. And I'm sure you guys will do something this summer." Ernie only wanted what was best for the family. I couldn't fault him for that, even if I wasn't interested in participating.

Poised to fight back, I thought better of it and kept my mouth shut, intentionally leaning toward the door so Ernie couldn't see me in the rearview mirror. I was also out of Hensley's sight, unless she turned around again. With my head against the glass, I closed my eyes, tried to enjoy the sunshine on my cheeks, and listened to my parents prattle on about all the things to do in the Cape. It was horrible, but part of me hoped the car would break down or that Cape Cod might have a monsoon and flood the town. Or maybe the bed and breakfast would accidentally get overbooked—anything to keep from enduring seven days in a shared bedroom with the boy I loved, who currently hated me.

JUDE HAD AVOIDED ME LAST NIGHT, AND THIS MORNING, HE'D DONE exactly what I predicted the moment we got into the car to make the three-and-a-half-hour drive from Carondale to Cape Cod—he put on his headphones and opened a book. Ernie and Hensley talked amongst themselves, so I got out my iPad and played word scramble until my eyes crossed.

The four of us checked in to the quaint bed and breakfast Hensley had arranged, and even though I knew it was coming, I was still shocked when Ernie handed me a key to the room Jude and I would share for the next week—alone. I'd hoped I would be paired off with Hensley and Ernie and Jude could do the boy thing. I knew better. They'd been clear that they intended for us to find a way through the issue at Christmas, and while *I* was willing to do what it took, Jude held fast to resistance. The guy was stubborn as a mule and always had been. God almighty couldn't make Jude Thomas do something he wasn't inclined to do.

I groaned as I walked down the hall, leading the way to our room. The door opened easily to a bright, flowery room filled with yellow blossoms on the two comforters and bright-green curtains. If I weren't in such an irritable mood, I might have found it pretty—right now, it just seemed to taunt me.

Jude totally ignored me and the décor when he tossed his bag on the floor and himself onto the bed he'd chosen to spend the week in. I followed, set my stuff down, and sat on the mattress opposite him. I wished I could pretend nothing had happened. If only I could lie down next to him, hit him with a pillow seven or eight times, and then wait for him to tickle me to convince me to stop. I missed playful Jude, but I didn't think the guy across from me would welcome my advances. Although, I wasn't sure I could spend the next week enduring this, either.

My eyes lingered on his freckles and then roamed to his copper-colored hair. His eyes were closed, but I didn't need them to be open to see the warmth of the brown hidden by his lids. Jude folded his arms behind his head, and I noticed with great detail the way his muscles tightened and their definition stood out. He'd put on a solid twenty pounds since he started his senior year, and every one made him look more like a man and less like a child. He crossed his ankles, drawing my attention down the length of his long legs, legs that weren't all that lanky anymore.

A knock interrupted my appraisal and came just before I started to pant. Jude hadn't heard it through the headphones. I huffed my irritation at his obliviousness and got up to answer it.

"Hey, sweetheart," Hensley cooed as she peered over my shoulder toward Jude. "Your father and I are going for a walk. We'll be back in time for dinner. I have my cell phone if you need me."

She leaned over and kissed my cheek and then wiggled her fingers when she caught Jude's attention.

And as quickly as Hensley had appeared, she was gone again. I resumed my spot on the bed and realized there was no television in the room. The more I thought about it, I hadn't seen a television anywhere in the place. If Jude wasn't going to talk to me, it would be solitary confinement. I could already tell by Hensley's "walk" that they didn't intend to entertain us—they were doing their best to force us into reconciliation. There was no way in hell I was going to watch the fan spin on the ceiling for seven days, and I wasn't exploring Cape Cod alone.

I picked up a pillow and threw it at Jude's head. I didn't care if it pissed him off or woke him up—I needed a reaction. Which I got.

He sat up straight, removed the pillow from his face, and glared at me. "What the hell, Portia?"

"So, you *haven't* gone mute!" Being a smart ass probably wasn't going to win me any points with my cellmate, but he'd said four more words than he had in months.

He quirked one side of his face, giving me a look that screamed, "You're an idiot" without actually speaking and collapsed back on the mattress.

"I can't do this, Jude. I can't spend the next week cooped up in this tiny-ass room with you and not speak. We're stuck. At the very least, we have to find a way to make this bearable. It's been over three months. Can't we just hash this out and move on?" I pleaded with him, but when he didn't so much as turn my direction, I figured it would be more of the same.

No sooner had I fallen back to stare at the ceiling, Jude finally spoke.

"Okay." His voice was rough and scratchy. "You want to hash it out. Fine. Just tell me why you told Ernie and Hensley instead of talking to me."

"I made a mistake, Jude. I can give you a laundry list of reasons, but none of them will hold any weight in your mind."

"Do you realize that the next morning I went looking for you to apologize and tell you I'd screwed up?"

"How would I know that? You haven't talked to me." I didn't have the courage to meet him face to face. Talking to the fan was the best I could muster at this point, and thankfully, their ceiling was clean.

"Exactly. You wouldn't know because you didn't give me time to talk to you, which is exactly what you've begged me to do since then. You didn't extend me—someone you *claim* to love—that courtesy, even though you expect it for yourself."

I didn't have a retort, because he was correct. I'd had reasons I believed were valid at the time, but now they just seemed like excuses. "You're right. I should have talked to you first."

He had sat up and, from my vantage point, I could see the top of his head, but not his eyes. "Then why didn't you? You had a reason; I just don't know what it was. Maybe if you shared that with me, I could find a way past the anger."

My tongue snaked between my lips and moistened them, while I pondered how to explain my thought process. There wasn't a pretty way to paint this ugly picture, so I opted for the truth. "I found my mom dead on our floor at age nine. *Nine* years old." I struggled to keep the emotion from my voice. Not because of her, but because of him. "The idea of a repeat with you is more than I can handle. And I'd rather have you hate me alive than love me dead."

"You realize tons of teens experiment with drugs and alcohol... including yourself?"

"You're right, but ecstasy isn't a beer or a joint. One pill can kill you. One." I wanted to sit up. I wanted to see his face. I wanted to be next to him. Instead, I closed my eyes and willed the tears away. The lump in my throat became painful to swallow around, and if I had to speak in the next thirty seconds, I wouldn't be able to conceal my turmoil.

"I get it. And I got it the next morning when I woke up wondering if death had settled in, which was why I wanted to talk to you. But you'd thrown me to the wolves before breakfast. Do you have any idea what I've had to deal with since then?" He paused as though he expected me to answer a rhetorical question. "Of course you don't, because you went back to school and left me to clean up the mess."

Technically, he'd made that mess, so I wasn't sure how I could have helped clean it up had I not returned to campus. But Jude referred to my helping make the mess with Ernie and Hensley. The same mess that didn't have to be created had I given him the chance to speak.

"For crying out loud, Portia, will you look at me?" He let out a heavy huff, and I sat up to find him pulling on his roots in frustration.

I noticed—although I didn't dare comment—how much darker his hair was, a much richer, strawberry color versus the copper it was this summer. Women all over the globe would pay top dollar for that shade of red. But not even the distraction of how Jude had changed in the months since I had last seen him kept the tears from falling. His eyes traced the trail down my cheek before they met mine. He wanted to be mad. He held onto the anger, clutching it like a lifeline, until the weight of it snapped his resolve. Jude's broad shoulders slumped, and his back arched slightly as he exhaled and dropped his head into his hands.

My touch might not be well received, but I couldn't see him in pain and not try to ease it. I hesitated as I closed the gap, waiting for him to flinch or give me a look of disgust, yet he never even raised his line of sight. The hardwoods were brutal on my knees when I kneeled in front of him and took his hands, wrapping mine around them. And when he squeezed back instead of pushing me away, I forgot about my discomfort and held on for dear life. The pads of my thumbs felt raw sliding back and forth against his fingers, and my chest tightened, waiting for him to respond. The threat of my heart pounding through my sternum left me anxious, and I couldn't stay quiet any longer.

I kissed his fingers, although I didn't move away from our hands when I murmured, "I'm so sorry, Jude." The tears trickled down my cheeks unseen, and I swallowed hard against my emotion. I didn't know what else to say if those words weren't enough.

And just as I was about to rock back onto my heels and leave the room to escape the tension, Jude shifted. He pressed a kiss onto my hair and then ducked his head to the side of mine. "I know."

"Are you ever going to forgive me?" I whispered against our hands, leaning into his face just slightly.

Jude's breath met my skin as I clung to his hands and waited for his reply. It was a reply I'd never hear. He pulled back and our eyes met. Mine swam with emotion, while his warred with it. His tongue snuck out and wet his plump lips just as his gaze dropped to my mouth. I didn't have a clue if it was an invitation or challenge, and the truth was, I didn't care. I'd fought with my heart and my head for longer than I cared to admit, and at that moment, I took a chance.

Our mouths met, and my lids closed. He let go of my hands to secure my lower back to draw me to him, and I went freely. He settled my hips between his thighs while he still sat on the edge of the bed. Without peeking, I wrapped my arms around his neck and tangled my hand in his hair. The second his tongue found mine, our hearts started to talk when words had failed. A kiss had never been more sublime, and when my toes curled and my fingers followed, I knew I had to break away before I gave myself to him.

Breathlessly, he put his forehead against mine. His shoulders rose and fell beneath my arms draped loosely around his neck. I didn't open my eyes. Instead, I took a deep breath and lingered in the high he'd just given me. Every part of me wanted more, regardless of the consequences, but I didn't know how to move from where we'd been for three months to where my soul wanted to go.

"I'd say that was a pretty good start." Jude's statement caused me to open my eyes, unsure of what he was talking about.

"Huh?" I breathed the word out on an exhale that was barely audible.

"You asked if I'd ever forgive you. That went a long way toward tamping my anger." He smirked, but it was playful, not arrogant. Nothing about Jude was ever cocky.

I sat back on my heels, breaking our embrace, and offered him a shy smile. "Is that the only way to get you to talk to me?" I couldn't bear the thought of having another encounter similar to the one I'd had with Chet.

He patted the mattress next to him and extended his hand to help me off my knees. "No. It just got my attention."

Once I sat on the bed, he leaned back on his hands. I turned to face him, drawing my bent knee in front of me. "I really am sorry."

He tilted his head to the side, considering me in a way only Jude ever had. I'd kill to know what ran through his head when his eyes glazed over and that distant expression transformed his features.

"I'm sorry, too. I was sorry *then*."

"Why wouldn't you talk to me?" I didn't expect him to answer, but it was worth asking.

"Because I've been stuck talking to someone else for three months."

I already knew what he referred to, but I asked anyhow. "Counselor?"

"Twice a week since the beginning of the year."

It would be easy to tell him all the reasons that was a good thing. It was also the fastest way to shut him down. Jude hated counselors, and he didn't think he needed to share anything with a professional.

"Do you want to talk about it?"

"No." His answer was short, but he placed his hand on my thigh and waited for me to look him in the eye. "I want to move on."

"From which part?" I wasn't sure if he was referring to what happened at Christmas, not wanting to see a counselor anymore, or the kiss we'd just shared.

"All of it, I guess." He shrugged.

I wondered if that was the best approach—ignore what we'd done to each other in favor of just moving on instead of discussing it. It worried me that Jude just wanted to sweep things under the rug as though they'd never happened. It was what he'd done with his mom's death, and that had led us here. There wasn't a psychologist in the world who would agree that was healthy, but I was so desperate to have him back in my life that I didn't speak up. I didn't insist that we talk further. I didn't make sure we were really okay. I took that kiss as the gospel because there was passion in it, and I believed it was more powerful than words. There was no way a person could kiss with that much feeling and harbor resentment or animosity.

So, I let it go.

And waited for the awkwardness I expected to come, yet it didn't. Instead, the easiness the two of us normally shared—well, prior to Christmas—had returned, and so had our good-natured attitudes.

WE HADN'T SEEN MUCH OF HENSLEY AND ERNIE SINCE WE GOT TO Cape Cod. They stopped by or sent one of us a text message to let us know where they were or what they were doing, but either they were having their own romantic holiday, or they believed shoving Jude and me together was the solution to our problems. I never would have thought it would work, yet it had—maybe too well.

In the two days we'd been here, we'd eaten dinner with them and that was about it. And even then, there were stolen touches and secretive glances. My mom was clearly proud of herself and her plan for forced isolation, although she didn't realize what those secretive glances between Jude and me actually meant. She had no idea the two of us were playing tonsil hockey in the room, or holding hands on the beach, or kissing when no one was watching.

Jude and I hadn't talked about what was going on between us. We just let it happen on its own accord, and it was better than anything I'd ever experienced. He was safe—his arms, how close we were, there were no secrets. I'd never had that level of security with anyone in my life other than Jude, and it had been that way since we were kids. Adding in the physical and romantic part only added to the depth of the love I'd had for him for years. And without saying it, there was no doubt he felt the same.

When we finished dinner, Ernie and Hensley excused themselves for the evening, and Jude and I did the same. It was too cold to walk on the beach at night, and we weren't old enough to do much of anything else. Without a television in the room, we were left with books, music, and iPads.

This was the part of the day that became stilted.

Where Jude and I frequently shared a bed in the past, that was now a huge step, even fully clothed. And when my mind started wandering—and wanting—to do the first without the second, I worried about how far the two of us might let this go. Just as quickly as the worry came, his touch would soothe it away and replace it with comfort.

"Why are you all the way over there?" I peered through my lashes from my spot on my bed.

He held up a book. "Reading." There was no way he was that daft. "Why are you all the way over there?" His eyes sparkled with innuendo, and the corner of his mouth lifted into the most adorable smirk.

I wanted to throw myself across the room as quickly as possible, but I had to maintain some semblance of dignity. Then, once I got there, I wasn't sure what to do with myself. Typically, I'd lie down on his right—on my side—and bug the crap out of him until he put the book down and paid attention to me. But that was when we weren't doing...*whatever* this was. I opted to prop the pillows up against the headboard and sit the same way he was with my legs outstretched. It was slightly awkward, but I figured this would just take getting used to. I had no clue what we would do once we left here and had to return to our lives, but I tried not to think past today.

The word scramble game I had played on my iPad for months didn't hold my attention, yet I forced myself to stare at the screen until my eyes closed with boredom. I set the device in my lap and rolled my head to stare at the freckles that marked his face and the smile that tugged at his lips when he realized I was watching him. "What are you reading?"

"The Kite Runner." He stuck his finger between the pages and flipped the book over so I could see the cover.

I'd never heard of Khaled Hosseini. "What's it about?"

Jude didn't respond; instead he grabbed his bookmark off the nightstand and exchanged it with his hand and set the book aside. "You'll have to read it. You're pretty far behind unless Hensley's been sending you an assigned reading list since the holidays." He rolled over to his side and adjusted the pillows when he slid down.

I giggled, wishing I'd never admitted that I read all the books he did. The truth was, I hadn't been able to keep up with that trend since I'd started college. Between my class load and homework, there wasn't a ton of extra time, and what little I did have, I spent with friends and not with my nose in a book in the dorm.

"I don't even want to admit how far behind I am. Maybe I can catch up over the summer." I sat up, adjusted my pillows, and mirrored his position. *This* was how Jude and I were naturally.

"What was the last book you read?" His eyes had warmed from

chocolate to whiskey, and his red lashes only further drew my attention in.

"Off your list? Or in general?"

"Both."

"*Wuthering Heights* for class, and *Alias Grace* from your list."

He jerked back just a hint, and he scrunched his face. His lashes weren't nearly as captivating when he looked like that. "I was reading *Alias Grace* when you left for school."

I lifted my shoulder in a bit of a shrug. "I've been busy. College is a lot harder than high school. And I didn't have a social life then, either. I'm doing good to keep up with my assignments and tests."

Jude nodded.

"Don't look at me like you're disappointed." I poked him in the side to get him to smile. "You didn't even know I was your groupie until right before I started classes." My giggle came off as humored, although it was more from nerves. I didn't want to let him down—and as dumb as it was, books were important to him. If Jude believed it was one more thing I hadn't made a priority, it might send us back in a direction I never cared to revisit.

He reached out and cupped my jaw with his hand. His thumb moved along my cheekbone as he studied my eyes. "I'm not." His words were barely a whisper. And when he leaned in to kiss me, he confirmed they were true.

Our lips didn't part; it wasn't drawn out. It was soft and sincere and perfectly timed. My heart beat faster, and a grin covered my face. I became shy every time we met in an intimate exchange. I had no experience, and neither did he, yet somehow, he became confident when I was timid. His fingers traced a path down my cheek and then my neck. The feather-soft touch tickled in an erotic way that sent a chill down my spine and heat between my legs.

Pushing himself up onto his elbow, he rolled to hover over me and peppered kisses from behind my ear down my throat. "I hope every kiss I place doesn't leave a freckle." The warmth of his breath against my skin only accentuated the warring heat and cold running rampant over my body.

I didn't want to think about his mom leaving all those marks all over his skin as a kid, when all I could envision was him taking off his clothes. I was like a cat in heat. Every brush of his arm or touch of his hand made me want to back into his hip, rub my ass on his crotch, and howl with desperation.

I elongated my neck, trying to entice him to lavish more attention on the places that tickled my fancy. When he obliged, he also snaked his arm around my lower back, pulling me against him. It was the only invitation I needed to slide my knee between his thighs to get as close to him as possible, and he welcomed my forwardness. His hand slid under my shirt, and he dug into my skin when he moved his lips from my neck to my mouth. As our tongues danced together, our bodies began to move in tandem, and I could feel his excitement growing as it pressed against my leg.

I tugged at the hem of his shirt, forcing him to sit up so I could remove it. And when I got his off, he reciprocated the gesture. He stared at me with wonder, and when he didn't move to take my bra off, I did it for him. I had no idea where this brazen streak came from, but hesitation didn't interest me. I craved Jude against me, inside me, all over me. I needed it as much as I needed my next breath, and I was completely sober. This wasn't a lapse in judgment or an alcohol-induced mistake.

"Holy shit," he whispered under his breath. His gaze lingered on my breasts and then slowly rose to meet my eyes. "I always knew you'd be gorgeous, but I had no idea."

While I had his attention and he remained enamored, I scooted off the edge of the bed. His focus followed my every move as though he weren't sure if what he witnessed was reality. He didn't stop me or say a word. Jude studied the curves of my body, the lines of my shoulder, and his jaw dropped just slightly when I shimmied out of my jeans and panties, leaving a pile on the floor at my feet when I stepped out of them.

I licked my lips and waited for a response. Slowly, he swung his legs off the mattress and stood before me. He leaned down to capture my mouth and unbutton his pants in the process. It might have been minutes or possibly seconds when his clothes joined mine, but I didn't know because time no longer existed. The only things on Earth were Jude Thomas and me.

He laid me down on top of the comforter and joined me. Our hands explored as did our mouths; our legs tangled, and our arms moved like octopuses. Every moment was perfect. And when he rolled on top of me, I wrapped around him, securing my ankles behind his thighs.

"Are you sure?" he asked in the most loving tone, his eyes widening just a hint.

I nodded with a gentle smile.

"I need to hear you say the words, Portia."

I huffed out a tiny giggle. "I've never wanted anything more in my life."

He stared at me with an intensity I'd never witnessed from him. "You know we can never go back from this?"

Taking in a deep breath, I took his flushed cheeks in both hands and lifted up to kiss him. "That's my hope."

When he still didn't initiate, I worried *he* didn't want it and that I'd pushed him into something he wasn't ready for.

Jude closed his eyes and dropped his forehead to mine. "I don't know what I'm doing, and I don't want this to suck. I've heard it's going to hurt you and that will gut me." His admission was honest, and I loved him for it.

I poked him lightly in the side, and his eyes popped open. "I don't know what I'm doing, either. And there's no one in the world I'd rather figure it out with than you."

A hint of a smile parted his lips, and he set his stare on mine. He reached between us and lined the head of his dick up with my entrance. I was nervous, worried it would be more painful than I was prepared for, but I wanted it, nonetheless. He eased inside and each inch filled me in a way I'd never thought possible. It was warm and tight, and when he stopped, I knew he'd reached the barrier he was afraid to pass. I took a deep breath and tried to relax, opened my thighs as wide as I could, and encouraged him with my heels.

Just as he broke through, he dropped his head next to mine, and with his breath heating my ear, he whispered, "I love you, Portia."

I couldn't stop the yelp as the pinch seared through my torso, and I probably drew blood from the way my nails dug into his skin with the pain. It lasted less than a minute, and Jude just held me until the tension no longer coiled my muscles. Our hips rocked, and in an awkward exchange of emotion and passion, Jude Thomas made love to me. It was awful and perfect all at the same time, and I didn't care how long it took for the two of us to get good at it as long as we practiced together.

We lay next to each other—my head on his shoulder and his arm wrapped around my waist—until our breathing returned to normal and the quiet was comfortable. He reached over and pulled a blanket on top of us and then switched off the light next to the bed. Submerged in darkness, I finally repeated his confession.

"I love you, too, Jude."

12

JUDE

Waking the next morning, I wondered if the previous night had been a dream. The heat of a body curled into my side confessed the truth. Portia's dark hair flowed in a river of black covering the arm I had wrapped around her, and my fingers danced on her bare skin. Every second of our time together was crystal clear, yet I couldn't quite bring myself to believe it was real. With her soft breaths prancing across my chest, I carefully lifted the comforter, verifying the two of us remained unclothed.

Portia stirred with the intrusive draft from the cool air in the room, and her hand slid along my side. I peered down my nose to see the smile begin to form, and even though she didn't open her eyes, the corners of her mouth lifted in happiness.

"Good morning," she cooed in a husky voice that made my dick twitch. Her fingers continued to explore my bare flesh until she cupped my ass in her hand and squeezed.

A sensual groan of satisfaction parted my lips and carried a word with it. "Morning." There was nothing I wanted more than to roll over and settle myself between her legs, but I needed more of a green light. "How are you feeling?"

Her lids parted seductively, exposing radiant pools glazed over with desire. "I'm good. You?" Portia raised her brows, asking more than how I'd slept.

Burrowing farther into the warmth of her embrace and the comfort of the blankets, I rolled to my side, bringing her to me, chest to chest. "Are you..." I hesitated, uncertain how to ask the question dangling on the tip of my tongue, "sore?"

Her nose brushed against mine when she shook her head. With narrowed eyes, I silently posed the question again, doubting her response.

"Okay, maybe a little, but nothing you need to worry about." Her crooked smile stole my heart, and the soft pink had returned to her voice. It seemed like it had been years since I'd heard the cotton candy in her tone, and I wanted to make myself sick consuming it.

Portia didn't give me the chance to ask for details or ensure she didn't need anything. Every square inch of her was flush with me, and she used that for leverage as she rolled me onto my back and straddled my waist. She settled, perched on my abdomen, and her hair cascaded in a waterfall over her shoulder and onto her bare breast. My hands cupped her hips, and she lifted of her own volition.

And where last night had been awkward and jerky, today was fluid and smooth, as though we'd rehearsed the choreography of this affair countless times. Portia's ravenous, green eyes never left mine as she rode me to ecstasy, and it wasn't until we both reached the peak, that her lids closed the curtain on the windows to her soul. But I didn't need to see her irises when I'd long ago memorized every striation that colored them. Watching her come undone on top of me, for me, and with me was far more decadent anyway. I could feast on her body, get drunk on her scent, and swallow her affection for days. There was no doubt in my mind, I could starve to death trying to survive on Portia.

Her sweaty frame collapsed onto mine, and her hair stuck to my skin as much as it did her own. Our chests heaved with exertion, and the tips of my fingers traced patterns along her spine as we both came down from the high we'd just experienced.

Portia picked up her head from my chest, and when she did, the morning sun came through the window at the perfect angle to temporarily blind her. She shifted to shielded her eyes with a hand, and in doing so, lost her balance and fell—less than gracefully—to my side, giggling.

The smell of sex and the sight of her smile first thing in the morning, made my heart strum. And the knock, followed by Hensley's voice, nearly sent me into cardiac arrest.

"Good morning," she sang through the door.

"Oh my God. What are we going to do?" The glitter that sparkled in Portia's eyes only moments before dimmed, and panic took over. She hid under the covers as though that provided a viable solution.

I could only hope Hensley hadn't heard Portia's muffled anxiety or her giggle. I sat up and covered her head with a pillow. "Morning," I called through the wood.

"We're going for breakfast. You and Portia get dressed and meet us downstairs in fifteen minutes." It wasn't a request, regardless of how sweet her voice came across.

Portia popped her head out from under the pillow and blankets. "Jude, I need more than fifteen minutes." Her cheeks burned a crimson red, and if Hensley saw her, there'd be no doubt about what we'd spent our morning doing.

"I need to shower, Hensley. Can you make it thirty?" The truth was, if I didn't wash my body, everyone within a ten-foot radius would be keenly aware of what we'd been up to.

"Thirty minutes," she confirmed.

My heart pounded in my ears, and swallowing blocked out all other sounds. I tried to listen for her footsteps retreating but was unable to hear anything other than blood pumping through my veins.

Portia whimpered—or maybe whined—snapping me out of a trance, staring at the door. The two of us were naked, had just had mind-blowing sex, and if Hensley had been two minutes earlier, she would have heard her daughter climax. It dawned on me the walls weren't soundproof, and we might have neighbors.

"Jude." Portia pushed on my bicep to get my attention. "Do you think she knows?"

I didn't, but even if I did, I wouldn't have told Portia. She'd spend the day freaking out about when they were going to confront us and how. "No. I don't think she would have given us thirty seconds, much less thirty minutes."

The adrenaline slowly left my body, and my hands stopped shaking. I finally thought it was safe to move without alerting Portia to my turmoil. Hensley was none the wiser, and as reckless as it might be, the only way the two of us could both shower and be downstairs in half an hour was to do it together. Another first with Portia Shaw that made my lip hitch and my cock twitch.

I grabbed her narrow waist under the white sheet, rolled over, and placed a chaste kiss on her sensuous mouth. Then I continued to roll until I was off the bed completely. "Come on. We don't have any more time to waste."

She took my extended hand and the linen she wore as a cloak fell, exposing her firm breasts and flat stomach. "Together?" There was a mischievous gleam in her eyes. Portia had a wild side she'd waited her entire life to unleash, and I was witnessing it claw its way to the surface to break free.

"Absolutely."

Portia took the lead to the bathroom—not that the ten steps to the other side of the room were a long trek. It provided me with the opportunity to watch her hips sway and her ass clench with each move she made. Her skin was flawless, from her neck to her ass and down to her heels. I reached out to smack her rear end, just as she leaned in to turn on the faucet.

She caught sight of me from her periphery and swatted my hand away in anticipation. "We don't have time for any of that," she warned. "I don't want to tip them off that we've done anything more than just made up. And we need to figure out how we're going to explain *that*. You know Hensley's going to ask."

She dipped under the stream without waiting for my reply and then held the curtain open. I joined her and shivered when the water bounced off her back and hit me like daggers of ice. Portia and I hadn't had enough time together intimately for her to be privy to shrinkage, and unless she moved quickly and gave me some heat, I'd have to explain that nuance of manhood. No thank you.

Finally, she stepped to the side to allow me to warm up. The damage had already been done, but she was in too great a hurry to scrub the scent of our sexcapades off her skin and didn't notice my shriveled package. I'd love nothing more than to linger in the steam, with every inch of her drenched body under my touch, and lavish her with kisses until she was drunk on ecstasy, but that wasn't in our near future. Shampoo and then towels were.

In all the years I'd known Portia, she'd never showered as quickly as she did when she believed her parents *might* catch us having done something they *might* consider taboo. I wanted to ask her about it, question how she thought we should approach this, but now wasn't the time. The two of us stole quick glances at the other, and each of us blushed when we caught the other staring. There was nothing sexier than a post-sex glow on Portia.

After our shower, she blew out her hair with the dryer, but with our limited timeframe, she wasn't able to dry it completely and ended up knotting it on top of her head and then got dressed. I pulled a shirt over my head, tugged on a pair of jeans and then tennis shoes, and grabbed a jacket. I didn't have a clue if we were eating here or going out, so I prepared either way.

Neither of us had spoken since we'd gotten in the shower, and I thought we should address the elephant in the room before Hensley or Ernie did.

"Portia, what are we going to tell them? I don't want to pretend we're still fighting."

She shrugged as though she hadn't been stricken with fear half an hour ago. "Just that we talked and both realized we made mistakes."

"That's it?" I shook my head. "Hensley will want more."

"Just play it by ear." She grabbed my hand to lead me out the door and then glanced down at our twined fingers. It took her roughly two seconds to break apart from me. "And maybe not touch each other like we just had sex." Her nervous laughter did nothing to ease my mind.

She was right. We had to act normal. The problem was, normal over the last three months had been ignoring and avoiding each other, and prior to that we had touched each other like kids who grew up together, yet more like siblings than lovers. I wasn't sure where the median was, but I had about three minutes to find it before we were face to face

---

WE MET ERNIE AND HENSLEY DOWNSTAIRS IN THE LIVING ROOM, which served as a makeshift lobby for the bed and breakfast. They both had on jackets, indicating we were going out for brunch.

Ernie grabbed my shoulder with a smile and then directed his affection toward Portia, scooping her into a hug. When they separated, he beamed. "Glad to see you two have worked things out and are on speaking terms again."

Hensley stood from her seat and clapped her hands together and then held them in a prayer in front of her mouth. "I knew this would be the perfect thing for you to mend your relationship. Siblings should never squabble, much less for months." Her smile grew behind her fingers, and then she dropped her hands to her side.

I cringed at her mention of the word siblings and wondered how Portia and I would ever break this to them or go public. Over the years, I'd made numerous comments about her not being my sister, just not enough to the two people who mattered. And as long as I'd loved Portia, I had worried about how our peers would see any type of relationship between us. I didn't want to hurt them. I also never believed Portia would return my affection, so in my mind, it hadn't mattered.

Clearly, I was wrong on all accounts.

"Where are we going?" I asked, needing to shift the focus to food and away from our reconciliation.

Ernie opened the door and held it for each of us to pass through so he could take the rear. "There's a little seafood place a block or so away that your mother and I found yesterday when we went for a walk. One of the locals told us it was the best place in town for brunch. We'd planned on breakfast, but time got away from us, so this works out well."

I was going to pretend he had directed his answer at Portia and not me since Hensley wasn't my mother, which would make Portia my sister. Instead of focusing on the words he chose, I allowed him to move ahead of me. Ernie laced his fingers with his wife's, and Portia and I followed behind. Our normal banter wasn't just stifled, the Shaws' presence silenced it. Truth be told, I wasn't sure either of us knew how to act with each other after the last twelve hours, much less other people—especially those who would be less than thrilled to find out we'd made up naked.

Ernie and Hensley yammered away as we traversed the street in the cold. Portia wrapped her scarf tightly around her neck and then hugged herself to ward off the chill of the morning air. Whoever thought the Cape was a great place to spend spring break clearly hadn't been here during unseasonably frigid weather. My hands hurt when I pushed them into the pockets of my jeans, and I contemplated how long it took for hypothermia to set in. It might have been a slight exaggeration; nevertheless, I was already uncomfortable, and the weather made it worse.

"Here we are," Ernie announced when he glanced up at the restaurant sign. "It's an Irish kitchen." He was evidently proud of his find, even though we'd yet to step foot inside or taste the food. In my mind, Irish and seafood didn't go together, but I was willing to give it a shot to get inside.

Hensley glanced over her shoulder. "I'm so glad we're all together again. It's been ages since we've done anything as a family."

There was another one of those words, "family." That one had never bothered me in the past, yet in light of having made love to their daughter, it was sandpaper to the heart. I had to find a way past this, or shit would get ugly fast. I couldn't let every word out of Ernie's or Henley's mouth grate on my nerves, or I'd drive myself insane. If I spent all my time second-guessing every syllable they uttered, I'd have to check into a mental institution before the week ended.

Portia didn't seem to be dealing with any of it any better than I was. The hostess escorted us to our seats, and Ernie and Hensley slid into one side of the booth, leaving us to sit together. The table linens pooled in our laps, and without thought, I slipped my hand to Portia's thigh. She jerked her head toward me in response, and her eyes widened in disbelief. Instead of removing it, I gave her a gentle squeeze and winked the eye opposite her parents so they wouldn't witness my attempt at calming her nerves.

Her pupils surged before they narrowed and then dilated, and the warm green I associated with her happiness settled, pushing away the cool blues. She left the menu on the table and tucked her hands under the veil of secrecy. I watched her from the corner of my eye as she peeked through hooded lids to see if her parents were watching, and when they were deep in their own discussion of eggs and corned beef —still no seafood—she tangled her fingers with mine, which remained on her thigh and dared to put her right hand high on my leg.

When she licked her lips and tugged her bottom one under her teeth, I inched our clutched hands toward her center, and she mirrored the movement with her right. I hadn't bothered looking at the menu; I was too busy studying Ernie and Hensley, while I teased their daughter under the tablecloth and she cupped my growing erection. Her parents were hidden behind the large menus they held in front of them which gave me a stolen moment to play. My fingers warmed next to the heat of her desire, and I coughed to keep from groaning when she gave my dick a firm squeeze. My knee hit the table, jostling the silverware and startling the Shaws. Portia giggled and jerked away, while my cheeks burned with embarrassment.

"Are you okay, Jude? You look a little flushed." Hensley stood enough to reach across the table and placed the back of her hand against my forehead. "You're terribly warm. Do you feel bad?" She was just as bad as Portia, checking for a fever.

I pushed her hand away and acted like any teenage guy would when a motherly figure fawned over them unnecessarily. "I'm fine. I just need to take my jacket off." Which I did and glared at Portia in the process.

Her eyes sparkled under the lights above, and she donned a spirited grin. Playing under the table was a dangerous game, and it was obviously one that turned Portia on. Even when the waitress came to take our order and her parents were distracted, I had to push her hand back to her side of the booth. I'd like to say it was irritating, although it was anything but. Her game of cat and mouse was flirtatious, and any other time I would have welcomed it. In front of her parents, I was terrified we'd be caught.

Just when I was about to come unglued, not out of irritation but rather uncontrollable arousal, Portia stuck her finger in my ribs and erupted in laughter when I jumped. She'd been doing it for years, and they all thought it was hysterical to see the studious bookworm get goosed. And their reaction was no different today.

"Jude, it's so good to see you smile. I worried we'd lost you there for a while." Hensley searched my face as though she might be able to, in a single glance, impart the love she felt.

"How have things been going with Dr. Vanderhugh?" Ernie sipped from the orange juice the waitress had just set in front of him.

They didn't ask about my counseling sessions often, and I never offered information unless they pried. I didn't care to discuss any of it in front of Portia, yet if I shut it down, it would only serve to draw more attention to the therapy I'd had to endure since Portia ratted me out at Christmas.

I took a deep breath, and Portia bowed her head in shame. Neither of us were comfortable. I nudged her in the arm with my shoulder. "It hasn't been bad. We've talked about college the last few times I've been there."

Portia's head snapped up, as did her widening eyes when she focused on me. "Have you applied anywhere?" Hope twinkled in her eyes.

I downed half of my tea to put off my response. I hadn't discussed this with anyone, not even Ernie or Hensley. No decision had been made, but they didn't even know I'd filled out applications. "Yeah."

Hensley put her forearms on the table and leaned toward me in anticipation.

My Adam's apple felt like it was being rubbed against a cheese grater each time I swallowed, and the tea hadn't helped—it had only delayed the inevitable. "The University of Maine, Columbia, and Carnegie Mellon."

Ernie crossed his arms and leaned back in the booth with pride.

He nodded slowly in agreement with my choices, I presumed. "All good schools, Jude."

Portia's jaw dropped, although I wasn't certain if it was because she wanted me to join her at UM or because she feared me leaving the state for four years after what we'd shared last night and this morning.

Hensley straightened her posture and asked, "Have you heard back from any of them? Why didn't you tell us, Jude? This is wonderful." Nothing in her tone or the way she held herself agreed with her statement. "I didn't have any idea you planned to go to college."

I coughed as I tried to down the mouthful of tea I had hoped would extinguish the burn in my throat. "Seriously? Why would you think I wasn't planning to go to college? I've taken the SATs, I'm in all AP classes, and I have straight As."

Hensley's face morphed into something akin to pity and reminiscent of remorse. She tried to wave off her response, but I stared at her, waiting on an answer. "I just didn't know if you would race off with everything you've been through this year. But I'm happy you've been thinking about your future, even if you haven't shared it with any of us."

"Yeah, yeah, yeah. Enough of that." Portia cut Hensley off. "Have you heard back from any of them?" Her eyes were intently focused on mine, and a flash of insecurity crossed her expression.

I nodded. "All three."

Portia turned and leaned back into the corner, still facing me. "Who the hell applies to colleges, especially those colleges, without telling anyone?"

"Ethan and Carson knew." That wasn't the answer any of them wanted.

I was afraid to move or take my focus off Portia. I couldn't tell if she was ready to pounce in anger or elation, and I wasn't sure I wanted to find out.

She hit her little fist on the table, shaking the silverware and the glasses. "And?"

I shrugged. "I got in." Most kids would celebrate that accomplishment. University of Maine was a state school, and it had a solid liberal arts program. Columbia and Carnegie Mellon were prestigious, and I'd been lucky not to have been waitlisted.

Hensley reached across the table and took my hands in hers. "Oh, Jude. That's fantastic. I wish you'd told us; we could have spent spring break seeing the campuses." The warmth of her palms threatened to make my hands sweat if I didn't get out from under them.

Pulling back, I kept Portia in my line of sight, still unsure of which way her reaction might go. I relaxed against the cushioned seat and tried to play all this off. "It's okay. I'm pretty set on U of M."

The tension in Portia's shoulders and spine ebbed, and she let out a sigh that I felt rather than heard. The air from her lungs brushed my cheeks, bringing the citrus scent of her juice with it. "You're joining me on campus?" If she weren't careful, the Shaws would see the tears in her eyes.

"If you won't think I'm invading your territory."

She shook her head in quick jerks, confirming she wanted me there as much as I wanted to be near her.

Ernie finally piped up and dropped his crossed arms. With his forearms next to his silverware, the way Hensley's had been only moments earlier, he eased across the table, maintaining eye contact. The vein in his forehead—the one that bulged when he was upset or thought too hard—became prominent when he started to speak. "Did you even consider Columbia or Carnegie? Jude, those are amazing schools to pass up for the University of Maine."

"Hey!" Portia expressed her displeasure at his crack at her college.

He held up one hand in her direction, stifling her objection.

"Maine's a good school, too. I just want to know why you chose it. Without having seen the other campuses, I don't think you're ready to make that choice."

"Ernie, I want to teach English. Even as a professor at a university with a PhD, I'd never be able to repay that kind of student loan debt."

Ernie used his index finger to trail the rim of his water glass. The vibrations stirred a gentle hum, but I thought Portia was about to knock it in his lap if he didn't stop. "What kind of cost are we talking?"

The waitress interrupted the discussion as she amassed piles of food in front of each of us. I'd need a nap if I consumed everything on my plate. With my fork in hand, I presumed I'd gotten out of any further discussion. No such luck. Ernie was like a cadaver dog with a scent.

"Tuition cost?" he asked, shoving a forkful of corned beef hash into his mouth.

I inhaled deeply and exhaled. The truth was I never should have applied to either without a concrete way to pay for one of them. "Carnegie Mellon is about seventy thousand a year with room and board, and Columbia is fifty." As high as my SAT scores were, even coupled with straight As and advanced placement classes, I hadn't gotten any type of scholarship money, and I could never ask the Shaws to foot that kind of bill.

Hensley nearly choked, and Portia laughed awkwardly. The Shaws were well-to-do, but they weren't rich, and I wasn't legally their responsibility after I graduated from high school.

I thought I would set all their minds at ease. "I want to go to the University of Maine. It's a great school, and Portia will be there. It's not that far from you guys. It just makes sense. Two to three hundred thousand dollars of debt for a teacher doesn't."

Portia tilted her head, and then she reached for her glass. "To Jude and the University of Maine."

The three of us followed her lead in a toast, and I appreciated her support. The truth was, she was the only reason I'd applied to U of M. And had things not changed between us, I had planned to accept at Columbia—regardless of the cost. But that was a secret I'd gladly take to my grave.

"Do you think Hensley saw us?" Portia craned her neck, peering around my shoulder.

"If she had, she wouldn't have kept walking." I could see the thrum of Portia's anxious heartbeat in the vein that ran along her neck. I'd be worried if she weren't grinning from ear to ear.

Her fingers dug into my sides as she practically climbed my body to bring my face low enough for her to reclaim my lips. I'd learned quickly over the last four days that Portia was big into public displays of affection. There was no doubt the two of us were together, and to anyone we encountered it appeared we had been for ages. We'd held hands all over town, taken a couple of little day trips to see shit neither of us cared about as an excuse to have time away from Ernie and Hensley, and even if they were around, we found ways to sneak in stolen kisses and quick glances. Part of me worried if the thrill of hiding from them held the appeal for Portia.

I pulled away from her kiss, distracted by my thoughts, as I leaned against the brick building we'd had lunch in. It had warmed up a little as the week progressed, but the chill still lingered in the air, just not as icy as it had been that first day we'd arrived. My breath mingled with hers in a fog. It was hard to force myself to stop when all I wanted to do was consume.

Her lips had become chapped from the additional moisture and cold weather, yet, for some reason, it made them all that much sexier. And her normally milky skin retained a rosy hue right at the cheekbones. The shamrock green of her irises were more vibrant than I'd ever seen, and she appeared truly happy. It was in her eyes, the way she carried herself, and the gentle way she acted when we were alone.

I cocked my head to the side, pushed off the wall, and laced my fingers with hers. My hand swallowed hers in size, and somehow, between that and our height and size difference, I felt like her protector. Her shield against the world. "Come on. Let's take a walk...in the opposite direction of your mom." I chuckled and tugged her along with me.

Personally, I could get lost in Cape Cod. Not physically, mentally. It was easy to be at peace here. The air was clean, the town was quiet, and nature was the only thing to ever disturb me. Even at seventeen, I could picture myself with a stack of books and an Adirondack chair out on the back porch of a Cape Cod-style house, maybe even overlooking the water. I enjoyed the pace here.

"Penny for your thoughts." Portia peeked up at me, shielding her eyes from the sun with her hand.

In some ways, Portia and I were very different. The hustle and bustle never appealed to me, and she'd become quite the social butterfly since going to college. I'd always kept to myself, whereas, she confided freely in Hensley and me. "What do you want to do when we leave here?"

She swung our hands between us and kicked her foot out, taking an exaggerated step. Without letting me go, she turned to face me and walked backward. "Sadly, I have to go back to school," she pouted.

"I meant about us." We stopped moving, and I brought her to my chest. "Was this just a spring break thing?" It would decimate me to hear her confess this had only been a fling, but I needed to know where we stood and how she planned to move forward.

Portia pulled her head back, and her expression fell. I couldn't tell if I'd hurt her feelings or offended her, but I'd elicited a strong emotion one way or another. Or she'd smelled something rotten that filled her nostrils with a pungent scent.

"Jude Thomas. Really?" She dropped my hand and cocked her hip. "You think this is just a fling to pass the time in a boring town?" The crease deepened between her brow, and the shades of green in her eyes were taken over by hues of deep blue.

Shrugging wasn't the best idea, which she made clear when she swatted at my stomach. "I don't *want* to think that. I also don't want to get home and not have a clue where we go from here."

Her hands fell to her sides, and a gentle smile eased the tension in her face. Any time she pressed her body to mine and stared up through the vast height difference, I always saw adoration reflecting back at me. And it was the most beautiful sight I'd ever witnessed... even more so than having her come undone in my arms.

"Jude..." My name lingered between us like a promise. "I don't know when it happened, or how I realized it, but somewhere along the way, it dawned on me that no one else would ever compare to you. Guys I met couldn't hold a candle to the connection we shared. And what I'd once believed was just us being best friends, turned into a love that is soul deep." Her eyes closed slowly, and her long, dark lashes drew me in, as I waited for whatever else she had to say. When she parted them again, the blue had cleared and strands of gold feathered the green. "The only thing I can tell you with any certainty is that I never want to go back to how we were before."

My chest heaved with the weight of her admission, and I was suddenly warm, where moments earlier, the frosty air had chilled me. "I don't, either. I've loved you for as long as I can remember, and I want to tell the world. But Ernie and Hensley aren't going to take it well."

Her shoulder lifted as she drew in a deep breath and lowered when she exhaled. "Then maybe for now, we don't tell them. You'll be eighteen next month, and then you'll be graduating and going to college. It will be a lot easier next fall when you aren't living in their house."

"I'm not sure they'll ever get past the idea of being parents to both of us, Portia. It's the whole reason..." I trailed off, thinking better of what I had almost admitted.

"The whole reason what?" She stepped aside when a pedestrian bumped her shoulder, and I moved with her.

A truck passed by, and I waited for the noise to disappear while I collected my thoughts. I didn't want to keep this from her. I also wasn't sure how she'd take what I was about to say. I raked my hand through my hair and sighed. "It's the whole reason I said no to the idea of adoption."

She laughed as though she hadn't understood. A gust of wind brushed by, plastering her hair across her face, shielding her expression from view. I watched as her delicate fingers reached up to tuck the dark strands behind her ear. "What do you mean?"

"Just what I said. I didn't want them to adopt me because of my feelings for you. Legally, that would make us siblings, and while I wanted to share a last name with you, it isn't Shaw that I want to scribble after mister and misses...it's Thomas." My chest constricted painfully, and I wondered if my ribs would break under the pressure before she spoke.

Her throat moved when she swallowed. "You want to marry me?" Tears pooled in her eyes and finally broke free when she blinked. She licked her lips, and when I could see the green again, I wiped away the emotion that trickled down her cheeks.

This conversation was far too heavy to have on a sidewalk in public, but there was no way I could divert where it went or how we got there. I had to face it head on and hope it didn't shut her down. And just before I opened my mouth, a car stopped at a light next to us, and through the closed windows, I could hear the faint sounds of "Hey Jude" on the stereo inside. Whether it was hokey or not, I believed it was a sign from my mom telling me this was safe.

"Not today, but eventually, yes."

"Is that why you chose University of Maine?"

No point in holding back now. I cupped her jaw, not even considering who might witness my affection. The chapped skin of her lips was rough on my own, and when she parted, our tongues tangled and stirred my arousal. Somehow, I needed to end this conversation and get her back to our room without anyone noticing.

I broke away with one more quick peck and held her gaze when I said, "Yes."

13

PORTIA

It was what he said, how he said it, the way he kissed me before he admitted he'd already made plans for our future. It might have been naïve to believe that two foster kids who'd been to hell and back could end up with a happily ever after that included each other, but it was a dream I wanted to fall into head first.

There was no resistance on his part when I linked my arm in his and redirected us back to our bed and breakfast. I'd rather hold his hand, but if we ran into Ernie and Hensley, us being arm in arm wouldn't rouse any suspicion. By the time we climbed the steps into the B&B, the quick pace back had left us winded. We hadn't seen or heard from my parents since lunch, and my best guess was they were off touring lighthouses or something equally as boring, which would allow us several hours before they would expect to have dinner. I planned to enjoy every minute.

Jude closed the door to our room and engaged the lock. The moment he faced me, my fingers worked the zipper on his jacket. I had his coat and mine off in seconds. I raised the hem on his shirt, and his skin pebbled under my touch. Even with my arms completely extended, I couldn't get the garment off, so he reached behind his neck, tugged on the collar, and yanked it over his head. Jude didn't immediately drop it to the floor. It stretched across his arms, leaving his shoulders exposed. It was like a spotlight shone down on him.

I'd noticed subtle differences in Jude every time I came home, but not having seen him since Christmas, the changes were huge. What was left of the scrawny, lanky guy during the holidays had vanished. In his place came a man with broad shoulders and thick, taut muscles that strained to be set free. The fabric fell to the floor, joining the jackets. The freckles were less prominent on his chest and were now shadowed by copper-colored hair, darker than that on his head. A patch hovered between his pecs and then reappeared under his bellybutton and highlighted a path beneath his jeans. As my sight followed the map that puberty had left for me, I couldn't help the sharp intake of air when he leaned back slightly and every muscle in his stomach flexed and accentuated the deep V in his lower abdomen.

Somewhere in the last year, Jude had become a walking sex symbol, and I'd missed the advertisement. When I licked my lips, still staring at his waist, he let out a deep, guttural laugh that drew my attention to coffee-colored eyes. It might have been the sun streaming through the windows or the lust-induced haze clouding my mind, but for the first time, I caught hints of cinnamon swirled with the brown.

He didn't let me dawdle or even seem to notice that I'd stalled. With a delicate touch, he removed my blouse and then unbuttoned my jeans. My tongue snaked out, and a rumble came from his chest when I drew the bottom one into my mouth. Chewing on it seemed to be an aphrodisiac for him. I shimmied out of the only clothing I had on, and he did the same. Jude's strong hands reached for my hips, and then he lifted me. Instinctively, I wrapped my legs around his waist, pressed his erection between us, and secured my arms around his nape. My lungs filled with the scent of lemon and cedar when I buried my face in his neck. And I held on when he carried me to the bed.

It hadn't taken Jude many tries to figure out what turned me on, where my erogenous zones were, or that I preferred it slow and deep. I didn't have anything to compare it to, but he was thick and the perfect length to thoroughly satisfy me with every thrust, each pull. His hips rolled in waves, and my spine arched in response. With my throat exposed, he pressed a kiss to the vein that pulsed in time with my erratic heart, and when his teeth grazed my skin, I called out his name and detonated around him.

I loved the sounds he made when he knew I'd exploded, almost as much as the ones that echoed around us when he joined me. They were seductive groans of pleasure that filled my dreams and made my day. I'd become as addicted to his body and our physical connection as I had to the idea of a relationship with him, regardless of how taboo some might think it was.

Lying there next to him, I dragged my fingertips along his ribs, while his drew intricate patterns on my back. I fantasized about a time where we wouldn't have to hide, where I could see him daily, and we would be free to explore who we were meant to be together as adults, versus where we'd come from as kids. I didn't want to consider the rough road we faced for the next few months or the turmoil we might endure when we came clean to my parents. In the end, I believed we'd overcome the obstacles.

I just had no idea how soon they'd come or how high the hurdles might be.

NEITHER OF US TOOK INTO CONSIDERATION HOW HARD THE separation would be, much less how difficult keeping our relationship a secret would be. When I got back to school, Jet honed in on the difference in my attitude before I'd left compared to when I returned, and I couldn't give her anything other than Jude and I had worked through our differences. I had to sneak phone calls to him and change my tone when she walked in the room. But it was the physical loss of not having him near that was the hardest to deal with.

She'd gone to class, leaving me in our room alone. I was biding my time until I could call Jude. As soon as I was certain he wasn't at school, I unlocked my phone and touched his name on my favorites list.

"Hey, babe." Those two words uttered from his mouth in a deep, rich baritone released my frustration and warmed my heart.

I never thought I'd crave hearing a common term of endearment, but something in his inflection, the casual way he said it, and how the words hit my ears made me swoon every time. "Hey." It also made me miss him even more. He was a drug I couldn't get enough of, and I needed the highs to last longer after each dose.

The radio played in the background, although not loud enough for me to decipher the song, just enough to be aware it was on.

"Everything okay?" His voice was distant, indicating he was in the car and I was on speaker.

I'd learned the hard way not to blurt out anything until I knew who rode with him. Not long after we'd gotten back from Cape Cod, I'd called, and when he answered, I told him all the things I missed about our time together—in graphic detail meant for his ears—only to find out Ethan and Carson were with him and heard every word. Jude hadn't cared. After they gave him a ration of crap about incest and ribbed him about losing his V-card—a term I'd thought only women used—they seemed happy for him and left it alone...with the understanding that it wasn't public information.

"Are you by yourself?"

"Yeah, I just dropped Ethan and Carson off. What's wrong?" If concern were tangible, I could have grabbed hold of his.

A heavy sigh echoed through the phone, and I realized it had come from me.

"Portia? Talk to me. What's going on?"

Any bit of truth I gave him would sound clingy and whiny, even if Jude wouldn't make me believe he took it that way. "I just miss you."

Without skipping a beat, he suggested, "Aren't you coming home this weekend for my birthday? If Bart or Jet can't drop you off, I'll come get you after school on Friday." The sound of him lifting the emergency brake told me he'd reached my parents' driveway. He'd sit in the car as long as I wanted to talk so that we were free to chat without being overheard.

"I'm sure Bart wouldn't mind, but do you?" My need for reassurance was annoying, even to me. I didn't need an invitation, especially not for his birthday, but I still craved one just the same.

He chuckled and then coughed when he tried to conceal his amusement. "You do remember that you live here, right? I'll come get you every weekend if you'll let me. It doesn't have to be for my birthday."

"We both know that would raise red flags. Mom and Dad would think I was unhappy at school or about to flunk out. Then I'd be at weekly sessions with Dr. Vanderhugh alongside you."

"Pfft. I'm down to bi-weekly meetings, thank you." His tone lilted in humor. "Point being, I want you home as often as you think you can come. Plus, Ernie and Hensley are doing some square-dancing thing on Friday night, so we'd have the house to ourselves."

It wouldn't have taken a promise of time alone to convince me to show up, but it definitely brought an unexpected smile to my face. "You're not going to be out with Ethan and Carson? Eighteen is a pretty big birthday."

His birthday wasn't until Saturday, but I knew my parents would take him out to eat and make him do the family thing that night.

They'd already expressed their desire for me to be with them, but I still needed Jude to tell me he wanted me there.

"It's easy to divert their attention. I doubt they even remember it's my birthday. Plus, I see them every day of the week. You, on the other hand, are the pot of gold at the end of the rainbow. Every time I think I'm close to reaching it, the rainbow disappears."

"I think your analogy is a little off, but I get the point. I'll see if Bart minds dropping me off."

He hesitated, and finally offered, "You know, if you don't want to come home, I can come there. I just won't be able to stay. We could have our own little celebration."

We'd talked about this countless times, and every time we did, he ended up hurt. But until his birthday, he was a minor. My friends also thought of him as my brother because that's how I'd introduced him. I didn't have a clue how we'd finagle that when he was on campus, but until he was legally an adult, it wasn't an option. Bart was the only person I had confided in about Jude, and that was only because he'd suggested there might be something there to begin with. Either way, I didn't think it was safe to make waves. Not to mention, I had a single bed in a room I shared with another person. At home, we could use any time we found ourselves alone to our advantage.

"Jude…"

"I know. It makes more sense for you to come here. Plus, it would make Ernie and Hensley happy." He didn't sound as bothered as he normally did, but maybe that was because he still had a promise of when we'd be together. "Hensley is standing on the porch, so I better go. Let me know if you need me to come get you tomorrow."

"I will."

"Love you, Portia."

And with a few measly words, he put Earth back on its proper axis. "I love you, too."

Twenty-four hours later, Bart graciously deposited me in my parents' driveway and told me he'd see me Sunday night for dinner. The four of us—Bart, Jet, Todd, and me—still met up in the cafeteria for most meals, but Sunday night was a ritual none of us missed. And as much as I enjoyed them, I wasn't praying for it to come quickly, because it would also signal the end to my time home with Jude.

The front door was unlocked, and Hensley's car was in the driveway. As soon as I stepped foot inside the foyer, I could smell freshly baked cookies and hear her humming in the kitchen. "Mom?"

"In here, dear," she sang from down the hall.

I dropped my bag at the base of the stairs. My feet moved, and I wasn't sure which I was more excited for, a warm, chocolate chip cookie or Jude's kiss. Since he wasn't home, the cookie would have to occupy my time until something sweeter came strolling in.

I gave her a tight squeeze and took the opportunity to grab a treat from the pan behind her. "Hey, Mom." The melted chocolate burned my fingertips, but it was worth every ounce of pain once I took the first bite.

She giggled when she released me. "When was the last time you ate?" This was an ongoing joke every time I came home. In her mind, if I scarfed down three perfectly good cookies, that meant I hadn't had a decent meal in a week.

"Lunch," I said through a mouthful of rich goodness. "I can't help myself. You make the best desserts in the world."

Hensley motioned for me to sit at the bar while she loaded another pan with balls of uncooked dough. "I'm flattered. Did Jude know you were coming home? You might want to text him. He usually goes to Carson's house after school. He'll be thrilled you made it for his birthday."

I wasn't surprised he hadn't mentioned it to her. It was his way of lying low, and he knew I'd call her myself, anyhow. Which I had, hence the baking frenzy in front of me. Instead of confessing that he indeed was aware of my pending arrival, I produced my phone from my back pocket and sent him a quick text to tell him I was here.

"He knows now." Technically, it wasn't a lie.

She tore a paper towel off the roll and handed it to me. "You can slow down to breathe between bites; no one is going to steal them." Her mock irritation was charming. Hensley Shaw loved nothing more than to watch her kids enjoy something she'd made...even if that meant seeing it all over their hands and faces.

I wiped the chocolate from my fingers and then picked up another cookie. Before I took the first bite, my phone vibrated on the counter. I stuffed the entire cookie into my mouth, smiled at my mom, and did a happy dance on the stool when she turned the other way. Jude would be home in less than fifteen minutes, and I couldn't wait to see him.

It seemed like I'd just set the phone down when the front door opened. I looked over my shoulder at the sound of it closing to find the most gorgeous guy I'd ever known waltzing toward us. He stood just feet away. In the few weeks since I'd seen him, his hair appeared darker, more of a rust than red, and I'd swear he'd gained another twenty pounds of solid muscle. Jude never worked out, so I had no clue where his bulk came from, but it looked incredible on him.

"Hey, sunshine." I wagged my brows, knowing my mom stood behind me and couldn't see the way my face lit up while I stared at him.

He narrowed his eyes, unable to respond to my innuendo. "Brat."

Hensley rounded the counter to make her way to Jude's side. "Now, now, you two. Your sister just got home. Don't start bickering before dinner." She wrapped her arms around Jude's waist and leaned up to kiss his cheek. "How was school, dear?"

"Fine." Typical Jude response. Idle chitchat didn't interest him. It was also a way for him to escape without fanfare and for me to follow behind him shortly after.

He grabbed a handful of cookies from the plate Hensley had arranged them on, turned back toward the hall, and pushed me off the stool with his elbow when he walked by.

"Be nice to your sister, Jude," my mom called out, shaking her head. She liked to pretend our behavior irritated her, but I knew for a fact she preferred this over the three months of silence she'd endured after Christmas.

She hovered near the counter, and I righted myself on the stool again. When I popped a third cookie in my mouth, she leaned over the granite and whispered, "You should probably go check on him. He's been pretty quiet since we got back from the Cape."

Music to my ears—not his being quiet, but her encouragement to chase him. She'd give us privacy in hopes that I could connect to him. I groaned to keep up appearances, when my inner self flipped cartwheels of joy. "Fine." I huffed and hopped down. I trudged out of the kitchen, down the hall, and then practically ran up the stairs as soon as I was certain she couldn't see me.

Once I hit the second floor, I could hear the Beatles behind his bedroom door, and I worried about his mood on the other side. Anything that reminded him of his mom sent him into a downward spiral, but when I knocked, he opened, poked his head out to look down the hall, and then snatched my wrist to drag me into his cave without being seen. The instant we were trapped inside his room, he flicked the lock, pushed me against the wall, and he bent down to cover my lips with his.

The tousle of our tongues left me gasping for air. My chest heaved, my thighs quivered, and my panties were uncomfortably wet. Jude had taken me from concerned to aroused in three-point-five seconds. He didn't wait for an invitation or even ask permission. Clothes flew in all directions, and before I knew it, we'd backed up to the bed. He sat on the mattress, helped me climb into his lap, and then dropped his gaze to watch every inch of his erection sink into my heat. With one arm wrapped around my lower back, he guided me to the rhythm he set, and he covered my mouth with his hand until he delivered the pleasure he wanted me to have.

With each thrust, my groans grew louder and his moans intensified. He dropped his hand to my ass when I buried my face in his shoulder. The reason for the loud music resonated with my release and subsequent cry. It was a signal for Hensley to leave him alone and a mask for the noises we created. The second my teeth hit his skin, his jaw tensed against my cheek, and he drove into me one final time, holding himself there while he pulsed into me.

When his grip relaxed, he didn't encourage me to get up, and I didn't make any indication that I wanted to leave. It wasn't until he softened and slipped out of me, that I leaned back, took his mouth in a slow, passionate kiss, and then met his loving eyes.

"Happy birthday, Jude," I whispered.

He smacked my ass and gave me a shit-eating grin. "That's not until tomorrow. But I'll be accepting those types of gifts all weekend." Jude flinched when I swatted at his arm, while I was still firmly nestled on his thighs. "Just from *you*! Damn, don't get all violent on me." With a peck to my forehead, he stood, taking me with him.

I slid from his grasp and down his legs until I stood on my feet. His body was slick with sweat, as was mine. I wanted to rinse off in the shower, but that would draw Hensley's attention. Instead, I stepped into his bathroom, found a washcloth, and took a whore bath in the sink.

Jude, on the other hand, didn't bother to cleanse any part of his body. He tugged his jeans back on—sans boxers—and went without a shirt. He was laid out on the bed in a post-sex haze when I reemerged from the bathroom.

"Do you want me to get you a towel?" I asked.

He crossed his arms behind his head. Then his long legs shifted when he put one ankle on top of the other. Jude was thoroughly sated and completely relaxed. "For what?"

The muscles in my face tightened into a grimace. "To get rid of…" I didn't have a clue what to call our juices without sounding crass. And I still wasn't comfortable talking about sex the way we performed it. "*Us.*"

He leaned up and over the mattress, grabbed my hand, and pulled me onto the bed. In a not-so-graceful move, I collapsed at his side, and he wound an arm loosely around my waist. "Not a chance." He didn't elaborate, and I didn't ask.

At Jude's request, we celebrated his birthday at the diner where his mom had worked when he was growing up. And when the dishes had been cleared, one of the older waitresses, who'd known him since he was a child, brought out what appeared to be the entire staff to corral around our table. Together, they sang "Happy Birthday" behind a lemon pie with one lone candle burning brightly in the center of the whipped cream.

When they were done, she set the pie in front of him, and he blew out the flame. His eyes glistened, but tears never formed. The lady leaned down and whispered something in his ear. He grinned when she patted his shoulder. I had worried that being here would set off emotions he wouldn't be able or ready to handle, but he soared through the night beautifully and appeared happy.

As we left the diner, I snuggled against his side. The smell of cedar and citrus wafted around me in a hug as tight as his actual embrace. And when he held the door open for me to walk through, he popped a kiss on my temple and whispered, "Lemon pie." Jude was high on life. He was also crazy for taking a chance that my parents might have seen his unusual affection.

Sometime after nine that night, we parked in the driveway. Hensley and Ernie wished Jude a happy birthday for the four-hundredth time today, and then they excused themselves for the evening. We lingered in the kitchen until we were positive they weren't leaving their room.

Jude held out his hand, and I took it willingly. Even in the dark, I trusted him to forge the way. But when we reached his room, I released his fingers. He flipped on the light, and I whispered, "I'll be right back."

I quickly stepped down the hall, changed clothes, and grabbed the present I'd brought. I hoped he didn't think it was stupid. I'd wrapped it at school and kept it in my bag, so the bow was a little mashed and the card was bent. I tried to fluff up the decoration and straighten the envelope, but it still just looked rather pitiful when I handed it to him.

He stuck his head out the door and looked both ways before he closed it behind me and asked, "What's this?"

I gave him a goofy look. "Umm…a present."

"But why? You've been giving me gifts all weekend." He winked, and I just about stripped right then and there to give him another.

"Just open it." Then, I shot my hand out to stop him. "You may think it's dumb."

He pushed my fingers aside and tore off the paper. Dropping the trash on the floor with one hand, he turned the worn book over and stared at the cover. His eyes remained there for an ungodly amount of time before he opened it. He traced the copyright, and while he studied the text, I started sweating with anticipation. And then the verbal vomit started.

"Jet and I went to a garage sale that the school had two weekends ago. A bunch of people donated stuff, and I looked through the books just to pass time." His eyes met mine, but I couldn't read them, so I kept talking. "It's not in the best condition, but it's a first edition *Huckleberry Finn*." Several pages were tattered and dog-eared, and the cover had been scuffed, but it was still a first edition.

"This was the first book you read from my shelf when we were kids…" He was correct, so I nodded.

Words were about to get messy, at least if I spoke.

He set the book on his nightstand, and without so much as a word, he tugged my body flush with his and held on for dear life. His lips pressed against my scalp, he planted a kiss there, and his breath fluttered on my ear when he leaned down without letting me go. "It's perfect. Just like you. Thank you."

I nodded against his chest, and when he finally released me, I gave him one more present—kneeled in front of him while staring into his eyes. The moment his head dropped and he fisted my hair, I expected to get a gift of my own. To my surprise, he gently eased his hips back until I released him. He undressed me, and then he finished removing his undone pants and tossed aside his shirt. He switched off the light, and we climbed into bed. There, Jude enjoyed his birthday until the very last minute, and sometime after midnight, I drifted off to sleep, safe in his arms.

The next morning, I startled, realizing I was naked in Jude's bed in my parents' house. Yes, we'd had sex multiple times when I'd come home, none of which they'd even been in the house for, but I hadn't been so brazen as to actually sleep this way. I'd always snuck back to my bed, fully clothed, in the middle of the night or early morning.

Jude didn't seem the least bit bothered by the situation. In fact, he grinned when I leaned back. He'd been awake for some time, based on the clarity in his eyes and the color in his cheeks.

"Oh my God, Jude. How am I going to get back to my room without Mom or Dad seeing me?"

His gaze roamed the room like he was looking for an answer he wasn't going to find. "The same way you have for ten years? Peek out the door and make sure no one is out there. It's not like they're going to be keeping watch."

The noose of guilt strangled me. "This is *so* different. And you know it."

"Only if you let it be. They don't know you're not in your room. It's like six thirty." He brushed the hair back from my face. "Although, I think we should tell them and stop sneaking around."

He had to be kidding, yet nothing in the way he held my stare indicated there was any humor in his suggestion. My heart accelerated with the idea of confessing to my parents that I'd been sleeping with—literally and figuratively—my foster brother under their roof.

The moment I began to shake my head to protest, he interrupted. "I'm eighteen. There's nothing they can do. I don't want to keep secrets, Portia."

I sat up, clutching the sheets to my chest. "We agreed on this. Not until you left for college." I wouldn't budge on the matter. I loved Jude, but I loved my parents, too. Now wasn't the time, and certainly not the day after Jude's eighteenth birthday. "You're insane. No."

Using his hands, he pushed himself up and back against the headboard. "You won't even consider it?" Incensed, irritated, confused, I wasn't sure which adjective best described his tone, but I didn't care for any of them.

"You're not thinking clearly. If they flip out—which I fully expect they will—there's no telling what might happen. You can forget weekend sleepovers. They'll never leave us alone in the same room again." I shook my head as I talked. "You have Ethan and Carson you can tell. I have Bart. Right now, that has to be enough."

At the point I finally stopped talking and studied his expression, I realized he'd conceded only because he loved me, not because he agreed with me. The chestnut hues that had lit up his eyes in recent weeks, darkened to a deep chocolate. He was hurt, and I'd done it to him.

"You know I love you, Jude. I just don't want to be kept from you. I don't want to create any room to allow that to happen until no one can prevent it, even if they try." I cupped his jaw and leaned in to kiss him.

He nodded, and the discussion ended. In the long run, he'd snap out of it and realize it was the right decision. I just hoped it happened before the fall semester started in four months. I couldn't stand a repeat of what had happened between Christmas and spring break.

JUDE

"I'D HOPED WE WERE DONE WITH DEBBIE DOWNER ONCE YOU AND Portia hooked up." Carson squinted to keep the smoke from his eyes when he took a drag off the joint.

"I don't have a clue what you're talking about." But I did. Ever since she went back to school two weeks ago, I'd tried to play it off, not just with my friends, but with Portia, as well. Evidently, I hadn't been all that successful.

Carson leaned back in his lawn chair and dropped one hand on the armrest, while still holding the joint with the other. He licked his teeth beneath his lips, and I studied him with odd interest as his facial expressions changed. They went from confusion to concentration and possibly curiosity. I watched him blink several times, open his mouth, close it, and he finally spoke in a relaxed, low tone. "You were you again. And then you weren't."

"That's profound. Thanks for clarifying the personality shift."

"You know what I mean. When you came back from spring break, you were the Jude you were when your mom was alive and healthy. It was as if Portia filled the gap your mom left. Now you're back to the sad sap you were after the funeral." He took another drag. "At least this time you're not pissy, too."

The smell of the marijuana and the tease of the temporary high started to get to me. He was right. We both knew it. A couple of tokes off that joint and I could be the jovial guy I was a few weeks ago. The problem was, I'd promised Portia I wouldn't mess with any of it anymore. It was a temporary fix. It only lasted as long as the high, and then I would be right back to where I was now. And while the appeal of a reprieve—however fleeting—was strong, my desire not to disappoint Portia was stronger. So when he held it out, I shook my head and watched him continue to smoke.

"You act like I was a whiny chick." I leaned to the side and attempted to get a contact buzz, unsuccessfully. "My mom had died. Surely my anger at the situation was excusable, or at the very least, understandable."

"I didn't say that I didn't get it, just that I was sorry to see it return."

Carson's garage was filled with a thick haze, and the sun being hidden by clouds did nothing to illuminate the space. It was dim and depressing to sit in there for hours. Add in the topic of conversation, and it created a recipe for suicide. I held my tongue and stared out the narrow windows at the top of the rolling door, watching the sky morph into various hues of grey.

From the corner of my eye, I saw Carson set the roach in the ashtray. He propped his elbows on his knees, and I knew from experience, it was the posture he took when he was about to get philosophical or play psychotherapist. "Why does it bother you so much that she didn't want to tell your parents?"

"*Her* parents," I corrected.

"That's just semantics."

"It's also the root of the problem."

He scratched behind his ear and faced me. "Do you not *want* to see her point, or do you really think it has no validity?" Sometimes I hated just how smart Carson actually was.

I'd thought about that very question more times than I cared to admit. "Both. Neither." My chest heaved with an exaggerated breath. "I don't want to believe she's right, because if I do, then I have to believe that what we're doing is wrong. And it's not. Regardless of how anyone wants to taint it, we aren't related. The only valid reason I had been willing to concede to was her being eighteen and me seventeen. Technically, I guess it was illegal for that reason, but hell, who was going to turn her in? I certainly didn't have parents around who would press charges."

The glimmer in Carson's eyes—could have been the glassy fog of marijuana—indicated his humor in my rationale. Nothing about this was funny, and I had yet to figure out why anyone thought it was.

"We're both eighteen. Why can't we do what we want?"

He shrugged. "Because even though you're not related, Portia's parents *are* your legal guardians until you graduate. You can sit here and pout all day long, but even if you disagree and don't care what happens the day after you accept your diploma, Portia *does* care. They *are* her parents." He leaned back again with a smug look on his face. "And if you love her, you need to respect it."

"When the hell did you become a fountain of wisdom?" I huffed, and a grin tried to take over, but I fought it hard.

"It's always been there. I just chose to save it for special occasions. People who appreciate it." His speech was slow and drawn out, making the statement somewhat comical. The inflection in his tone and the rhythm of his dialect made him sound like a burnout, regardless of his brilliance.

Carson smiled, and his eyes disappeared behind hooded lids. Even if he'd managed to lift my spirits temporarily, I desperately wanted to join in his state of bliss. If I didn't take off, I might give in to temptation, and that wouldn't make things any better with Portia.

Once I stood, I folded the chair I always sat in and put it on the shelf. "I'm going home. I've got homework to do."

"You're welcome to do it here."

I clapped his shoulder and then lifted my hand to raise the garage door. "I appreciate it, but I'll see you in the morning."

It was a short drive from Carson's house to the Shaws', but no sooner had I gotten behind the wheel than I replayed our conversation in my mind. Portia wasn't asking for a lot, just a few more months, but no matter how I tried to rearrange that in my mind, I either came out feeling she was ashamed of our relationship, or that I was a dirty secret—neither of which sat well with me.

After we'd gotten back from Cape Cod, I'd managed to convince Ernie and Hensley that I didn't need to see Dr. Vanderhugh anymore, and as much as I hated sessions with him, I wondered if I'd made the wrong decision. Carson was right, Portia filled some void. When I was with her, especially sexually, nothing else existed—including my grief. The moment she was back at school and I was home, I fought the darkness continually. It was exhausting, and so was the façade I tried to maintain.

The house was empty when I arrived, so I hiked up to the second floor to do my homework. No sooner had I opened my history book than a message lit up my phone.

Portia: Just thinking about you. ALL of you.

Seven words allowed her light to shine through my cloud. A smile spread across my cheeks at the innuendo.

Me: Yeah? Which part are you thinking about most?
Portia: Definitely your eyes. ;)
Me: Oh yeah? Do they turn you on?

My dick twitched, and my pants squeezed my growing erection. All it took was a hint for me to visualize Portia naked in front of me. And that quickly turned into me buried inside her. My fantasy went from Nicholas Sparks to E.L. James in mere seconds. I'd read them both.

Portia: They swim with hints of gold just before they turn into molten chocolate…right before you come.

I wondered if Portia might have been reading a little smut of her own. Never in my wildest dreams had I imagined her being into phone sex, or tempting me with erotic text messages. Yet she did both, and she did them well.

Me: I haven't noticed you staring at my eyes.
Portia: Maybe you should let me show you.
Me: FaceTime?
Portia: Nah.

Well, that was a bucket of ice water down the sexual pants. I was lost as to how to respond. She'd started this being flirty and then shut it down just as quickly. I sat there, phone in hand, staring at the screen, trying to figure out what I'd missed.

Portia: I had something else in mind.

My hopes for the evening were squashed, and so was my erection, but I'd play along to satisfy her.

Me: What's that?
Portia: Jet's gone tonight. Why don't you come see me?

One simple request produced heat between my legs and made my balls tighten. She'd never asked me to come to the dorm.

Me: Now?

Portia: The faster you get here, the more time we have to… enjoy each other's company.
Me: It's a school night. What am I supposed to tell Ernie and Hensley?
Portia: I'll call Mom. You start driving.

It might not go over well, but I trusted she'd take care of her parents. I had homework to do, but I'd stay up all night if I had to. If I didn't go tonight, I wasn't sure if I'd get to see her again before graduation, and that was still a few weeks away. Consequences be damned.

Me: On my way.
Portia: Be careful. Love you. <3
Me: Love you, too.

Fifty-one minutes and several traffic violations later, I parked in the same place I had the day I'd dropped her off. It was hard to imagine that in a few short months, I'd call this place home. It wasn't New York or Pittsburg, but Portia was here, and it was less than a third of the cost of Columbia or Carnegie Mellon—Portia made it priceless.

I didn't waste time hanging out in the car or checking out the people I passed on my way into Sander Hall. The only thing in my sight was my destination, not the distractions along the way. A group of girls hovered in front of the elevators, so I opted for the stairs. Taking two at a time, I reached her floor, slightly winded. I tried to calm my pounding heart before I knocked, yet the instant I saw her, I was on the verge of cardiac arrest.

It never failed. Every time Portia came home from college, she became more stunning than the last. When I saw her daily, I didn't notice the subtle changes in her hair or how she wore her makeup. Her eyes lit up with a different kind of love than I'd seen in them as a child, and today they were hooded with desire, intensified by the smoky shading of her eyeshadow. I'd never seen the silky robe she wore, tied loosely at the waist, and when the fabric slipped to expose her skin, I was instantly aroused by the sight of the knot on her shoulder I'd admired growing up. A coy smile played on her shiny lips, and I was in a trance staring at her, wondering how I'd gotten lucky enough to call her mine.

The plaguing void of her absence vanished, and everything in the world faded away, except Portia Shaw. It was as if the lights in the hall dimmed in her honor, and the chatter of voices silenced to give her center stage.

"Wow." It was one syllable and more of a moan than a word.

She grinned with embarrassment, tucked her hair behind her ear, and grabbed my shirt in a fist. One tug was all it took to bring me inside, and the door closed behind us with a thud. It was almost as loud as the thump inside my chest.

"You look pretty good yourself, sunshine." Her voice was sultry and seductive, or maybe my own lust distorted the sound. Regardless, I had trouble controlling my urge to strip her down and have my way with her.

I didn't bother to ask how she was. Instead, I wrapped my arms around her waist and drew her close. No sooner had we started to kiss, than she retreated. One glance at the expression on her face, and I was painfully aware something was wrong. Her nose wrinkled, her brow furrowed, and I was rather confident her jaw ticced. Before I could confirm that her teeth were clenched, her hands hit my chest, and she pushed away, separating the two of us with a foot of space.

"Where have you been?" The accusatory way in which she spoke didn't bode well for me. And when she crossed her arms under her pert breasts, there was no denying she was pissed. But just in case I'd missed her cues, she cocked her hip to the side and tapped her toes.

The cadence of her foot drew my attention from her face. I passed her chest and down to her toes before I dared look up. This wasn't good. And I had no idea what I'd done. "I was at home."

"Before that?" she quipped.

I hadn't done anything wrong, nor had I been anywhere that might upset her. "I went to Carson's after school, but that's it."

Portia whipped around, her inky locks fanning in a circle as she went. It took her precisely four steps to reach her bed, turn as quickly as she had the first time, and then plop down on her mattress in a huff. "What were you doing there?"

The interrogation had me on edge, and I was afraid to answer for fear that anything I said would only further upset her. "I go there every day after school to drop him off." None of this was new information. I'd been doing it all year.

Her lips pressed into a thin line, erasing all the beauty I'd admired only seconds earlier, and her darker makeup accentuated her displeasure when she scowled. "You reek of pot."

I shrugged. "Carson smoked in the garage like he always does." This shouldn't be a shock. And then it dawned on me. "I didn't do it with him, if that's what you're insinuating." Thankfully, I could say that honestly.

Portia's thin shoulders relaxed and so did the tense muscles in her face, yet the unhappiness lingered in the lines around her eyes and mouth. I took a seat on her mattress with one knee bent in front of me and the other foot planted firmly on the floor. Facing her, I took her hand, laced our fingers together, and let her see the truth in my eyes.

"I'm sorry." She cast her gaze to her lap. "I shouldn't jump to conclusions."

I wanted to tell her it was okay, but before I let her off the hook, I needed to hear the "but" that would follow. And when she began to stroke her thumb over the top of my hand, it wasn't far from coming. So I waited.

"After everything that happened at Christmas…" she trailed off.

I refused to put words in her mouth, although I didn't mind helping her articulate what was going on in that gorgeous head of hers. "You think…?"

She lifted her focus when I gently squeezed her hand. "It's just a hard limit for me. I know you don't think pot is dangerous and that it's nothing like heroin, but for me, there's no difference. Not after my mom." Her green eyes shimmered with unshed tears.

"You're right. I don't think they're even remotely close. But I didn't do anything, so you have nothing to worry about."

When she blinked, a tear slid down her cheek, washing away a thin line of the blush that had been painted there. "I just don't like the idea of you being around it."

I appreciated her honesty, even if it wouldn't change anything. "Portia, Carson and Ethan are my best friends. Just because they do something you don't approve of doesn't mean I'm doing it with them." I grazed my hair in frustration. This wasn't what I'd come here for. And that gaping hole she'd filled when I saw her started to open again as I defended myself. "I don't like the idea of you drinking at frat parties when I'm not around to protect you, either, but not once have I asked you not to do it. I trust you to be safe and faithful. I need the same from you."

"I *do* trust you. And if you want me to stop going to frat parties, I will." Her warm palm caressed my jaw, and she tilted her head slightly. The emotion in her eyes shifted from anger to remorse and then adoration.

"That isn't necessary. Just put as much faith in me as I do in you. Please."

She nodded her acceptance, and I prayed we were done with this topic. "I love you, Jude." Portia leaned in, sealing her declaration with her lips on mine.

My eyes drifted shut until she pulled back, without engaging in a passionate kiss, yet it was still tinged with emotion. "I love you, too." The gaping valley worked its way back together until it was a crevice instead of a divide. I tipped my forehead to hers, holding her stare. "I need you, Portia. In a way I'm not sure I even understand. Everything about you makes me better." A tiny smile crept up her cheeks, and I kept confessing, hoping to earn a crooked grin. "You create sunshine in a bleak world. You fill my heart and touch my soul. I'm invincible with you at my side."

They weren't just words to feed her ego; they were my truth. I might have had my man card revoked for leaving my testosterone at the door, or talking to her like a girl, but I didn't care. Portia was as critical to my life as air was to my lungs. One didn't exist without the other.

Silently, she stood. Portia turned on the lamp by her bed and then strolled across the floor where she engaged the deadbolt and flicked off the light. The soft glow in the room highlighted her delicate features, and the shadows accentuated her soft curves.

Portia climbed onto the bed, and I adjusted my position so I could face her. She nestled her legs between my widespread thighs, and I stared at her fingers as they untied the knotted belt of her robe. The sash fell to her sides, and she shrugged. The fabric slipped from her shoulders, down her arms, and finally pooled behind her. The love of my life modeled her impeccable body and enticed me to indulge.

She pinched my chin between her thumb and fingers and tilted my head. "Make love to me." The pink I'd always heard in her voice had gone from pastel to jewel tone, cotton candy to raspberry sorbet. Light to rich.

I'd never deny her anything I could provide, but this didn't take any coaxing. Portia was my religion, and I'd worship her body like a goddess. And when we united in communion, the hallelujah chorus sang out in our song of love.

I HAD STARTED TO FEEL LIKE A BOUNCY BALL WITH ONE FLAT SIDE. When I was with Portia, it was as if someone had launched me high into the air. Yet the moment she was out of reach and I couldn't smell the scent of her shampoo or taste the hint of soap on her skin, I crashed to the ground and flew off in odd directions, springing erratically around until I finally settled into a pit of despair in a dusty corner. With no one around to chase my proverbial flight path, I was forgotten until her face lit up my cell phone screen or a text message lifted me from the cobwebs.

Ernie and Hensley were on my ass about going back to Dr. Vanderhugh—a fate worse than death. I argued vehemently that my emotional swings were related to stress and not at all connected to grief. I'd long since packed that into a tidy box and stored it in the recesses of my mind, never to be opened again. Even still, every time one of them brought it up, it ripped off the emotional packing tape and exposed the loss again and again.

I couldn't confide in them. And Portia had made it clear—more than once—that disclosing our relationship wasn't an option. So, while admitting that Portia's absence was the cause of my mood swings could completely ease Ernie and Hensley's troubled minds, it wasn't something I could do without losing her. It wasn't my mom's death that sent me staggering into bouts of depression, it was not having Portia around. Phone calls, text messages, and FaceTime only went so far. And she wouldn't be home again until graduation.

Her class schedule and looming exams made visits impossible, and I had schoolwork of my own and finals before I could walk across the stage. It would put me one step closer to the fall and having her back in my world daily. So, for now, I just had to endure it. Only, I wasn't doing it with any semblance of grace.

As the weeks passed, my daily visits to Carson's house became more difficult to navigate, and my ability to resist temptation waned on more than one occasion. I just wanted to feel good, to escape the loneliness and heartache. Ethan and Carson were no help. Both believed Portia's stance on marijuana was over the top, and they lured me with the fresh smell of pine and their state of nirvana.

I dropped Ethan and Carson off at Carson's house while I ran home to help Hensley move furniture around in her bedroom. I had no interest in doing it, but it was sheer laziness, not a real objection. So, I conceded since Ernie was working late. I should have stood my ground, told her I had too much studying to do, anything other than walk into the house.

I didn't bother to take the keys out of the ignition and left my backpack and cell phone in the front seat. Hensley assured me it wouldn't take more than ten minutes; she just couldn't move the bed in their room without help.

The second I'd pulled into the driveway, she'd appeared on the porch. "Hey, sweetheart." It was like she had watched for me out the window. "How was school?"

"Fine." My response was terse, and she flinched slightly at my tone.

After a kiss on the cheek, Hensley pushed inside and then ushered me through. Once she passed me, squeezing my shoulder as she went, I followed her up the stairs. She took each step so slowly, my thighs burned by the time we reached the second floor and so did my agitation.

I nearly lost my temper when I stepped into her bedroom. There was stuff everywhere. Piles of clothes. Stacks of books. Picture frames lined the baseboards. Boxes stood four feet high in the corner. Except for the lack of smoke and fire damage, I'd swear a bomb had gone off. Standing in the doorway with my hands on my hips, I realized there was no way I'd be out of here in ten minutes, or even an hour. The clutter that littered the space had to be moved to rearrange the furniture.

Hensley faced me, clearly reading my irritation, and then she looked around. "I guess this little project got out of hand." Her eyes shimmered with remorse. "You don't mind, do you?"

Hell yes, I minded. I just wasn't going to say that, even though it clung dangerously close to the tip of my tongue. Lashing out at her would only result in another conversation about counseling. "It's fine. What do we need to do?"

She offered me a kind smile and an unspoken thank you, and I let the tension ease from my shoulders. The faster I got this done, the faster I could leave.

"Those boxes"—she pointed to the stack in the corner—"need to go in the attic. The clothes need to be bagged for donation and taken to the garage. And then, once we load the books onto the new shelf"—I hadn't seen it on the far side of the room—"then we can move the bed and dresser. I'll hang the picture frames later."

Maybe it wasn't as bad as it seemed.

Hensley continued to chatter, but I only half-listened and grunted at the appropriate times as I carried boxes to the base of the pull-down attic stairs. A few minutes later, I had them arranged in the storage space, climbed back down the ladder, and pushed it closed with a clatter.

"I know you have other things you'd rather be doing. I appreciate your help."

I was an ass. This woman gave and gave to me, and I couldn't do anything other than huff and blow with every step I took. I stopped and gave her a hug. "It's not a big deal."

She smiled against my chest and patted me on the back. "I'll go get the trash bags."

Four large, black bags later, the two of us lugged the heavy plastic down the stairs and into the garage.

Hensley stopped in the kitchen, waving me on. "I'm going to grab a duster. None of that stuff upstairs has seen a rag in ages. Why don't you start organizing the books into piles?"

That I could do with finesse. My shelves were more organized than the public library, and I had scads more than the few dozen that Hensley had accumulated on the rug upstairs. Grabbing the rail for leverage, I took the steps three at a time. Even with my mind some-where else, and my heart away at school, this was something I could enjoy. The feel of a novel in my hands and the pages under my fingertips always made me happy. It wasn't just the stories I got lost in; I loved the smell of worn paper.

Her collection was eclectic at best. There was no rhyme or reason to why she bought or read anything sitting on her floor. So, instead of categorizing them by genre, subgenre, and then author, I skipped the first two in favor of the last. I moved around on my hands and knees and started with Alcott on the far left. When I came across one I didn't recognize, I stopped to flip it over and read the back. Hensley baffled me. From classics to Harlequin romances to books on the psychological mind, I couldn't identify what held her attention. I set the novel in the *J* pile for Johansen and shifted back to the unsorted mess.

I froze at the site of the white cover, and my throat closed. My chest constricted so quickly and painfully that I worried I'd broken ribs. My heart thrashed under my sternum, and my mouth became as dry as the Sahara desert.

I'd seen that book more times than I could count.

I knew every dog-eared corner.

Every scribble and note in the margins.

And there wasn't a single tear on the jacket that I didn't associate with a memory, because I'd put most of them there.

But even if I were mistaken about the scars and wear and tear, the pitiful excuse for a submarine done in a red, permanent marker would be enough to confirm who it had originally belonged to.

My mom had saved for ages to buy the hardbound Beatles trib-ute. And when she had finally brought it home—after admiring it for what equated to years in my five-year-old mind—she spent even more time poring over the pages, reading the lyrics to every song out loud, taking notes in any blank space she could find, and telling me all about the inspiration for her favorite ballads. She'd been furious when she caught me with it, creating my masterpiece. When she snatched it from my hands, the marker streaked out to the spine, and my finger had snagged the edge, ripping the corner. It was the one and only time I could remember her being too upset to speak.

Even after the artistic mishap, she'd adored that book. Yet, it wasn't until this moment that I realized that I hadn't seen it since before she died. I leaned over, taking it in my hand. My fingers traced the raised title, and my palms began to sweat. I couldn't swallow past the knot in my throat, and tears not only stung my eyes, they streamed down my cheeks.

I hadn't heard Hensley enter the room, just the gasp she let out when she stood next to me. "Oh, Jude. I didn't realize that was in the pile." She might have been waiting for a reaction, I just didn't have the ability to speak.

With Hensley hovering over me, I tuned the world out to thumb through the pages. Due to the years of reading, it opened naturally to the song my mom had named me after. It was her favorite, and mine, too. No matter how many times she read it, she always started there. Her handwriting was as painful to see as a picture. And when I reached the front, I found a note. Not to me, but to Hensley.

"If you need to reach him, try lyrics. They speak to Jude the same way I would." And she'd signed her name in a verbose gesture, as though *Carrie* were regal—which she was.

Her voice rang through my head as if she spoke in my ear. God, I missed her...the way she'd run her hands through my awful, red hair as she sang from each page, and her arm around my shoulders when she told me why she loved George Harrison better than McCartney, Starr, and Lennon. I could smell the phantom scent that hours of working in the diner had left on her clothes.

What I couldn't do was breathe.

The edges of my vision narrowed with black shadows. Silver twinkles of light danced before my eyes. And the stabbing pain in my heart only increased with every intake my lungs managed to accomplish. The book hit the floor with a thud. Stumbling to my feet, I half-crawled and half-lunged toward the hall, desperate to escape the walls closing in.

Hensley called out after me. I heard the words. They just didn't register.

I flung the front door open, barely catching it with my hand, and slammed it shut behind me. I dashed to Portia's car, got inside, and turned the ignition. I wasn't in any condition to drive, but I had to flee. As soon as I hit the street, the tires squealed, and I took off through the neighborhood. At the first stop sign I came to, I grabbed my phone from the seat next to me and called the only person who could ease my pain. When Portia's voicemail picked up, I ended the call and dialed again and again. At the sound of her greeting the third time, I swung the car in an illegal U-turn and went straight to Carson's.

Neither he nor Ethan asked any questions. Nor did they dish out any smart-ass remarks about my emotional state. I held my hand out, and Carson raised his brows to silently ask if I was sure.

Consequences or not, I needed an out.

And I took it…with the joint pinched between my fingers.

THE BEST I COULD HOPE FOR, UNTIL PORTIA CAME HOME FOR THE summer, was to stay numb. I'd successfully managed to plan our phone calls around going to Carson's house, but she knew something was wrong. I tried to convince her it was just me missing her, although I was fairly certain Hensley told her about the book and my subsequent meltdown. Then, all manner of hell had broken loose last night when I'd given Hensley and Ernie my report card.

It was a good thing I hadn't planned to attend Columbia or Carnegie. After my fourth quarter grades, the offers probably would have been rescinded. I didn't give a shit. If I hadn't had straight As going into exams, it would have been far worse. As it was, I ended up with Bs, Cs, and an F for the quarter, which didn't affect my overall GPA enough for the University of Maine to care. It did, however, send the Shaws into a tailspin. Hensley threw out the word suicidal—laughing at her probably wasn't the best response. My "indifference concerned them," and Dr. Vanderhugh's name came up again. I was eighteen and done with high school—they could no longer force me to do shit counseling.

Which also happened to be the last thing I said to them that night before storming out of the house. I found myself in the same spot I had every afternoon and evening since finding that damn book...in the garage at Carson's. It was the only place my mind relaxed and pain didn't exist.

I had to get through today, and Portia would be home tomorrow. My world would right itself again, and I could enjoy the summer. There were bikinis, pools, and sex in the near future if I could get through tonight. Tomorrow, I could steal kisses from her sweet lips and stroke her until she purred. I didn't want to talk or hash out my emotions. All I needed was to bury myself in her body and get lost in everything that was her. It was selfish and slightly barbaric, but she was the only salve that could heal my wounds. Once I had her, *then* I could deal with the rest.

I sucked in a lungful of smoke and passed the joint to Ethan. He hadn't been at Carson's last night when I came back, so he'd missed out on hearing how things went down.

"How the hell did you manage to drop to Bs, Cs, and an F from straight As?" Ethan squinted at me, and the space between his lids was so narrow I couldn't see his eyes.

Talking to someone with their eyes closed was odd, but so was Ethan.

"Basically, bombed exams. It was just grades for the quarter, not the entire year." I shrugged and dismissed it without much thought.

I coughed on the smoke that took over every square inch of fresh air in the garage.

"That's what I don't get. Did you just not take the tests? Damn, you were present for class. You knew the first three-quarters worth of material. Statistically, you should have at least gotten Cs, not an F."

I shrugged one shoulder. "Yeah, apparently you don't get points for signing your name. They want you to actually answer questions."

He nearly choked, and Carson laughed at him in the seat to my right. "You left it blank? What the hell were you thinking? Dude, your entire future is on the line."

"Ethan, don't be an idiot. Jude's future is U of M and Portia."

"Chicks are shady, man." Ethan didn't have a clue what girls were or weren't. He'd never so much as been on a date. His virginity was firmly intact. And he had no prospects on the horizon. Girls used him to do their homework and help them cheat on tests— then promptly forgot his name...so maybe he did know they were shady.

"My decision about school wasn't driven by Portia." *Lie.* "I can't justify the tuition anywhere other than at a state school." It was the story I'd maintained with everyone, and I wouldn't change my tune now.

Ethan bought my lie. Carson just chose not to call me out on it and handed me the joint instead.

I didn't need any more, but I took it just the same. By the time I went home, I wouldn't even know my name if I kept this up. And while that should have been a deterrent, it only served as an incentive. The further away from reality I could get, the better. I had about twenty hours before I'd be whole again. The more of those I could forget, the better off I'd be.

The outside world ceased to exist in Carson's garage. His parents knew what we were doing and left us alone. We kept the garage closed so we didn't bother the neighbors, but we could still see through the windows at the top. So, when headlights appeared in the driveway, none of us thought anything of it. Ethan continued to ramble about shifty females, Carson sat in his chair with a dopey grin on his face, and I took another puff of the joint just as the door into the house opened.

I turned to glance over my shoulder—assuming it was one of Carson's parents—only to get the surprise of my life. There, mere feet away, stood Portia Shaw in all her glory. With her hair knotted on top of her head, she had on a tank top that showcased her thin shoulders and the tightest jeans I'd ever seen. But after I scanned her body and my eyes landed on her face, her angry scowl jolted me from my seat.

Her irises almost glowed in the dim garage—a fierce, basil green. My attention followed hers, landing on my hand. The smoke wafted from my fingertips, and the burning paper warmed my skin. The singe hit me the moment she spun and raced back inside.

Neither Ethan nor Carson realized what had just happened, nor were they paying attention when I tried to hand them the joint she'd caught me holding. I finally threw it in the ashtray and tripped over the leg of Carson's chair as I attempted to chase her. Before I could put my hands out to lessen the force, I absorbed the impact of the floor through my chest and thighs.

"Portia!" I screamed after her, desperate to stop her.

My friends both sat with haunted expressions as I picked myself up off the ground, dodged Carson's dad in the foyer, and then leaped onto the porch. My reflexes were delayed and so was my coordination. My stumbling feet couldn't keep up with the stairs, and I was a hair away from busting my ass when I caught her wrist.

She stopped and jerked herself free from my grasp. Streaks of dark mascara lined her cheeks in vertical stripes, and the whites of her eyes were bloodshot. There was no trace of the vibrant green, much less the love I'd waited weeks to see.

I dropped my hands to me knees and hunched over, trying to catch my breath and my bearings. With my eyes pinched closed, I shook my head. When I reopened them, the purple, metallic paint on her toes caught my attention. Her flip-flops were a reminder of how close the summer was and how soon everything would come together.

Portia had yet to say a word. The sounds of her sniffling were the only indication—other than her feet—that she was even still in front of me. I hated to hear her cry, seeing it was worse, knowing I'd caused it was crushing.

Once I was finally able to stand upright, I put my hands on my hips and dared to speak. "What are you doing here? You weren't supposed to come home until tomorrow." The moment the words fell from my mouth, I wanted to take them back.

"Mom told me about last night. I wanted to surprise you." She used the back of her hand to erase the tears. All it did was smear the makeup more. Even with her face in total disarray, Portia was still a work of art. "Guess the surprise is on me, huh?"

I closed my eyes slowly and shook my head. "Portia, just let me explain. Please?" When I dared to open them to receive her response, the light in her irises—the glitter, the gleam, the glow—was extinguished.

A gentle breeze brought the flowery scent of her shampoo, or maybe perfume, to my nose. It was refreshing and bright, clean and vibrant. It was everything I loved about Portia and all that I wanted to submerge myself in.

She twisted her hands together in front of her. Another tear slipped down her cheeks, and she finally spoke. "I'm going to go home. We can talk tomorrow."

My defenses engaged, and I immediately drew my proverbial sword. "Am I going to wake up to a family meeting around the kitchen table where I'm the focal point of the discussion? And you bail to leave me with the fallout of your noble deed?" I wasn't going to win friends or influence people with *that* tone.

Her lips pressed together and tilted up, but it wasn't a smile; it was a smirk of disbelief and, quite possibly, disappointment. "No. Your secret is safe."

If she wasn't going to rat me out, and she didn't want to talk, then I couldn't figure out the reason for the theatrics on Carson's lawn. Thankfully, there had been no yelling, just quiet condemnation. "Portia, don't be like this. Just talk to me." My tongue stuck to the roof of my mouth and muffled the last part of the sentence.

"Don't be like this? Are you kidding?"

"I just—"

"No. I'm not doing this here. I'd suggest you sober up and come home when you can safely operate a vehicle." Portia pivoted on the ball of her foot and stomped the remainder of the way to Ernie's SUV. Her slim fingers wrapped around the car handle and she yanked the door open. In the blink of an eye, she was in the driver's seat, backing out of Carson's driveway.

The whole thing was over as fast as it began. The high that normally brought a smile and eased the strain of life away, now bogged down my thoughts in a loop I couldn't break. The night I'd gone to see her at school, she'd made her position on drug use clear —recreational or otherwise.

I'd also promised her back in the fall that I wouldn't do them again. Then Christmas happened. We managed to come back from it. Now, regardless of the fact that I'd been honest, sitting in her dorm that day, she'd never believe I'd ever stopped. My only two alibis were as stoned as I was—not that she would have trusted them, anyhow.

Her taillights glowed in the distance, and when I couldn't see her anymore, I turned to go back inside. It didn't matter that I wanted to chase her. I wasn't in any condition to get behind the wheel of a car, and I had to wait it out until I could.

15

PORTIA

I'D LAIN IN BED WITH THE LIGHTS OFF FOR HOURS LAST NIGHT, waiting for him to come home. There hadn't been any point in trying to close my swollen eyes, sleep wouldn't have taken over, anyhow. Not until I knew he was safe. While I stared at the ceiling, my eyes drifted out the window. It never ceased to amaze me that no matter how much turmoil took place on Earth, the moon and the stars didn't lose their luster. They shone just as bright, and they hung safely in the sky where they'd been for ages, unaffected by any raging storm below. If I could have found a way to reach one of them, I would have.

It was funny in a non-comical sort of way, ironic, maybe— until I heard Jude close the front door and pad up the steps. I worried I'd been too quick to pass judgment. I wouldn't have been able to live with myself if I'd left him, knowing full well he was too high to drive, and something had happened. Yet, the sounds of his shoes taking the steps two or three at a time suddenly cata- pulted me back to anger. I had a hard time deciphering between that, hurt, and betrayal. There had to be a word in the English language to describe all those emotions wrapped into one, but I didn't know what it was. And when I went to get up to ask Jude what it would be, I gave myself a mental slap and rolled onto my side instead.

Our rooms—mine and his—shared a wall. I put my back to that wall, covered my head with a pillow, and tried to drown out the sounds of him getting ready for bed. He moved at a more lethargic pace than usual, which either meant he was still high or he hurt as much as I did. My heart made this strange thump in my chest, as if it were trying to beat correctly but sputtered or skipped a note entirely. It ached for Jude as much as it did me—traitorous organ. Not even the muscle that gave me life could remain loyal.

Somehow, when the thuds and the bumps on the other side of the barrier between us had slowed, and then stopped altogether, I had been able to close my eyes. I hadn't slept worth a damn, and this morning, I felt as though I'd been the one strung out last night. And when I went to the bathroom, I realized I looked like it, as well. Mascara colored my washed-out cheeks. Bags large enough to carry mine and Jude's issues to a foreign country hung under my lashes. And the whites of my eyes had so many red lines crisscrossing in every direction, they could be mistaken for roadmaps.

Discouraged, I leaned down, splashed cold water on my face, and attempted to scrub away the stains. When I glanced back in the mirror, I'd managed to remove the black streaks, just not the hurt. It was on display, and anyone who knew me would see it clearly. My eyes weren't their typical green. They'd muddied into a color I didn't recognize. The one person who'd always had the ability to right my world from any horrible twist couldn't fix it this time.

And I couldn't repair him.

It hadn't been clear last night. But now, my brain waffled between mixed emotions. Then, staring at myself in the mirror, not recognizing the girl I'd become, I realized that the hurt, the betrayal, the disappointment I fought wasn't my own. It was Jude's. And until he could reconcile that, I had to let him go. Not because I wanted to. God knew it would be a soul-crushing blow to us both.

We'd been *it* for the other more than half our lives. But instead of being each other's helping hands and shoulders to lean on, I'd become his crutch.

The urge to slump on the floor, cross my legs, and cry overwhelmed me. I couldn't image a life without Jude. Deep inside, I knew there would never be anyone else for me. Jude was *it*. He held every piece of me in the palm of his hand, but he couldn't give me the same because he didn't know where all his pieces were. He'd shattered into so many fragments and shards when Carrie passed away, we'd missed some, trying to clean up the mess. And others were so small they'd turned to dust, lost forever. There was no picture on the top of a box to indicate how his life should look after death, and we hadn't put the puzzle together so that it interlocked.

Agony engulfed me. A dense weight pressed on my shoulders and squeezed my ribs; it was difficult to breathe under the pressure. The fabric of my clothes scratched at my skin, leaving me raw. I wasn't sure what I'd say to Jude when the time came or when I should say it. Today was supposed to be the next step in our journey toward an open relationship. He'd worked so hard and overcome so much, and last night only served to taint the finish line.

My thoughts ran a thousand miles an hour as I started the shower, and they didn't slow once I stepped into the stream. The water didn't soothe my distress, and even being clean didn't wash away the truth. It clung to me like a wet T-shirt, just as ugly and uncomfortable.

I didn't linger under the spray. There was no doubt in my mind Jude would be anxious to talk. I debated putting it off until after the graduation ceremony, and in the end, decided that was cruel. It would give him false hope that he'd be able to weasel his way out of this. The only person he could talk to in order to fix it was a therapist. I didn't have the skills or the qualifications to deal with it. I prayed he wouldn't ask me not to attend the ceremony this afternoon, but if he did, I would honor his request.

The beauty ritual—which normally layered me with armor to fight the day—acted as nothing more than a mask to conceal my hurt. Once I finished, I appeared just as I always did…on the outside. I took a deep breath, walked out of my bathroom and then my bedroom, and down the hall to Jude's room. When I raised my fist to knock, I squared my shoulders and tried to swallow past the boulder lodged in my throat. The first was uncomfortable and the second was impossible.

Each rap of my knuckles on the wood sent splinters to my heart. There was no way to prepare to decimate my best friend, much less the boy I'd loved since childhood, and whose last name I'd hoped to carry one day.

He opened the door, and I had to stop myself from wrapping my arms around his waist and pressing my cheek to his bare chest. My heart wanted to wave a white flag. The possibility of never again feeling his muscles flex when he hugged me, or never witnessing him come undone with me, or having him hold my gaze with one that assured me he loved me more than anything else in the world was crushing.

Jude's pec flexed when he lifted his hand to his head and dragged his fingers through his auburn hair. The muscles on his stomach tensed when he clutched the nape of his neck. And the *V* I'd traced with my tongue screamed at me to make another choice. He was my drug, the only high I'd ever need. Mentally, physically, emotionally, he was my world. And I'd wait, no matter how long it took, for him to realize he was on a path to self-destruction and needed help to heal.

An awkward silence lingered between us, but he finally broke the spell. "Hey." A word, three letters, one syllable—and nothing but hopelessness.

"Hi." I took a deep breath, my chest rising and then falling as I exhaled. "Can I come in?"

Jude didn't answer. He merely waved me through. He closed the door behind me and reached for his stereo remote when I took a seat on the mattress. When the Beatles came through the speakers, it was evident Jude knew he'd need his mom. My eyes filled with tears when I thought back to the number of times I'd promised her to always take care of him and be his best friend for life. It was naïve, but I believed it then, and I still believed it now.

I thought I knew every Beatles song ever recorded, but the one that played wasn't something I'd heard before. If I asked, Jude could tell me everything about it.

"Can we talk about last night?" he asked hesitantly.

I nodded, and he joined me on the bed.

He opened his mouth, and I thought he was going to speak. Instead, he took a deep breath and then released it with a heavy sigh. Three Mississippis later, he let go. "I need you to hear me out before you say anything."

It was the least I could do. In the end, Jude would need to know he'd been allowed to say what was on his mind.

"Okay." My natural inclination was to push to my side of his bed, face him, and put my hands under my cheeks the way I always did. But I forced myself to stay rooted where I was.

"Did Hensley tell you that she asked me to help her move furniture in her bedroom a few weeks ago?"

I wasn't sure what that had to do with anything, but I shook my head since I didn't know what he referred to.

His brow drew in, wrinkling his forehead. "Seriously?"

"Yeah. I didn't know until I got home that she'd done anything in there."

When Jude shifted on the mattress, the scent of cedar and lemon brushed by me, tempting me once again to stop the confession and just move on. Our bodies could do the communicating for us—they spoke a perfect language that outsiders would never understand.

"I'd been kind of irritable since you'd been gone. It hurt that you wanted to keep hiding our relationship. And I missed you. But I was getting by. When I came to your dorm and told you I hadn't done anything since Christmas, it was the truth. I need you to believe that."

The thought certainly crossed my mind that he hadn't been honest. But if Jude made a point to clarify that, it was real. "I do," I confirmed with conviction.

"This past year has been hard. Anyone who's come within ten feet of me could attest to that." He paused and rubbed the back of his neck.

I tried not to stare, but I wanted to memorize every detail so I could recall them in my dreams until I could have him again. I wished the strands of gold were highlighting his irises; the rich brown always appeared so sad.

He tilted his head from one side to the other, cracking it both times. Jude was stalling. Whatever he had to say would ruin him. It would also probably be the most real emotion he'd expressed since Carrie had decided not to undergo treatment. "I miss my mom. Every day. And when she enters my thoughts, I force them away because it hurts too much to face them."

I reached out and held his knee to ground him and possibly offer a shred of comfort. And while he didn't brush it aside, he didn't cover it with his own.

"The fight at the start of the school year, the ecstasy at Christmas, and the pot the last few weeks were my attempt at warding off demons. They offered temporary relief, but an hour of laughter carried me through days of suffering." He scratched his temple and stared at me as though he waited for me to interject.

But I'd promised to listen, which I intended to do. And Jude needed to guide this part of our discussion, not me. My eyes never left his, so there was no doubt he was aware of my undivided attention.

"Christmas sucked. I was madder than hell at you for telling your parents about that party. They lost all trust in me, sent me to that quack, Dr. Vanderhugh, and watched me like a damn hawk. And every week when I had to walk into that guy's office, it ignited my anger all over again. I played the game. Went along with the sessions, but I didn't allow them to work."

Sometimes I wondered if it were possible for me to keep my mouth shut. "Why not?" I posed the question softly, more out of curiosity than accusation.

"Truthfully? I don't know. Best guess is…I didn't want them to. I *wanted* to be angry. I felt justified in it. That one feeling hadn't failed me when my mom was sick or when she died. Every other one had." He lifted his shoulders slightly and then allowed them to fall. "Then spring break happened."

I smiled. I couldn't have stopped the toothy grin even if I'd wanted to, which I didn't. I'd never regret anything about that week.

He huffed through his nose, and his eyes lost focus. It was clear he was reminiscing and maybe even wishing he could go back to that place in time. "It was as though God answered a prayer and gave me a blessing all at once. Other than my mom, you are the only thing in the world that makes me truly happy…core deep."

That was a heavy burden to carry, and one I wasn't equipped to hold. "Jude…"

"When you went back to school, and every time I saw you after that, it was like losing my mom over and over. I couldn't see you. I couldn't touch you. And hearing your voice only reminded my heart of how far away you were. Yet each time, just as I was about to break under the strain, you'd come home and patch me up until the next visit."

Patch him up.

I was a Band-Aid when he needed a tourniquet. He was bleeding out, and instead of stopping the loss, I merely mopped up the pool. And I hadn't seen any of it. I knew there was something wrong, but I had let him convince me it was just our being apart.

"So the day Hensley asked me to come home after school to

help her move the bed, I was irrationally agitated. I should have told her no. I could have admitted I was barely holding it together and had a hard time being in this house. Hell, anything would have been better than what happened." His cheeks flushed red, making his freckles appear to multiply.

My imagination took off with scenarios of what could have possibly taken place. My mom was about the sweetest person I'd ever met, and she adored Jude. She'd do anything to fix whatever was going on, if she knew about it.

He blinked slowly. Once. Twice. And on the third, he held them closed, pinched them together, and a tear managed to escape, despite his determination to keep them away. He had the most beautiful eyelashes—a rich ginger with honey tips—but when they were wet, they appeared muddy in color, and his fair skin tinted easily. An angry, scarlet line now surrounded the fine hairs. And when he finally looked at me again, the chocolate had darkened to coal. "It shouldn't have been a big deal." His voice cracked, and the dam broke. Jude didn't try to stop the flood of emotions. He seemed to just wade through it and hoped he didn't drown. "We moved boxes, bagged a bunch of old clothes, and then she asked me to organize the books for her new shelf."

I fought—literally sat on my hand—to keep from reaching out to cup his jaw. One kiss would stop the hurt. And if we came together completely, part of him would heal. But all that was a lie I wanted to believe, because that's what it did for me—not him.

Sex wouldn't heal him.

I couldn't heal him.

Jude had to heal himself.

He hiccupped, but he didn't try to hold back. Jude didn't wipe away the tears. He continued to expose himself, ripping off every foolishly placed Band-Aid and poorly placed stitch. "She had my mom's Beatles tribute book in a pile on the floor, Portia." My name tore through the room on a guttural howl. "And just seeing the cover, I was back on the couch, listening to her sing with her hand in my hair and her arm around my shoulders." His volume continued to rise, but I made no attempt to silence him.

Whatever was coming had been festering for the better part of nine months. The poison Jude needed to expel could be lethal if he didn't cleanse the wound. And if my parents were concerned by the noise, the moment they heard him sob, they wouldn't intervene. They'd wait until an opening presented itself.

If cries could reach God, Jude's were humming in His ear. It wasn't a tune I wanted stuck in my head. I doubted I'd ever be able to forget his contorted face, his eyes haunted with memories, or the torture he'd been living with for who knew how long.

I'd stake my life that this was a defining moment in both our lives.

His Adam's apple bobbed as he struggled to swallow. The color on his face now worked its way down his neck, and his shoulders and stomach were spotted with the same horrible red-wine glow. "I couldn't breathe. Blackness crept in, leaving nothing more than a pinhole of light. I couldn't get out of there fast enough."

Clarity returned to his eyes, and his focus shifted back to me. "I tried to call you, Portia. I called three times, but you didn't answer."

I'd been in a lab and hadn't had my phone. As soon as I saw Jude's missed calls, I tried to reach him. And when his phone went to voicemail, I'd called my mom who told me he'd gone to bed early. That was the point I had started questioning him. It all began to fall into place.

"And when I didn't answer, you went to Carson's house?"

He nodded, and his chest jerked with a sob he attempted to conceal. "I didn't plan to. And when I got there, he didn't ask any questions. I didn't smoke to get high; I smoked to stop the panic attack that I believed was going to end my life."

His calls had almost become scheduled after that night. And his voice was different, but not enough to really know whether something was wrong or school just kept him busy. With as much time as we'd spent between visits, I allowed myself to believe that it was the latter.

When he stopped speaking, it dawned on me that the room wasn't silent. I allowed the music to reach my ears, and the chorus to "Help" filled the space. Never, in all the years I'd known Jude, had I hated the Beatles as much as I did in this moment. It was like a plea from his mom on the other side of eternity.

I couldn't maintain eye contact. Guilt dragged my attention to my lap, and I finally pulled my hand from his knee to twist my fingers together. "I'm sorry, Jude."

"For what?" His tone was gruff and rubbed my frayed nerves.

"Letting you down. I could tell something was off with you. I should have pried. Done a better job of getting you to talk." Tears of my own now dripped from my chin. "I just thought everything would be okay once I got home. From that point on, there was no reason we wouldn't see each other."

"Don't do that, Portia. I intentionally kept things from you to ensure you wouldn't know." He'd stopped crying to comfort me. "I never lied to you. Not directly. But I did what I had to do to cope."

And this was the point where I had to tell him my side. I expected resistance and doubted I'd leave this room with my heart intact. It'd been pretty well beaten up already, but this would be the final dagger. "But you did deceive me."

He immediately went on the defensive, and his subdued posture jerked into one of aggression, causing me to look up. "To protect you."

My curt smile received an uneasy glare. "It wasn't to protect me. It was to protect you. I've been very clear about drug use and how I feel about it. It doesn't matter if you agree with my stance or not, I didn't hold back when I told you it was a deal breaker. I didn't give you an ultimatum."

"Then what the hell would you call it?" he sneered.

I searched for any sign of the guy who loved me, but there was nothing hidden in his blank stare. "Preservation?"

Jude narrowed his eyes, and his head cocked ever so slightly. The tip of his tongue poked out and lingered there while he contemplated what to say. "I don't want to know where this is leading, do I?"

I gave in, cupping his cheeks in my hands. The stubble tickled my palms, and I wondered how long after this it would be before I felt his skin against mine. A storm brewed just beyond the windows to his soul, and I wished I could be his shelter. My eyes drifted shut when I leaned in. Jude's lips were soft against mine, and I hated saying goodbye.

"I love you. So very much."

He pulled out of my grasp, putting distance between us, bracing himself. "But?"

"I can't do this," I whispered.

Jude blanched.

But I had to keep going. "Not like this."

The fucking Beatles continued to play in the background, and I wanted to beat that damn stereo with a sledgehammer. They could join Janis Joplin on my list of most-hated bands.

He pleaded. "Tell me what you need. I'll do anything."

A somber smile twitched at the corners of my mouth. I tried again to touch Jude's face, but he stayed out of reach, and I dropped my hand to my lap. "I need you to find the boy I fell in love with and bring him back to me."

I couldn't be certain if the expression I witnessed was uncertainty, confusion, or anger...maybe it was a mixture of all three.

"What if he doesn't exist anymore?"

"As long as I'm still breathing, I'll hold out hope that you'll find him. Even if it's an older, more mature version." My cheeks ached as I tried to reassure him with a hopeful expression.

Jude didn't respond, not verbally, anyway. He stood with his back to me, and the muscles along his spine and in his shoulders flexed when he put his hands on his hips. Casually, he took two long strides toward his nightstand. His elbow swung back, and his fist went through the drywall. The unexpected impact caused my entire body to jolt.

My eyes never left him, and I tracked his hand when he reached for the knob. The twist of his wrist wrung my heart. And when he stepped to the side, opening the door alongside him, there was no question it was over.

I still sat in the same spot on his mattress where I had when this conversation started. I didn't need an engraved invitation asking me to leave; he etched the request in his posture. Defeat hung in his slumped shoulders, and rage lingered in his balled fist. Jude wouldn't raise a hand to me, but he *would* escort me out.

Nothing had ever hurt as much as walking toward the door, not even finding my mother with a syringe in her arm or the uncertainty that had followed. But before I got into the hall, I needed to make Jude a promise. I stopped in front of him, craned my neck to stare into the eyes he tried to avert, and placed both my hands on his bare chest. If he hadn't already been slumped over, I never would have been able to whisper in his ear. "Never doubt how much I love you...or how long I'll wait for you. My heart is yours to keep."

His jaw ticced, but it didn't deter me from placing a seal on that vow. I kissed his cheek and dropped my hands. The instant my palms left his skin, my blood ran cold, and a chill raced up the length of my spine. The loss was immediate.

I had barely taken a step when the door slammed behind me, shaking the pictures that hung on the wall.

I RETREATED TO THE SECURITY OF MY BEDROOM. IT WAS EERILY quiet. Jude had turned the music off or put on headphones, and I hadn't so much as heard footsteps outside my door. There had been no sign of Ernie or Hensley, either. It was as though I were the only one in the house.

Curled into a ball on my bed, I picked at Woobie's knotted fur, keeping the little bear close to my face. He reminded me of Jude, and if I closed my eyes and tried hard enough, I could smell Jude's scent on him. Or maybe that was my mind's way of comforting me through the most excruciating pain I ever remembered experiencing.

When my mom died and I was in protective services—before I'd been placed with the Shaws—a counselor told me that with each day that passed, the hurt would subside a little more. Even as scared as I had been, I just never missed a mother who hadn't really existed. But the fear had done the same thing the lady said the pain would do. And I got to where I longed for the sun to come up just to inch my way toward something normal.

It was going to take an infinite number of sunrises to gain any distance from this blow. I didn't want to be away from Jude. I didn't want to take a break. I didn't want to hurt him. I wanted him to deal with his grief, to learn to cope with his loss. Not just for us, but to make him a better man. A happier one. I just wasn't sure I'd pulled the trigger soon enough. I refused to believe that Jude was too far gone; however, if he wasn't willing to help himself, there'd never be a future for us together.

The strum of knuckles on my locked door startled me. It seemed as though I'd been lying here for an eternity and that somehow my parents had deserted me in that same span of time. Part of me hoped it was Jude, while another dreaded the notion.

"Portia, sweetheart. Can I come in?"

When I sat up, I glanced at the time on my phone and realized I'd lost hours in the fetal position with a stuffed animal that had seen better days. I tossed Woobie onto the mattress. I needed to get up anyway to get dressed for Jude's graduation.

"Yeah. Hang on." Thankfully, I'd sounded asleep, not upset.

There was no way I could lie to Hensley, and I couldn't tell her the truth.

The grim look on her face shocked me. "What's wrong?" As soon as I asked the question, Ernie appeared at her side.

He spoke over her shoulder. "We need to talk to you."

If either one of them told me someone had died or brought more bad news, I might lose my ever-loving mind. I couldn't handle anything else today. The ceremony and dinner would be difficult enough to get through. The summer would be torture.

They came in—always a united front—and sat on my bed. My mom pointed toward my desk chair, indicating I should sit, which I did. And then I waited.

"Jude has decided not to attend graduation." My dad delivered that punch as calmly as possible.

My attention swung back and forth between them, and I attempted to read what was going on. "What?" I wasn't able to get out more than a whisper.

"Portia, sweetheart." Not even Hensley's calming voice could tone down the alarms sounding in my head. "A lot has happened in the last few weeks that we haven't shared with you. You needed to focus on school, and it's our job to take care of Jude."

I couldn't stop shaking my head in disbelief. "He can't skip graduation."

Ernie leaned forward and placed his hand on my forearm, giving me a gentle squeeze. "He's asked to see Dr. Vanderhugh. We don't know what triggered it. He's resisted every bit of contact with a counselor, but something broke in him today."

"No." I was adamant. "No, he can't miss it. He's graduating with honors. You can't let him do this. He'll regret it for the rest of his life."

My mom stood and came to kneel in front of me. Her eyes glistened with unshed tears, and her voice shook when she spoke. "Portia, baby, we're afraid it won't matter if we don't get him the help he asked for."

"So what do we do?" I was baffled. I didn't think Jude would take what I had to say well. His being upset wasn't surprising. *This* reaction had me wondering what the hell I'd done.

My dad patted the mattress next to him, and I moved to take the seat he offered. My mom flanked my other side seconds later. "Didn't you mention that a group of your friends from school are going to Panama City?"

For the life of me, I couldn't figure out what the beach had to do with Jude. "Um, yeah. They left yesterday." I had wanted to go, just not as much as I wanted to see Jude.

Bart, Todd, Jet, and a couple of other guys and girls rented a house on the beach for ten days. Rather, their parents did. Based on the pictures, the place was huge and sat right on the ocean. I hadn't bothered to ask what it would cost to get in on it, although I was certain it wasn't cheap.

My parents glanced at each other. I huffed a nervous laugh while waiting for one of them to connect some dots for me. Hensley got to be the lucky one to paint that picture. "Why don't you call Jet. See if one of them would be willing to pick you up from the airport. We'll give you a credit card and money to cover your expenses."

"I don't want to go to the beach!" They were insane. "Why are you trying to send me away?" I was about to play a card that I knew would cause Jude to hit the roof if he heard it, but I didn't care. "That's my brother. He needs his family." I hated calling him that, knowing what existed between us. Unable to tell them the truth, I'd use whatever means necessary so he wouldn't feel abandoned. I may burn in hell for lying to my parents, but I'd fight for Jude... even if it meant I had to do it dirty.

They continued to glance at each other, and I lost my cool.

"What?" It came out louder than I intended. I was on edge and freaked out about whether or not this was a result of what I'd asked him to do, or if he had given up on himself.

The bed shifted when Ernie repositioned his legs to face me. Neither of them ever acted this...vague. "Jude doesn't want you to be a part of this." Well, *that* was pointed.

My mouth gaped.

Dad halted my objection. "Portia, he's embarrassed and doesn't want you to think less of him. He just needs a few days to meet with Dr. Vanderhugh so they can formulate a plan to get him feeling better. By the time you get back, we'll have things situated."

If he patted my arm one more time, I might unleash on him. He was talking to me the way he did when they told me Jude was coming to stay with us...when I was *nine*. My parents weren't normally rigid people. They were flexible and willing to negotiate on just about anything, yet there was no denying, this wasn't open for discussion.

I stared at him like he'd sprouted a third head, but I finally conceded. "I'll call Jet."

Four hours later, I boarded a plane to spend the next nine days with my friends. When I left the house, Jude was nowhere to be found. I didn't have the courage to ask for fear my voice would crack, and I'd break down.

Once the river of truth started to flow, I would spill every secret I'd kept behind the dam.

16

JUDE

FOR THE LIFE OF ME, I COULDN'T RECALL WHAT I'D SAID TO ERNIE after Portia left my room that day. From the moment she told me to find myself, until the time I walked into Dr. Vanderhugh's office, there were only fractions of time I could clearly visualize. The same thing that had happened when I found the Beatles tribute book in Hensley's room happened again when Portia gave up on me. Only this time, I didn't have anywhere I could run.

The walls had closed in as the darkness narrowed my field of vision. My chest constricted, my heart raced, and I had kept it hidden so Portia wouldn't see how truly broken I was. The slamming door sparked impending doom, and I was certain my death was imminent. Ernie's panic-stricken face was crystal clear when I got downstairs, yet how I had arrived there was a mystery. Once I had gotten out of the house, the possibility of death by suffocation waned. It might have been something Ernie had said, it could have been escaping the torture chamber, or possibly fresh air and sunlight. I doubted I'd ever know.

The first thing that was familiar was the silver-streaked hair and wire-rimmed glasses of Dr. Vanderhugh. My ability to breathe began to return. My heart and chest still hurt, but the pressure faded.

It was the most terrifying experience of my life, dwarfing the loss of my mom and Portia. I remained aware of the physical pain and anxiety, fearing I wouldn't take another breath, yet my surroundings and what brought me out of it were a mystery.

It was late afternoon by the time we had arrived, and I spent about two hours with Dr. Vanderhugh. After seeing me on such short notice, he assured me that I would survive, gave me a prescription for Xanax, and diagnosed it as a panic attack. He didn't make light of it. He did, however, tell me that I needed to make some changes. It wasn't the first or even the fifteenth time I'd seen him. I'd given him enough information in each session that I'd attended to say I'd adequately participated, just nothing of substance that might have led to any real healing.

That day, sitting on the couch in his office, I committed to him, and to myself, to get serious about processing my grief. I also told him the truth about Portia, our argument earlier that morning, and about my drug use. Given the circumstances, he and I agreed that my living situation wasn't ideal during therapy. He had managed to work me into his schedule for a session a day while Portia was gone, and at the end of the week, we called Ernie and Hensley in.

My knee bounced, and Ernie tried to pat it. Even his smile and the gentle way he'd always loved me didn't do much to settle the butterflies in my stomach. I wasn't just anxious to tell my foster parents what I was about to do, I was scared as hell to actually do it.

Dr. Vanderhugh clapped his hands together once everyone settled into a seat. I was startled by the stark noise, and it occurred to me just how edgy I had become. "Jude and I have spent a lot of valuable time together this past week. He has some things he needs to tell you, and we agreed this would be a safe place to do so. That way, I can help guide him through anything he might get stuck on."

Ernie and Hensley faced me. This already proved to be more than I wanted to deal with. I got up and moved to a chair across from them, where they weren't quite as close. And where I could better see their expressions.

"Jude, you want to start?" Dr. Vanderhugh asked.

No. I didn't.

There wasn't a delicate way to dump this on them. And I wasn't willing to discuss another option. For now, this was it. I licked my lips, practiced the breathing techniques I'd learned in the last few days, and then took the plunge. "I need to get out of Maine for a while."

Hensley's mouth fell open, but Ernie's hand on her knee kept her from speaking. He held his poker face firmly in place, prepared to listen.

"Carson and Ethan left last weekend after graduation. They got an apartment in Berkley and plan to spend the summer getting to know the town, finding part-time jobs, and settling in before the school year starts. I've talked to them, and they have a couch for me to crash on." Another deep breath where I focused on the air entering my lungs and then visualized it exiting. "I'm leaving in the morning."

Now that I had that part out, answering their questions would be easy. I refused to defend myself or what I needed, but I owed them the respect of hearing their concerns. They also needed to have the reassurance from my therapist that this wasn't me running from my problems.

Hensley leaned forward, desperate to get near me, and I was glad I'd chosen to sit across the room. It wasn't that I didn't love her. Right now, I just needed to love *me*—and I didn't want to be touched. "Oh, Jude, what about college?"

"This isn't permanent. It's just for the summer. A change of scenery while I work through therapy." I sounded like an after-school special.

"I don't understand, sweetie. How are you going to participate in therapy if you're across the country in California? You don't have a car to even get to appointments."

They were valid questions. "Dr. Vanderhugh went to school with a guy who has a practice in Oakland. They're going to work together while I'm there, and when I come back, I'll resume my sessions here. There's public transportation. Ethan and Carson have cars"—they just never drove them here—"and remember, I have the money from my mom's life insurance policy, so it won't cost you anything." She hadn't had much, but she left me enough to share a couch in someone else's apartment for a while.

Ernie recognized Hensley's pending frenzy and spoke on their behalf. "Dr. Vanderhugh, with all due respect, is *now* the right time for Jude to make this kind of life decision?"

"Actually, Ernie, I think it could be very beneficial for him." He wouldn't mention Portia, although if the Shaws were aware of the relationship dynamic between us, I was certain they'd agree this was best for everyone involved. "Lots of kids do adventurous things after high school. Jude doesn't have any plans to delay college in the fall. He will continue therapy twice a week in Oakland. And in my professional opinion, a little time away might be the breath of fresh air Jude needs." That was a nice way to put that I'd been fucking their daughter, and that being in the same house with her would only increase my anxiety.

Hensley slumped back on the couch next to her husband, clearly not planning to put up a fight. "You think he needs to be away from family right now?"

She was hurt. I got that. And I hoped at some point down the road, I could give her all the pieces of the puzzle she was missing.

"You guys, I appreciate everything you've done for me since we met. I'm not walking away from you. I promise. Right now, the house haunts me, and I have to figure out how to deal with that." It was a true statement, even if it hurt them. "Every time my mom got sick, I came to your house. When she passed away, your house. I never saw it as my home because I had a home. Then it was ripped away, and I was back in the place I associated with heartache." Those were true words. I just didn't amend them to include Portia's role in my need to go.

"Your sister's going to be devastated, Jude." Ernie wasn't trying to convince me to do anything different than what I'd presented. He merely pointed out what he believed to be true.

I didn't want to put Portia in a position to have to explain anything to her parents, but I couldn't leave that statement hanging in the air. "I think she might be relieved. She's been just as worried as the two of you. It might comfort her to know I am doing something to find myself again." I hoped he would quote that last part so Portia would be confident I'd heard her words. But even if he didn't, Portia would know why I'd left.

The four of us chatted for the remainder of the hour, and I was grateful for Dr. Vanderhugh's ability to ease their minds. I also appreciated everything he left out. Like the fact that I'd consented to weekly drug tests with his colleague to ensure I didn't allow Ethan's and Carson's choices to become my own. And Dr. Vanderhugh had only agreed to the arrangement because I didn't have an addiction to drugs. I needed to accept the loss of my mom, come to terms with the nuances of facing the truth with Portia, and find a path that was my own. It had to all be for me, not to be close to a girl. All of which he believed I was doing by going across the county. The distance would give me space and prevent me from being distracted by Portia.

By the time we left, Ernie and Hensley resigned themselves to my decision, and I'd bet money that they'd see I made the right decision in a few weeks. I wasn't gallivanting off to the sun and the surf to avoid my problems. I was going somewhere I still had a support system. Aunts, uncles, other family members—none of those were options for a guy in my position. I had my two best friends and the Shaws.

When we got home, Ernie went out to the garage, Hensley baked, and I went upstairs to pack. I wasn't planning to take a lot. Clothes and toiletries were about it. I had two suitcases ready, and I'd stuffed my backpack with Hensley's cookies, my laptop and headphones, and a journal I'd kept since I'd started to see Dr. Vanderhugh again. I glanced around my room. I didn't take any of the pictures off my desk, not even the ones of my mom. It was my way of letting her go and showing Ernie and Hensley that I planned to return. She wasn't behind the glass, anyhow. She also wasn't going to ring the bell and surprise me, either.

The more that thought had rooted in my mind over the last week, the more determined I became to find peace with it.

It was late, and I needed to get into bed. I found Ernie and Hensley in the living room watching television, and I told them both goodnight. The lights were off in the hall upstairs, and I didn't bother to switch them on. Just as I reached my room, I paused and then bypassed it. Even though I hadn't heard a sound, I stole a quick glance over my shoulder to make sure no one had followed me upstairs.

And I slipped into Portia's room.

I couldn't stop myself from stepping into her world one more time before I left, even if I shouldn't. I flicked the switch and bathed the room in light. Everything sat in its place, the same way it always had when she would leave. Inhaling deeply, I took in her flowery perfume that never faded completely, and I dragged my fingers along the wood of her desk. Completing a full circle from the hall to the closet to the bathroom and back toward the door, I noticed that dingy bear she'd thrown at me when she packed for college.

Wooly—I think that's what she called the damn thing— appeared haphazardly forgotten and discarded onto the stack of pillows. It didn't matter that the stuffed animal was worthless. Stealing was stealing, but I would add that to my list of issues to work on with this new guy in California. Regardless, it was a piece of Portia, and I was taking the smelly thing with me. I snatched him up, flicked off the light, and went to my room. Wooly fit perfectly in the front pocket of my backpack, and I'd be long gone by the time Portia missed him.

CALIFORNIA WAS AN ADJUSTMENT. I'D ONLY BEEN THERE A FEW days, but the heat was a killer, and the people were different. Not in a bad way. Actually, I loved how liberal Berkeley seemed as a whole.

Ethan and Carson both found menial jobs near the campus, which was within walking distance of the apartment, so I spent most of my days alone. I had met with Dr. Sarratt twice since I'd gotten here. He encouraged me to get out and walk around, see everything I could find that held any interest, and start writing. I wasn't certain I bought into the belief he had about journaling, but I committed to giving this my all. That meant playing by the rules. And I hadn't set the rules in this game.

I tried to treat my notations about my excursions like a documentary on paper. When I viewed it as an exercise in evaluating my surroundings instead of my feelings, the words covered the pages. If I tried to analyze the ink on the page—zilch. It only took a couple of days before that notebook became my bible, and I wrote compulsively any chance I got.

Hensley called. I wrote it down.

Ernie texted. Noted.

Watched a dog shit in the park. Check.

Silence from Portia. Check. Check.

That last one came up frequently in the margins, across the top of an already packed page, and any other place I could find space. I hadn't counted the number of times I'd mentioned her, yet it stuck out like a sore thumb to Dr. Sarratt. Along with my dependence on

Portia and the need for her approval and love. I was a work in progress.

"Hey, dude. How was life as Mark Twain today?"

I shot Carson the bird when he walked in. "Probably as good as the world of Gordon Ramsey."

He worked at a fast-food health bar or something. I didn't understand the concept. I equated fast food with grease, burgers, and fries. This place served kale and fish...only in California. "I'll be Cat's sous chef any day of the week. That girl is smokin'."

"Sous chef? Is that a synonym for janitor that I'm unaware of?"

A grin spread from one ear to the other, and Carson's eyes danced with humor. "It's good to have you back, man." He tossed his dirty apron onto the kitchen table and wandered off down the hall.

I wasn't back to who I was, but the light was chasing away the dark...at least it had started to. It was just easier to breathe here, without any expectations. No one knew my name, every day was something different, and I got to focus solely on me. My only obligations were to show up for therapy twice a week and drug tests on Fridays. I'd passed the first with flying colors. When I had called Hensley to tell her how well I'd done peeing in a cup, and that she could be proud to have her honor student back, she laughed and then cried.

If I'd been home, she would have handed me a warm cookie and patted me on the cheek just before she chided me for thinking my comment was funny. That was the first time I'd thought of the Shaws' house as the place I'd go back to. Since my mom's death, it had always been our apartment and her arms. The moment I'd recognized the slip, I grabbed my journal and lost myself in whatever garbled mess came out.

"It doesn't have to be well-written, Jude. You're not sending it to an editor. No one other than the two of us ever has to read any of it.

Just let go." Dr. Sarratt's words were so much easier to accept than Dr. Vanderhugh's.

I'd analyzed the hell out of that in the second notebook I'd started. At this rate, I'd need to buy stock in Mead and possibly BIC. I went through pens as fast as paper, but that might be Ethan stealing them to stir his pot. Once the tip of an ink pen had been stuck in the tar of burned marijuana, it was pretty much useless. Yet, instead of using the same one over and over, he'd grab the first one he saw and take it to the balcony. There was no telling how many had fallen through the slats.

"I'm going outside; you want to come?" Carson returned from a shower.

I set the journal aside and put the pen on top of it. I shouldn't bother. I might as well bring it with me. Ethan would snatch it the moment he walked through the door.

Carson slid the heavy glass to the side and stepped through, leaving it open for me to follow. We had four chairs on the porch. It was surprisingly large. Real estate in California was astronomically high, so I hadn't expected much when I got here. It wasn't the Ritz Carlton, but it was comfortable. The patio was probably my favorite spot in the place.

Carson and Ethan's parents weren't well off, they were just middle-class Americans. But Ethan had gotten a full ride, and Carson had managed to string together several smaller scholarships I hadn't even been aware he'd applied for. He was sneaky like that. For a guy who smoked pot like a chimney, he was surprisingly resourceful. Anyway, with the help in tuition, their parents were able to take care of the apartment. And Ethan used his graduation money to buy the patio furniture—rather domestic for an eighteen-year-old.

When I had first arrived, he showed me the apartment in less than five seconds. There wasn't much to see. It was two bedrooms, two baths, a kitchen, and a living room. The dining room was just a corner that connected the rest of the space. But the patio—it took time. It was his sanctuary. He bought potted plants and some kind of bushy tree. Strategically placed candles adorned the glass tabletop and the railing, and he kept it spotless. It was a pretty nice gig.

We both pulled out chairs, swiveled them toward the courtyard, and then took a seat. Carson produced a joint from his shirt pocket. "You okay with this?" He held it up to ask.

I shrugged with indifference. "I'm good."

Carson came across as aloof because he was easygoing, but he was one of the most thoughtful people I'd ever known. He raised his brow, held it high, and waited for confirmation.

"I swear. Go ahead."

He relaxed, kicked his feet up on the rail, and sparked the joint. "How are you doing? I know it's only been a couple of weeks." Carson was the only guy I knew who could check on my mental health and not sound like a girl.

I bobbed my head. "Surprisingly well. I miss her, though."

"Portia?" he asked at the same time he inhaled the joint, and her name came off pinched.

"Yeah."

A cloud of smoke exited his mouth, and then he puffed out rings with what remained. "Still no word from her?"

Carson provided a safe place to vent, and I needed to exhale the emotion. It was my greatest struggle in all this…talking. "I'm sure she's pissed. Her parents shipped her off to the beach, and I was gone without a word when she came home."

"You made the right decision, Jude. Portia loves you. She'll get over being mad if this does what you need it to."

Dr. Sarratt had said the same thing.

"She can't be my motivation though. I'm having a hard time moving past that part."

He glanced at me and cocked his head to the side. "I'm not a shrink, so my personal opinion is pretty much worthless. Nevertheless, I don't think your motivation right now matters. Just bringing yourself back from the brink is what's important. Once you're in a better place, then worry about why you're there."

I made a mental note to jot that down and explore it later. "What if my motivation never changes?"

"Dude, I don't have a clue. All I can tell you is that I don't believe it matters whether you process the loss of your mom because you wanted to, or if some chick asked you to. Once you do it, it's done. Come to peace with that first."

I chuckled because he made sense. It was simple logic. Puzzles had to be put together one piece at a time, and sometimes you had to search through a huge stack to find the one you needed. It didn't make the rest of the stack any less valuable in the overall picture. "You ever thought about going into counseling?"

Carson choked as he laughed and inhaled smoke at the same time. "Right, I'm sure people want to pay a pothead to give them life advice."

"Then quit smoking pot, dumbass."

He dropped his hand onto the arm of the chair with the joint between his fingers. My gaze followed his as he stared out across the courtyard. The sun had started to set, and the held a gorgeous canvas of pastels. I still hadn't gotten used to how different the colors of the sky were compared to Maine.

"Dude," I said, "I didn't mean anything by that. I meant it as a compliment."

He waved me off as though I hadn't hurt his feelings.

I straightened my back and angled toward Carson. It was a chick thing to do, but this whole therapy gig had me expressing way more than I ever had. I wondered if it was affecting my hormone levels. "You may think what I'm about to say is melodramatic, because I *wasn't* suicidal, but you saved my life. Don't take that lightly." My eyes burned as I fought tears. I'd cried in front of Carson more times in recent weeks than I cared to admit.

His eyes narrowed as if he were about to argue. "I didn't do anything."

"You didn't have to offer me your couch. Or pick me up at the airport. Or put up with my blubbering shit when I got here. I'm sure it's been like living with a teenage girl going through puberty, except without the tits or wet dreams." I tried to chuckle and keep it lighthearted. I was fairly certain I'd failed.

"You would have done the same for me."

"My point is, you have a way of putting people at ease. You're easy to talk to. And you give sound advice instead of rash horseshit or flowery psychobabble."

"That's just because I'm not trained in the art of psychobabble. If I were, I'm sure I would have mastered the language." A smile played on his lips, and I was confident I hadn't ruffled his emotional feathers, so I leaned back to enjoy the sunset.

The two of us sat there until it got dark. It didn't escape my attention that Carson had extinguished the joint shortly after I suggested he might want to consider counseling as a career— without taking another drag.

"So tell me about this Cat chick you work with."

"You don't want to hear about my girl trouble."

"If she's already trouble, she's not the one." I snickered.

He stared into the distance long enough that I didn't think he would provide me any insight into the girl who'd caught his attention. I should have realized he was formulating the words to paint the picture he wanted me to see.

When he closed his eyes and slowly shook his head, I knew he was in deep water. I just hoped she was actually in the pool, too. Otherwise, he'd drown. "She's the nerdy-chic type. Fifties pinup vibe and hot as sin. And dude"—he swatted me on the chest to get my attention, or maybe accentuate a point—"she's crazy smart and witty. Her snark and banter get me more worked up than porn."

The glassy sheen hadn't disappeared from his eyes, but it wasn't the pot—it was the girl.

"Have you talked to her?" Typically, guys of our social standing admired women from the sidelines. We learned more about them than they would ever actually share because we watched and listened. It was easy to take in the details when you weren't part of the conversation.

He slowly nodded his head. "Every day. Well, every day that I'm at work."

"Like a co-worker kind of vibe?" I didn't want to come out and ask if he was dreaming of a girl who believed she was out of his league. No such girl existed. Most just didn't take the time to get to know a quiet intellectual, even one who smoked pot and looked like a Gucci model. Although, that whole model look had kind of happened in the last year, and the girls we had gone to school with were blind.

Carson shrugged. "I think she digs me. Hell, who knows? I'm hardly an expert on the subject. And clearly, I don't have a lot of experience in this department. But she gave me her number tonight."

"Seriously? That's awesome. Are you going to ask her out?" I seemed to be far more excited by this than Carson.

And then I caught the look in his eyes. He feared Cat would say no. "I'm just going to play it by ear."

"Did you ask for her phone number, or did she give it up voluntarily?"

He grimaced and pulled his head back, making his jaw blend in with his neck in a deformed way. "Seriously?"

"Stop doing that with your neck. You look weird as hell. Yes, seriously. It is within the realm of possibility that you asked a girl out."

"Just not terribly likely." He stared at me in disbelief. "You shouldn't play the lottery...or gamble...ever. You clearly suck at reading people, and your luck is as good as mine."

I crossed my arms over my chest, lifted my ankle to my knee, and donned a smug grin. "I'd say your luck is changing, my friend. If she gave you her number without you having to ask, much less beg, then you're already in."

"Nothing personal, but your history with women isn't exactly tried and true."

Carson was right. And just like he thought he was the last person to give life advice, I was the last one on Earth to counsel anyone on the ways of the female world. "Fair enough. Still, if she gave you her number, she wants you to call."

"I could send her a text."

Hell, no. "Don't be *that* guy."

"What guy?"

"I don't give a shit how little I know about women or how inexperienced I am. I realize Portia doesn't count since we grew up together through the 'courting' phase. But I'm a firm believer that chicks dig old-school romance. Even when they say they don't."

Suddenly, Carson ducked out of nowhere, and a flash of white blew by. It was followed by a strangled caw.

I stood abruptly. I hadn't seen it coming, but I sure saw it leave. "What the fuck was that?"

He sat up, hesitantly. "A fucking suicidal seagull. I hate those damn things."

"This far from the beach?"

"I guess when you have a death wish, you're willing to travel." He brushed himself off as if the bird had touched him. "That damn thing whizzed by your head. How the hell did you not hear it?"

I couldn't stop laughing. The flight path of an out-of-control bird left Carson traumatized. The longer the muscles tensed, the more my stomach burned, and I slumped over, trying to ease the ache. But once Carson started chuckling, it became uncontrollable. I gasped for air. I couldn't remember the last time I'd been this carefree and sober.

By the time I finally calmed down and could breathe well enough to talk, I'd forgotten what we were saying before the bird of death had swooped in. "What the hell were we talking about?" I questioned.

"Cat."

Right, the art of seducing women. "Don't text her. Call her. Ask her out and plan a real date."

I could see the wheels churning in his mind. He didn't put himself out there often. Guys like us were aware of how fast we'd be turned down. Without another word, he got up, slid the glass back, and disappeared inside. I followed when I realized he wasn't coming back.

Going to sleep was pointless. Not that I had anything better to do. But Ethan would be home in about an hour, and when he came through the living room, he didn't attempt to do so quietly. Ethan was simply oblivious to the nuances of living with other people. He'd come in chattering about work, talking to himself more than us.

My notebook—already worn from days of writing and carrying it with me everywhere I went—sat where I'd left it when we went outside. It was funny how a pad of paper could become such an integral part of who I had become. And by the time Ethan came through the door, I'd filled several pages, mostly about Portia and my motivation to be in California. When I set the pen down, I realized I was going to come out of this okay. I didn't know when or where the path would take me, but I prayed it led back to her.

———

"IF YOU'RE SO BORED, WHY DON'T YOU GET A JOB? I KNOW YOU don't have to have the money, but it would give you something to do." Ethan had found the first semblance of a social life—Carson had, too, for that matter—when he'd become gainfully employed.

I'd always heard that life after high school was totally different, and that my social status prior to college was meaningless after my senior year. I'd just found that hard to believe when the same kids who held the spotlight in high school then went on to the colleges we attended after. Yet somehow, it was true. The clicks faded, and people were generally more accepting. I wasn't experiencing it myself, but both Carson and Ethan had quickly found friends here. And Carson and Cat had even gone out on a couple of dates. He kept the details a closely guarded secret. Any minute now, he believed she'd start laughing at him with her friends, and he'd find out it had all been a big joke at his expense.

I had met her once when they stopped by the apartment to get his wallet. She was exactly who he had portrayed her to be, except when I pictured pinup, I expected scantily clad. Cat was not. Her hair was retro as was her makeup, but her clothing was tastefully appropriate and spirited to match the decade. But she wouldn't be gracing any calendars to lure men in with her cleavage.

"It seems kind of counterproductive to get a job when I'm going home in a week."

Ethan hovered near the bar in the kitchen, with his head down, making coffee. "Then don't go home."

I scoffed, "I have to." The summer had flown by and been a breath of much needed fresh air, but I didn't live here.

He lifted his eyes to meet mine. "Says who?"

"That was the deal when I left, Ethan. Ernie and Hensley expect to pick me up at the airport in a week."

Steam rose from the liquid in his cup as he lifted it to his mouth and then took a sip. "So call them and tell them your plans have changed."

"It's not that easy," I countered.

"Only because you're making it difficult." He set the travel cup down and screwed on the lid. "Look, I gotta go. But if you want to stay in California, make it happen." Ethan was so nonchalant about the whole thing, as though my future weren't at stake.

"And just ditch school?"

He grabbed his cup and lifted his backpack from the floor. The guy was as attached to it as a woman was a purse. Although, I had to admit, I did the same because I took my journals and Wooly everywhere I went. "Look around, Jude. There are schools everywhere. Plus, are you ready to be on a campus with Portia? You haven't talked to her since you left, and your parents haven't mentioned her once. Do the math." He lacked all social graces.

When he reached the door, he stopped with his hand on the knob. "Call your parents and talk to them. You might be surprised."

I nodded, and he left.

One of the biggest things I'd worked on with Dr. Sarratt all summer was not worrying about tomorrow and living in today. That had been great when there were tons of weeks in front of me, and I didn't have a flight to catch in eight days. But at some point, I had to consider my future and how I planned to get there.

I loved it here. The sun. The people. But living on Ethan and Carson's couch wasn't ideal, nor was it reality. People had to earn a living or go to school or something. Existing in a space as if it were purgatory couldn't be healthy on a long-term basis.

But after my session with Dr. Sarratt that afternoon, I had a plan. And it wasn't one I believed the Shaws were going to care for.

At six o'clock eastern time—when Ernie and Hensley would both be home—I picked up my phone and made a call that could change my future.

"Hey, Jude." Hensley's singsong voice rang through the speaker, happy to hear from me. I had tried to call her regularly throughout the summer so she wouldn't worry. It had been hard for her to let me leave, and I hoped she heard improvement in my voice.

I was about to find out.

"Hey, Hensley. Is Ernie around?"

"Yeah, hang on. I'll get him for you."

She called out to him in the background. "Are you looking forward to coming home?" she asked while she waited for Ernie.

"Actually, that's why I called. I wanted to talk to both of you. Can you put me on speakerphone?"

She struggled with basic cell usage. I heard her ask Ernie for the phone, and then he explained to her how to use it. The silence shifted to white noise when the speaker engaged.

"Hey, bud. How's California treating you?"

"It's good, Ernie. Thanks for asking."

No one spoke for an awkward amount of time after. I realized I'd called them, and they were waiting for me. "I had an appointment with Dr. Sarratt today."

More silence. Apparently, Ernie and Hensley weren't going to even acknowledge my statements with a grunt or "oh, yeah."

"We discussed my coming back to Maine." Might as well just rip off the Band-Aid. "And I've decided to stay in California." They tried to interrupt, but I refused to let them interject until I said what I had called to say. Most of that was dispelling their fears and objections. "I'm going to defer school until next fall. That doesn't mean I'm not ever going to go to college. I'm just not going right now."

Ernie interjected, "Jude—"

"Hear me out, please."

"Fair enough." I could visualize him putting his hands in the air apologetically.

"Things are going well here. Counseling is productive. I've met some people. Carson and Ethan are here. And right now, I think it's more important for me to stabilize than get an education. College isn't going anywhere in the next twelve months."

"Sweetheart, I don't think that's a good idea." Hensley missed the point. I wasn't asking for permission.

I sighed and tried to keep the bite out of my tone when I spoke. "That's disappointing, but not unexpected. I'm aware neither of you

thought my coming here—based on how I left—was a smart decision. But I don't think you can argue that it hasn't been good
for me."

Ernie was a thinker. And he could be swayed with a well-formu-
lated argument. Hensley would lean in whatever direction her
husband believed best. "You're right, son. We can't argue that
you've seemed happier than when you were here. But you can't run
away. This is your home."

"Guys, kids leave. They go off to school, and then they end up
all over the country when they take jobs and start careers. I'm just
doing it in a different order."

"But you aren't going to school. What are you going to do? Just
live on your friends' sofa?" Hensley sounded scared, not mean.

I raked my hand through my hair, realizing how badly it needed
to be cut, and then I stood and paced the living room. "I'm going to
get a job. Keep going to therapy. Continue journaling. Basically,
figure out what my next step is."

"And that's not U of M?" Ernie already knew the answer. I
could hear it in his tone.

"Not right now, no. And if it doesn't work out, I'll come home. I
want to give it a fair shot, though. I can breathe here. I haven't had a
panic attack once since I got to California, and I had two in a matter
of weeks in Maine."

I stared at the floor and traversed the same small circle around
the living room, over and over. I wondered how long it would take
to actually form a path in the carpet. Since I didn't pay rent here, I
changed my pattern and moved down the hall and through the
kitchen, listening to them ramble.

Once they'd finally stopped talking—mostly to each other—I
told them both I loved them. And then I held my ground. "I'll keep
you posted on the job hunt. I just wanted to let you know that I
wouldn't be on the plane next week."

Hensley cried. Ernie confirmed what I already knew by assuring me I always had a place in their home.

And we disconnected.

It was time to get focused on moving forward instead of just enjoying a walk in the park. And that started with a job.

17

JUDE

"WHAT THE HELL ARE YOU DOING?" I SNATCHED MY JOURNAL FROM the hands of a nosy co-worker.

She shrugged and contorted her face into an expression of equal indifference. "Just wondering what you spend so much time working on."

I tucked the notebook into my backpack and slammed the locker. When I turned around, Lacy wore the same unbothered look. "So, you went through my locker, dug it out, and just thought you'd have a look around my private thoughts?"

Lacy pulled out a chair from the table and placed herself in it with more fanfare than called for. "We work in a bookstore. Do you know how many people here are writing the next great American novel?" She paused, waiting for my answer. When she didn't get one, she popped a grape into her mouth and continued. "All of them. Including the ones who run the place."

"And how does that justify breaking and entering?" I didn't have a clue what she'd read, or how deep into my thoughts she had been able to dig. My heart lay fully exposed on those pages without so much as a filter to shield them.

The eccentric girl who talked too much and wore too much

makeup pressed her forearms onto the table in front of her and leaned forward, causing her dark hair to fall around her arm. "I'm no expert, but I've never read anything like that. Are you planning to publish it?" And clearly, she was a moron as well.

I wasn't a famous actor or politician. No one gave a shit about Jude Thomas or my memoire scribbled on hundreds of pages of notebook paper. It also dawned on me that Lacy thought what she had read was fiction. "Hadn't planned on it."

"It's quite the love story. Angst, heartache, broken pasts." Another grape flew from her hand into her mouth, and she talked around it as she chewed. "I'm just saying, I think you have something unique."

Two other employees walked into the breakroom, chattering between themselves and oblivious to Lacy and me. I lowered my voice and said, "It's not open for discussion. Please stay out of my things."

She flung herself back into the chair, wiped her hands on her pants, and then crossed her arms. "Why is it that the people with something to say won't share, and those who fill the world with mindless chatter won't shut up?" Oh, the irony in that statement. "I'd love to read more." Then she stood, grabbed her trash, tossed it in the basket, and walked out.

I shook my head and decided to get a padlock. I didn't carry anything valuable in my backpack, so I hadn't thought one would be necessary. But I'd been wrong. Prying eyes and grabby hands could result in total exposure. I'd made a lot of progress in the months I'd been in California, but I was nowhere near ready to face the world. I still struggled with my mom's passing. And in a way, Portia felt dead to me right now, too.

Dr. Sarratt and I had been unpacking, in a particularly painful way, both of those relationships. And I had started to come to terms with just how unhealthy my addiction to Portia was. And how unfair that burden was to the girl I loved. I'd taken several steps backward in the therapy process by the time I asked Dr. Sarratt if that dependency meant I couldn't ever have her again. I hadn't been prepared for him to tell me that I might not want her when I broke away all the pieces of my carefully crafted, emotional wall. It was possible that I'd see her differently. It might also happen that when I was healthy that I wouldn't need her the way I had before. There were so many dynamics that *could* change that I didn't care to consider what *might* change. And I struggled with whether or not I actually wanted them to.

Portia had been a part of my identity since I was eight. Letting her go would mean losing Hensley and Ernie, as well. And while I loved Ethan and Carson like brothers, the Shaws were my family. It took a lot of hours to come to terms with the possibility that I might have to sacrifice them all to save myself.

As I stacked books on shelves and reorganized the mess that customers had left behind in the aisle I currently worked on, my mind raced, and every thought I'd shared with Dr. Sarratt the day before played in my head. This was how it always was. I didn't know if anyone else's brain worked this way, but mine broke down every sentence, one by one, and evaluated the impact of that partic-ular thought on my daily life and my future. Having a mindless job, surrounded by things I loved, aided in my therapy process.

It had taken me weeks to find employment. I couldn't have picked a worse time to look for an entry-level job than the week the college students flooded Berkeley. There wasn't a place within a mile that didn't have their regular staff—that had gone home for the summer—back on hand. During my job hunt, I'd reached a point of desperation, and I set out with no destination. Almost two miles later, I had found the bookstore.

There were no "Now Hiring" signs, and I didn't go in looking for employment. I had only pulled on the metal handle with the intention of enjoying the one thing I'd always found comfort in—books. I'd wandered the store aimlessly, touching the spines and enjoying the smells. Every once in a while, I stopped and plucked one from the shelves to read the back before returning it to the same spot. An employee had stopped to ask me if I had any questions or needed help. That sparked a conversation, and before I knew it, the manager offered me a job.

I'd been here ever since. The duties were easy and lacked skill, but it gave me an endless stream of people to talk books with. Authors, plots, characters, genres—it didn't matter. Every shift brought more interactions with customers who didn't know I was broken or hurting. It provided me with an income and an outlet. And lots of time to think.

I was more myself here than I was anywhere else. And the end of each day brought sadness about going home and leaving the job behind, which seemed unusual. Just one more thing to add to my ever-growing list of topics to discuss with Dr. Sarratt. I'd never get through all the things I thought were wrong with me, which only made me believe that Portia got further away rather than closer to reaching.

I closed the shop down with Lacy and Ed, the manager. Ed locked the door with the three of us standing on the sidewalk together. I moved to head home and made it a few steps down the street.

Lacy called out, "Jude, you should seriously consider what I said about your book."

I stopped and faced her. She might as well be a neon sign the way she stood out. Her outfit was more suited for prom than work. "Yeah. Thanks." I waved to be polite and left without giving it another thought.

When I reached the apartment, I stuck my key in the lock and realized it was already open. Carson and Ethan stood at the counter in the kitchen, talking. They both stopped as I closed the door behind me.

"Did I interrupt something?" I asked and set my backpack on

top of my suitcase next to the couch. Living in someone else's home for an extended amount of time was less than ideal. I didn't have a dresser or a closet, much less a bed.

Ethan glanced at Carson, and I wondered what they were about to throw at me. Dread wrapped its hand around my heart and began to squeeze. I hadn't had a panic attack in months, but the telltale signs crept into my future.

Carson rolled his eyes at Ethan, although he still took the cue. "Ethan and I are going home for Thanksgiving and wanted to see what your plans are for the holidays."

The fingers of anxiety slowly released their grasp on my heart, and my breathing returned to normal. "I haven't thought about it." I also didn't have the money to fly home. There was no way they were driving. That would be a four-day trip, and they had to be back in time for school.

Ethan finally found his backbone. "Why don't you call Hensley and see what their plans are? That way we could all get flights together. We're going to buy tickets today."

The Shaws did the same thing for Thanksgiving every year. An elaborate spread over lunch that extended into dinner and left me wanting to sleep for a week. They hadn't said a word to me about Portia since I'd left, and I wasn't ready to find out what she'd been doing by showing up at the dinner table. "Do you guys care if I stay here? I haven't asked for any time off at the bookstore, and I'm sure everyone else has."

I didn't know if anyone had or not. I didn't care. I intended to work whatever days they scheduled me. There was also the matter of counseling, which I refused to miss. My plan was to go back to Maine this coming summer and start school at the university in the fall. In order to do that, I had to stick to the regimen as outlined, or I'd never survive Portia.

Carson shrugged, and Ethan gawked at me.

It was Carson who stepped into the living room first. I took a seat on the couch, waiting for their response, and he sat in the recliner. "Fine with me." He kicked the footrest out and relaxed as the chair leaned back. "But you know, at some point, you're going to have to face the music. You can't hide out here forever, Jude."

There was a part of me that acknowledged that truth and a bigger part that hid from it. I wasn't there yet. "I'll get there."

"Then I guess you have the place to yourself for a few days." He smiled and picked up the television remote, ending the conversation.

SPENDING THANKSGIVING ALONE HADN'T BEEN ALL THAT BAD. Christmas was torture. The Shaws sent me a box of presents, and I opened them by myself on the morning of the twenty-fifth. Somehow, they'd managed to package the scent of their home and mail it to California. As soon as I had unfolded the cardboard, the familiar smell rolled out in waves. It was the first time I'd missed home since I'd left. I'd longed for Portia, but I'd talked to Ernie and Hensley enough that their absence didn't seem any different than it had when I lived with my mom. There were times I'd go long stretches without seeing them, although not often.

I hadn't been able to unwrap a single package for nearly an hour. And when I finally regained my composure, every piece of paper I tore, tape I removed, and ribbon I untied, took me further into longing. Even though I wasn't sure I was ready to go back just yet, that box convinced me that there was nothing I wanted more. With the last gift opened, I stared at the bottom of the box. There hadn't been anything from Portia included—not even a card.

That night, with the trash littered all over the living room floor, I made a list of the things I needed to do—to get right in my head— so I could reclaim the part of my heart that had gone silent the day Portia walked out of my bedroom. I might have destroyed any hope of ever having her again, but she'd promised me she'd wait. I just had to make sure I returned whole.

There were nine, five-subject notebooks filled to the brim with my thoughts, fears, and every detail of my life since I'd arrived in California. I started with the first one. Reading through it, I highlighted passages, drew lines through others, and created a list of questions that remained unanswered. The task was daunting; akin to sifting through documents that had gone through a shredder to try to tape them back into a readable format. At this rate, it would take me weeks to accomplish my goal, but I hoped by the time spring rolled around that I might have my project completed.

The next day at work, I bought a thick, leather-bound journal and a set of black pens. And day by day, I transferred bits from my spiral notebooks to the blank pages. I made sure to use the same pen for every entry so the final product would flow as though it were written in one sitting. I didn't have any intention of publishing it, but I couldn't get Lacy's comment out of my mind. This had the power to be the greatest love story of all time...or the greatest tragedy. That determination lay in the hands of someone I hadn't spoken to in months.

It was tough to separate what I was working on while doing counseling. Dr. Sarratt and I continued to push through my lingering issues. And I finally admitted to him what my goal truly was and the timeframe I hoped to accomplish it in. The weeks became months and the two sessions I had per week expanded to three. He believed I'd be ready to go home this summer, if I still wanted to.

My happiness no longer depended on the dark-haired girl I grew up loving. I'd found my own niche. I'd miss my mom for the rest of my life, but coping with it became far easier once I let go of the anger and resentment I carried. Instead of hating the force of nature that took her from me, I hated the disease. I hadn't done a single drug since I'd gotten here, and I had cultivated an outlet that was far more cathartic than any illegal substance. I had never planned to be a writer, then or now. I had, however, grown to love and appreciate the process of transforming my emotion into words. Which was exactly what I did when I filled the leather journal.

At the end of March—between the bookstore and counseling—I finished what I'd been working on. I'd painstakingly chosen every word and line that now stared back at me from the pages in black ink and my crummy handwriting. I read through it, happy with how I'd conveyed something so personal and private, yet sad to remember just how morose I'd been when I arrived in the Golden State.

Dr. Sarratt thumbed through it during our next session. I spent most of that hour biting my fingernails, waiting for him to respond to what he'd read. Five minutes before our time was up, he pushed the book across his desk.

He slid his glasses from his nose and laid them on his desk. "This is an awfully bold move, Jude. Are you prepared if it doesn't go the way you hope?" His tone was inquisitive, yet encouraging.

The truth was, my answer was yes. It would hurt like hell if Portia kept her distance, but I refused to live in the shadow of doubt any longer. It was time to pay the piper. And either way, I had already planned to return to Maine at the beginning of June. The bookstore cut back on staff when the college students left for the summer because their sales tanked with the dip in the local population, so it was the perfect time for me to leave.

I nodded slowly. "Obviously, I hope the dream I had for my future is attainable. But even if Portia's gone, I'm ready to go home." And that was the hardest hurdle I'd had to overcome— accepting that my life might never include the girl I loved.

"When do you plan to send it to her?"

I still had to write a note to put with the journal, get a box or envelope to ship it in, and then take it to the post office. "Probably tomorrow."

"Are you ready for the wait that will come once you drop it in the post?"

The two of us continued to talk at length. He reaffirmed that silence would be the next stage I would deal with. "I am." The ball had been in my court since I got on the plane to fly out here. She'd given me the space to do what I needed to do. I just hoped she'd kept her promise—to wait.

Dr. Sarratt stood and rounded his desk. He did the same thing at the end of every session to signal that our time for the day was over. As he walked toward the exit, I got to my feet and followed him. We both stopped when he opened the door.

"I think you're ready. But I'll still see you back at your next appointment." He shook my hand, and I went to the apartment.

THE NEXT DAY, AFTER ETHAN AND CARSON LEFT FOR SCHOOL, I SAT at the kitchen table and wrote a letter to Portia. I didn't have her address at school, and I hadn't wanted to ask Hensley for it. Then I considered how long it might sit at the Shaws' house unopened, or worse, opened by Ernie or Hensley, so I caved and called. Hensley didn't ask any questions, and she made certain not to say too much. Nevertheless, I didn't miss the exuberance in her voice.

"I'm planning to come home the first week of June, if that's okay?" There was no doubt in my mind that Ernie and Hensley would welcome me. Even still, I believed I owed them the courtesy of sharing my plan.

She gasped into the phone. "Oh, sweetheart. Of course, it is. We can't wait to have you back. Just let me know what date. I'll book a flight for you."

"It's okay. Carson's parents are renewing their wedding vows, so he's planning to drive home. I'll ride with him. Once I have all the details, I'll let you know."

"Perfect."

"I've got to get to work, but I'll call you in a few days, okay?"

"Sure. Sure." Hensley didn't say goodbye. Instead, she took a deep breath, and I waited. "Jude?"

"Yeah?"

"I know how hard this has all been on you and that I wasn't thrilled with you trying to conquer it on your own." Not new information. "But I'm so proud of you. So so proud." Her voice was soft and tender, and each word came straight from the heart. "I love you."

"Love you, too, Hensley."

We disconnected. I grabbed the leather journal and stowed it safely in my backpack along with the note I'd written and Portia's school address. I took a deep breath and walked to the post office on campus. My heart strummed a rapid beat, and my palms sweated as I scribbled out the address. I'd remember the *swoosh* of the heavy, padded envelope sliding down the metal shoot for the rest of my life.

In that moment, I let go of my past and turned toward my future.

18

PORTIA

Jet flew into our dorm room with her usual dramatic flair. "Mail call." Her lyrical voice tumbled into the room, and she followed. It was clear she didn't plan to stay when she left the door open, tossed a few envelopes on her desk, and held a package in my direction.

I sat up and swung my legs over the edge of my bed. "What's that?"

I never got mail. Everything I received went to my parents' house, and I didn't get care boxes because I went home often enough for Hensley to load me up with baked goods to tide me over for weeks.

Jet snatched the thick packet back and held it against her chest like a treasure. "It's from California," she teased and then wisely handed it over.

An uneasy feeling landed squarely in the pit of my stomach. Butterflies didn't flutter; vultures swarmed. I'd no sooner taken the parcel than the greedy bastards started pecking away at my insides —starting with my heart.

My roomie's expression softened, and the emotion she held for me was written all over her gorgeous face—pity. When the school year first started, she'd made the mistake of asking about Jude. It hadn't gone well, and she'd only dared one other time to mention his name. I wasn't quite as raw at that point, so I told her what little I knew, which wasn't much. He'd gone to California, deferred college, and he talked to my parents regularly. To my knowledge, he'd never asked about me, and I hadn't heard from him since the day I broke his heart.

Jet tilted her head toward the hall. "I'm going to leave you alone, but if you need me for anything, I've got my cell. Okay?"

My head barely moved when I nodded, but somehow, she saw it. She left with far less grandeur than she had entered.

The walls seemed to close in around me, and I swallowed hard past the lump that took up residence in my throat. There was nothing I wanted more than to rip into the seal and see what Jude had sent, but part of me wondered if I'd ever be the same after.

He'd waited over ten months to reach out. There hadn't even been so much as a goodbye. In fact, he'd forced me out of my own house so he could escape unseen. Upon my return from the forced vacation, my parents said very little. And anytime he called over the summer, they left the room. I never dared to ask for anything more than they offered. Whatever he needed, it didn't include me. Now I wondered if it ever would.

I ran my fingertips along my name, written in his hand. I'd always loved the way Jude made the *P* so dramatic and the letters that followed artistic. He said it was sloppy. I thought it was unique. He'd painstakingly placed every number and letter in order to ensure they were legible, and other than my name, I wouldn't have recognized it as his.

The ache in my chest grew when I glanced to the left corner. There, I finally learned where he'd been. I had assumed it was with Carson and Ethan, and now I had an actual location. I wasn't sure why an apartment number and street address seemed so profound. They just were.

Using scissors instead of tearing the paper, I cut the envelope carefully. It felt more like open heart surgery than mail. And without peeking, I reached inside to pull out the contents. There was nothing more than a leather journal and a folded piece of white paper with the same power *P* that started my name.

I set the journal and the packing aside absentmindedly, wanting nothing more than to read the words he'd selected to send me.

DEAR PORTIA,

I was already in tears. I could hear his voice speaking the written words. It was the first time in ages I'd allowed myself to remember the way he sounded, or to believe that he might come back. My chest rose as I took a deep breath and started again.

I found the boy you were looking for.

Love, Jude

I flicked the page over. That couldn't be it. There had to be more. But the backside was blank. That was all I got. A greeting, eight measly words, and a salutation. I pushed the book aside, grabbed the envelope, and opened it with both hands to search inside for the rest. There was nothing. I snatched the letter again, reread it, and each time I did, I got angrier.

All the pain I'd endured alone while he had run across the country, and I got eight stupid words. I hadn't had a single person to talk to since he left. I never told Ernie and Hensley. I refused to discuss it with Jet. And Bart just hugged me and offered to lend an ear if I ever wanted to talk—I hadn't. What I had done was wait.

For a phone call.

A letter.

Any sign of life.

And for ten months, I got nothing.

Abruptly, I stood, accidentally knocking the journal off the bed. When I kneeled to pick it up, it had fanned open, and I realized it wasn't an empty book meant for me to fill. My knees were pressed into the hard floor, and I sat back on my heels as I flipped through the pages. Every page, from top to bottom, was lined in Jude's best handwriting. Tears prevented me from stalling on any one paragraph long enough to read it.

I didn't have a clue what lay between the pages of that leather binding, but whatever it was, I was certain it was important. Clutching the book to my chest, I leaned over to grab the envelope. The date stamp was four days earlier. The months of silence had been horrific, and there was no doubt in my mind, the last four days had been the same for Jude.

This could be his final goodbye, and I might find that he not only wasn't waiting for a response at the end but that he'd moved on completely. But my heart told me that if he'd found the boy I was looking for, then he was ready to come home.

When I finally got to my feet, still holding his words against my chest like they were the holy grail, I glanced in the mirror. Makeup ran down my cheeks, and I was a hot mess. There was no salvaging it. I'd have to wash my face and start over. Neither of which I wanted to waste time doing. Instead, I pulled three makeup wipes from a package and took it all off. I'd never left this room without a coat of war paint, but I wasn't preparing for battle. I hoped this was a peace treaty.

I needed to find a quiet place where there wouldn't be any inter-ruptions, which was almost an impossibility on a campus this size. When people all shared the same resources, realty was sparse. I set the journal down long enough to dump the contents of my backpack onto my bed. Then I folded a blanket, placed Jude's book on top, and slid them into the bag. With the weight of the world and the hope for my future strapped to my shoulders, I raced out of the dorm to find a nook to hunker down in peace. I didn't want to risk interruptions or a roommate who would pry.

I needed to do this alone.

THERE WAS A HUGE TREE JUST BEHIND CAMPUS THAT TYPICALLY went unoccupied and far enough away from the bustle of the crowd that I could escape. I didn't have a clue what I was getting myself into, and I didn't want to be exposed to onlookers or passersby. I trotted across campus, through the quad, and past the bookstore. When people attempted to stop me to talk, I waved and said hello, but I kept the course to my destination.

As I'd hoped, there was no one around. I unzipped my backpack and took out the blanket I'd packed, careful not to accidentally toss the journal on the ground. There wasn't anything ornate or special about the cover itself, although I was certain it had been expensive. The leather was soft like suede yet worn like a jacket. While I assumed it was new, it appeared aged. The words on the pages screamed at me to read them, but even if Jude hadn't written what was inside, I'd still covet the book for its beauty.

Once I settled onto the blanket, I grabbed the notebook and leaned back against the trunk of the tree. It wasn't the most comfortable place to be. The bark was scratchy against my thin shirt, and the ground was hard under my ass. But the sun was shining, and it was a gorgeous day.

I caressed the spine and finally opened the cover. I wanted to be able to absorb everything inside without having to spend hours reading, except Jude didn't work that way. In the months that had passed, he could have provided me with whatever I was about to learn. Instead, he'd disappeared, which was even more painful than him slamming the door behind me.

It didn't take long to succumb to the manuscript. Although it wasn't a novel. In the first couple of pages, I realized Jude had chronicled his time in California. It didn't matter whether he'd done it for me or if the book was a byproduct of therapy. Sharing it took courage. I forced my feelings of abandonment and anger aside, and I tried to open my heart.

"I've never been more terrified than I am now. Even when my mom died, the familiarity of the Shaws, of Portia, their house...it all kept me from floating away. Now, even with Ethan and Carson here, I'm utterly alone. And the pain has only intensified. Instead of just having to face my grief over my mom, I have to accept that I might have lost the only girl I've ever loved."

Ernie and Hensley had kept a tight lid on whatever took place the day I went to Panama City, and it broke my heart to find out—even months later—that Jude couldn't remember it, either. The only thing he could recall was the fear of dying and the way those emotions gripped him, blinding him to everything else. And he blamed me.

"She didn't even try to understand. All she could see was what her mother had done—as if heroin and pot were one and the same. Portia couldn't grasp that without her, my nights never ended. The sun never rose. Days without her light weren't days worth living."

He was wrong.

I knew he struggled, just not to what degree, because he never wanted to burden me with his truth. Tears streamed down my cheeks as I acknowledged just how much he'd kept hidden in order to keep me happy. Jude truly believed that once I came home for the summer, suddenly all the pain would disappear. His happiness depended upon me. And I wasn't there.

I stuck my finger between the pages and closed the cover. My face was wet, and the breeze had already begun to chap my cheeks. With the back of my free hand, I swiped away all that I could. I wasn't sure how much of this I'd be able to absorb in a day. Jude had been gone over ten months, and I was only in week one of his journey. If he had indeed found the boy I needed, it was bound to get worse before it got better.

After I regained my composure, I stared out at the open sky and watched a bird soar without flapping its wings. A squirrel rustled in the branches above, dropping debris onto my head. I brushed it off and started Jude's journey again.

The anger toward me that came off the pages shouldn't have been surprising, although the reasoning was. Jude couldn't rectify in his mind how I equated recreational pot use to my mom's overdose. He didn't see the relationship or the discomfort it brought me. All Jude recognized was me trying to control his life when I wasn't around to prevent it. Selfish, obtuse, detached—all adjectives he used to describe his view of how he believed I saw things —saw *him*.

Gone were the tears the earlier pages brought, and in came the irritation and desire to defend myself. I yelled at the words as though they might fight back, and a couple who strolled by asked me if I needed help. Politely, I thanked them and said it was an infuriating book. The girl laughed, and the two kept moving.

In the distance, a bird chirped a happy song, and I wished I had a slingshot to knock it out of the tree it taunted me from. Nature didn't deserve to pretend it hadn't had a hand in this nightmare when, in fact, it was the sole cause of Jude Thomas's demise. Clearly, my ranting hadn't deterred the bird from its song, so I doubted yelling at it would, either.

I tucked the journal's leather cord between the pages and closed the book. Somewhere in my mind, I'd believed this was an apology ten months in the making. There wasn't a piece of me that truthfully thought he'd dump the blame in my lap. Not entirely, anyway. He had to see it was his life, and therefore, he played a part in the destruction. As it stood, the responsibility fell solely on my shoulders. Not his mom dying. Not his inability to control himself. Not his refusal to get help. *Me*.

There was only so much emotional distress a girl could take in one day. I'd hoped to hear about his time in California, to know what he'd been doing while I suffered his silence. I got nothing. Part of me regretted even trying to read what he sent, and a larger part knew that no matter how much I hated what he had to say, or what he believed the truth to be, I'd read it till the last word in hopes of a happy ending. Just not today.

This was one of those stories where I desperately wanted to skip to the last page to make sure my heart would get a reward at the end for enduring the harsh beginning and angsty middle. Yet, without the meat, a sandwich was just two pieces of bread. So I slid the book into my bag, stood, and then gathered the blanket. I shook off the dirt and carefully folded it so it would fit comfortably next to the book without damaging it. I may hate the words I'd read so far, but it was still a gift from Jude. And regardless of what happened, I had never stop loving him.

It took me three times as long to get back to the dorm as it had to reach the tree. Not because I ran into people or stopped inside the bookstore. My feet refused to budge. It was as if the weight of Jude's words and the depth of his emotion and blame bogged me down, making it hard to move—difficult to breathe. My arms and legs tingled, tears stung my eyes yet never came, and there was a lump in my throat that wouldn't go away. The muscles in my neck constricted, ensuring that knot wasn't able to move. Somehow, my subconscious had sided with Jude, accepting his words as the gospel and reaching out to hold onto the responsibility of what had happened to him.

The room I shared with Jet was empty when I returned. It didn't appear she'd been here since I left. It was just as well. With the mood I was in, I wouldn't be good company and would probably end up lashing out simply because she was the one around to hear it. When I marched across campus, I promised myself I wouldn't open the journal again until tomorrow. It had exposed enough wounds for one day. Yet once I got comfortable on my bed, I began to pout. My arms were crossed, and no matter how many times I huffed and puffed, the pity party didn't shut down.

Against my better judgment, I started reading again. I skipped dinner. Ignored Jet when she came in. And then I kept the light on long after she'd gone to bed. Delving into this with her around proved to be a better way to contain my emotional outburst since I couldn't share any of our history—Jude's and mine—with her, anyhow. It forced me to stay quiet, and it silenced my arguments against everything he wrote. I became immersed in the black handwriting, page after page.

Shards of his broken glass slowly started to come together as he took me day by day, week by week, through the process of self-discovery. It wasn't pretty. The mess was unsightly, and at times, seemed pointless to try to clean up. Yet somehow, he kept going to counseling two and three days a week. He took drug test after drug test, each one coming back clean.

He'd claimed to need to get high to see the sun, and then he fled to California during a self-imposed blackout. When I told him I couldn't continue, he'd shut everything down to search for any glimmer of hope. Where I'd believed he'd run to avoid dealing with his issues, he'd actually dove headfirst into fixing them.

With each page I flipped, it was like witnessing his transformation in real time. And when Jude reached the end of the summer— when I thought he'd be home—he'd just started to accept his own role in his past.

The sound of my alarm startled me, and I realized I'd stayed up all night. I had to put the book down to shower and get ready for class. I forced myself to step back into the present, and I mentally kept repeating that I'd have more time to read when I got back this afternoon. Every part of me wanted to forgo my morning ritual to get in a few more weeks of his story, but I was tired and couldn't let go of my own responsibility to figure out how he'd dealt with his.

Jet didn't stir in her bed. I was grateful I wouldn't have to answer any questions when I replaced the leather cord between the pages. When I got up, I tossed the journal onto the spot I'd just vacated and gathered my things to get ready. But just before I left the room, I caught sight of it again and snatched it up to find a hiding place for it. In the two school years we'd lived together, Jet had never given me any inclination that she'd snooped through my things, but this wasn't something I could risk falling into anyone else's hands. Nevertheless, I slipped it under my mattress and smoothed out the comforter to make sure it wasn't noticeable.

But when I came back after class, Jet sat at her desk, studying. Neither of us left the room except to get dinner together. I couldn't skip meals—even though it was tempting—without raising suspicion. And it wasn't until after she fell asleep that I was able to retrieve my secret from its hiding place. Unfortunately, by that time, having stayed up the night before had left me exhausted. I owed it to Jude to get to the end; it just wasn't going to happen today.

Or the next.

A week later, I'd only reached the halfway point. It was agonizing to have to hide it instead of devouring what Jude wanted to share. It was like being left with a cliffhanger every time I set it down. Yet with the semester coming to a close, my professors had stacked the projects and reports on top of one another, and homework ate up my time. Although, my heart could only take small doses at a time; so in a way, I was grateful for the distractions.

It had been two weeks since Jude dropped his confession in the mail, and each day that passed without a response was another day he might believe he'd lost me forever. There was a reason Jude hadn't mailed this to my parents' house. He hadn't wanted me to have to wait to receive it. And if he'd needed me to have it now rather than later, I had to believe there was a reason. Except I couldn't get to that without finishing it.

Although I didn't want to admit it, the slower pace forced me to consider in tiny detail how he had endured each day. The comparisons of our mothers' deaths—something we shared in common—was a point I pondered for two days. Yes, they'd both died, but the circumstances were different. Jude didn't lose a mother he was never close to due to drugs. He'd lost a woman he cherished beyond all else, to a disease that destroyed her over several years. I'd always thought of addiction and cancer as silent killers, but one was self-induced and the other was unavoidable. I'd found the Shaws shortly after the cops pulled the needle from my mom's arm. I was nine when my agony ended. And while there were pieces I remembered, the only vivid details I carried were of that one day. Jude had seventeen years of memories. The majority of them good. And he'd believed she'd beat cancer. I hadn't known conquering drug addiction was even a possibility.

I'd been relieved when my mom died. Jude had been devastated. I welcomed the Shaws. He resented them. Other than the fact that they both died, nothing about them was even remotely similar. None of which I'd bothered to understand when he faced it. I expected him to be grateful he had the Shaws already embedded in his life. And even though I knew he loved them, none of us helped him to cope with his loss the way he'd needed. Intentional or not, it was what had happened.

The plain and simple truth was that there was no comparison between his loss and mine. His words didn't try to devalue or negate what I went through; they just served to enable me to see the two from a different perspective—one that made his dependency upon me and the recreational use of drugs, make more sense.

And as slowly as I read, I began to see his growth from week to week and month to month. The boy I'd loved as a child made appearances on the pages, and if it had been possible, I would have reached into the black ink to hold him. Since the day we'd met, the two of us had never been separated this long. I missed the smell of cedar and lemons and the way he stared at me across a room. It had been too many months since I'd fallen asleep in his bed or had his arms around me.

At the time, I'd become Jude's drug of choice, and the resemblance to my mom's dependency was too great a burden for me to carry—and an unfair one at that. Yet now, as I neared the end of the months I'd missed while he was gone, it was clear… Jude no longer lived for me. His counselor had prepared him to lose me. But most importantly, he'd come to the realization that he hadn't done this all to get the girl. During his time away, his focus and motivation shifted from getting me back to finding himself.

Regardless of how much I'd wanted to reach the last page, I wasn't prepared for it when I got there. There were still details I didn't have about friends he'd made, his job at the bookstore, why he'd chosen this method of communication. This list went on and on. And I assumed there were some things I'd simply never know.

Then, when I flipped the final sheet of paper, I took a deep breath. My eyes blurred with tears thinking all this had been a tease. Just enough to entice my mind back into a world where I didn't want to exist without him. A place where I was in Maine and he was in California. There was one final paragraph I'd yet to read—one separated from the abrupt ending, or possibly the start of a new beginning.

My gaze traveled the page, and the salty mix of emotion clung to my chin as I considered whether or not this was goodbye. When my heart stopped pounding, and my breathing returned to normal, I let myself accept whatever came next.

"I don't know where we stand or if we even still stand together. I will be home the first week of June, and I hope—no, I pray—that you'll meet me, talk to me, give me a chance at loving you the right way. Whether we're in a relationship or the best of friends, I never want to do life without you again…"

Signed, *"The boy you've been searching for."*

JUNE WAS TOO FAR AWAY. THERE WAS NO WAY I WAS WILLING TO

wait for Jude Thomas to show up on my parents' porch and see him again for the first time with an audience. It just wasn't going to happen. Consequences be damned. Without their knowledge, I booked a flight using their credit card and found a way home.

"Hey, sweetheart. What are you doing here?" My mom stuck her head out and looked around. "And why are you ringing the bell?"

I didn't bother with any pleasantries. "I didn't want to alarm you by coming home during the week unexpectedly." I pushed by her, and she shut the door behind me. The kitchen was the place we did our best talking, and that's where I headed without further fanfare. "Where's Dad?"

Her tense expression and creased forehead articulated her confusion and concern, although she didn't question me anymore. "Ernie?" She dashed to the bottom of the stairs, leaving me on the bar stool. "Ernie, can you come down here?"

The heavy clump of his feet on the steps sounded like a time bomb. I was about to pull the pin and hoped it was a dud that didn't explode.

My mom spoke in hushed tones. It didn't take a rocket scientist to figure out she had prepped him at the bottom of the stairs. Together, they joined me in the kitchen, and both took stools across from me.

"I need to talk to you guys." The words rushed out. The only way I'd make it through this was without interruptions. I had to confess everything I'd hidden while I dared to do it, and I didn't have a lot of time to spare. One look of disappointment from either of them would throw me completely off balance and likely cause me to miss my flight. "There are some things I need to tell you." Stalling wouldn't help, so I just spit it out with far less finesse than intended. "I'm in love with Jude."

Ernie dropped his chin to his chest, and Hensley's audible intake of air rushed through her parted lips. Neither of them spoke. They waited, which might have been worse.

"I think I always have been, but the two of you referred to us as siblings so often that it took me longer to realize it than it did Jude." They didn't need *all* the gory details, just enough to understand this wasn't a fling. "Bits and pieces of our feelings started to come together when I left for college. And after you guys offered to adopt him, it clarified more than it confused."

My mom couldn't help herself; she had to ask because the whole adoption thing had bothered her mercilessly. "What do you mean? What did it clarify?"

There was a part of me that worried Jude would be upset that I had exposed his secret, but a bigger portion realized this was what he'd wanted a year ago and I'd refused to give it to him. He needed transparency, and I'd forced him to hide. "If he allowed you to adopt him, then legally, we would have been brother and sister." I took a deep breath, knowing this would rock their world. "He wants us—me and him—to share the same last name eventually. *His*, not Shaw." They could think about that later. It was hardly the wave that would rock the boat.

"I don't understand," she said.

I held up my hand and closed my eyes to focus. When I reopened them, I started again. "You forced us together over spring break. And you can be mad all you want, but I'm grateful you did."

Ernie chuckled. "What would we be mad over?" Apparently, he assumed I'd missed the point if I thought they'd be upset that Jude and I had reconciled on that trip.

The one thing no child ever wanted to admit to their parents was about to part my lips. "We made up. We also made out." Deep breath. "And we had sex. A lot." Exhale.

I couldn't watch both of their expressions at the same time. Swinging my gaze back and forth between them would only serve to induce a headache that I couldn't afford to have.

My heart pounded against my sternum, and I lifted the heel of my hand to press against my chest as though that might quiet the anxious organ. "It was the first time we both admitted how we felt. And we hid it from you. All week." My lungs expanded as I grabbed as much air as possible. "And for months after." And then deflated with my admission.

Hensley just blinked. Over and over again. Slowly. Ernie nodded at the same pace that my mom blinked. I'd expected to argue and possibly yell.

Silence wasn't on my radar.

And I kept trying to fill it.

"Jude had a hard time with me being at school. He did some things I couldn't handle." I skipped over what exactly that entailed. There was no telling what Jude had told them since he'd been gone, and I wasn't about to be the bearer of that news on top of this. Nope. If he wanted them to know about the drugs after Christmas, that was on him. "The day you took him to Dr. Vanderhugh's office and sent me to Panama City...well, I—uh, I had broken up with him."

Ernie no longer kept his mouth shut. Anguish lined his forehead, and a frown seemed to engulf his features. His shoulders slumped, and the one emotion I couldn't handle poured from his body. Disappointment. "Why didn't you tell us?" It was almost a whisper.

I shrugged. That wasn't an answer or an explanation. "Jude begged me to for weeks. When he turned eighteen, he wanted to come clean. I refused." I pursed my lips and then tugged the bottom between my teeth to chew on it. When they continued to wait, I released it. "I was afraid you'd think there was something wrong with us. And that you'd push us away or force us apart."

Hensley touched my shoulder, softly at first, and then her warm hand tightened in a reassuring squeeze. "Why would you think that?" The glitter that normally sparkled in her eyes quit shining. They were dull and lifeless.

"Because you both constantly referred to Jude and me as brother and sister. I thought you'd think we were freaks. That we were sick.

And besides, I was already out of the house. Jude wasn't. It wasn't just a risk of not being able to see him or be with him. I worried that you'd cut him off or kick him out."

Ernie laughed. It was more of a nervous chuckle at first, and then it sank to his stomach and became guttural and hearty. No part of this was funny, yet the longer he went on, the more Hensley released the distraught emotions glued to her face. Either they'd been doing drugs, or I was hallucinating.

"Why are you guys laughing?"

Ernie shook his head and covered his mouth. The more he tried to regain control, the harder he had to fight.

I crossed my arms over my chest, and I would have tapped my foot on the ground in irritation had I been able to reach the floor from where I sat.

He finally calmed down and tried to wipe the smirk from his lips. The corners of his mouth continued to dance while he tampered his grin. "First of all, just because we referred to you two as brother and sister doesn't actually make it so. When you were growing up, it just seemed natural."

"Then why do you think this is so funny?" My frustration turned to pouting, and I dropped my arms and balled my hands into fists instead.

It might have been the tone of my voice or the fact that I was upset, I didn't know which, but something caused him to relax. "Portia, I think somewhere in the back of my mind, I've always known even if I never admitted it. And if I look at the last few years carefully, it was obvious. Yes, it's unconventional, but neither of you are doing anything wrong by loving each other differently than people expect."

"Your dad's right, sweetheart." Hensley never failed to take Ernie's lead. There were times that trait had annoyed the ever-loving crap out of me; today, I was grateful. "There's not one ounce of shared blood or lineage between the two of you."

This wasn't at all how I expected any of this to go. And the change in the outcome threw me off-kilter.

They looked at each other and, I guess somehow, communicated that my mom would continue the discussion. "We're disappointed the two of you thought you had to lie and hide. I'm concerned that you didn't use proper protection, but based on the fact that you haven't told me you're pregnant and how long Jude's been gone, I assume you took care of that on your own."

I nodded. I did not elaborate.

"Portia, all your mom and I have ever wanted for you and Jude is to be happy. You've both had difficult pasts, and we just wanted to make your futures easier."

"I thought it was odd that you never asked about him." Hensley's comment came out of nowhere. "And he never once asked about you." She looked up as though the ceiling might hold an answer she hadn't yet considered. "Well, until a few weeks ago when he asked for your address at school."

"So you knew he reached out to me?"

Her fingers came to rest on top of mine, and the warmth of her skin flowed through me. "I didn't ask any questions, Portia. I gave him space and time to do what he needed. It was hard to let him go in the first place, but once he was there, I had to trust him to take care of things." She patted the top of my hand before taking hers back to rest in her lap.

I'd arrived with only my backpack. Jet had dropped me off, and I assured her I could get back to school on my own. It was Thursday afternoon, and I had contacted my professors to tell them I'd be out of class tomorrow. That gave me three days to do what I needed, and then get back to campus in time for Monday classes. Now I had to bring my parents into the loop.

"I need you to take me to the airport." That was one way to go about it. Information dumps always seemed to be the best solution. It typically took people days to sort through a massive number of details, and I'd be long gone by the time they figured out what questions they really had. Repercussions would follow. That I was certain of.

Ernie stood and walked to the counter to grab his keys. "Okay." That was too easy. "Let's go."

Hensley followed behind him and snatched her purse. I hopped down from the stool and slung my bag over my shoulder.

We'd been in the car for more than ten minutes when Ernie finally asked me what airline I'd booked, just not my destination. And when we arrived at the terminal, they both got out to hug me. It was the oddest thing I'd ever experienced, and it left me unsettled when I turned toward the terminal.

"Hey, Portia?" Dad's voice carried over the bustle of other travelers and the rumbling of engines clogging the airport. "Bring him home."

My eyes burned and filled with tears that I didn't want to cascade down my cheeks. The salty wetness would ruin my makeup, which could scare the other passengers. I bit the inside of my cheek and nodded. Seconds later, I was swept into the sea of moving people and on my way to claim my destiny or let go of my past.

One way or another, my life would change direction when this plane touched down.

19

JUDE

THE KNOCK AFTER ELEVEN AT NIGHT STARTLED ME. I FIGURED
Carson or Ethan left their keys at home, locking themselves out. I
didn't bother glancing through the peephole. Instead, I kept my nose
rooted in the book I was reading, disengaged the deadbolt, and then
grabbed the knob. I didn't take notice of who stood on the other side
when I flung it open, and I returned to my place on the couch.

The weight of the metal latching itself in place resounded
through the apartment. After sitting down, I realized neither of them
had come inside. Irritated by the disruption—and ready to fire off a
smart-ass comment about one of them needing an escort or an invitation—I ripped back the door.

And every thought fled my mind.

If I'd been asleep, then I would have believed I was dreaming.
As it stood, the vision before me was as real as the book I'd thrown
on the sofa. My Adam's apple bobbed in painful exaggeration as I
swallowed back my surprise.

There.

Within arm's reach.

Stood Portia Shaw.

She clutched my journal in one hand, and a silver tray with a plastic top in the other. My mind hadn't done her justice. Her inky hair had grown longer, and the pools of green glowed a brilliant shade I couldn't identify.

Her lips twitched. And then they parted. A toothy grin of nervous excitement finally broke free. My heart soared, and I stared, scared if I took my eyes off her she'd vanish.

She licked her lips, and I recalled—in graphic detail—what her tongue was capable of. My mind slipped back to a memory of her on her knees with my hands in her hair, but just before I reached the climax, she interrupted my thoughts.

"Can I come in?" she asked in a gentle tone.

Holy mother of God, the pink of cotton candy.

I moved back, unsure of what to say or do. I'd hoped the two of us might talk when I got home. Never, in my wildest dreams, did I suspect she'd fly to California. All I could do was watch and swallow and blink. Over and over.

Portia took a few steps away from the entrance and toward the kitchen. There, she put the journal on the bar, and then she set down the aluminum dish. Finally, she let her bag slide down her arm and land on the carpet. Not once since I'd let her in had she taken her eyes off mine. She didn't give me the once-over or even mention that I stood before her half-dressed.

Determination smoldered her gaze, and I prepared myself for her to chew me out and leave. It had been several weeks since I'd sent the journal, and her continued silence—then and now—didn't bode well for me. But I was afraid to speak for fear of what she might say back.

Her left foot moved forward, followed by her right. And again. Until she was inches from my overheated body. The door closed behind me, but not even the loud thud distracted my attention. The heat of her breath burned the skin on my chest and then rose up my neck.

"Portia..." It was a plea for forgiveness, a sigh of frustration, and a moan of relief.

She closed the little space that remained between us. One hand fisted the waistband of my basketball shorts, and her other wrapped around the nape of my neck to pull me down. I went willingly, and there I was met with a perfect kiss. She answered my request for absolution, squashed my discouragement, and offered me release.

No questions.

No conversation.

No hesitation.

She'd come to make amends, and my heart came home. There wasn't anything better than wrapping my arms around her tiny frame as she deepened the kiss. Her nails dug into the skin on my sides, and if I'd let her, she would have climbed my torso.

I wanted all of it.

Needed every inch of her.

And I hoped we got there sooner rather than later. But we couldn't go from almost a year of separation to sex on Ethan and Carson's couch—nuh-uh, no matter how badly I wanted to rip off her clothes and sink into her until neither of us could remember the other's name.

Winded with my chest heaving, I broke away. Clearly, she'd expected it, although a lust-filled storm still brewed in her eyes.

"What are you doing here?" It was the first sentence I'd managed to utter since she'd shown up. It seemed like hours ago, when in fact, it quite possibly was less than three minutes.

She moved her hand to my chest, right over my heart, and smiled. Her tongue ran across her lips, moistening them with a sheen I wanted her to trail down my abs. "You didn't think you could send me *that*"—she tilted her head toward my journal—"and me keep quiet, did you?"

I hadn't expected anything. "Honestly, the best I hoped for was that we could sit down and talk when I got home next month." I didn't want to get my hopes up. Talking was realistic. Her hopping on a plane to California—or driving—wasn't on my radar. "How did you get here?"

Her fingers tangled with mine, and she dragged me toward the couch as though we hadn't been apart a single day. She wasn't the least bit apprehensive or shy, whereas I didn't have a clue what to make of the situation. Portia sat on one end, and I took the other. If I continued to touch her, I'd end up buried inside her. And that wouldn't help either of us—not yet.

"I flew. Then I took a cab to the only bakery in town that didn't have a vegan reference in their online ad. And now I'm here."

I glanced at the container she'd set on the bar when she came in. It clearly resembled a pie tin now that I wasn't enthralled by Portia materializing out of thin air. "What did you need at a bakery?"

The shy look I'd seen on her face countless times in the past made an appearance, and she raised a shoulder and then her eyebrows. "Lemon pie."

My lungs struggled to take in fresh air. She'd brought the one tangible thing in my life that she knew meant everything good. It wasn't from the diner my mom had worked at, but it was her peace offering just the same. I didn't have a clue where she'd found a bakery open this late, and it didn't matter. The gesture alone eased my anxiety.

"And I brought you...*me*," she said wistfully.

The space I'd intentionally put between us now served as a nuisance. I snatched her hand and tugged her between my legs as I leaned back. Chest to chest. "And you," I confirmed. She was the greatest gift I'd ever received. Twice.

There was so much I wanted to say, things I needed to tell her. Yet at that moment, nothing mattered but holding her. I tucked her head into my shoulder and secured a firm grip around her waist and lower back. She'd have to fight me to ever let go again.

Portia wiggled a bit under my hold, and finally grunted out, "Jude...you're squishing me." The sound of her giggles were music in a world that had been silent since the day I'd left Maine. As she struggled to break free, writhing in a fit of childlike amusement, she suddenly stopped.

Her stare lingered over my shoulder, and I strained my neck to find what she gawked at. It landed squarely on Wooly, tucked into the side pocket of my backpack.

"Is that Woobie?" Her voice was animated yet filled with dismay. "I wondered where he ran off to." Then she glanced down at me from the spot she'd settled into on my chest and waited.

Wooly, Woobie…his name didn't matter. He'd been the only physical part of Portia I'd had to hold onto in California, and he'd gone with me everywhere. "Maybe."

"You *stole* him?"

"Borrowed is a better term." My sheepish grin sparked a sassy look from her in return. Eleven months ago, it would have been an expression that had me reaching for the hem of her shirt, now I was clueless as to what it meant or how to react.

I didn't know what to do with her. I'd spent the better part of a year sleeping on a couch in a living room of an apartment that wasn't mine. We needed to talk, but I didn't want to do it here. There was no way in hell I wanted to share her with Ethan and Carson when they got home—not so much as a glimpse. She hadn't told me how long she planned to stay, but I wanted to monopolize every second of her time.

With a smack on her perfect ass, I motioned for her to get up, and Wooly was promptly forgotten. "We need to get out of here before the guys get home."

"You don't want them to know I'm here?"

"Babe, don't get offended, but hell no. I want you to myself. There's not enough money in the world to get me to agree to anything different. Let me grab my wallet. There's a hotel not far from here."

I GOT DRESSED AND TOSSED HER BACKPACK ON MY SHOULDER, AND together, we set out. Portia held my hand as we walked down the street, and she carried the pie in the other. We didn't speak, but her thumb caressed the top of my hand and spoke a language all its own. Ever since we were kids, she'd done it to reassure and calm me, and now I was grateful for all those years so I understood its quiet meaning.

It wasn't the Ritz Carlton, but I wasn't Donald Trump. The hotel was within walking distance, didn't charge by the hour, and most importantly, didn't ask for ID, so I was sold. Portia set the pie on the nightstand, along with the two forks I'd grabbed on our way out the door. I set down her bag, and it dawned on me that I hadn't brought anything of my own. Not that it mattered. I just wanted time with the girl I'd seen every night in my dreams yet hadn't been able to touch. She sat on the mattress and peered up at me with large, curious eyes. I didn't move, and I wasn't sure how to proceed.

"Are you just going to stand there?" She patted the bed.

My feet moved, and I found myself sitting next to her. I eased my leg onto the mattress between us and angled my torso away from Portia to prevent touching her. I had so many questions, and I was sure she had a laundry list of her own.

I raked my hand through my hair, and she grabbed my wrist. She tugged it toward the space between us. Together, our twined fingers rested there.

"Why are you so nervous?"

Either Portia had been hit upside the head on her trip here, forgetting all that had happened before I'd left Maine, or she was totally clueless.

Words floated around in my mind while I tried to formulate a response. I finally admitted that I was lost. "I'm dumbfounded you're here. I'm wondering how we go forward." My chest rose as I took a deep breath and then deflated when I released it. "I don't know what you're thinking or why you came." It wasn't poetic, but it was honest.

The pink of her lips deepened, and her pupils dilated just a fraction and constricted again. "I came to bring you home."

"Just like that? Don't you think we should talk?"

Portia's thin shoulders rose in a shrug. "Not really. I mean, I don't have to. Your journal was pretty eye-opening. It detailed the months you were gone." She stopped, seeming to consider something further. "I don't believe you need to relive this nightmare over and over. You did what I asked. That was all I needed. Is there something you left out?"

I shook my head. Everything of importance had been cataloged on those pages.

"Don't get me wrong. I want to hear about the people you've met and the bookstore you work at. But none of that has to happen tonight."

Portia hadn't made anything simple in the last eighteen months, so I couldn't figure out why she would now. "What about you?"

"What about me?" she asked.

I leaned back on my hands and kept my focus on her fierce, green eyes. "Portia, I don't have a clue what you've been doing since I left town. Ernie and Hensley haven't told me a thing, I haven't heard from you, and I'm still stuck on the day you walked out of my bedroom. It's like someone paused *us* and hasn't bothered to press play again."

A smile appeared, and I couldn't help but reciprocate when her crooked tooth showed through. "I haven't been dating, if that's what you're asking."

That wasn't what I meant, but I was glad I didn't have to ask that question.

"I told you I'd wait on you, Jude, and that's exactly what I've done."

I cocked my head in disbelief. She might not have dated, but I was certain she hadn't joined a convent and committed to a life of boredom in my absence. When I quirked my eyebrows, she giggled.

"I don't mean I've sat around wasting away. Don't get me wrong, I missed you. God, did I miss you. But I focused on school. Straight As." I think she might have curtsied had she been standing. Portia was proud of herself, and she should be. "Other than that, I've hung out with Jet and Bart. Nothing out of the ordinary or even worth retelling."

"Do they know?" My question was purposely ambiguous. I didn't want to lead her into an answer; I wanted her to tell me the information she wanted me to have—good, bad, or indifferent.

Her gaze fell to her lap. "Bart does. Jet doesn't."

I reached up and lifted her chin. "It's okay, Portia."

"You're not mad that I told him about us?"

Surprised, yes; mad, no. It wasn't a secret that she and Bart were close. I just assumed she was closer to Jet, since they'd lived together for two years. "Why would I be mad? I wanted to scream it from the rooftops." And then something dawned on me—the issue that had ultimately led to my breakdown back in Maine. "Do Ernie and Hensley know about us?"

She nodded, but her intent stare never wavered. Portia gave no indication of how they had taken the news, and I was afraid to question it. Now I feared *that* was why she was here. If they hadn't taken it well, I had no idea where that left us—or me. She would never cross them. Fear seized my insides, and my internal organs seemed to clench under the weight of worry. Seconds felt like hours. I had to ask before my spleen ruptured or my appendix burst. Neither of which would have been pretty or endeared her to me.

"And?" I questioned hesitantly. "How'd they take it?"

The soft smile I loved to see grace her face slowly rose into place again. Her hand settled on top of our laced fingers. "Honestly, they weren't all that surprised."

The boulder of shame lifted from my shoulders when I let out a sigh of relief. "Seriously?"

Portia released a nervous bit of laughter. "Hensley was concerned we hadn't used protection, but once she did the math and realized I wasn't pregnant, she was okay with it. Although, I'm sure they'll have a thousand questions after they've had time to think about it."

I blinked several times, processing her words. Leave it to Portia to turn over every stone and unveil every secret. Not only had she admitted that the two of us had hidden an affair of sorts, but she'd also told her parents that we'd had sex. I prayed there hadn't been details involved, but that wasn't a subject I was willing to broach. I didn't want that answer—ever.

"You told them we had sex?"

She shrugged. "I was nervous." Her eyes danced with amusement, and the skin crinkled at the sides of her widening smile.

"Anything else you want to share with me before I have to face the firing squad?" My tone was light, and I tried not to laugh. I couldn't imagine the look on Ernie and Hensley's faces when Portia dropped that bomb. And I silently thanked God for allowing me to be across the country so Ernie couldn't chop me into pieces for deflowering his only daughter.

She tapped her chin in thought. "Nope," she said, popping the *P* in her usual Portia way. "That's about it."

This was all surreal. It didn't seem possible that in the eleven months I'd been gone that life had somehow righted itself. Yes, I'd worked my ass off to deal with my issues, and I had hoped it would pay dividends, but never, in my wildest dreams, had I believed the outcome could be this blissful. I wondered if I'd spend weeks or even months waiting for the other shoe to drop or if I could accept that my family welcomed me back with open arms.

"So what does this mean for us?" It shouldn't be my top priority; nevertheless, it was. I'd prepared myself for Portia not to be there when I came crawling back. I had never considered the possibility of a future for fear it would catapult me back into darkness if it didn't happen.

Portia settled her hand on my jaw. She cupped my cheek in the most tender embrace, and the soft smile returned. Her eyes shined and radiated with love. "I can't predict the future, Jude. What I can do is promise you my heart. I don't know how we will navigate life at home or school; I just know I want to wade through the water with you."

She sealed her commitment by pressing her lips to mine. When she reached for my cheek, I took the initiative to wrap my arms around her waist and draw her in. One touch was all it took, and the kiss deepened. A glorious chill rolled down my spine and brought goose bumps to every inch of my heated flesh. Each swipe of our tongues together left me warm and aching in the places that had been in hibernation since I'd come to California.

The timing might not have been right, and Dr. Sarratt probably wouldn't have approved, but I didn't need to hear anything more from Portia. All I needed was her. There, in a hotel room a few blocks from the apartment where I'd spent the better part of a year trying to heal, Portia wiped away the months of pain. Together, we connected in a way neither of us would ever experience with anyone else.

And when I sank into her warmth, I found peace.

SUNDAY AFTERNOON CAME FASTER THAN EITHER OF US WANTED. Three days hadn't been nearly enough time to reconnect, and even though I'd made myself sick on lemon pie, saying goodbye proved to be painful. I'd give anything to freeze time in that hotel room with the dessert tin between us, forks in hand, simply enjoying each other's company and catching up as we shoved pie in our mouths.

Standing in the airport, I held Portia's face and softly kissed her. "Don't cry, babe. It's only a couple of weeks," I whispered with my forehead pressed against hers.

Her eyes were bloodshot, and no amount of consoling would change her anguish. It was inevitable—her displeasure and our circumstances. She had exams to finish, and I had to fulfill a two-week notice at the bookstore. We'd be back together in no time; however, having spent the majority of a year apart, those weeks seemed unjust. A harsh penalty neither of us wanted to serve.

"I don't want to go." Portia's whimpered words tore at my heart.

My thumb moved along her cheekbone as I tried to remind her that this wouldn't break us. "I know, but you've worked too hard to throw away school. Just because I'm two years behind you doesn't mean you need to stay there an extra year to be with me." I chuckled, thinking about her becoming a delinquent. It wasn't possible, although the thought humored me all the same. Portia had a goal, and I refused to derail it.

She pulled back and swatted at my arm. In return, I locked my arms and squeezed her at the waist, pressing her against my growing erection. I couldn't touch her without getting aroused, and I had no doubt she could feel the evidence of my attraction. The airport wasn't the place to demonstrate just how much I cared about her, but I hoped it gave her something to long for during our separation.

I hated to do it; regardless, I had to say goodbye. The crowd around us only grew larger, and the longer we stood there, the less time Portia had to get through security and to her gate. Even recognizing the multitude of people in our midst, it was easy to drown out the sounds of passengers talking and suitcases being dragged on the floor. The announcements over the intercom didn't faze me, and neither did the guy who bumped into us.

"Promise you'll text me as soon as you land, and call me once you get home?" The last word sounded stiff as a lump formed in my throat, making it difficult to speak. I wasn't about to cry, but it hurt to let her go. I kept reminding myself that this was the start of something good. Unlike the last time we had separated, when I had no idea how things would turn out, this time, I was certain I was headed toward forever.

Portia nodded and pulled me down for one final kiss. Her lips were soaked with tears, and they left a briny flavor on my mouth; I hoped I would never have to taste it again.

"I love you." Those words didn't say enough. They didn't express the depth of my devotion to the girl in front of me. "You're my lemon pie." *That* did.

Her eyes flooded again, but this time, a smile threatened to split her cheeks in two. "When you get home, you can put the whipped cream on top." She winked, sending the tears past her lashes, and turned toward security.

Her ass swayed with each step she took, and when she reached the TSA checkpoint, she stopped, glanced over her shoulder, and called out, "Hey, Jude?"

I lifted my head to acknowledge I'd heard her instead of shouting through the crowd.

"I love you, too." She waved, and then the sea of travelers swallowed her from my view.

Cotton candy.

EPILOGUE

PORTIA—FOUR YEARS LATER

"Portia, stop squirming or I'll never get you into this thing." Hensley hadn't quit complaining about my fidgeting since we'd arrived at the bed and breakfast in Cape Cod.

"You're pulling too tight," I whined as she cinched the corset of the dress. She'd been laboring to get me in it for the better part of twenty minutes.

Her hands stilled, and her breath blew against the back of my neck before I heard her words. "Do you want it to fall down in the middle of the ceremony?"

I shook my head, but she didn't wait for a response. Instead, she tugged on the satin strings like they were shoelaces and my body was merely a foot inside the sneaker.

"Jet, sweetheart, can you lift the top of the dress?" Hensley requested.

Jet didn't think twice before sticking her chilly hands into the front of my gown, nearly slicing off my areola with a fingernail to hoist it into position. The second I winced, Hensley took that as her cue to eliminate any remaining slack in the bodice. I wasn't sure I'd be able to sit, much less breathe, once she tied the bow.

"Good lord, you need mittens. Your fingers are like blocks of ice." I swatted at Jet's hands to get her to move.

Jet took a step back and appraised me. Starting at my bust, she worked her way down the ivory lace and crystal beads to the short train. When she found my eyes, hers were filled with tears. "You look spectacular, Portia. You and Jude deserve this." She hiccupped, trying to keep her voice from cracking.

My mom circled me to get the full picture. As Jet moved aside, Hensley took my hands. My gaze flitted between the two most important women in my life. I wasn't good at being the center of attention, and their fawning over me only caused my apprehension to rise.

"I wondered if we'd ever actually get you here." Jet had been to hell and back with me once I'd finally come clean and told her the truth about Jude. She'd been hurt that I hadn't confided in her, but eventually—after a lot of pleading on my part—she came around.

When I came back from California, I expected my parents to have questions they hadn't been able to come up with at the time I'd made my confession; however, I hadn't prepared myself for what my relationship with Jude would actually do to our daily lives.

Hensley cocked her head and crossed her arms in what would be a defensive posture on anyone else. It just made me giggle when her focus flip-flopped between Jet and me. "That's not fair," she responded to me laughing at her. She sounded like a child trying to prove her innocence. Her voice rose an octave as she objected. "Your father and I were rather accepting, given the circumstances."

I didn't even try to hold back the fit of laughter that started in my stomach, rose through my chest, and erupted past my lips. "Yeah, if you consider that 'accepting' means the two of you kept watch at our doors like soldiers. I couldn't wait for that first summer to be over to go back to school where I wasn't under constant surveillance. At any given moment, I worried about another interrogation coming." I kept my tone light so I didn't hurt her feelings. We'd talked about it at length since, and the older I got, the more I understood the predicament Jude and I had placed them in. Now we all joked about it in good fun, although that had not been the case four years ago.

"We did what any good parents would do." Hensley straightened her spine and dropped her arms to my waist, fiddling with the beadwork.

The effort I put into not rolling my eyes was in vain. I couldn't stop the natural response. My lids fluttered as I tried to mask the gesture. "You guys sat between us on the couch…in the living room." I giggled remembering just how awkward things were then.

It was my own fault. I'd given up far too much information when I'd unloaded in the kitchen that afternoon. If I'd never told them Jude and I had sex right under their nose, there wouldn't have been a reason for them to hover. And I'd refused to lie when I got home from school, regardless of the questions they'd asked. Jude and I had hidden long enough. It wasn't fair to either of us. Honesty seemed like the best policy…until it didn't.

Hensley raised her brows, and her nose tipped just slightly when she calmly replied, "We were supportive of the relationship."

I loved getting her riled up. "Just not the sexual part?" It was tense back then, but it was funny now.

Jet's jaw dropped a hair, and Hensley flat-out gaped at my brazen response.

"You were *nineteen*, Portia." Every mother thinks their daughter is too young for sex. It didn't matter that I was the only virgin I knew in college.

I shrugged. "We were careful…and have been ever since."

My friend snickered while my mother blushed. "Portia Shaw, I do not need to hear this." Any minute now, Hensley would stick her fingers in her ears and start humming to drown me out.

I could stand here all day—because I certainly couldn't sit with this dress on—and ruffle her feathers, but the truth was, she and

Ernie had done the best they could in a difficult situation. Despite never leaving us alone in the house that first year, forbidding us to step foot in each other's rooms, and insisting Jude and I "date" properly, they'd fought off rumors and comments about our relationship. Their friends weren't nearly as accepting, and they'd lost several over their support. Yet even through navigating treacherous waters and hateful glares, somehow, for the last four years they'd maintained their alliance with Jude and me as a couple.

Jet twirled a strand of hair near her face, and a serene expression engulfed her features. "I think you've all done pretty well. And I'm honored to be here with you guys today."

Hensley patted my shoulder and then gave it a gentle squeeze. "She's right. We've weathered a lot of storms, but today marks the day that you and Jude get to start your happily ever after."

"It's not a fairy tale, Mom."

A tear made a sudden appearance and danced down her cheek. She swiped at it with the back of her fingers. Love and joy radiated from kind eyes. "I disagree. And I don't know two people who deserve it more."

There was a knock, interrupting the Hallmark moment this had become. Jet stepped around me to answer it, and when she opened the door, Bart winked at her. I kept hoping they'd quit tiptoeing around each other and acknowledge what the rest of us noticed between them. I couldn't see her face from where I stood, but I could tell by the way his softened that something passed between them.

"Is the bride ready?" Bart glanced my direction for a fraction of a second before shifting his attention back to the bombshell before him.

He and Jet were my two closest friends. He'd graduated before we did but ended up sticking around to work on his masters. Jet and I had joined him in the graduate program the following year while Jude completed his undergrad. It was funny how things had all come together in the end. Jude and I ended up graduating together, him with his bachelor's degree and me with my masters. We'd tossed around the notion of waiting another two years to tie the knot, but when it was all said and done, neither of us wanted to postpone our future.

I had a new job with a counseling practice waiting for me when we got back from our honeymoon, and Jude planned to work on his masters at night while teaching high school English. The next two years would be hectic as I established a client base and he worked while going to classes, but starting our lives together would make it worth the struggle.

"She is," I called out, even though he wasn't paying a bit of attention.

Hensley reached for the bouquets and handed one to me and one to Jet. She had a simple corsage pinned to her dress as the mother of the bride, and her dress was a lighter shade of lavender than Jet's but designed to coordinate. I hadn't seen the setup on the lawn, but none of that mattered. I'd loved the idea of having the wedding at the same bed and breakfast where Jude and I had established our relationship. The ceremony would be small, and the guest list was even smaller. I had Jet and Bart, and Jude had invited Carson and Ethan. The only other people in attendance were my parents and the minister. Our tribe was tiny, but we were all very close. Each one of us played critical roles in each other's lives.

Bart had disappeared, and Ernie stood in his place. I'd been fine until I caught sight of him in his tuxedo. He and Jude were the two most important men in my life, and both were in it by choice. I struggled to see clearly through the water gathering in my eyes, so I fanned my face, hoping to keep the moisture from falling and ruining my makeup. Hensley must have seen it coming because she had a tissue in hand ready to dab the emotion away.

Her arms wrapped me, and she brought me to her chest in a

motherly embrace. There she whispered, "I'm so proud of you, Portia. Your dad and I love you very much."

Words would have been messier than the tears, so I nodded, hoping she understood that I reciprocated her sentiment. I hated to give up the last name Shaw after all they'd done for me, but I couldn't wait to become a Thomas, either.

I pulled my shoulders back, straightened my dress, and then walked toward the only father I'd ever known. At my dad's side, I threaded my arm through his and allowed him to lead me toward the only man Ernie would ever deem worthy of my hand.

THE CEREMONY WAS A BLUR, AT BEST. THE ONLY THING I RECALLED with any clarity was the boy I'd loved almost my entire life and the way he watched me as I approached. Long gone was the tall, lanky, awkward kid from my youth. In his place was a man with confidence. His smile was perfect, his tux was dapper, and he was virtually edible. Throughout our vows, he never took his eyes off mine, and he hadn't even tried to erase the sheer joy that overtook his features. I'd long since memorized every freckle on his skin, every streak of color in his irises, and every strand of hair on his head, but nothing had prepared me for the expression Jude wore as he committed his life to mine.

Once it was over, and I was officially a Thomas, the world came back into focus. After the minister announced us as husband and wife, Jude and I started across the lawn toward the bed and breakfast. It was then that I noticed two empty seats amongst the six in the audience. Hensley had insisted on doing something to commemorate the mothers Jude and I had lost. And there, in the white chairs, lay two yellow roses—one for each—tied with a lavender ribbon. I stopped and picked up the one closest to me, and Jude mirrored my action. I could have moved on without hesitation; instead, I brought my nose to the bloom and inhaled deeply. Maybe she hadn't been the perfect mother, but she'd given me the perfect life. With the two blossoms in hand, we continued down the aisle and inside.

After the obligatory pictures—something I was certain I would love later yet currently loathed for keeping us from enjoying each other and our guests—we finally made our way to the dining room. My parents had rented out the entire place, rooms and all, so the staff was there to dote solely on us. I hadn't remembered the food being so good when we'd stayed here before, but that likely had more to do with the fact that I had dined on Jude during that trip—a Michelin-star chef wouldn't have outshined him—than it did with the quality.

"Hensley, you outdid yourself with all this," Jude praised.

While we had been busy with exams and graduation, Hensley had planned a wedding with virtually no help from either of us. She waved him off. "It was nothing. I'm just so happy you are legally part of the family." She'd wanted that for years, and now she'd gotten her wish.

"You're welcome," I announced casually from across the table. The comment did exactly what I'd hoped it would. It lightened the mood when Ernie laughed and shook his head.

The head waiter ducked down to whisper something in Hensley's ear. She leaned toward him and nodded. "Is everyone ready for dessert?" There was never a time when dessert wasn't welcomed.

I gripped Jude's hand and did a little whispering of my own in his ear. "I don't think she wants to see the kind of dessert I have in mind." I nibbled on his earlobe for good measure…just to give him a glimpse of what was to come when we were alone. I'd made every effort to keep the affection relatively hidden from onlookers. To my surprise, he didn't shy away or blossom into a crimson red.

A low rumble only I could hear brewed in his throat, and without so much as batting a lash, Jude turned his head, and his giant hand engulfed my jaw. His lips swarmed mine, and he held nothing back in taking them with passion. If I'd thought about it, I might have realized just how many people at the table blushed. However, none of that came to mind when I opened to allow his tongue in, or when I reciprocated. It wasn't until I broke away, breathless, that it occurred to me that we had an audience.

Carson cleared his throat. "I'm sure your parents would love grandchildren, but I doubt they want to see them conceived." It was a comment I'd expect from Ethan, not Carson. And while it shouldn't have been funny, it was.

Ethan lobbed a piece of a leftover roll at Jude. "We all know you love her, but seeing you make out with your sister is a little gross, dude."

And the second Jude went to open his mouth, we all chimed in with the response he'd given for years. "She's not my sister." It sounded like a well-rehearsed chorus.

"Nah, she's your wife." Ethan sat back in his seat with a shit-eating smirk on his face. "Try *that* word on for size." His banter was playful, and everyone at the table knew it. It had become a game with Jude, and regardless of how much he swore up and down he hated it, I knew the truth.

Some part of it—the whole twisted sister motif—made us who we were. And neither Jude nor I would trade that for the world. It made us unique. It was our story. We were just two foster kids who fell in love.

I relaxed onto his shoulder, and he lifted his arm to place it around my back. Once I'd settled into the safest place on Earth, I leaned in so only he could hear me. "I love you, Jude." I cooed the words in his favorite shade of pink and prayed he never grew tired of cotton candy.

The waiter reappeared with dessert, and Jude placed a kiss on my temple. Lost in the smell of cedar and citrus, I hadn't paid attention to the plates set before us. I hadn't had any hand in picking out the cake. Hensley was a master at baking, so I was confident she wouldn't let us down in this department. But when silence engulfed us—it was so quiet I could have heard a feather fall—I pulled away from the security of my groom. Unable to see his face, I knew the instant he saw the same thing I did. His body stiffened and so did his hold on me. I shifted, craning my neck to see Jude's face. The lone tear that trailed his cheek nearly tore my heart in two.

My eyes darted to Hensley, who definitely held her breath, anxiously waiting for a response. I didn't have a clue what to do. The room was so quiet, it might as well have been empty. But the tension was so thick, it was claustrophobic. It could have been two seconds or two minutes, I didn't know. Nevertheless, I had to do something.

I tried to paint my words in his favorite shade, but the ache in my heart made them more magenta than pastel. "Jude…"

He hadn't taken his eyes off the plate until that moment. The molten browns shifted to Hensley, then Ernie, and finally dropped to me. It was difficult for him to swallow, and the motion appeared to stop midway in his throat when he choked out, "Lemon pie."

Peace teetered at the edge of his lips and then tipped the corners up in happiness. Glitter sparkled in his irises and wrinkles of fond memories danced on the skin near his temples. Carrie would have appreciated the gesture just as much as she'd loved Jude. The unexpected presence of the pastry didn't mean it was unwelcome; it just took Jude a minute to recognize the significance of everything good in his life still being right at his fingertips, despite what he'd lost.

The vacuum that the final course created was lost the moment Jude took a bite of that bright-yellow filling and fluffy, white whipped cream bordered by flaky, golden crust. "This is perfect, Hensley. Thank you," he said around a mouthful of pie.

As if on cue, we all let go of the proverbial breath we'd been holding, and conversation resumed. I glanced at the people I loved, who all sat around the table, and I wondered how I'd gotten so lucky after such a rough start. The day I'd found my mom with a needle in her arm, I never dreamed I had a chance in life. Now, here I sat years later surrounded by family and friends who were all determined that Jude and I would succeed.

Our family tree might have started off with different roots, but over the years our trunks had grown together until the branches now wove an artistic tapestry of love. It wasn't born from DNA or bloodlines but by choice. And we were all connected by those family ties.

THE END

ABOUT THE AUTHOR

Stephie Walls is a lover of words—the more poetic the better. She lives on the outskirts of Greenville, South Carolina in her own veritable zoo with two dogs, three cats, the Mister, and Magoo (in no preferential order).

She would live on coffee, books, and Charlie Hunnam if it were possible, but since it's not, add in some Chinese food or sushi and she's one happy girl.

ALSO BY STEPHIE WALLS

Bound

Freed

Redemption

Metamorphosis

Compass

Strangers

chimera

Beauty Mark

Fallen Woman

Girl Crush

Unexpected Arrivals

Label Me Proud

CO-WRITTEN AS STELLA WITH LEDDY HARPER

Third Base

Home Run King

Dr. Fellatio (releases July 25, 2018)